# THE INVOCATIONS

# THE INVOCATIONS

## KRYSTAL SUTHERLAND

NANCY PAULSEN BOOKS

**NANCY PAULSEN BOOKS**
An imprint of Penguin Random House LLC, New York

First published in the United States of America by Nancy Paulsen Books,
an imprint of Penguin Random House LLC, 2024

Nancy Paulsen Books & colophon are trademarks of Penguin Random House LLC.

The Penguin colophon is a registered trademark of Penguin Books Limited.

Visit us online at PenguinRandomHouse.com.

Library of Congress Cataloging-in-Publication Data is available.

Printed in the United States of America

ISBN 9780593532263 (hardcover)

ISBN 9780593696286 (international edition)

1st Printing

LSCC

Edited by Stacey Barney with assistance from Caitlin Tutterow
Design by Suki Boynton • Text set in Laurentian Pro

This book is a work of fiction. Any references to historical events,
real people, or real places are used fictitiously. Other names, characters, places,
and events are products of the author's imagination, and any resemblance to
actual events or places or persons, living or dead, is entirely coincidental.

*For all the angry girls*

# PROLOGUE

**A GIRL** walks home alone at night.

It's All Hallows' Eve in London, and the street that stretches before her is empty, quiet except for the soft thud of her boots on the sidewalk and the rustle of autumn leaves plucked by the wind. Hazy sodium lights struggle to shift the dark.

The girl is dressed as a witch. Cartoon-green skin, pointy hat, a fake wart on her nose. She is coming from the Electric Ballroom, where, at a Halloween concert with her housemates, she saw the boy she likes kissing a girl dressed as a sexy angel. It immediately made her regret her costume and want to go home.

Now she slips through the gap between two buildings, past the canal-side pub she goes to with her friends in the summer. A girl sits on the other side of a window decorated with bat decals, her face smeared with blood. A couple in matching hot-pink jumpsuits are breaking up on a bench.

The girl takes a few steps onto the footbridge that leads over the water and down onto the towpath on the other side.

It is here, on the bridge, that she pauses. The canal beneath her is a thin snake of shallow water. On a clear day, you can see the algae-coated detritus that collects at the bottom: the bicycles, the shopping trolleys, the tires. Tonight it is black and impenetrable. If you didn't know its depth, you might think it fathomless.

Across the water, the bars and restaurants of Camden Market are still busy with the Halloween crowd. Men and women in costumes cluster around the spaceship-red glow of outdoor heaters, laughing, drinking mulled wine out of steaming mugs.

Ahead, the footbridge slopes down to the towpath that winds alongside Regent's Canal, below street level.

The girl hovers at the edge of the dark, weighing her options.

Usually she avoids the canal after sunset. It is unlit. It is the kind of place she has been told all her life to avoid for the simple fact that she is a girl—but tonight she is cold and drunk and sad and hungry for the leftover pad thai she knows is waiting for her in the fridge. The path by the water is the shortest, fastest route home.

Yet something tells her not to go any farther. Perhaps it is the memory of what happened to her on another night like this one. The stranger waiting in the dark, all the warnings she had been given growing up suddenly manifesting as flesh and breath and muscle.

Then the girl remembers the words at her wrist and runs a fingertip over the cool metal letters sunken into her skin. Words that took her a year to find. Words that mean she no longer has to fear the night or anyone who might be lurking in it.

She crosses the bridge. She plunges down into the blackness.

The first part of the walk is fine. The path is narrow and cobbled. The canal is bordered on both sides by converted warehouses turned into blocks of fancy flats. Light from their windows reflects on the smooth surface of the water, creating an eerie mirror world just below the real one. Houseboats sit snug against the canal's edge, the smell of woodsmoke clinging to the air around them. A huge, fat dog sits atop one, watching her as she passes. The sounds of revelry dissolve into the distance, but there is still life here. Still people to hear her, if she were to scream.

She crosses beneath a bridge. It is mauled with graffiti and lit with shocking blue light to discourage drug use. Combined, they make the place feel dangerous. She moves on quickly, back into the waiting shadow.

The next stretch of the walk is worse. There are no more houseboats. There are no more fancy flats. There is no one to come to her aid. There's more greenery along the side of the path, vines and brambles that don't lose their foliage as the nighttimes turn to frost. She moves closer to the water, wary of attackers hidden in the creepers.

The girl crosses under a second blue-lit bridge, and then a third that's rancid with the stink of urine. She makes it to the base of the stairs that leap up out of the darkness and onto the brightly lit street above.

A girl walks home alone, but not alone.

She feels him before she sees him. There's no sound, or movement, or smell. Just some primordial response left over in the blood from a time before humans were humans. A sudden prickle of fright in her gut. A displacement of energy that makes her gaze snap back over her shoulder and brings her footsteps to a stop.

Her eyes find the figure immediately, standing stationary on the path. He's a slip of shadow, nothing more. No face, no weapon, nothing to indicate that he might do her harm. Just a man.

But she is a girl. And she is alone. And it is night. And that is enough.

She ducks her head and takes the stairs two at a time, but tries to do it casually, the way women do when they're afraid but trying not to look rude. She forces herself not to run. There's no need for desperate measures. Not yet. He's just a man on the towpath at night. It would be rude to run.

And sometimes.

Well.

Sometimes, if you run, the monster chases you; this she learned the hard way.

So she climbs, step after measured step, up, up into the light. The staircase spits her out on Gloucester Avenue, only one street from her flat. She waits under a streetlight to see if the man will follow her, but he does not. She breathes a sigh of relief and turns for home. It's a sloe-black, moonless night. The kind that beckons demons out of the liminal world and brings them into this one, hungry to feed on the souls of the living. London is full to bursting with magic, dark and dangerous, if you know where to look . . . and she knows, now, where to look.

A dog barks.

The girl looks up and stifles a yelp with her hand.

The figure from the canal is somehow standing on the sidewalk directly in front of her. Closer than he was the first time.

The girl stops again. Stares. Her heart crashes inside her chest. She takes small, gasping breaths as she tries to understand the logistics of what has just happened. How could he have followed her? How could he have overtaken her? How could he have moved so quickly? There's no way. There's no way.

Then she remembers the words at her wrist.

There's no need to fear anymore.

There's heavy shadow to her right, the deep, wet shadow that trees cast in the forest. The girl moves toward it, into it, lets it devour her, and—

She steps from a bank of shadows on the next street over. A little out of breath. A little frazzled. She looks around. She's alone again. She went where the figure could not follow. Into one shadow, out of another.

A small smile on her face now, she again heads toward her flat, only a few buildings away. The price she paid for this power—blood and money and soul—was worth it to feel safe.

The girl climbs the five stairs up to her blue front door and unlocks it. When she steps inside and turns to close the door behind her, she finds the figure once more, now standing at the bottom of the stairs. He is unmoving and close. So very close to her now.

It is impossible. Men cannot use magic. This is what she has been told. This is what she has been promised. Men cannot write spells. Men cannot sear invocations into their skin. Men cannot bind their souls to demons in exchange for power.

Men cannot use magic.

And yet. Here he is. Again.

They stand still, staring at each other. Though—is he staring? She cannot see his face, cannot make out his eyes, his nose, his hair. He is empty space, a black hole from which no light escapes.

The girl slams the door closed and scrambles backward. She doesn't bother with the stairs that lead up to her flat on the third floor. She lunges into the shadowed corner of the hall, falls out of another shadow in her kitchen, then fumbles in the sink for one of the dirty knives her housemates are forever leaving to soak.

The blade quivers like a water reed in her white-knuckled hand as she watches her front door and waits. Waits for a bang against the wood, a turning of the handle, a horror-movie moment worthy of a scream.

It does not come.

It does not come.

It does not come.

And then, when she thinks perhaps she is safe, perhaps he was no more than a Halloween prankster out for a laugh, a pair of strong hands close around her throat.

# ONE

**EMER BYRNE** sits in a far corner of the dining hall of Brasenose College, curled over a plate laden with food. Students move in and out of the wood-paneled room, their trays neatly set out with eggs and toast and tea, not noticing the stranger in their midst. They watch their phones with sleepy eyes. They listen to AirPods. They highlight lines in textbooks as they eat. Oxford students tend to be more alert at lunch and dinner, more suspicious of faces they do not recognize, which is why Emer only ever eats in college halls for breakfast. Nobody bothers her. Nobody tries to make conversation. Nobody cares when she takes a second muffin for the road.

Outside, she unlocks her stolen bicycle from where she left it chained against the fence of the Radcliffe Camera. Emer has heard passing tourists remark quizzically at the name—"It doesn't look like a camera"—but it has never stumped her. The word *camera* shares its roots in Greek and Latin with *chamber*. To a girl fluent in Latin and a dozen other old languages, it makes perfect sense.

As she wheels her bike through the square, she tests herself. Behind the Camera is another extravagant building: a palatial wall, beyond which rise turrets shaped like spear tips. All Souls College. To her left, a boxier more fortlike building, also of pale stone and topped with turrets. Bodleian Library. To her right, an ornate spire. University Church of St. Mary the Virgin. Oxford students are expected to know the names of these buildings, and so Emer has learned them, too.

It was a confusing place when she first arrived two summers ago, frantic and afraid that she was being hunted already. She expected the university to be one big campus, not a collection of halls and buildings—residential colleges—scattered throughout the city, each with its own history and charm. Some are very old: Balliol was founded in the thirteenth century. Some are much newer, like Linacre, established in 1962, which is where Emer cycles to this morning.

Cool air needles her skin as she rides. Autumn has descended over the streets. The gutters are laden with leaves the color of honeycomb, and the sandstone buildings are dipped in blanched sunlight.

Linacre College has a gym in the basement. Emer scans an ID card that is not hers, then heads to the locker room to get changed. There, she pulls her workout gear from her backpack. A navy Oxford-branded hoodie and shorts, both stolen from a merchandise store. The clothes are musty and damp with sweat from last night's workout, and the workouts before that.

Emer runs, hard and fast, for forty-five minutes, until her head spins when she steps off the treadmill. Her muscles feel heavy, in a good way. She likes to be able to feel the meat of them when she walks. All that muscle, just beneath the skin, encasing her bones. That is power.

After her run, she goes back to the locker room and gets into the shower fully clothed and rubs soap over the fabric of her clothing until it lathers. Then she stands under the stream to wash away the sweat and grit of the past few days and the faint smell of sulfur that seeps from her skin. She takes off her sopping clothes and washes them properly, washes her underwear, too, all three pairs, then wrings them out and hangs them up on the hooks where people sometimes hang jackets or accidentally leave their towels. When all the cleaning is done, she stands under the water and turns up the heat until it sears her white skin pink. It is a stupid luxury. Even now, so many years after Nessa found her half-feral in the woods, having access to a shower makes her want to laugh and weep at the same time.

She dries herself with someone else's towel and considers her naked body in the foggy full-length mirror, admiring the thick cords of muscle in her arms and legs, the six-pack that has bloomed across the once-soft plane of her stomach. There are two toes missing from her left foot, an unhealed two-inch wound on her left forearm, and an angry red rash below her collarbone where her lead pendant rests against her skin.

Linacre women leave their deodorant here, their shampoo and conditioner, their foundation and lipstick and mascara. Emer uses what she needs, then changes back into the clothes she wore here. A tan wool coat, a black turtleneck, a tweed skirt, black tights, black boots. The same clothes Nessa shoved into Emer's backpack two years ago as she pushed her out the door and told her to run, run, they will come for you after this.

At midday, Emer goes to her first and only "class" for the day. It is a lecture on mathematics. She does not understand mathematics beyond what she learned from her mother, and her mother died when she was seven. Addition, subtraction, and multiplication are concepts that make sense to her, but she struggles to put them into practice without counting on her hands. Nessa sometimes tried to teach her in fits and starts, but Nessa herself had never gone to school, had learned only what had been deemed useful for Byrne women to know: when to plant seeds in the spring, how to turn plants into tinctures, how to speak the tongues of the dead.

Emer would prefer to attend a lecture on languages, the older the better, but those are delivered in small rooms to small classes— and they do not serve food. At the mathematics lecture, they are serving bánh mì, a pork version on one side of the room, a vegetarian option on the other. The sign above the food reads PLEASE TAKE ONLY ONE. Emer takes two of the pork sandwiches, then leaves the auditorium, comes back in another door, and takes two of the vegetarian sandwiches.

The lecture is so full that she has to sit on the side of the room, on the carpeted floor. There's a young guest speaker talking about a scholarship she won to study at an elite university in America. Emer wonders what the food is like there. Then the lecture begins. The professor writes all sorts of strange symbols on the board, as he does every week. Egyptian hieroglyphs she understands, but not these. Emer listens, and watches, and eats all four of her sandwiches slowly. When the attendance sheet is passed around, she looks at it and pretends to fumble for a pen before passing it on without writing her name down. Nobody notices. She has become proficient at being a ghost.

The lecture goes until midafternoon. When it is over, Emer

returns to the Camera and goes to the Bodleian Library and sits at a dark wood table among the dark wood stacks.

The library is why she is here. It is why she decided to hide in Oxford instead of anywhere else when she fled Cork in the night two years ago.

Here, Emer reads. The sun slants long and golden through the windows. The air smells of leather and old paper. It is Emer's favorite place in the world. It is here that she finds books left for her: at her feet, on the chair next to her. She never has to go looking for them; they just appear, as if by magic. Books about protolanguages. Books about sigils and runes. Books about Sumerian, Hattic, Elamite, Hurrian. Books about Linear A. and Cretan hieroglyphs about syllabaries and logograms and constrained writing. Emer reads them all, cover to cover, taking extensive notes as she goes. While she works, she fiddles with the pendant around her neck, twisting the tightly rolled scroll of lead, beaten as thin as silk, between her fingers. A subconscious gesture to make sure it is still there.

At the end of a book on protolanguages, Emer undoes the necklace and unfurls the scroll to review her work. Into the lead are engraved all the worst words Emer has found in every dead language that ever had a writing system.

Every word for *blood*.

Every word for *hatred*.

Every word for *vengeance*.

She adds a new word today, a tiny thing scratched at the very edge with a scriber, and then she looks up to watch the other people in the room, their heads buried in books and laptops in silent contemplation. They are all so clean. They all sit so straight.

They are all so sure they belong here. Emer studies them carefully and tries to emulate them. The lines of their spines. The way their eyes squint when they work through the problems on their screen, frustrated but confident in their ability to prevail in the end. The women are bright faced, with neat ponytails and little makeup. The men have freshly cut hair and shiny shoes. Humans are pattern-recognition machines, and Emer must try hard to fit the pattern. To not arouse suspicion.

When a man gets up to go to the bathroom, Emer stands, puts her pendant back on, and walks past his workstation. He has left his wallet in his open backpack. It still surprises her how freely Oxford students leave their belongings unguarded. How freely they trust each other. Emer pretends to drop something next to the backpack and bends down. She does not take the whole wallet. Just the things that will help her around the city. His student ID card. His cash.

In the evening, Emer eats the muffin she saved from breakfast, then goes back to the gym and lifts weights for another hour. No one questions her presence in the small room meant only for Linacre students. Why would they? Emer's workout gear is still drying, so she wears an Oxford Medicine hoodie that someone left scrunched up in a locker. Sometimes men stare at her as she passes, and she thinks it might be because she is pretty, striking even, with her red hair and brown eyes, but that is not useful when you are trying not to be noticed, not to be remembered.

*What did the girl look like?* Emer imagines the police asking her neighbor back in Cork. *The girl who killed your husband?*

After the weights sessions, Emer goes to the Linacre common kitchen and makes herself a coffee, drinks it, then makes another one. The drawers here are filled with tea bags and packets of brown sauce and coffee pods and individually wrapped biscuits. So much food. She thinks of the nights she spent in the woods around Lough Leane as a child, cold and starving and wild, when there were drawers like this at Oxford the whole time. She takes four biscuits and puts them into her backpack. Then she takes four more, two for each pocket of her coat.

It is night now. The sky is clear, the college gables bleak and Gothic in the gloaming. Emer rides to Franco Manca and lingers outside, waiting for a table of students to leave. It does not take long. Three girls stand and wander out, chatting and laughing as they go. There is still half a pizza on their table, a plate of salad, a beer that has barely been touched. Emer slips inside the restaurant and sits where the girls were sitting and eats everything they left behind. She takes her time. She savors the pizza. She sips the beer slowly. When she is done, she leaves. Nobody stops her, because the bill has already been paid.

Outside, the town is dark and cold in the November chill, late autumn settled heavily over the streets, lulling them into an early hush. The streetlights are yellow and look like gaslight. It reminds Emer of the candles her mother used to burn all throughout the house when she was small.

It is at night that she watches men. In the day she dips her gaze from theirs, smiles at them coyly when necessary, shrinks her muscular frame to look smaller, weaker, more petite. Now she pulls her shoulders back to reveal the full extent of her broadness, feels the weight and surety of the muscles she has cultivated. Under her warm clothes she looks soft, but she is strong, and this, she has learned, makes her dangerous.

Emer follows men on her bicycle. Men do not know what it feels like to be hunted. Men do not walk alone on dark streets and think about fingers closing around their throats or their skulls thudding dully against the pavement.

They do not think about strangers coming to their house and slaughtering their entire family.

Emer likes to find them where they sit or stand or walk, comfortable, unafraid. Because there is no need to fear if you are a man. You own the darkness. It is your space.

Emer slows her bike on Christ Church Meadow Walk, across from a low stone bridge. Folly Bridge. It is her favorite spot in the whole city, apart from the library. The River Thames is surrounded by a medley of mismatched trees; faded eucalyptus, rich emerald evergreens, and impossibly bright oaks in autumn tones of candy red and sherbet orange. It is close to 9:00 p.m. There is only one other person here. A light-haired man sitting on a bench, watching the water as he eats a burger. Emer sits next to him, too close to him, and stares and waits.

Men think she looks like prey.

They do not know she is bait.

"Can I help you?" the man asks. There is no fear in his voice, no fear in his eyes. "Are you okay?"

Emer continues to stare. "Andy?" she asks. It's been two years since she left Ireland, but her accent is still strong.

*Try me*, she thinks. *Try to hurt me.*

*See what happens.*

*See what I can do.*

"No. My name is John." The man looks confused. Concerned. He says nothing more. Emer stands and backs away and leaves him be.

She rides for three more hours, until her fingers are numb with the cold and the city is quiet and there are no more men to stalk.

At midnight she goes back to Brasenose, where she ate the muffin this morning. It is Tuesday night and there is a party going on in the common room. There is food and alcohol, and Emer weaves through the crowd and takes both. Nobody notices. She belongs here. A boy tries to talk to her, asks her name, but it is too bright, and Emer has her shoulders hunched again. The boy waits for her to reply, but she does not, and soon he goes away, looking at her like she is strange.

Stupid. Flirting is part of her camouflage, her disguise. She cannot be the weird girl. She cannot be the girl people think of if anyone comes asking questions.

There are bathrooms down the hall. Emer sits on a toilet lid and eats curry puffs and sips another beer and waits for the party to end, which it does at 1:00 a.m., because there are noise restrictions. The students must be well rested if they are to rule the world one day.

Emer washes her face in the bathroom and drinks five handfuls of water from the tap. In the fluorescent light, her skin is bilious. There are blue half-moons beneath her eyes. She makes a mental note to eat more broccoli, then drinks five more handfuls of water.

When the lights are turned off and everyone is gone, Emer takes out her ring of stolen keys, which is heavy because there are dozens of them on there now, and unlocks the common room. Inside, it is messy, strewn with crumbs, the furniture askew, but it is warm and enclosed, and that's enough. That is more than enough.

Before she goes to sleep, she takes the knife from her backpack and slides the blade down her left forearm, reopening the partially healed wound that she cut last night, and the night before, and the night before, and several hundred nights before that. The blood bubbles to the surface of her skin and begins to trickle down her arm. Emer flicks droplets of it at the walls and recites the wards her mother taught her as a child as she walks the perimeter once, twice, three times.

Then she lies down on a couch, her wool coat still on in case she needs to run, and takes solace in the sound of demons licking up her blood as she falls into a shallow sleep.

# TWO

**IT'S 8:00** a.m. when Jude Wolf wakes, fully clothed, gasping for breath in her bathtub.

The water she jolts up in is cold and black as ink. The room—her bedroom—is trashed, glass shattered everywhere, the Persian carpets that cover her hardwood floors waterlogged.

Jude heaves a few more breaths and tries to remember what happened. The pain had started around sunset. A dull sensation in her leg at first, teasing twinges of the storm to come. She started drinking soon after dark, when the pain became blinding, brilliant, and she could no longer control the desire to claw at the wound in her flesh, to try to excavate the source of agony with her own fingernails. That's when she drew a bath and sank her rotting flesh into the hot water to try and find some relief—there was none.

Jude knocked herself out shortly after with the world's most boring magical spell: the ability to render herself unconscious.

"You miserable bastards," Jude says as she hoists her dripping body from the tub.

Jude is still dressed, as she was yesterday, as she is every day, in a finely tailored black suit, the kind her father so dearly hates because he prefers her in a dress. Prefers her black hair long, too, despite the fact that she's had it cropped in an ear-skimming bob for years.

"It makes you look like a lesbian," he said to her once. Lawrence Wolf failed, rather spectacularly, to realize that was precisely the point.

The thick sludge in the bathtub clears and turns back into water as soon as Jude is no longer submerged. She bends down and touches the surface with a fingertip. Immediately, a glob of black drops into the water. It begins to swell and cloud and boil like a Satanic bath bomb until Jude removes her finger, and then it clears once more.

She flips the bird at the bathtub, then grasps the wet fabric covering her right thigh as a sudden punch of pain lands there. It's not over yet. The aftershocks will twist in her flesh for days. She collapses back onto her bed and tries to breathe through it.

When she can move again, she stands and peels off her damp clothes carefully, as if removing wadding from a wound, then hobbles to the gilt-framed mirror on the other side of the room. There's a gruesome lesion on her thigh, swollen and gangrenous. The skin from knee to groin looks remarkably similar to a log of wood that has been chewed up by fire. It's desiccated and hard to the touch, cut through with bone-deep fissures that leak pus and sulfur. In the wound there is writing, metallic letters melted into her flesh, but the skin is so warped that the letters no longer form words. It's no normal injury. It's old, and doesn't heal, and sometimes, in very quiet rooms, Jude can hear it whispering to her.

It whispers to her now. She breaks out into a sweat and presses her palm over the foul thing, screaming from the white-hot pain, but at least her screams drown out the voices.

It's a language she's not supposed to be able to hear.

The language of demons.

The human body has a visceral reaction to it. Moments later Jude is vomiting, half from the demon language and half from the dazzling hurt of touching the lesion. The pain beats through her body in waves, washing over her and over her, radiating out from the husk that was once her thigh.

"I get it, I get it, don't mess with the occult," Jude gasps as she sinks to the debris-strewn floor.

More minutes pass. She lies still and examines her hand. Touching the wound for a moment has left a red welt across her palm. She uses the back of the same hand to wipe away a thread of spittle dangling from her lips and sits up to survey the damage to her body in the mirror.

*Jesus Christ, they're going to suck me dry,* she thinks as she takes in the big-eyed alien creature staring back at her. Once, Jude Wolf was as handsome as the devil and dressed even sharper. Tall and ballerina-limbed, like her mother, the late beauty queen Judita Nováková, she knew she was a total smoke show. Many girls—and some confused guys—wanted to take their knickers off at the sight of her. Now her body has grown so weak, so thin. A cut at her hairline has sent blood down one side of her face, dried and sloughed away into a rusted mosaic. There's a crust of yellow sulfur on her tongue and several wobbly teeth at the back of her mouth where the bone has begun to soften.

Jude knew there was a price to pay for magic—there always had to be a price—she just didn't expect it to be quite so . . . gruesome.

Jude's phone rings. She answers.

"Hey, Jude," Elijah sings.

Jude cannot help but smile, annoying as that godforsaken song is. "I will never forgive Paul McCartney for writing that."

"You know, I was thinking the other day about the first time we got drunk. Do you remember? At that wedding where I requested the band play 'Hey Jude' and you screamed at them until they stopped?"

They had been young. Jude eleven, Elijah thirteen, the two of them left unsupervised at the wedding of one of their father's business associates. They went around the tables while the adults were dancing and each took a sip from every glass of alcohol they could find, not realizing they were getting absolutely hammered in the process until it was too late.

"I remember," Jude says. "I vomited on the bride. That was so metal."

"That's when I knew you were my favorite sibling."

"It took you eleven years to decide I was better than the Horsemen?"

"You were an exceptionally annoying child."

"That's not true. I was an angel."

Jude hears muffled voices in the background and wonders where her brother is, who he spends his time with now that she's not there.

"Yes, thank you," Elijah says to someone else, then back into the phone: "I gotta go, Judebug. I was just checking you're still alive."

"I am," Jude says, but Eli is already gone. "Okay," she says to herself. "We play to the buzzer, Wolf." The creature in the mirror doesn't look convinced—but what other choice does she have but to give her demons hell?

Jude moves to her feet, pulls on a silk smoking jacket and mismatched brogues, then heads off to take in the damage to the rest of the house.

She lives alone in a nineteenth-century printing factory in Hoxton that has been converted into a house. There are Persian carpets on the floors, taxidermied flamingos in the reception room, a six-seat home theater with red curtains and purple velvet chairs, three bedrooms (each with its own freestanding copper bathtub), two roof terraces, and a room in which the entire south-facing wall are Crittall windows that look out over the city in the distance. The bookshelves are packed with leather-bound tomes. There is a six-oven AGA range in the kitchen.

It's a gilded prison.

The house was given to—or rather forced upon—her two years ago, not long after her fifteenth birthday, along with a monthly stipend that allows her to live in it alone. This arrangement came with some provisos: Jude was not to contact her family again. Jude was not to speak to the press. Jude was not to be photographed in any more compromising situations. Jude was not to go back to school. Jude was to sort her life out and quit bringing shame to the Wolf name.

The rest of the place is in the same state as her bedroom. Glasses lie shattered on the floor. What little furniture she has is upturned. There are holes in the walls, some putrid-smelling dark ooze—pus from her wound?—smeared on the windows. The first time this happened, Jude thought she'd been robbed while she was blacked out. It was only after installing surveillance cameras and reviewing the tapes from the next episode that she realized she had done this herself. Or rather, an invisible and very pissed-off demon had dragged her unconscious body around, slamming her into things.

There is a battle going on inside Jude. A literal battle for her very soul. Two demons want her alive so they can suck her spirit dry. One wants her dead so it can be free of her for good. She has to live with all three of them fighting for supremacy.

In the kitchen, the fridge is open, smashed bottles of sauce congealing on the floor—but the coffee machine has mercifully been spared.

Jude makes two espressos, as she does every morning. "One for you, one for me," she says to the floor-to-ceiling photograph of her mother as she slides to the ground cross-legged and pushes one of the coffees toward it. Judita looks down at her with bright, clever eyes—the same eyes as Jude's—and Jude wonders what became of her mother's soul. She knows very well that demons are real and that the devil is, too. The rest, she is unsure about. What happens to people after they die?

After coffee, Jude begins her day: She opens her laptop and checks the messy Google Doc of private investigators she's currently paying—there are thirteen now—then she calls each of them, one after the other, for a status update. Most don't answer, because most don't believe what Jude is looking for can be found. They take her money, sure, but will they actually do the work? Unlikely.

Usually, this frustrates Jude, but today it infuriates her.

Three of the thirteen end up answering. Saul, the only PI who consistently takes her calls, delivers his update in a bored drawl; he's been calling psychic hotlines and has racked up a £600 bill he wants Jude to pay before he delivers any intel. Jude resists the urge to call him an idiot and explains, for the third time, that she's not looking for a psychic, damn it. Marta is more useful (this time at least; she has a tendency to go dark for months at a time); she has a lead on a young slam poet she saw perform at one of the venues she's been casing. It's a long shot—but what isn't a long shot in Jude's situation? The final contact who picks up is Harry, who isn't a PI so much as semi-competent on-the-ground surveillance. There are rumors of good curses coming out of Oxford at the moment, and Harry is studying English literature there. Jude hired him to scope out his classmates.

"So no one is particularly interested in Latin?" Jude asks him.

"It's Oxford. Everyone pretends they can read and write Latin. You need to be more specific."

Again, Jude gives him the pitch, with more information and less patience than the first time: She's looking for a writer, most likely a poet. They will be fluent in Latin at the very least, but are probably proficient in other classical and ancient languages. What she didn't tell him before: There is—how to put this delicately?— likely to be a faint stench of sulfur to them. Jude is reluctant to be more specific than this, because as soon as you start using words like *curse* and *witch*, people immediately laugh or hang up. Or— and this is the mistake she made with Saul—they start sending every penny-dreadful psychic they find her way and expecting her to pay for the pleasure.

"Sulfur?" Harry asks.

"Yes, Harry. Sulfur. What I'm asking is, do you know any budding poets who reek of rotten eggs?"

"I don't know, I lost my sense of smell when I had COVID. Why would they smell of sulfur?"

Jude pinches the bridge of her nose and decides *screw it*. "A witch, Harry. I'm looking for a witch. Two years ago, I accidentally yoked an angry demon to myself against its will. Now that demon and I are bound together until I die, and it is *quite* pissed off about that because it's starving. Demons expect payment for their services in the form of a human soul to snack on, but instead of feasting on me, it's turned my soul necrotic, and I'm going to be totally and utterly miserable for the rest of my short, cursed life—unless I can find a very talented witch to fix me."

Harry hangs up. Jude throws her phone across the room, yells, "TWAT," as loud as she can, then kicks things with her left leg until she's breathless.

After that, she trawls through Reddit forums looking for certain terms—*cursewriter, voces mysticae, demonic possession*—hoping for another diamond in the rough but finding none.

Midmorning, she begins the arduous task of cleaning and repairing the house. It's a never-ending battle against the corrosive force of the curse. The dark magic has settled into her flesh and bones, but it has also seeped out of her and poisoned the walls and floors. When she moved in, the place was pristine, but like her, it has decayed. It's always cold here, no matter how high she turns up the heat. The walls sag inward as if the bones of the place can no longer bear its own weight. Paint bubbles and peels beneath her fingertips. The electrics have had to be rewired several times, because the wires melt and fray behind the walls. There are leaks everywhere, so many now that Jude has given up on having them repaired: buckets of water dot every room, collecting drips. The lights convulse off and on of their own accord. Wind moans through cracks in the windows.

That the house is melting around her is not even the worst of it.

To be cursed is to be haunted. Dying things come to Jude in the night. Spiders crawl from their holes and contort into twitching knots as she sleeps. Flying insects fall out of the air in her wake. Plants yellow in her presence, their leaves puckered like leather.

Today there are dead birds on each of the terraces, their feathers coming out of them in clumps. Jude picks them up barehanded and feels the powdery coating on their feathers. When she was growing up in her father's tower apartment, pigeons used to hit the windows all the time, leaving tiny snow angels on the glass.

Jude sweeps and vacuums the whole house, pushing all the broken glass and dead insects into a pile for easier collection. She plasters over the new splits in the walls, spreads grout between the cracked tiles in the bathroom. When she first moved in here at fifteen, her long-fingered hands were soft. Now they are rough and callused. It's the only thing she likes about this version of her life.

As she works, Jude thinks of herself as a modern Sisyphus, cursed to forever roll a boulder up a steep hill. Tomorrow, there will be more leaks requiring more buckets. There will be more dead animals seeping from the walls.

Once, Jude was practically a princess, the spoiled daughter of a very rich man. Now she is walking nuclear fallout in the form of a girl.

It's early afternoon when an email arrives from Saul.

*There's a woman with strange markings on her arm working in Harrow. Meet her here in two hours.* The next line is an address. Then: *I think I found you a witch.*

Jude grins and grabs her keys.

# THREE

**ZARA JONES** draws a precise circle around the word *curse*, then looks up, for perhaps the hundredth time, to make sure that no one is watching her. The book she's reading, stolen from a store last week, is nestled inside her science textbook, which is what she's pretending to study. It's mostly dreck, all new-age drivel about healing crystals and the power of beeswax candles, but the chapter on curses and demons holds her attention. It's why she stole the book in the first place.

*Tether*, she circles, then looks up again. Tethered to what, though?

It's late in the afternoon on a Wednesday. The corridor outside the principal's office is mostly deserted at this hour, the students long absconded, the teachers weary and ready for home. A tween couple walks past, their arms linked, but apart from them, Zara is alone. She pushes her metal-rimmed glasses further up her nose. They're for reading and only have a slight magnification, but the blue light filter stops her head from aching when she's been staring at a computer screen for hours, which happens almost every day of her life.

It's hard to know how much the book in her lap has gotten right and how much is guesswork on the part of the author. Over the past year, Zara has been able to piece together a vague idea of how curses work, or at least how she thinks they might work, if they're even real. The idea of tethers is something she stumbled across only recently, but now that she knows about them, she can't get the concept out of her head. Tethers. A tether between a person and a demon, maybe?

Zara's phone buzzes in her pocket.

**Another one**, the message reads. It's been six weeks since the last. Zara was almost starting to believe it was over.

A second message follows the first: **£500 to see it this time.**

Zara tips her head back and exhales in exasperation. The first was £200. The second was £350. An absurd amount of money. An almost impossible amount of money.

Zara thinks about how much cash she has in her room, tucked away in an envelope. There might be £50 or £60 there, she isn't sure.

**I'll see what I can do**, she sends back, even though she knows she won't be able to raise that kind of money. **Where and when?**

**Primrose Hill**. An address follows. **Meet here at 9pm sharp.**

Come up with £500 in a handful of hours? It might as well be £5,000. Or £50,000.

"Zara?" Zara looks up. A man, the principal's administration officer, is looking at her. "Principal Gardner is ready for you."

Zara tucks her science textbook and Wiccan tome into her

backpack and follows him. On the other side of the door she finds Gardner, expectant. The woman is Black and stylish as hell, considered a fashion icon by her students. They rarely see her without her signature red lipstick and some form of neon on her body: neon-pink suit jacket, neon-green earrings, neon-blue slingback pumps. Some of the senior girls are trying to convince her to start a fashion TikTok.

There are three books laid out on the desk in front of Gardner, all facing Zara: *Magic and Witchcraft in Ancient Rome: A Sourcebook* by Harriet Owens; *A Brief History of Women and Magic* by Anna Alexander; and *Black Magic and Forbidden Rites: Necromancy for the Modern Witch* by Elizabeth T. Lee.

"Oh hell," Zara says.

"Indeed," Gardner replies. "Take a seat."

Zara does.

"You really—" Gardner stops to take in Zara's outfit. "What *are* you wearing? I've told you before, you don't have to dress like that."

Zara looks down at her outfit. Camden School for Girls does not require its students to wear uniforms, a policy that Zara scorns. Aunt Prudence would turn in her grave at the thought of what some of Zara's classmates wear. Ripped jeans and hoodies—in a place of learning!

Today, like most days, Zara wears a box-pleat pinafore dress over a dark turtleneck, all under a smart tartan blazer, all in tones of brown. Leather loafers and chunky wool socks complete the look. She ties her hair—blond, thick, cut in a long bob to her shoulders—back with a ribbon. It is a kind of armor. A shorthand message to the world: Zara Jones is a serious and learned young woman, meant for the hallowed halls of somewhere like Oxford or

Cambridge. What she hopes the world doesn't see is that the blazer is inherited from her dead aunt and is two sizes too big for her, and the leather loafers are thrifted and have holes in the soles so that when it rains, her socks go soggy.

Zara clears her throat. "As we have discussed previously, I find the uniform policy at this institution sorely lacking. I'm setting an example for my peers on how to dress for success."

"You look like you're cosplaying Sylvia Plath."

"Thank you."

Gardner looks very much like she wants to say, *That wasn't a compliment*, but restrains herself. Instead, she motions to the books. "For an aggravating follower of rules that don't exist, this is somewhat of a surprise. Care to explain?"

Zara sits up straight and smooths out the pleats in her skirt. How to wend her way out of this one? "Well, they're research sources for a history assignment," she tries.

"I care less about the content and more about the fact you were caught stealing them. A police officer dropped them here earlier today and asked me to give you a stern warning."

The cop had threatened to come to Zara's school, but she thought it had been just that: a threat.

It wasn't the first time she'd been caught shoplifting, wasn't the first time she'd been forced to sit in the back room while an employee called the police. Zara was compliant when she was busted, mostly because she felt so ghastly when it happened. There was no thrill in it for her, no attempt at rebellion, unlike some of her classmates, who pocketed lipstick from Boots or earrings from Primark. When she did it, her hands were always sweaty and shaking. There was always a sloshing pit of acid in her stomach. Zara was not a natural thief. She stole because she needed things and she had no money to buy them.

Yesterday, she'd gone to a boutique used bookstore in Bloomsbury. The closest Waterstones had books by witchy Instagram influencers and thick volumes on pagan rituals and Neolithic druids, but never anything that felt relevant to her project. So she'd gone to the bookstore, where the floor and walls and ceiling were all dark wood and the books were covered with vellum and locked away behind glass. It was the kind of place Zara felt most at home, among the almond-sweet pages of old tomes.

Zara hadn't even known she was busted until the officer, a man, tapped her on the shoulder several blocks from the store. Zara had sighed and nodded and handed over the three books she'd spent the last twenty minutes slipping—skillfully, she'd thought, though clearly that was wrong—into her backpack.

"Ms. Jones," Gardner continues. "This is incredibly serious and incredibly disappointing."

"Yes, I was quite disappointed in myself for getting caught."

"Zara."

Zara looks at her hands, cupped in her lap. The way people say her name now is so full of sadness. Nobody says *Zara!* with a smile on their face. Nobody snaps *Zara* when they're furious with her. It's always said with weight, with grooves of concern carved into the speaker's forehead. It's always said like an apology.

"The last time I saw you in this office—"

"I would rather not talk about that."

"No. Of course not. What I'm trying to say is that the last time you walked in here, you were our best student. You were exceptional. Now your teachers are worried for you. Your grades . . ."

Gardner keeps talking, and Zara lets her thoughts drift, as she does whenever anyone tries to give her a pep talk. Many have been delivered to her over the past year. *Keep your chin up. Things will get better. It won't always hurt this much.* But it does still hurt, and it never gets any better. Each day is like the first. The wound is not healing—nor does Zara want it to. She will not allow it. The rawness of the pain is what keeps her going.

Truth be told, she only comes to school anymore because of the library. Zara is the first person here in the morning and the last to leave. Most of that time she spends in the stacks, reading about curses and demons and tethers on the school computers or in the books she steals. Occasionally she goes to class, and teachers say her name in that sad, heavy way—*oh, Zara*—and she sits and tries to concentrate, but often she ends up laughing. Laughing at all the silly things she used to take so seriously but that now mean nothing. What use are English essays now? What use is speaking French now? What use are good grades now that her world has ceased to exist entirely?

"What do you think?" Gardner asks.

Zara has no idea what she has said.

"Yes," she answers. "I think that sounds good."

"Is everything okay at home? I know you're with your uncle now and—"

Zara's nostrils flare. "Everything is fine. Peachy. I've been distracted by a big project I've been working on, that's all."

"I wasn't aware that our curriculum covered dark magic and necromancy."

*If only it did,* Zara thinks. *Then I might know what I was doing.* She forces a smile. "May I be excused? I really should get back to my schoolwork."

Gardner dismisses her with a nod. Then, when she's at the door: "Ms. Jones. Zara." The weight. The concern. Zara stops. Gardner takes a breath. "A terrible thing happened to you. A heartbreaking, unimaginable thing. No one would be shocked if you let it ruin your life—but I'm asking you not to. You are only seventeen. You have so much of that life left in front of you. Now, if there is anything I can do to help—"

"I need five hundred pounds, right now, no questions asked."

Gardner blinks a few times. There is a long silence. "That's a lot of money," she says eventually. "It would be wildly inappropriate for me to—"

"Everyone is always telling me, 'If you need anything, just ask.' So I'm asking. I need five hundred pounds. That is how you can help me."

Zara doesn't think Gardner will do it, but the next moment she goes digging in her handbag and comes up with a handful of coins and some notes. "I have"—she counts it—"forty-seven pounds. Oh, wait." She fishes in her coat pocket (killer neon tartan). "There's an extra five," she says, holding up another note. "Fifty-two. Will that suffice?"

"If the answer on a math exam was five hundred and I wrote fifty-two instead, would that suffice?"

Gardner leans back in her chair with her lips pursed, cool as hell.

Zara knows she's taken it too far. "Sorry. I apologize, that was rude of me. Thank you. I do appreciate it. I'm trying to . . . I am trying. I promise."

"Are you? Because it sure doesn't look that way to me."

"I am. In my own way. I'm trying to—" Zara stops, because

there's no way to explain what she is trying to do without sounding like she's unhinged. "I'm going to fix everything."

Gardner frowns. She looks worried. "It's very type A to think that you can fix everything." She picks up a pen, writes something on a piece of paper, slides the paper across the desk. "My personal phone number. Any time of the day or night you need someone to be there for you, you call me, okay? You need to know that there are people in your life who care if you succeed."

Zara takes the paper and shoves it in her jacket pocket, knowing full well she'll never use it. "I need to keep the books."

"For your project."

"For my project."

"The cop brought them by because he was very concerned about their content. Wanted me to have a strong word with you about how damaging demonic themes can be for young ladies." Gardner stacks the books up and slides them across her desk, too, along with the money. "The school can pay for them and add them to the library when you're done. I don't want to see you in here again, and I don't want any more visits from the police. Understood?"

Zara nods and then leaves Principal Gardner's office £52 and three books richer than when she entered. Not a bad afternoon, all in all.

She walks home quickly. It's Wednesday, November 1, the day after Halloween, and there are still decorations out everywhere. Shop fronts are painted with hollow-eyed pumpkins and bent-branched trees. Houses have fake spiderwebs cast over hedges and CAUTION DANGER tape crisscrossed over doorways. The weather seems to have changed overnight, the last of the autumn warmth giving way to bruised skies and gusting winds, a dusting of nicotine-yellow leaves tossed across everything.

Zara lives not far from her school in a one-bedroom flat with her uncle in an ex–council estate in Camden. Uncle Kyle bought the place fifteen years ago and thought he was very smart at the time, twenty-one years old and already on the property ladder. Then his career as the front man of an emo band failed to gain traction—shocking, really—and Kyle Jones has been stuck paying off his interest-only mortgage ever since.

Zara looks up at the window of Kyle's flat. The curtains are drawn, the room beyond them seemingly dark. She calls the landline. (Who still has a landline?) When no one picks up, she figures it's safe to go inside. It is not until she has her keys in the lock, not until she's turned the door handle and heard the electronic pop of a machine gun that she realizes Kyle is home and it's too late to back out now. Kyle is sitting on the couch with the lights out, buried in the nest of blankets he sleeps in every night, playing *Call of Duty*. The place stinks of weed, as per usual. Kyle is still in his pajamas, as per usual.

"Where have you been?" he asks without looking away from the TV.

"At school," Zara says brightly as she slips past him into her room. The only bedroom. "You know, the institution I go to every day."

"Yeah fucking right."

Zara closes the door and waits. Sometimes, when he is very angry with her or with the game or with the state of his life, he will throw down his controller and storm in here. Zara never knew why it was called storming before she came to live with Kyle last year, but now she thinks she understands. When Kyle doesn't come, Zara lets out her breath. She wishes the flat was on a lower floor so she could shimmy in and out without ever having to see him. It's something she fantasizes about often. A year ago, she daydreamed about being the youngest woman to win the Nobel Prize for physics (Marie Curie was thirty-six—a difficult record to beat, certainly, but one Zara was sure she could surpass). Now this is what passes for fantasy: having a room slightly closer to the ground.

Zara goes to her bed and pulls out the suitcase from underneath it. It is neatly organized and contains things she wants to keep hidden from Kyle: her research journal, Prudence's old chessboard, a vacuum-packed bag of Savannah's favorite clothes, a bottle of Savannah's perfume, and everything she has collected over the past year. Everything she thinks she will need for her project. There are candles and bags of salt and crystals (back from when she thought they might work—she knows now that they won't).

The envelope is there, on top where she left it, but now it's empty.

It's empty.

Zara slams her door open so hard she hears the knob crack the plasterboard of the wall behind.

Kyle looks up, a bolt of anger already wedged between his eyebrows.

"Where's my money?" Zara demands.

"What money?"

"The money I keep in an envelope under my bed."

"Oh, that money. That's your rent money."

"You took it. You went through my things."

"You think you can live here for free? Eat my food? Use my electricity? I put a roof over your head, Zara. You can contribute."

"I sold things online to get that money. I sold *Savannah's* things."

All sold on Vinted, strangers sending her messages asking, **Hi, would you sell this for £5?** like they weren't buying sacred shrouds of the departed.

"Good," Kyle spits. "Not much use in keeping a dead girl's stuff around, is there?"

Zara thinks about killing him. She thinks about the IKEA knife in the kitchen, the silver one that is barely sharp enough to hack through an onion these days, but pointy enough that it could surely sink into Kyle Jones's gut deep enough to do some damage. Zara curls her fingers into a fist and lets herself imagine how deliciously satisfying it would feel to stab him.

"Give it back," Zara says through gritted teeth.

"Bugger off, Zara. I'm busy."

*"Give it back,"* Zara says again, more forcefully this time.

Now Kyle is pissed. "Don't you tell me what to do. What's all that weird shit under your bed, anyway? I want that out of my house. You hear me? You better clear all that shit out or I'll burn it. I'll burn every goddamn thing in there."

Zara stalks past him—she doesn't storm, only Kyle storms—and heads for the front door.

"Where do you think you're going?" he asks her.

"Out," Zara says as she slams the door behind her. She will pay for this later. Kyle hates slammed doors. It's disrespectful, he says, like respect is something he deserves. Soon, once he has finished his stupid game, he will go and inspect the cracked plaster in her bedroom, and because he has nothing better to do with his time, he will let his anger about it fester. Then it will spill out of him in a torrent the next time he sees her, even if she stays away overnight.

Downstairs, Zara punches Kyle's junk box of a car so hard that her knuckle splits. The car is undamaged. Zara sits in the gutter and watches her blood drip onto the concrete as the sky darkens overhead. People pass by and see her. They mind their own business. It's that kind of neighborhood.

If Aunt Prudence could see her now! She'd no doubt call her behavior boorish. Beneath her. That was the very worst insult Prudence could muster.

Zara sucks on her split knuckle and inhales deeply.

*I did not come this far to only come this far,* she chants in her head, a motto borrowed from Pru. *I did not come this far to only come this far.*

With her eyes closed, Zara pictures Prudence, all six foot two of her. Her pale, papery skin, her hair in rollers, her teeth always slightly smudged with lipstick. A large woman in every way: in height, in intellect, in presence. She took up every room she walked into, enlivened every conversation. There is a picture of her on Zara's phone, taken several weeks before she died. In it, Pru, eighty-two, drinks whiskey on the rocks and smokes a cigar. "Refreshing for the lungs, I do not care a lick what young doctors think they know now." She died, of course, from lung cancer.

God, Zara had loved that woman.

What would Pru do? What would she tell her, if she were here?

*I did not come this far to only come this far.*

Zara knows that she's not grieving like a normal person. Zara knows she is not grieving for Savannah in the same way she grieved for Pru. Pru was old. Pru was sick. Pru was ready to go. Pru saw death as a mercy and welcomed it when the time came—but Savannah was ripped from the world against her will.

It is not fair.

It will not stand.

When it comes to Savannah, if there really are five stages of grief, Zara has never made it past the second: anger. She is furious. It bubbles and boils inside her, barely contained by her neat exterior. Fury is what drives her, what fuels her, what flows through her veins and keeps her heart beating. Before, Zara used to think that if anything ever happened to Savannah, she would cross into the afterlife and snatch her back from the jaws of death—and then something did happen to Savannah, and Zara discovered that she was powerless.

But maybe not for very much longer.

Pru would not give up on something she cared about (heck, she didn't even give up smoking, even at the end)—and neither will Zara.

She wipes the mist from her eyes, opens the stolen Elizabeth Lee book that Gardner let her keep—*Black Magic and Forbidden Rites: Necromancy for the Modern Witch*—chooses what she deems the most promising ritual, then stands and heads toward the cemetery.

*I did not come this far to only come this far.*

Zara Jones is going to bring her sister back.

*I did not come this far to only come this far.*

Zara Jones is going to raise the dead.

# FOUR

JUDE HAS met two honest-to-God witches in her life. One was a retired doctor who specialized in pain magic. The other was the lead singer in a band who moonlighted as a cursewriter to pay her bills. Neither had advertised their services with neon signs (neither had advertised their services at all), so when Jude arrives at the address Saul gave her and sees, in screaming-pink neon, the words TAROT CARD READING AND PALMISTRY! she is deeply displeased.

Jude parks her car across from the run-down house in Harrow and calls Saul. It goes to voice mail. "Saul, you utter prick," she spits. "Stop sending me to psychics you find advertised in the newspaper or you're not getting paid!"

Jude knows she should leave. Real witches are hard to find because they don't want to be found. Plus, magic isn't something that can be controlled or divined through tarot cards or crystal balls or rat bones cast into bowls in heady rooms that stink of incense. Once upon a time, it might've been, but those days are long gone. There's very little left of magic anymore, and what remains is bitter and strong and dangerous. It is kept hidden from the world. That is the only way for those who practice it to survive.

Still, there's something raw and hungry inside her. It is desperation. It is hope—hope that this time, maybe, she will find the person who will fix her, who will open a door back to the life of warmth and luxury and belonging and comfort that she lost—and hope has a way of making smart people do stupid things.

"Screw it," she says as she gets out of her car and walks toward the door, the memory of champagne on her tongue.

The Wednesday afternoon sun is drowsy, the air laced with winter. Jude shudders, hikes her shoulders up to her ears, draws her coat tighter across her chest. She feels the cold in her bones now. The wind spears through the fabric of her clothes into the wound nestled beneath, where it shoots up her femur and into her hip socket. The joint there is stiff and swollen with some ungodly supernatural arthritis that makes her skeleton actually creak like the bough of a tree in a storm. Jude moves slipshod across the layer cake of sodden leaves collecting in the gutter and on the footpath.

The front door is half-open. "Hello?" Jude calls into the hall. There's no answer. She steps inside. The place smells, predictably, of sandalwood incense and burned sage, undercut with cigarette smoke. Dumb hope pushes Jude farther, lures her deeper. In that moment, she despises herself. Despises how vulnerable and pathetic her need has made her. The air in the house is warm and stagnant, the heater turned up too high. Wind chimes plink from somewhere nearby.

"Hello, Jude," comes a woman's voice. "I've been waiting for you."

"Oh hell," Jude says when she sees her, because the woman is ridiculous. She's a generation behind the modern Instagram mystics, whom Jude has also met a handful of, sleek young businesswomen who charge £100 an hour for card readings and sell crystals and shells in their online stores. This woman is dressed like a fortune-teller you'd hire for a child's birthday party, complete with a headscarf with a row of coins dangling across her forehead.

"I'm Cassandra," the woman says. Of freakin' course.

"I'm leaving," Jude replies.

"You're a skeptic. That doesn't bother me. I've changed the minds of skeptics before."

"Trust me, Cass, I'm the furthest thing from a skeptic there is."

"What can I do for you?"

"What *can* you do for me?"

"Saul told me you're looking for someone like me. That's all I know."

"You're the psychic. Can't you figure it out?" Cassandra says nothing. "Fine. Let's give you a whirl. Why not, since I came all this way. I'm plagued by demons, Cass."

"Personal demons? Addiction, depression?"

"No. Not personal demons." Jude takes a step forward. "Two years ago, I cursed myself. I was fifteen and interested in magic. Ouija boards, communing with the dead, that kind of thing. I found a very old book with a very specific set of instructions on how to do a spell. On how to bind my soul to a demon in exchange for power. I performed that spell, but because I'm an idiot, I messed it up."

The first time was the worst, because it went so catastrophically wrong. When Jude accidentally yoked a demon to her soul against its will, her body bore the brunt of the damage. The force of the curse cracked her femur—the strongest bone in the human body—in four places. There was bruising from her navel to her ankle. ER doctors assumed she'd been in a car accident. She was hospitalized for three months and endured having her leg wound debrided—stripped of the rotten flesh. Nurses often vomited when they changed the dressing. They always apologized when it happened. It wasn't like them, they said, to be squeamish—but Jude knew that this was no normal wound. It smelled of sulfur and sewage. Even she was repulsed by the sight of it, the smell of it.

Those were long, lonely months spent in appalling pain and punctuated with the daily sting of regret that she'd done this to her bloody self. The only person who came to visit was Elijah, who told her it was *so cringe* that she'd decided to become a heroin addict because it was cliché. It was the first time Jude had heard the cover story that her father had concocted. What Lawrence Wolf believed had really happened, Jude wasn't sure.

Elijah kept visiting in secret, because their father had already forbade the family from reaching out to her. Each time, he brought with him a new book because he knew Jude was bored and loved reading. "But I don't want you to think I've forgiven you for being a tragic idiot, hence all of the books are from the list of the worst ever reviewed on Goodreads," he told her. "Two stars or under. That's what you get." It was the same reason he'd only bring her Double Decker bars as a snack, because they'd both once agreed they were the worst chocolate.

So, during her long convalescence, Jude read much of L. Ron Hubbard's back catalog, a gay conversion manual, and a truly terrifying children's book that attempted to educate kids on the ineffectiveness of vaccines.

By the time she was released from hospital three months later, she'd decided that Double Decker bars were, in fact, the finest chocolate the UK had to offer. She was, thankfully, still very gay.

"Jude," Cass breathes. "I have to say, I don't sense evil energy around you at all."

A slow smirk spreads across Jude's face. "Is that so?" The second time she offered up a slice of her soul to the devil, it was an attempt (a fruitless one, it would turn out) to bind the pain caused by the first stupid curse. The only thing it *did* do was make Jude's vision crack. Her normal vision is unaffected, but if she closes her left eye and squints in gloomy rooms, she can sometimes, in the sliver of space that appears between her broken sight, glimpse the realm beyond the veil. Jude does this now, and sees the blurred shapes of the three demonic creatures tethered to her soul. They are clustered around Cassandra, circling her closely. "There are three demons in this room right now, Cass. They like the look of you. Or rather, the smell. Did you cut yourself recently? A nicked kneecap when you were shaving, maybe? Even a paper cut will do it. They're like sharks. A whiff of blood, and they're all over you."

Cassandra swallows and runs her thumb over the Band-Aid on the tip of one of her fingers. "I think . . . Maybe you should go."

Jude blinks her left eye open. "Just for shits and giggles—show me the mark on your wrist."

Cassandra looks reluctant but pushes up one of her sleeves to reveal an ordinary tattoo that reads *LIVE, LAUGH, LOVE* in a cursive font. Jude groans.

On her way out, she calls Saul again and leaves another message: "You're fired, you useless old git."

---

HOLLAND PARK ISN'T exactly on the way from Harrow to Hoxton, but it's not *not* on the way, either. Jude is halfway to the Wolf home, guided there by muscle memory, before she realizes where she's going. Rain comes down hard against the windscreen, and she feels a sudden sharp ache for her old life. Because there was a life before this one. A life with a family, however screwed up they might be. A life in which Jude moved through her days with ease. A life spent in pursuit of pleasure and joy. A life with school and friends and a brilliantly glowing future.

Now that she's close, Jude wants to see the place, even though she's banned from being anywhere near there. She drives through the streets she knows well and parks across the road. The house is unassuming from the outside, or at least as unassuming as a £40-million property in Holland Park can be. It's three levels of red brick with white window frames, a black door, and neat hedges in the small front garden. A plaque by the front door reads WOLF HALL because her father read the book once and soon began claiming to be distantly related to Jane Seymour, the third wife of Henry VIII.

Nobody lives here. At least not full-time. Cousins host parties here, and aunts and uncles entertain business associates here, and Jude's brothers sleep here sometimes, to get away from their wives. Beyond the restrained façade is a vast sprawl of hidden luxury. There's a cinema, a heated indoor swimming pool, an extensive garden, multiple staff quarters, a gym, a sauna, a surveillance room filled with CCTV screens. There's also a panic room with walls made of steel that is, weirdly, a popular place for the younger Wolf family members to bring dates ("I don't know why women think it's so hot," Elijah had told her once, "but they do"—TMI, Eli) and a terrifying fortification system that could withstand a nuclear blast or a zombie apocalypse or, like, the Purge. The family flocks here for dinners and birthdays and Sunday lunches. Many of Jude's happiest memories took place in this house.

The cover story—at her school, for her family, in the media—is that Jude has a drug problem, Jude was in a car accident caused by a drug overdose, and Jude has been in and out of glamorous rehab facilities ever since. If only. She tried heroin once, to see if it would cut through the pain in her leg. It didn't. Instead, it royally pissed off her one starving demon. If it was in pain, then damn it, Jude would be in pain, too. It spent the night throwing her drugged-out body around her house like she was in *The Exorcist*, shoving her down the stairs, then dragging her back up the stairs, then shoving her down again. Jude was too high and then too concussed to care much. Sure, why not, get it over with, she remembers thinking. If she died, the putrid tether that bound them would break and the demon would be free.

By the time Jude woke in the morning, sprawled out and bleeding on her reception room floor (nothing new), her entire house was trashed (nothing new) and the gut-deep, nerve-plucking, slowly spreading rot pain in her thigh (nothing new) was worse than ever. Jude has sworn off opioids ever since. That did not stop the manufactured rumor that she was a habitual drug abuser from spreading. Even her brothers believed it. It made more sense and required far less explanation than the truth, so Jude went with it. Played into it.

"Bollocks," Jude whispers as a car pulls into the driveway of Wolf Hall. She sinks low in her seat and waits to see who gets out. Her eldest half brother, Adam, more than twenty-five years Jude's senior, followed by Dove, his daughter, a lanky blonde who emerges from the back seat wearing her school uniform.

There was a time in Jude's life when she wore the same uniform like a second skin. A time not so long ago when putting on that skirt, that jacket, that hat meant she got to spend her days reading Shakespeare and kissing pretty girls in the library stacks at lunchtime.

That is the life that she lost. That is the life that she's supposed to be living. That is the life she wants back.

More cars pull into the drive. More Wolf family members emerge. Three other older half brothers, Seth, Matthew, and Drew, and their wives. And then him, in the flesh. Lawrence Wolf. Everybody waits for him under umbrellas. No one goes inside before the king.

Even from this distance, even through the rain, Jude can see his eyes. Light blue, almost milky, like moonstones. They belong to a man with a long, thin face atop a long, thin body. He's old—in his seventies now—and impeccably dressed. The others straighten around him, their spines snapped to attention. Jude remembers that feeling, of Lawrence walking into a room, always with Adam a pace behind him, and the oxygen suddenly turning thin.

Drew darts over to him now with an umbrella. Lawrence brushes him off, continues walking through the rain with Adam at his side. Drew stares after them, his expression somber. It changes so quickly with their father. You can be bathed in the golden light of his favor one moment, outcast the next—but damn, does it feel good when he throws a bone your way, tells you you are good, shiny, worthy, loved. It's like a drug, and they all take hits of it, all of the siblings, because no one can make you feel more invincible than Lawrence Wolf—until he tears you down.

All her life, Jude has heard fantastic and terrible stories about her father. Lawrence Wolf is cutthroat, they say. Lawrence Wolf is unscrupulous. Lawrence Wolf is a monster. Many of the more sordid tales she does not accept—*cannot* accept. After all, how could her beautiful mother have fallen in love with a *monster*? How could Jude have come from a *monster*?

When Jude was moving out two years ago, she came across some old boxes of her mother's things stored in the attic. Inside were pieces of clothing from some of Judita's short-lived modeling career: early 2000s couture from Chanel and Jean Paul Gaultier and Versace, all stored in tissue paper. The next box was shoes and accessories. The boxes farther back in the attic contained books and paperwork and stacks of different-size photographs bound with elastic bands.

There were pictures of Lawrence and Judita on their wedding day. Jude had never seen them before. Judita was young and enigmatic-looking, her cheeks notched, her black hair slicked back against her scalp in a tight ponytail, her clever eyes staring just above the lens of the camera. Lawrence looked old enough to be her father, because he was old enough to be her father. Judita was twenty-five and Lawrence was already past fifty. Yet even Jude had to admit that they looked . . . happy. Judita had her hand on Lawrence's chest, her shoulder angled toward him seductively— and Lawrence was smiling. *This* was the man Jude longed to know, to be loved by.

Lawrence Wolf does not smile, not anymore.

If the couple looked happy, Jude's older half brothers most

certainly did *not*. They made no attempt to mask their loathing, solemn as pallbearers at a funeral.

Less than four years later, Judita fell off Lawrence's yacht and drowned.

There's a sudden rap at the passenger-side window, a face pressed close to the glass.

"Jesus," Jude says as she jumps in her seat.

"Unlock the door," Elijah orders.

"No."

"I've already caught you stalking me, so why don't you make this less embarrassing for yourself and just open the door."

"Fine." Jude unlocks the door, and Elijah slides inside.

Even though they are half siblings, they look alike. All of Lawrence's eldest sons are golden-haired and classically handsome, but Eli and Jude are both sharp, gaunt, pale. The black sheep, they call themselves.

Elijah looks her up and down, sips a breath, and—dear God, Jude could die from the shame of it—immediately winds down the window to let in fresh air. Jude has gotten used to her own stench, the vapor that rises from the puckered basin of wet skin on her thigh.

"How's your junkie mother?" Jude asks him.

"Still alive. More than I can say of yours."

"Ouch."

Jude's mother was a dark-haired, lissome model from the Czech Republic. Elijah's mother was a dark-haired, lissome model from some other Eastern European country (Lawrence Wolf has a type). Unlike Judita, though, Drahoslava is still alive enough (though barely) to show up in the tabloids from time to time, spending her chunk of their father's fortune on champagne and younger men.

Jude has a soft spot for that mess of a woman, just as Drahoslava has a soft spot for the boy she squeezed out between coke binges.

Of her five older brothers, Elijah is Jude's favorite. The four eldest boys, from Lawrence's first marriage to his college sweetheart, are much older than them. They have wives and children and perfectly respectable jobs at their father's company, none of which Jude finds particularly interesting (except, perhaps, for the wives—total bombshells, all of them).

There have been more women since her own mother. More lovers and more wives. More siblings, too. Younger ones, cuter ones. Three? Four? Five, maybe, by now? Jude isn't sure. She doesn't make a habit of keeping track of who her father is sleeping with, or how many squirming, unfortunate human life-forms result from the fact that Lawrence Wolf, rich and educated and powerful as he is, has apparently never heard of a four-hundred-year-old invention known as the goddamn condom.

"You look dreadful, and you smell *disgusting*," Elijah says.

"Lovely to see you, too."

"Pray tell, why are you here?"

"I was in the area. Thought I'd swing by and say hello to the family."

"You're lucky I spotted you and not one of the others. You need to leave. If he sees you here, he'll cut you off entirely. However will you keep yourself in Double Decker bars if you're poor?"

"Prostitution, probably."

"I truly don't mean to offend you, but I doubt anyone would pay to sleep with you in your current condition."

"Maybe I could try OnlyFans. The screen would hide the smell."

Elijah rubs his eyelids with his fingers. "*God.* To think, there was a point in my life when I was really excited about having a sister."

"What are you even doing in London? Did Oxford kick you out already?"

"I wish." Oxford was not Eli's idea. He'd wanted to break tradition, to study painting at Zurich University of the Arts—but breaking tradition is not an option for the children of Lawrence Wolf. The children of Lawrence Wolf go to Oxford and study something Lawrence deems useful, so that is what Elijah does. "I was summoned. Compulsory family meeting. Shit's going down: Adam is taking over as CEO of the company, and Lawrence is getting married again." Elijah watches Jude for her reaction; she manages to keep her face expressionless.

"I can't believe Lawrence is retiring," she says eventually.

"His fiancée is, like, twenty-three and pregnant with twins. He wants to move to the countryside and—I quote—'finally have a family.'"

"Wow. It's almost like he doesn't have a dozen children already. How did the Horsemen take the news?"

"Oh, it was all very *Succession*. Seth lost his mind when Adam made the announcement, disappeared for three days. We finally found him camped out in the Forest of Dean, half naked and hypothermic, high on magic mushrooms."

"As if it was ever going to be Seth."

"I know, right? I'd almost feel sorry for him if he wasn't such an abominable prick."

Elijah has never had an easy time with the Horsemen. They tolerated Jude, were sometimes even kind to her, especially Adam, whose daughter is the same age as Jude. The others—Seth,

Matthew, Drew—were not so charitable. They called Eli "Gollum" and "the bastard," taunted him, tormented him constantly. When he was a child and they were old enough to know better, they put a python in his bedroom while he slept. A freakin' *python*. Elijah woke to the snake in his bed, its polished scales cool against the bare skin of his chest. Eli panicked, shrieked, thrashed. The snake, no doubt also terrified, bit him once on the face before Eli managed to roll out of striking range. He still has puncture scars on the left side of his jaw and has never forgiven his brothers for the attack. Jude doesn't blame him.

"So when's the wedding?" she asks. "Maybe I'll crash."

"Sunday." Elijah is quiet for a moment, and then he asks the question he's been waiting to ask: "Jude. Are you . . . okay?"

"Whyever would you think I'm not?"

Elijah looks her up and down again, then checks the time on his Patek Philippe. (Lawrence bought one for each of his sons upon their acceptance into university. Jude has—*had*—been looking forward to receiving her own. A tangible token of affection from a man whose approval she still wants, despite everything.) He sighs. "Now I'm late. You know he hates that." Elijah grips Jude by the shoulder. "Whatever you did to piss him off—please fix it. I miss you. Don't leave me alone with these intolerable psychopaths."

"I'm working on it. Believe me."

"Don't come here again, Judebug. Don't risk it." Elijah gets out of the car and runs through the rain. A staff member opens the front door for him and then they're both swallowed by the cavernous house along with the rest of the family. The night will be bright with champagne and plates of colorful food prepared by the small army of private chefs who follow Lawrence everywhere he goes.

Jude's phone vibrates in the center console.

**Another one**, the message from an unknown number reads. A second message follows: **£1000 to see it this time.**

**About bloody time**, Jude types back.

**Primrose Hill** comes the reply, followed by an address. **Meet me tonight at 9pm sharp.**

# FIVE

NIGHT HAS swallowed the sky by the time Zara reaches the cemetery where Savannah is buried. Groceries clink in her satchel as she moves: a little bottle of wine, a jar of honey, a pint of whole milk, a bottle of water, and a bag of pearl barley, all *borrowed* from a nearby M&S. The ritual, which is inspired by the one performed by Odysseus in *The Odyssey*, also calls for the sacrifice of two goats, which she doesn't have, so she's improvising with a shrink-wrapped packet of lamb.

The cast-iron gates are locked, but there's a tree that sags low over one of the walls, low enough for Zara to reach up and haul herself into its branches. The bark bites into her palms, leaving her skin feeling jagged and gritty as she stands on a thick bough and weaves through a snarl of branches that nip at her stockings. There's a sucking whistle nearby, then the pops of cheap fireworks going off. Zara stops for a moment and watches them through the leaves. It's Guy Fawkes Night in a few days, and people are testing their rockets. London will smell like gunpowder for the next week.

Zara drops to the ground. It's cooler on this side of the wall, all that cold stone pressing close. Mist clings to the earth. The air smells of fox excrement and sweet lilies left on graves. Headstones push through the soil as though they've sprouted from it, tilting left and right like organic things instead of stone. There is a carpet of amber leaves across the grass. The paths through the graveyard are gravel and mud, pocked with puddles from the recent rain. Zara no longer needs a light. She knows her way there in the dark. She feels no fear of the dead. If anything, she would welcome a visit from a ghost—any ghost—to confirm that she's not crazy, that what she hopes to do is possible. As it stands, whatever happens beyond the veil has remained hidden to her, frustratingly out of reach. It's the only puzzle she's been unable to solve.

It was Prudence who first introduced her to puzzles, albeit by accident.

It had been storming when Zara's mother dumped her and Savannah at Pru's house. The thunder had been so loud, Zara had thought it sounded like something trying to slam through the sky from the other side. It was a terrible night. The storm scared her, her mother scared her, Pru scared her, the house itself scared her. Everything creaked. Everything smelled of woodsmoke and tobacco. Every corner of every room was dark, the firelight unable to reach the edges of the shadow.

Zara and Savannah were made to wait in the reception room while their mother argued with Prudence in the kitchen. Savannah watched TV, but Zara couldn't concentrate on the cartoons. She kept catching snippets of the conversation, a version of which she'd heard from many other relatives over the last few months: "No, Lydia, absolutely not" and "There must be someone else" and "I am sorry for your troubles, truly I am—but you cannot dump your children on me."

Prudence had all sorts of wooden boxes and trinkets on display in her bookshelves, the likes of which Zara had never seen before. She pulled one down and began to tinker with it, captivated by its interesting pattern and strange shape.

In the kitchen, a deal was eventually reached: Zara and Savannah could stay the night. In the morning, Prudence would call social services and have them placed in foster care.

Lydia left. It was the last time Zara would see her mother. Prudence came into the reception room at the exact moment the box Zara had been fiddling with broke apart in her hands.

"I'm sorry," Zara wailed, scurrying away from the pieces. Breaking things around Lydia never ended well. "I'm sorry, I'm sorry."

"It's quite all right," Prudence replied. "That's enough crying. Come here. Look, see? You didn't break it; you solved it."

Zara frowned.

"Have you seen one of these before?" Prudence asked as she gathered up the pieces of the cube.

"No."

"Did somebody teach you how to solve this?"

"No."

"Did you watch a video perhaps? See it in a movie? Read about it in a book?"

"No."

"Do it again, please. Walk me through your thinking."

To Zara's surprise, when Prudence handed her the cube, it was once again intact, all of its wooden pieces interlocking as they had been when she'd found it.

"I thought . . ." Zara whispered.

"Speak up. You have to make your voice heard."

Zara talked a little louder. "I thought it looked like it had a secret. I wanted to know what it was hiding."

"Go on."

"Then I thought . . . if I had built it and put my secret inside, where would I have started?"

"Show me."

Zara walked Prudence through the seventeen steps she had taken to dismantle the box. By the end, Pru was smiling.

"Do you like puzzles?" Pru asked.

"Yes," Zara answered, though she'd never seen a puzzle box before that night.

"Try another." Prudence pulled down another box and placed it in front of her.

It took Zara several minutes to figure it out. "Do you have any more?" she asked when she was done.

"I do," Prudence said.

One by one, Zara solved her great-aunt's puzzle boxes, until Pru went upstairs to fetch her most prized one. It was beautiful, a big, smooth cube made up of hundreds of rectangular slivers of different colored wood.

Zara tried for hours. Pru made them a late dinner, served dessert, and even placed a steaming cup of peppermint tea next to her while she worked. "I can't do it," Zara said eventually, tears slipping down her cheeks.

"There's no need to cry. This box was made by a master puzzle maker. There are three hundred and thirty-four intricate steps to solve it. It normally takes months, years even. It took me close to six weeks. You are halfway there already."

Zara rubbed tears from her sleepy eyes. Halfway didn't seem very far at all.

"How old are you?" The storm had long since passed, and the night was now quiet, cooler than it had been before the rain. A breeze crept though the half-open windows, carrying with it the scent of Prudence's summer garden: lavender, rosemary, jasmine. Savannah slept on a chair by the fireplace, her long blond hair swept across her face.

"I'm eight," Zara answered.

"Do you know how to read?" Prudence asked.

"Of course I know how to read."

"My apologies. I didn't mean to offend you. You have a sharp mind and a natural gift for strategy."

"Oh." Zara had not realized, until that moment, that what she'd been doing had been anything other than playing.

"Have you played chess before?" Pru asked.

Zara shook her head.

"A lesson for another day, perhaps. It's well past midnight. A girl your age needs her rest. Come on. Let's find somewhere for you and your sister to sleep."

Prudence didn't call social services the next morning. Instead, she called a nearby school and informed them that Zara and Savannah would be enrolling, effective immediately.

It took Zara only three more weeks to finish the final puzzle box and unlock its secrets.

They lived with Prudence for the next seven years.

BEFORE SAVANNAH DIED, Zara used to apply her disciplined mind to mathematics and sciences and languages. There was little that escaped her understanding if she threw herself into it. It was one of the things she liked best about herself, that ability to wrap her head around any problem. It wasn't like things came to her easily—calculus, chemistry, conjugated French verbs, none of it was instinctual to her—but she believed in the power of her brain to eventually master these things if she spent enough time unpicking them. It had made her an exceptional student. For a decade, that had been the spine of her identity: Zara was the smart one, the brilliant one, the girl genius.

Zara Jones was going places. Oxford, Cambridge—wherever she wanted.

Now she directs her brainpower toward one subject alone: the occult. Before, she had never been interested in magic. Even when she was little, she never believed in fairies or unicorns or Santa. The instant she knew Savannah was dead, all that changed. The occult became Zara's only option, and so she threw herself into the study of it with the same diligence and fervor that she'd once reserved for school.

When she reaches the place where her sister is buried, Zara kneels in the wet grass and unpacks everything in her bag: the groceries, the matches, the lighter fluid, the trowel, the book on necromancy from which she is taking the ritual, her school laptop. Savannah's headstone is simple and modern compared to the old Gothic tombs that surround it. SAVANNAH LYDIA JONES, it reads. BELOVED SISTER. Zara didn't want to give her sister a headstone at all. Sav won't be buried long enough to need one, she'd thought at the time. Eventually, the cemetery had insisted on marking the grave, so Zara had selected the cheapest option she could find, a piece of slate from Etsy that arrived with a sharp chipped corner on which Zara had sliced open her thumb.

"I know, Savvy," Zara had said to herself as she sucked the wound. "I'm sorry. It's not for much longer." Savannah hadn't wanted to be buried. It was something they'd talked about casually, when death felt decades away. Sav wanted to be cremated and have her ashes scattered in some exotic place she hadn't been to yet. The Amalfi Coast. Santorini. Somewhere warm.

The final item Zara takes out of her backpack is an Instax photograph of Savannah, the same one she'd shown to police the morning she woke to find Sav missing. They didn't do much with the information. Savannah was nineteen and had a life of her own, they said. What they didn't know was that she would never leave Zara on her own without telling her where she was going. Zara had gone to school that day, back in the days when she thrived at school, was good at it, saw the point of it. A queasy feeling of wrongness had settled in her stomach as the hours wore on and Savannah didn't make contact.

Something bad had happened.

After school, Zara had caught the tube to Sav's friend's place. The queasy feeling had bloomed into full-blown dread, a thing with black fur and insect legs that was unfurling inside her.

Then, at the friend's flat, peering through the slot of glass in the front door, Zara saw Savannah's shoes. Savannah's shoes. On a body. On the floor.

"Savannah!" she screamed, everything in her hoping that those feet didn't belong to her sister and yet already knowing that they did. The kitchen window was unlocked. Zara slid it open and tumbled inside, sending a rack of plates and glasses drying on the counter to the floor. The air smelled soiled with death. Zara could see from the gruesome pallor of her sister's skin that Savannah was dead and had been dead for some time, but in that moment it didn't compute. Zara scrambled to her sister's side and pressed her lips to her sister's and started CPR. Savannah's body was stiff with rigor mortis, so her rib cage barely gave beneath Zara's compressions. Zara kept up the CPR—one hundred compressions a minute, just like she'd learned in the first-aid course at school—until emergency services arrived. Later, she wouldn't be able to recall dialing them, though her phone would bear the evidence of a ten-minute call to 999, so she must have.

When they came, Zara was aching with the effort of trying to restart Savannah's stone heart. The paramedics stood at the window, calmly asking Zara to let them in, but she didn't. Once she let them in, she knew they would tell her that Savannah was dead, and Zara wouldn't allow that, so she kept compressing, kept breathing into her sister's cold mouth, until a woman followed her through the kitchen window and unlocked the front door and pulled Zara away from Savannah's corpse. They didn't even try to revive her, though Zara begged them to. Give her oxygen, give her a shot of adrenaline in the chest, shock her with a defibrillator.

She could not be gone, *she could not be gone*.

It was Zara that the paramedics ended up attending to, Zara who spent the night in the hospital. There was a gash in her leg that she hadn't even noticed—she must have cut herself when toppling the drying rack. Normally a wound requiring a dozen stitches wouldn't necessitate an overnight stay, but Zara had gone rabid with grief and could not stop screaming and shaking, so she was admitted and administered drugs to ease her into a numb sleep.

The police had come the next morning to take her statement. They suspected Savannah's new boyfriend, naturally, and asked a lot of questions about him. Zara could answer none of them. She didn't even know the guy's name, had never met him. They'd only been dating a couple of months. Eventually he was cleared—airtight alibi—and that was that.

Frankly, Zara didn't care who had killed Savannah. The desire for revenge never took hold. Retribution felt feeble, nowhere near enough to cover the cost of what had been lost. They were one soul split into two bodies. Often, Zara didn't know where she ended and Savannah began.

Though they were three years apart in age, they'd gotten their first period on the same day, an event too miraculous and impossible to feel anything less than foreordained. Zara had been twelve, Savannah fifteen, both of them eating breakfast before school when they felt it, felt something, a disturbance in the Force. The cramping, the strange sensation of wetness, the startling slick of bright red on light underwear when they checked.

How was that possible, if they were not cosmically linked? *How?*

That night, they made popcorn and ate pizza, and Prudence said they could watch any movie they wanted.

"Something bloody," Savannah insisted. She chose *The Texas Chainsaw Massacre*, which Pru tried to bargain her out of, but Savannah was resolute: "You said *anything*."

They had both been too young to watch it, but it affected Zara more profoundly; Leatherface imprinted on her psyche, the blood on-screen forever linked to the blood coming from her body.

In the hospital after her sister's death, as the sedatives in Zara's blood began to thin, a plan was already forming in her head.

She was going to bring Savannah back.

In the cemetery, Zara's fingertips linger for a moment on the image of her sister's face.

Death stumped her in a way that nothing else ever had. Sure, she grasped the fundamentals: the cessation of electrons in her sister's brain, the process of decay, the dispersion of Savannah's atoms back into the universe. Fine. But how could *Savannah* be *gone*? It didn't compute. Still, now, when she thinks about it, it fails entirely to make sense.

Zara puts on her reading glasses and opens her laptop, balances it on a headstone, brings up the spreadsheet that has become her magnum opus over the past year. Months and months of work, investigations into the occult and demons and necromancy, spells and curses and witchcraft, all distilled here into one sprawling document of columns and lines and cells. What has worked (nothing) and what hasn't (everything). Each ritual, tweaked a dozen times, tried beneath full moons and blood moons and no moons. She's been to the cemetery dressed in Savannah's clothes. She's drunk a hallucinogenic potion of henbane, jimsonweed, and mandrake that was supposed to help her commune with the dead, but instead gave her vomiting and diarrhea. She brought Kyle's neighbor's cat here and sat with it on her lap for an hour at dawn.

Tonight, she takes notes, as quick and efficient as a scientist in a lab. Date, time, ritual. Everything must be recorded accurately so it can be adjusted and tried again. In the wet earth over her sister's corpse, she digs a small pit, then she squirts the ground with lighter fluid and strikes a match.

Necromancy has proved a more slippery skill than Zara first anticipated. It's never taken her this long to master anything else. There are established rules for trigonometry that everyone agrees on. You only have to pick up one textbook to learn everything you need to know. The necromancy books she has at her disposal— none of the authors writing them seem to have actually *raised* the dead, and therefore no one agrees on how exactly it should be achieved. It's maddening.

There are, however, a few clues that make her feel like she's on the right track: Fire appears in almost every ritual, as does blood and some sort of sacrifice. Zara no longer bothers with rituals that call for crystals or salt or going on juice fasts to "cleanse the spirit" beforehand.

What concerns her most right now is that several books give a tight time frame in which resurrection of the bodily form is possible: twelve months. Beyond that, the flesh has decayed too significantly for reanimation.

The one-year anniversary of Savannah's death is in two weeks.

Zara has two weeks left to bring her sister back before it's no longer possible—and she feels no closer to achieving her goal than she did two days after Sav was killed. Tonight, though—something about this particular ritual seems promising. Zara knows that the word *necromancy* comes from the Greek *nékyia*, the classical name for Book 11 of *The Odyssey*. Odysseus's journey to the underworld is the oldest literary account of necromancy. It's where the very idea of communion with the dead began. Surely that has to count for something.

In a cup, she mixes the honey, milk, wine, and water, then she sprinkles the pearl barley over the top. She tears open the shrink-wrapped lamb and adds a few cubes to the mixture. It's a libation that's supposed to tempt Savannah's ghost into the open.

Finally, it's time for the sacrifice. Zara takes a razor dislodged from a disposable shaver, disinfects it vigorously with hand sanitizer, then slides it down the back of her forearm. The skin puckers and snags beneath the blade. Zara winces, stops, grits her teeth, then drives the razor deeper, until blood beads in its wake. She holds her arm over the flames and lets it drip, drip, drip into the fire. There must always be payment, of that she is sure. There must always be payment for magic, taken in the form of pain and blood.

Everything is ready. Everything is done.

Zara sits still in the cold and listens. At Savannah's funeral, she tucked a bell into her sister's hand. Already, she was planning for Savannah's eventual return. How else would she know that her ritual had been successful? What a grim fate that would be, to be resurrected in your own coffin and then to die again shortly after of asphyxiation because your necromancer hadn't realized their spell had worked.

The fire burns down to nothing. Zara's cut clots and grows sticky. The bell does not ring. Savannah does not come back.

Still, Zara waits.

And waits.

And waits.

Then she inhales deeply and screams. It is long, piercing, ragged—but it is only once, and when it is done, she wipes her mouth, clears her throat, straightens the pleats in her skirt, smooths down her hair, and takes some notes in her spreadsheet. She does not cry. Scientists do not cry when their experiments fail. They assess their method, figure out what went wrong, then try again—even if they want to tear out their own hair and beat their fists against the ground.

"I did not come this far to only come this far," Zara says to herself as she closes her laptop and checks the time.

More information. What she needs is more information—and the only place to get that right now is not here.

Zara stands, satchel in hand, and heads for Primrose Hill.

Two weeks. She has two weeks to bring Sav back before her sister's corpse is beyond resurrection.

Before she's gone for good.

# SIX

JUDE HATES Primrose Hill. It's the kind of neighborhood bougie rich people flock to; i.e., it's the kind of neighborhood her family owns multiple properties in, the kind of neighborhood her brothers' wives swan around in, in activewear, the kind of neighborhood Jude would be spending her time in if she hadn't ruined her own life so catastrophically. Jude hates Primrose Hill because she feels, desperately, that she belongs here.

It is long dark by the time she parks in front of a deli and pauses for a moment to hate-admire the autumn display in the window. There are crates of pumpkins in all sizes; a tray of knurled and knobby decorative gourds; rhubarb stalks in pink and sherbet red; tubs of tulips and other hardy flowers with waxy-looking petals. It's fucking beautiful.

Jude walks past a mural of the royal family posed like ABBA, then down the street, past Chalcot Square, a fancy little park surrounded on all sides by pastel-colored Italianate terraced houses. She's always thought they look like sugar eggs, pretty jewels frosted with white icing. She snaps a picture of one and sends it to Elijah.

**Don't we own one of these?**

She is joking, but Elijah replies immediately.

Adam lives in the big gaudy
one on the corner.

**Seriously?**

Paid £12 million for it—then
painted it pastel orange.

**Pastel orange?**
**What a twat!**

Indeed. Money really
can't buy taste.

Jude doubles back to the corner and stands in front of the pale orange house there. It is lovely, even in all its four-storied tangerine glory. The windows spill rectangles of gold onto the road through gauzy curtains that keep the rooms beyond them hidden from the prying eyes of passersby. An autumnal wreath hangs on the front door. The single tree in the tiny yard—shadowy, colossal—shivers in the honeyed light, its few remaining leaves dangling like delicate glass baubles. The air smells damp but inviting, laced with greenery and dinners cooking in the oven.

Jude imagines Adam inside, sitting in a leather armchair in a dark-paneled drawing room—because of course he would have a drawing room—reading and drinking a glass of amber liquor, his tie undone and feet up after a long day of being rich and powerful. His eldest daughter, Dove, is sitting next to him in a second armchair, still in her school uniform, her black-stockinged feet tucked up underneath her as she twists a curl of blond hair in her fingers. Adam's wife brings his smallest children, both blond and pajama-clad, in to say good night, and he bends to kiss each of them on the crown of their perfect head.

Jude's heart twinges.

After her mother died, Adam offered to adopt her, or so she had been told. Lawrence had no interest in children, and Adam already had Dove. Why not raise them together in a loving home? Lawrence apparently had vetoed the idea, even though he seemingly had little interest in being Jude's father himself. Jude has never known why.

Jude and Adam have never been close the way Jude and Elijah are close, but—despite Eli's vehement hatred of all four of their older brothers—Jude has always viewed Adam as a kind of father figure. A friendly face in an otherwise completely batshit family of narcissists (Eli excluded, obviously).

After Jude's "accident," though, Adam distanced himself from her. Sure, he sent flowers to the hospital, but he never visited, never called. Why would he? Jude is tainted with the stench of scandal, and Adam Wolf—clean-cut, handsome, and driven as he is—has been gunning for his father's job his whole life. It is better for his image, better for his family, better for his career to distance himself from his "junkie" sister, so that's what he's done.

In another life, Jude would be sitting with Adam and Dove in that glowing room. Whole and well and un-bloody-cursed.

A car crawls by. A private security company. The man at the wheel looks at Jude suspiciously.

"Yeah, yeah, all right," Jude says to herself. The wind creaks through the trees, creaks through her aching bones. She turns and sets off into the night once more.

Past the square, farther down Chalcot Road, the houses become more standard: London stock brick and white window frames, only the occasional red or green door for some personality.

Jude's heart beats faster at the thought of what she's about to see. She's not too squeamish—you can't have a gangrenous leg/soul without developing a strong stomach—but her mouth still goes slick with the thought of bloat-bellied corpses and the stink of maggot-ravaged flesh.

"I hope it's a fresh one," she says to no one. Which is a messed-up thing to hope for, but whatever.

Jude spots a blonde in a dark academia costume—tartan jacket, pleated skirt, leather loafers—and takes a few moments to delight in the woman's physique. Then, when the woman ascends the stairs of the same building Jude is bound for, she grins and races to catch up.

"What's a nice girl like you doing in a place like this?" Jude asks the blonde as they wait at the door together.

The blonde turns. She's younger than Jude thought she would be—Primrose Hill is notorious yummy-mummy territory—and cute in a schoolgirl way. Her cheeks are full, and her face is dusted with baby freckles. Mostly, though, she looks anxious. There's a haunted quality to her wide gray eyes.

"Are you hitting on me?" the girl asks.

"That depends," Jude says.

"On what?"

"On if you're interested."

The blonde tries not to smile, but those cheeks go as pink as rose petals.

The door buzzes and they both go inside.

"Visiting a friend?" Jude asks as they climb the stairs. She moves tenderly, the ache in her thigh and hip fully awake. The pain is often worse after dark, when her demons are most active. It is not always as unbearable as it was last night—the hungry demon's tantrums are sporadic, to keep her on her toes—but the pain is always there, always rotting away inside her.

The blonde shakes her head. "I wish. Can you imagine living somewhere like this? Sylvia Plath used to live on this street. I saw her blue plaque when I was walking over."

"Plath. Now there is a woman who might be able to help me. So hard to find a decent poet these days. Instagram has every second person thinking they can bang a few words out and call it poetry. Maybe the fact that Plath lived here is a good omen."

"What do you need a poet for?"

"I'll admit they're not useful for much. Mostly because they don't even know what they could be useful for."

Jude wonders if Plath did the kind of work she's looking for. Probably, the saucy minx.

It's not until they stop in front of the same door and the blonde reaches out to knock that Jude realizes they are both here to see Reese Chopra.

Jude frowns while they wait, trying to work out who she is. "Are you a cop?" she asks, though she already knows the answer. The girl is too young.

The blonde shakes her head. "Do I look like a police officer?"

"Interesting. New lover, perhaps? Reese keeps telling me I'm too young for her. What a dirty liar."

The door opens, and there is Detective Reese Chopra in a hooded white coverall, overshoes, face mask, and gloves.

"Reese, darling," Jude says. "You look as ravishing as ever." And it's true, she does. With the bedroom-iest eyes Jude has ever seen, how could she resist a little flirting?

"You're late," Chopra says to Jude, then she turns to the blonde and says, "and you're early."

"You said nine p.m., peach," Jude says. "So I'm here at nine p.m."

"You said nine p.m. to me, too," says the blonde.

"Did I?" Chopra asks. "I need to get more sleep. You're not supposed to be here at the same time. Screw it. Hurry up, we don't have long." She lets them in and hands each of them the same gear that she's wearing. Jude has never seen her without PPE on, but she has looked her up online, and knows that she is in her early forties, dark-haired and dark-skinned, with a jawline that makes Jude feel a little weak at the knees. She's married to—and separating from—a petite, angry-looking lawyer named . . . Bridget? Brooke? Something starting with a *B*. "You both know the drill. Money first, then you can have a few minutes. Don't touch anything. Don't take anything. No photographs. The team will get back from their break soon."

"How's the divorce going, Reese?" Jude asks as she snaps on her gloves.

Chopra must catch the scent of her then, because she scrunches up her nose and says: "Would it kill you to take a shower once in a while?"

"Not well, I take it, considering you've doubled your fee. I, for one, am thrilled to hear that you're back on the market."

The blonde has not started to put on her PPE. Chopra notices. "Hurry up, Jones. We haven't got all day."

"I could only get fifty," Jones says, "on such short notice. Well, fifty-two, to be exact. I need more time—but I can pay you later, I swear."

"Jesus," Chopra says. "I'm not a charity. I'm risking my career here, letting you trample all over a crime scene."

"I'm sorry. Really, I'll find a way to—"

"I'll spot you," Jude says. Why the hell not? "A thousand a pop, yeah?"

Jones looks confused. "No, five hundred."

Jude turns to Chopra. "You're charging her half what you're charging me?"

"I know who your father is, Jude Wolf," Chopra says. "I do not feel the slightest bit of guilt taking advantage of you."

"Rude," Jude grumbles as she counts out the cash and hands it over. Chopra shoves it down her coverall, into her bra. "Last time I paid you five hundred pounds to take a gander at an overdosed junkie in an alleyway," Jude reminds her. "This had better be the real deal."

"First of all, we don't call them junkies, okay? She had a *substance abuse problem*. Secondly, she was sliced up. How am I to know exactly what kind of wounds you want to look at? Thirdly, this *is* one of them. A perfect bright red rectangle of skin cut out of her wrist. The flat is full of weird stuff, too, hocus-pocus candles and potions and all that garbage—and, well, something new."

"Something new?" Jones asks.

"Something new," Chopra says again.

Of the five murder victims (and one overdose) Jude has paid Chopra to see, only three have been what she is looking for. The first, a high-profile CEO who was killed in her office nine months ago, had a two-by-four-inch piece of skin cut from her chest. That had caught Jude's attention when it popped up on her newsfeed. Chopra busted Jude breaking in to the crime scene and briefly believed that she might be the murderer, especially when Jude panicked and told Chopra about curses and demons and the witch she needed to find to save herself. Chopra assumed she was high or psychotic or both—until Jude mentioned who her father was, offered her a wad of cash to see the dead woman's office, and said there was more where that came from. A lot more. When the next body showed up two months later, this one with three rectangles of skin flayed off, Chopra had asked Jude for her alibi (it was solid) and then offered to let her see the dead woman—for a price, naturally.

Thus began their strange business relationship. Jude pays Chopra to see mutilated corpses, and Chopra goes along with it, in no small part because of the lack of evidence and the glaringly obvious fact that there are more to these crimes than she or the police understand.

"It hurts me that you've been seeing other people behind my back, Reese," Jude says as she and Jones put their face masks on. "I thought we had something special."

"Follow me," Chopra says to them both as she opens another door. "Let's get this over and done with."

There's no stench of death yet. The heating in the flat is off and the air is cool and the body has not begun to stink the way some of the others did—alas, the scene is no less horrifying for its lack of smell.

"Jesus," Jude whispers when she takes in the room. She knows her way around a crime scene now. Chopra watches her—watches them, Jude and Jones both—as they move through the room. There are little platforms set up on the carpet like stepping stones. They use these to navigate the space without trampling on any evidence.

Jude forces herself to look at the body. It's a woman. They're always women, of course. She's dressed as a witch, green skin and all, which feels like a giant screw-you. As Chopra said, there's a perfect rectangle of flesh cut from her wrist. The woman's eyes are wide with fear, the pupils blown out to the size of coins. Around her and beneath her, drawn in blood that has soaked into the carpet, is a massive pentagram and a line from the Bible.

"'Thou shalt not suffer a witch to live,'" Jones reads quietly, her voice quavering.

Fucking hell.

"You weren't lying," Jude says. "That is new. The bastard's getting angrier."

Jude steps closer to the woman's body, her expression dark and her teeth gritted. A needle of fury punctures through her, makes her curl her fingers into fists. There's a crackle of something electric and acrid in the room as all three of them stare at the dead woman.

They understand what they are looking at. They understand that it could have been them. A wrong turn onto the wrong street on the wrong night, and it could have been them. There is no sense to it. That you can be going about your life, minding your own goddamn business, and suddenly become prey.

Jude runs the gloved pad of her right thumb over the curse on her opposite wrist.

There had been Bible verses left at the other crime scenes, but they had always been . . . well, a bit more subtle. Nothing so overtly "Satanic panic." So what's the killer playing at now? Why the sudden drama? The giant bloody pentagram? What do they want?

*Attention,* Jude thinks. *They want attention.*

Chopra looks gloomily at the blood writing, her hands on her hips. "The press are going to have a field day with this."

The spell of rage is broken. The storm recedes to corners of the room. Jude shakes out her fingers and takes a deep breath, smells only the powder of latex gloves, the hospital-clean plastic of PPE.

"Press?" Jude asks. "I thought the Met was keeping it quiet?"

Ever since the gory details of the CEO's murder had been leaked—"Woman Skinned in Sickening Slaying"—the cops had kept the particulars of the other murders out of the papers and the crimes had not been publicly linked.

Chopra lets out a long sigh. "The decision's been made that it's unethical to keep a serial killer secret. There's going to be an announcement, a public safety campaign warning women not to go out after dark on their own."

"A curfew for women? That's gonna go down real well."

"*Not* a curfew. A suggested set of behaviors to enhance personal safety in these uncertain times."

"Wow, you're really toeing the party line, huh? That's what they want, you know. The killer. That's what the pentagram is for. They want this to be in the papers, and you're just going to give it to them."

"It's out of my hands."

"When are you and your buddies planning on doing your job and actually catching this guy?"

Chopra glares and checks her imaginary watch. "Look at that. You have three minutes left."

Jude turns and goes back to scouring the crime scene—and is immediately thrown off guard by Jones, who's now wandering the perimeter of the room and—

"I'm sorry, are you actually stroking your chin?" Jude asks.

"It helps me think," Jones answers, unfolding her arms to reveal a spiral notebook in her other hand, "and distracts me from vomiting."

*"No vomiting,"* Chopra warns. "I do not want your DNA at the scene."

"So what got you hooked on checking out dead bodies?" Jude continues. "Does being so close to death make you feel alive?"

Jones doesn't answer. "What's her name?" Jones asks Chopra. "How old is she?"

"Nineteen. Name is—" Chopra checks a piece of paper on the kitchen bench. "Rebecca Wright."

"Cause of death?" Jones asks, but it's pretty damn obvious: The woman has a wide necklace of bruising around her throat.

"Choking, over a long period of time. The skin was cut out just before death, like all the other victims. The precise nature of the wounds suggests that she was unconscious by that point, likely on the verge of death."

"Four victims now, Reese," Jude says as she begins to sweep the room, looking for evidence not of murder but of something else: magic. Real magic. "Tut tut."

"Five victims," Jones says.

Jude frowns. That is more new information.

"Yes, five victims," Chopra says.

"Which one was her bedroom?" Jones asks.

Chopra nods toward the hallway. "First on the right."

Jones goes into the girl's room. Jude and Chopra follow behind her.

Jude feels a sudden, surprising pang of jealousy for the dead girl, for the life she led before she died. The walls are painted a chalky forest green and lined with books upon books upon books. A puckered leather armchair sits in one corner, next to an ornate black metal bed that looks like it's been there since the Victorian era. On the wooden writing desk is a stack of textbooks: *The Oxford Companion to English Literature*, *The Norton Shakespeare*.

This is a life Jude wants desperately. A life Jude could have in the future, if she can fix herself.

"You mentioned hocus-pocus candles," Jones says. "Where's the occult evidence?"

Chopra stares. "You mean besides the big pentagram and the fact she's dressed as a witch and her bedroom looks like a *Buffy* set?"

"Yes. Please point out anything specific."

Chopra scowls and takes Jones on a little tour of the room, showing her crystals and jars of dried rose petals and a cushion embroidered with suns and moons. Jones shakes her head at each of them and says, "No. Next item," before Chopra has even finished. The only thing she seems interested in is a book: a copy of *Pseudomonarchia Daemonum*, which she writes the title of in her notebook. Jude knows it to be a catalog of demons and devils, written in the 1500s, that gets 95 percent of everything wrong.

So Jones is looking for magic, too, then. Huh. Jude wonders why.

"Why these women?" Chopra wonders aloud.

Jude thinks it's pretty damn obvious. *Thou shalt not suffer a witch to live.* Like, duh. They were witches; they were killed because they were witches. Jude tried explaining as much to Chopra after the first two murders, but would Olivia bloody Benson listen? Chopra's reply had been something along the lines of *Don't try to mess with me, you juvenile delinquent, I'll have you arrested*, and Jude hadn't raised the theory again.

And there, on the desk, out in the open, Jude sees what she's been searching two years for. She almost chokes when she spots it and covers her surprise with a cough. Both Chopra and Jones glance at her, but she clears her throat and waves them away. Nothing to see here.

"No coughing," Chopra warns, then she turns, long enough for Jude to lift the thin coil of lead—no bigger than half a cigarette—from the desk and slip it into her pocket without the detective noticing. Jones, however, sees everything. The two young women lock eyes. Jude thinks that Jones will rat her out immediately—she seems the type, a real Goody Two-shoes—but Jude is wrong. Jones gives a singular nod acknowledging their secret and then goes back to taking notes.

"Okay," Chopra says a minute later. "Time's up. Take off your PPE and get out of here."

"We really need to stop meeting like this," Jude says to Chopra on her way out.

"Goodbye, Jude."

"Farewell, Reese. Until next time."

"Hopefully there won't be a next time."

Jude can't tell if she means hopefully no more women will get murdered, or hopefully she just won't see Jude again.

Jude follows Jones down the stairs and falls in step beside her on the sidewalk, trying to ignore the sickening sensation of pus seeping from her leg as she moves. "Wouldn't it be a wild twist if Chopra turns out to be the murderer and she's been killing all these women as an excuse to see me?"

Jones frowns but doesn't say anything. Sheesh. Tough crowd.

Jones walks for a while, hands held behind her back like she's Sherlock Holmes, then stops in front of Chalcot Square, in front of Sylvia Plath's old flat. "You took something," she says.

"I did indeed. Thanks for not ratting me out. Chopra was in a mood."

"What was it?"

Jude holds up the curl of lead. "You seemed very interested in the demon book, so I assume you know what this is."

Jones shakes her head. "No."

Weirder and weirder. "What exactly were you doing there if you weren't there for this?"

Again, Jones doesn't say anything. Like talking to a brick wall.

"Ever been to Bath?" Jude asks her. "Familiar with ancient Roman curse tablets?"

"I have not, and I am not."

"Well, let's take a look-see, shall we?"

Jude unfurls the soft metal, which has been imprinted with a jumble of letters and numbers, and rolls her eyes. Witches. Always so crafty. At least this one is written in the Latin alphabet. The last one she came across was in bloody Sanskrit.

"Do you have a mirror?" Jude asks Jones.

"No."

"Jones, you are proving to be a completely useless assistant so far."

"My name is Zara, and I am *not* your assistant."

Jude thinks for a second, then holds the writing up against a car's wing mirror—and grins as the secret message reveals itself.

"Hello, Emer," Jude says. "You have no idea how long I've been looking for you.'

*Emer Byrne*, the mirrored writing reads. *Cursewriter.*

"What are the numbers?" Jones asks.

"If I had to wager a guess, I'd say they're time frames and coordinates."

"Coordinates to what?"

"Not to what, Jones—to who."

"To who?"

"Yes, to who."

"No, I mean—who to?"

Jude smiles. Jones is cute when she's baffled and a little bit angry. "A poet, if I'm lucky. This"—Jude rolls up the thin sheet of metal again and puts it in her pocket—"is a business card for one Emer Byrne, cursewriter. A witch, my dear. A very special kind of witch." Jones's eyes are big and unblinking, but she doesn't seem to think Jude is joking, which means she knows at least a little bit of the truth. "Fancy grabbing some dinner, Jones?"

"I told you: My *name* is *Zara*."

"Yes, you mentioned that. I'm electing to continue calling you Jones. Jude and Jones, girl detectives. It has a ring to it, don't you think? Let's go. I've a hankering for something carb-y."

# SEVEN

**A WITCH.** *A witch. A witch.*

Jude found the business card for a *witch*.

Zara's thoughts tumble and crash. There are too many puzzle pieces for her to hold in her mind at once but it feels like there is an answer here somewhere—and maybe Jude can help her find it.

On the table in front of her, Jude has already ordered olives and grilled sardines and stuffed vine leaves. The kitchen was on the verge of closing when they arrived, an inconvenience quickly solved with three fifty-pound notes from Jude, casually counted out and handed to the greeter.

Zara's stomach is unsettled. She can never eat after seeing a dead body. It doesn't get any easier, seeing women frozen in the moment of death. Seeing women frozen as Savannah was frozen, the same fear carved forever on their faces.

Jude, apparently, is not turned off food at all.

"Are you planning on closing your mouth at any point this evening?" Zara asks as Jude chews another sardine with her mouth open. "Or are your lips repelled by each other?"

"What?" Jude asks, her mouth stuffed full to bursting.

"You eat like a wild animal."

"I have several loose teeth in the back of my mouth, okay?" Jude manages to say once she swallows. "The less chewing I do, the better."

Jude is wealthy, that much is clear. Zara knows her type; she went to school with girls like her when she lived in the countryside with Pru. Jude aims for as unstudied an air as possible—wrinkled clothing, slouched spine, appalling manners, questionable personal hygiene. That was the general rule at Zara's old school: the worse the behavior, the sloppier the clothing, the richer the family. None of them were as generous as Jude, though, or so kind to strangers. Zara can't imagine any of them doing what Jude did and offering to pay her way. Then again, Zara can't imagine any of them paying to be at a crime scene to begin with.

The more she observes Jude, the more certain Zara is that Jude is wealthy beyond her wildest understanding. Zara knows about fashion—you need to when you wear clothing as armor—and Jude is finely dressed. Her structured black greatcoat, which makes her look like an haute couture Jack the Ripper, is, Zara saw when Jude handed it to the greeter, from Valentino. The white shirt she wears beneath it—hideously crumpled as it is—is pure silk. Her lace-up boots are the very same ones Savannah had lusted over—and laughed at the obscene price tag of—when she was alive.

*I know who your father is*, Chopra had said.

Why is a girl with those kinds of resources snooping around murder scenes looking for the business cards of witches?

Jude swallows another enormous mouthful practically un-chewed and scans the drink menu. "Bollinger? Or are you more of a Clicquot woman?"

They're in a Greek restaurant on Regent's Park Road, a place with a glass greenhouse roof and a cascade of plants suspended from the ceiling. Zara has never seen the inside of such a fancy place before, though Prudence prepared her to move in these kinds of circles. She sits up straight, her legs tucked neatly to one side of her chair.

"I'm seventeen," Zara replies. She's also never had real champagne before. Savannah let her have two glasses of prosecco from Waitrose once, on one of their last nights together. The bottle had looked like it was made of cut crystal and had glittered in the moonlight. "Things are going to be different now," Savannah had promised when they'd clinked their glasses together. They'd been celebrating Savannah's new job as an HR administrator for a media company. It would pay her more than twice as much as she was earning as a beauty consultant at Boots. To mark the occasion, they'd pooled their resources and spent £20 on the prosecco—an outrageous extravagance, but worth it, because their luck was changing and their lives were about to begin. Or so Savannah kept insisting.

Jude shoves another sardine in her mouth and swallows it whole. "Me too, but I've never let that stop me," she says. "Pick one."

Zara looks at the menu and feels doubly sick. Both bottles are over £80. A wild, inconceivable amount of money to spend on anything—other than crime scenes, that is. "I obviously cannot afford this."

"I obviously gathered that. Dinner is on me."

Zara clears her throat. "I should make it clear—I'm not . . . I mean, I'm not attracted to you in a romantic way."

Jude rolls her eyes. "Christ, woman. I'm not trying to get in your pants. I mean, if it happens organically, I won't complain— but you don't owe me anything for a souvlaki wrap. Now, if I take you to the Araki or Le Gavroche, we may need to renegotiate." Jude wiggles her eyebrows.

Zara flushes. "Bollinger, then."

"Excellent choice."

Zara's met plenty of rich kids before, but never a girl quite like Jude, someone who walks through the world exuding such force. Jude is very . . . beautiful? No, that doesn't feel like the right word to describe her. Jude is striking. Yes, absolutely. Jude is . . . hand-some, maybe? That fits, too. Jude has black hair, pale skin, light blue eyes, and eyebrows that look like dark, silken caterpillars have been glued to her face. Jude is built like women Zara has only ever seen in magazines before, all angles and limbs. Her shoulders are broad and sharp, as is her jaw.

Beneath the veneer, though, Jude is unwell. Something is . . . *wrong* with her. Zara can sense it, can see it, can smell it. There are bluish circles under her eyes and a faint rotten stench lifting from her skin. She walks slowly and often seems to wince when she puts weight on her right leg.

Zara lifts her backpack onto her lap, takes out her laptop, and slides her glasses onto her nose. Next she opens the Voice Memos app and puts her phone on the table between her and Jude.

Zara hovers her fingers over the keyboard of her laptop, ready. "Tell me everything you know about witches," she says.

"Wow, you're just going to dive right in there, huh?" Jude eyes the phone as it records.

"I don't have a lot of time."

"Busy lady. I like it. I'll tell you what, why don't we do a trade? You give me an answer, I'll give you an answer. You said five victims." Jude says all of this around another massive mouthful, this time of olives. Zara nods. Jude eats another olive and goes on. "How do you know that and I don't?"

"My sister was murdered last year." Zara doesn't talk about Savannah's death with anyone, yet it somehow feels okay to tell Jude. Jude has seen the other women. Jude has borne witness to the dead bodies with flayed skin. They are bound by that horror. "She was the first, I think. I couldn't find any news articles that mentioned crimes like that before she died—though it's possible those details were kept out of the media, so I don't know for sure, but Chopra hasn't mentioned any earlier victims. Her name was Savannah."

"Jesus. I'm sorry. I assume Chopra was—"

"One of the investigators on Savannah's case, yes."

"How'd you get roped into paying her?"

"It was her idea. Though I'm guessing, now, that she got the idea from you. The second victim—I'd been badgering Chopra for a while to give me more information. She asked me if I wanted to come to the morgue and see the body. She thought they were linked. I went, I paid her. She called me from the next crime scene. I'm guessing we've been ships passing in the night for a while."

"Charging the sister of a murder victim." Jude shakes her head. "Chopra's a real piece of work."

The bottle of Bollinger arrives then. The waiter pours a mouthful of it into a champagne glass for Jude, who tastes it and says, "Yes, thank you, that's fine." The waiter fills each of their glasses. Zara is still watching for her reaction, but it looks like Jude is thinking, mulling something over. "Normally I would suggest we toast to something, but considering what you've just told me, it seems like poor taste."

The flutter of a smile tugs at the corner of Zara's lips. Savannah would have liked Jude; she is sure of it.

Savannah.

Sa-van-nah.

Zara rolls the name around in her head. It sounds strange to her now, like a word said so many times in a row that it loses its meaning.

Savannah, Savannah, Savannah.

Sa. Van. Nah.

The word has come unstuck from the girl it belonged to.

Then the imagery begins, as it always does when Zara lets herself think about her dead sister for too long: Savannah, in the summer sunshine, her blond hair falling past her shoulders in loose barrel curls. These are Hallmark moments. Zara isn't even sure if they're real. They are a glossy Hollywood reel of grief. The mourning coats her insides quickly. It is viscous and dark as it fills her lungs, makes it hard to breathe. She grips the edge of the table with such force she thinks the wood might crack. In a fair world, it would crack. In a fair world, Zara would be able to harness the power of her grief. She would use it to shatter every glass and plate in this restaurant. She would use it to scream so loud that everyone in the city could hear her. She would use it to tear open the world and reach back through time and pull Savannah from the jaws of the universe. Her grief-power would make her stronger, make her more capable of doing what needs to be done.

Zara cracks the knuckles on her right hand and hovers her fingers over her keyboard once more. "Tell me everything you know about witches," she says again.

Jude ignores her. "So you're out here Enola Holmes-ing the situation. Solving the crime. I respect that. What are you going to do when you find the bastard? Vengeance?"

"I'm not looking for the killer."

"What? Why not?"

Zara ignores her question. "*Tell me everything you know about witches.* You owe me two answers now, by the way."

"Fine. Sure. What do I know about witches?" Jude leans back. "Double, double toil and trouble; Fire burn and caldron—"

"I want cold, hard facts, Jude."

"You are annoyingly persistent."

"A lot of people tell me that. I take it as a compliment."

"You're about to fall down the rabbit hole into Narnia. Once you know, you can't unknow. You think you're ready for that?"

"The rabbit hole didn't lead to Narnia."

"Whatever, I never saw the movie." Jude takes a swig of champagne, then pushes up her sleeve to reveal the pale skin of her wrist. "Have you seen one of these before?"

Zara glances down at her tattoo. "A tattoo? Yes, Jude. I have seen a tattoo before."

"Not one like this you haven't. Look closer."

Zara's gaze drops again to the black ink on Jude's skin—except it is not ink. Zara leans forward, takes Jude's forearm in both hands, pulls it closer to her face, adjusts her glasses to the tip of her nose to increase their magnification. "What . . . the *hell*?" she breathes. The "tattoo" is . . . Well, it looks like scratchy metal letters and images have been melted into Jude's flesh. There is a tiny depiction of Sekhmet at the center, the ancient Egyptian goddess of medicine, with sigils in a halo around her. Then minuscule, tightly packed words in . . . Latin, Zara thinks. Zara runs the pad of her thumb over the markings. They are cold to the touch, their outlines red and sore-looking. And then—

Zara gasps and shoves Jude's arm away. "It *moved*." Sekhmet, the lioness-headed goddess, had definitely *looked at her.*

"It's called an invocation," Jude explains. "You take a paper-thin piece of lead, you engrave some Latin and sigils into it, you burn the words and pictures into your skin, you tether your immortal soul to a demon, bada bing, bada boom: magic, baby."

Zara looks up. *Tether.* "You tether your soul . . . to a demon?"

"Not all of it. That would kill you. So you slice off a chunk. Big old juicy soul steak for them to sink their teeth into. It's a nasty process. Each invocation costs you maybe five to ten years of your natural life—and it hurts like hell. *All the time.* I mean, there's the initial suckiness of feeling years of life being drained from every atom of your being, but the hangover never goes away. You always feel like you're on the peak day of the flu. Headaches, fevers, aching bones and muscles, general malaise, exhaustion. A surprising amount of dysentery. Food doesn't taste like anything. You chew and you chew and you chew, and maybe you get a ghost of flavor, but mostly it's like eating gruel." Jude holds up her champagne glass. "Drinking too. Delicious sparkling gruel. You gonna write any of this down?"

"Oh." Zara looks down at her laptop. Her fingers are frozen

"Okay, Jones. You're not looking for the killer. Why?"

"I don't care who killed Savannah—I'm more interested in bringing her back to life."

Jude raises her eyebrows. "Jesus H. Frankenstein, you just came right out and said it, huh?"

"Yes." What's the point in hiding it? Maybe Jude knows a way to help her.

"Why?"

It is Jude's turn to answer a question, but Zara decides to give her a freebie. "The night Savannah died—we fought."

"Ah." Jude seems to understand immediately. "That old chestnut."

"I said some things"—Zara pauses and closes her eyes, remembering and regretting for the thousandth time. "I need the opportunity to take them back. To have one more conversation with her. To make it right."

"Seems like a lot of effort for a sisterly spat. I'm sure she knew you loved her and all that."

"You don't know what I said. My turn. Your invocation—what does it do?"

"*Invocations*. Plural. I have three." Jude points to the one Zara has already seen. "This one is supposed to stop pain, but it doesn't work, because I'm an idiot and I went to a charlatan to get it done. Waste of money and time and soul, but unfortunately there are no Google reviews and no refunds in the occult. Which is why I got this one." Jude pulls up her other sleeve to reveal a second complicated array of sigils and symbols and pictures and words, all crammed into an area the size of two matchboxes. "Means I can knock myself out when the pain gets too bad. I can knock others out too. Crude but useful."

"What causes you so much pain?" Zara wonders.

"It's my turn," Jude says. "A part of your sister's skin was taken?"

Zara nods. "From her neck. She'd just gotten a new tattoo and—" Zara stops when she realizes, almost laughs at herself. "It wasn't a tattoo."

"Nope. It was the terms of a deal she made with a demon. A slice of her soul in exchange for power."

Zara closes her eyes. The whole reason their fight had started was because of that stupid tattoo.

"Any idea what she asked for?" Jude asks.

Zara thinks back. "In the two weeks before she died . . . Savannah kept *finding* things. I thought it was odd. Like, when we were short on our rent, she knelt at a random storm drain and pulled out a fifty-pound note. Then a woman lost her toddler at a grocery store and Savannah just walked out, walked to the playground across the road, and found the boy there. It felt . . . uncanny. It kept happening, every day."

"Useful skill but not necessarily something I'd sell part of my soul for. Do you know someone who went missing, maybe? Is that why she'd want that kind of power?"

Zara shakes her head. "No."

"Weird. Try your champagne."

Zara does.

"Good, no?" Jude asks.

"It's good. Who's your father?"

Jude, for once, pauses. She swallows her mouthful of champagne slowly. "Who's *your* father?"

"I don't know my father."

"Yeah? Well, you're lucky. My father is Lawrence Wolf."

Understanding floods in. "Oh," Zara says quietly. She isn't sure she could pick Lawrence Wolf out of a crowd—he's not *that* kind of famous—but she knows his name, knows he's a billionaire, knows there was a Netflix documentary a few years ago about the death of one of his wives. Zara didn't watch it, but it was all people talked about for a while—until the next documentary about another dead woman came out a few weeks later.

"Yeah."

Zara clears her throat. Best to change the subject. "What do you know about necromancy?"

"It's my turn to ask a question."

"Actually, you owe me an answer because you asked me who my father is."

"You are really not a fun date, Jones."

"You said this wasn't a date."

"Yeah, well, it certainly isn't now that we're talking about *necromancy*." Jude shrugs. "I don't know anything. It hasn't been on my radar. I might've seen a book or two about it, but I haven't read them. I have buyers who purchase whole libraries from estates and sift through them looking for occult books. To be honest with you, though, I only found out about all this a couple of years ago. I'm not an expert. Obviously. But this person—" Jude holds up the piece of lead she stole from the crime scene. "Emer Byrne. She's just might be."

"How did you know you'd find it at the crime scene?" Zara asks.

"Because the killer is killing witches. Cursewriters make women into witches. Ergo, a witch—living or dead—must have had contact with a cursewriter at some point in time. Find a dead witch, and you might just find one of these." Jude twirls the small piece of lead in her fingers. "A path back to the cursewriter who gave her magic. They're damn hard to track down. All solitary women, working in secret."

"Wait, I thought witches and cursewriters were the same thing."

"Oh, they are. *Witches* is kind of like the catchall term, you know, for anyone associated with the occult."

"So you're a witch?"

"Guilty."

"Which means my sister was a witch."

"It does." Jude stares at her, her light eyes slightly narrowed. "Don't play coy with me, Jones. You must've known. Why else would you keep paying Chopra to see crime scenes? You were looking for something, right? You just didn't know what."

Of course Zara knew *something.* Suspected *something.* Knew the occult was linked to the crimes *somehow.* There was the weirdness of Savannah's newfound ability to find anything she wanted exactly when she needed it—and then there was the Bible page screwed up in a ball and shoved into her mouth when she died. A page from Exodus. The killer was not so obvious then, did not draw a pentagram or underline the passage at 22:18—*Thou shalt not suffer a witch to live*—but Zara guessed that that was the message.

It is why she keeps going to each fresh murder scene: She is looking for clues that will lead her to magic, because a) she strongly suspects Savannah was messing with the occult, and b) Zara herself desperately needs magic to be real. To hear it laid bare like that, though—*The killer is killing witches*—hurts in a way Zara did not expect. Because if it is true—if Savannah was a witch—it means that she kept a huge secret from Zara.

*Why?*

Jude yawns and picks something crusty from her eye. "I'm beat. You want a lift home?"

"No, thank you. I'm not far from here, across the train tracks. I can walk."

"The coordinates are for a bookstore in Oxford, by the way. I'm going to drive out tomorrow. Want to come with?"

"To meet a witch?"

"To meet a witch."

"Yes," Zara says emphatically. "I want to come."

"What's your address? I'll swing by in the morning."

Zara sits on her own for half an hour after Jude leaves, drinking the rest of the champagne. At a table nearby, waiters and chefs sit eating and laughing after their shift. They don't ask Zara to leave, so she stays in the warmth. While she sips, she tries to remember what Prudence taught her about wine tasting. She knows from movies that you're supposed to smell it first, which she does—it smells like wine—then she takes a sip and tries to think about what it tastes like (apart from wine). Honey, she supposes, and maybe . . . nuts?

There's still a light on when she gets home, so she does what she does whenever she returns late and Kyle is still up: She sits down in a nook by the entrance to the building, her back against the brick wall so that no one can see her, and waits until the window goes dark. Sometimes he's up until two or three in the morning. Sometimes, in the summer, Zara would nod off in the balmy night air and wake suddenly at dawn, disoriented and aching from having slept slumped on the concrete—but it's gotten too cold for that now. Now she sits and shudders, her teeth chattering, the cold wicking through her skirt and stockings.

"Come *on*," she says.

A little while later, the lights in Kyle's flat go out. Zara is tipsy by then, the champagne pushing her over into a groggy half sleep, but she waits a few minutes more to make sure he's really gone to bed. Sometimes—this has happened once or twice before—sometimes he waits for her in the dark, lures her in like a pitcher plant and then flicks the lights on and berates her for whatever she has done to annoy him that day.

When she can no longer stop her head from lolling forward and snapping back every few seconds, Zara stands and forces her heavy legs to carry her up the stairs. She knows, already, that she will spend tonight with Savannah. It's a special treat she has only allowed herself three or four times in the year since Sav died, but tonight she is craving it, craving the smell of her sister, craving the feeling of being close to her.

Zara tiptoes past Kyle where he sleeps on the couch and locks her door behind her. She pulls out the suitcase she keeps under her bed and opens the vacuum-packed bag. A plume of Sav's scent wafts out. Her favorite perfume was Hypnotic Poison by Dior, bottles of which she stole occasionally while she was working at Boots. The scent is intense and distinctive, heady-sweet vanilla with jasmine and almond. Men had loved the way she smelled. It came in a little red potion bottle that looked like a poisoned apple. Zara always knew when Savannah was home, because a luscious cloud of sweetened air followed her wherever she went.

Zara takes out each item one by one and lays it on the floor. A denim miniskirt that Sav wore most days, bare-legged in summer and over woolen tights in winter. A red crop top. A long brown suede jacket with fake wool lining and a fake wool collar. A mustard newsboy cap. Savannah looked like a 1970s rock god when she wore this outfit. These are the only pieces of her wardrobe Zara hasn't sold to fund the task of bringing her sister back.

Zara lifts each piece to her nose and inhales. She lets the memories tumble in with the scent. She is seven years old, and they do not yet live with Prudence.

"I think Mum forgot it's my birthday," Zara whispers to her sister when they leave the house to walk to school.

"She's very forgetful," Savannah says, "but I'm not." She pulls out a pair of silver chains, each with half a heart dangling from it. Both sides of the heart read *Sisters*. Zara wears hers for three weeks straight, until the metal turns her skin green, then she takes it off and stores it in a pouch that is still under her bed to this day. The second half of the heart is buried with Savannah.

When she is done with the remembering, Zara takes off her own clothes and puts each piece of Savannah's clothing on like it is a religious vestment. They had different body types—Savannah was even taller, even leaner—so nothing fits quite right. The skirt sits tight on Zara's thighs, the crop top cuts into her armpits, the coat is too long—but it's close enough. In the low light, with her hair cut in a shaggy blond bob the way Sav's was, Zara looks remarkably like her older sister. They have the same storm gray eyes, the color of a swollen sky just before it hails. They have the same bow-shaped lips. The same dusting of freckles across their noses that lingers long after summer.

Zara sits in front of the mirrored wardrobe and stares at herself. Stares at Savannah's ghost as it imitates Zara's movements. She smiles. She frowns. She laughs. She gives her body over to her sister and allows her to live for another hour in her own flesh.

What would Savannah be doing now, at twenty? What would her life look like, now that she had a good job and a decent flat that didn't have mold in the walls, mice in the ceiling, a creepy uncle on the other side of the door?

What if Savannah had found whatever it was she sold a piece of her soul to go looking for?

# EIGHT

**WHEN EMER** wakes, the room is full of demons.

In the common room, a sea of pit-eyed monsters stare at her, waiting. This is not new. They always gather in the night. Like a flock of seagulls at the shore, they have been fed enough that they have come to expect it. Now they converge around her and wait for the next drop of blood to be flung their way.

Emer's eyes sting and begin to water. The sulfur that leaks from their skin has poisoned the air. The creatures are roughly human in shape, though much taller, with longer, thinner limbs. They have bones and plum-dark organs visible beneath translucent skin. Their mouths are filled with sharp teeth, their eyes deep black craters. They cluster in the gloomier parts of the room: under tables, in the corners, clinging to the ceiling like bats.

Emer sits up. Her bare foot lands on something damp and glutinous. There's a moment of tension and then release as it bursts and squelches between her toes. A black banana, so rotten that its insides have liquefied. There is other garbage heaped in a pile, too. A dead mouse. A half-eaten pot of berry yogurt turned on its side.

A bag of compost. Several apple cores. A handful of cooked rice scattered over the top of everything.

Emer groans and wipes her foot on the carpet. "You idiots," she says. She points at the garbage and says, "Satis! Nolite me purgamentum adferre! Bring me a bowl of muesli or something."

The demons do not react or respond. They have brought her an offering, and as far as they are concerned, it is suitable. They cannot differentiate between a stale loaf of bread, a dead animal, and edible food. It is all organic matter to them. All human sustenance.

Emer tries not to feel ungrateful for it. This behavior begins every year when winter approaches and the weather starts to turn cold. Once, demons kept her alive during the bitter months. They came to her the same winter she plucked off her own frostbitten toes like bruised grapes. She had taken shelter in a cave in the woods around Lough Leane. There was no food and no warmth. She was starving. Emaciated. A rattling cough had settled in her lungs and made it hard to breathe. She was tired all the time and only wanted to sleep. She was seven years old, and she would have died there if not for the demons she began to see trailing her through the woods.

"Me salvate," she whispered to them. *Save me.* She knew she was dying, and she was afraid.

After that, whenever she woke, there would be some dead thing left next to her. Little forest creatures, caught and slaughtered and left open-bellied within her reach. At first Emer recoiled from these offerings. A fever burned through her and left her weak, but she was not yet desperate enough to eat raw squirrel. Besides, there was no such thing as a gift from a demon. This she knew. There was only an exchange.

The fever passed. Somehow, Emer was still alive, but the cold had already gotten into her bones.

"Ignis," she croaked to no one. Her grasp of Latin was immature then. She had been learning since she could speak, but the old language still felt unwieldy on her tongue.

Demons do not like fire or heat. They prefer cold, gloomy slips of space. It was the first test of their tenuous alliance. Emer needed warmth to survive the winter.

When she next awoke, there were the ingredients for a fire. Dry wood, kindling, a box of matches. A blanket had been laid over her small body. Demons would not start the flames themselves. No matter: Emer had been building fires since she could walk. A storm seethed outside, but soon the cave was dry and warm.

"Aqua," she rasped. Again, when she next awoke, they had brought her what she asked for. A bucket of stream water was sitting by her head.

Emer was the child of a witch and had grown up with a healthy fear of the creatures beyond the veil. Her mother had taught her how to see them. Emer had instead chosen to ignore them. Now, though, she wanted to see what was bringing her food and water and warmth.

There were three of them, in the beginning. They were monstrous things, their bodies stretched long and thin like sinew. Their skin was dull glass and clung to their bones like wet fabric. They walked on two legs but were just as comfortable loping on all fours like a predator. When you opened your sight to them, you also opened your other senses: smell, hearing. They stank of sulfur and sour rot. They called to each other like animals, the pitch going from low to high like hyenas. They bickered and snapped at one another. They were grotesque.

They were also the closest thing she had now to a family.

Demons saw Emer through the winter. Demons nursed her back to health.

In the months that followed, her demons—and she did come to think of them as hers, in a way—continued to feed her. Later, when she was stronger, one of them began to bring her books. Books stolen from libraries and private collections. Books about language. Books on Sanskrit. Books on Pali. Books on ancient Greek. Books on Hebrew, old Persian, Avestan, middle Persian, Chinese, Arabic. Many, many books on Latin. All left at her feet while she slept, along with paper and pencils to practice writing in these languages.

For three years, demons nourished her. Demons educated her. She was not so foolish to think they did it out of love or caring. It was an investment. Emer was the daughter of a cursewriter, the granddaughter of a cursewriter. Demons needed cursewriters so they could consume souls, and cursewriters were a dying breed. Every dead squirrel, every stolen book, every night they kept her alive, all of it was an investment in their own survival—and they did survive. Of the three who'd saved her, she had already given heartspace invocations to two. They left greedily and without hesitation. They did not love her, and she had not been sad to see them go.

The third demon who'd saved her, Bael, is here this morning. The one who brings her books. It has been with her every morning since she was seven. It is waiting for its turn, but there is only one soul it wants, only one soul she could offer that would sate its hunger: Emer's own.

Emer looks around the room at the rest of the demons who

have come. They have heard from other demons what she is, what she can do. They bring her gifts and offerings in the hope that she will feed them a human soul. They are all reedy things, gaunt. Demons are the batteries that provide power to spells, and none of these are particularly powerful.

"No," she says, this time to Bael directly. None of them are good enough. None of them are suitable for cursework. They will not be allowed to lurk around. "Eos dimitte." *Dismiss them.*

Bael moves slowly. It huffs sulfur dust from its noseholes and drags its long arms along the floor as it unfurls itself from slumber. It always appears unwilling to follow her orders in front of other demons.

Emer rolls her eyes. Such a *poser.*

Reluctantly, the demon does as she says. Emer covers her ears. Bael begins to speak in voces mysticae: the language of demons. There are no discernible words, only a string of foul tones that pluck at her nerves. Bile rises in her throat. The room cants sideways. There is hissing as Bael dismisses the creatures that have tried to win Emer's favor. They are angry. They want to be fed. A cacophony of noxious sounds erupts. Emer hangs her head between her knees and focuses on not vomiting.

Bael's voice rises even higher. The other demons fall quiet. Then it is over and only Bael is left. Just the two of them, as it has been for some years now. A wild young witch and the demon who raised her, each gilded in the soft morning sunlight that floods the room.

"Was that so hard?" Emer asks.

Now that they are alone, the creature crouches before her and huffs again.

"Good job, Bael," Emer tells it in Latin. She hovers her hand near the side of its pale skull, where its ears would be if it had them. How it hears, she does not know. How it sees, she does not know. The creature is far hotter than a human. Its skin feels like the dwindling coals of burned-down fires.

On the morning of Emer's tenth birthday, Bael brought her a scavenged cupcake and a pointy paper party hat. Emer ate the cupcake and put the hat on Bael. The paper did not last long against its furnace-hot skin. It is still one of Emer's favorite memories, the glum-faced hell creature with a striped pom-pom-topped cone strapped under its chin. Nessa found her less than a month later. Took her from the woods of Lough Leane to Cork. Rehabilitated her from a wild thing to a . . . well, a slightly less wild thing.

She begins her day. She cleans up the pile of garbage left by the demons. She washes the banana from between her toes in the bathroom. She uses a stolen student card to access breakfast at Brasenose. She rides to Linacre. She works out until her legs shake. She showers and washes her clothes. She puts on the disguise that allows her to move freely in this golden sandstone world: deodorant, makeup, clothes without holes in them.

Today, something tells her to go to the coordinates she puts on her business card: Blackwell's bookshop, where she sits on a balcony in the occult section. Emer only goes once or twice a month, but whenever she does, a woman finds her there. It is some kind of intuition. Some of kind of inherited magic, in her blood since before she was born, because her mother was a witch, and her mother, and her mother before that.

Cursewriting is a slow trade, existing only in the underbelly and at the edges. For good reason. It is dangerous to whisper beyond the veil and call demons into this realm. It is more dangerous still to bind these demons to desperate women, to let them feed off women's souls in exchange for a flicker of power. Most cursewriters sell their skills to wealthy entrepreneurs looking for a leg up at work or infatuated lovers hungering for a relationship with the object of their affection.

Emer's business caters to a different clientele. Perhaps it is too generous to call it a business at all, because Emer refuses any payment for the work she does. They come to her bruised and crying, fearful for their safety. They come to her injured and wrathful, determined to protect themselves. Emer warns them of the danger, which she has seen firsthand: Men may come for you, if you take this power. She never denies those who seek it, if that is what they want. She is not a gatekeeper or a governess. She believes women have the right to choose.

Emer understands the necessity of taking the risk. The ability to hide. The ability to escape. The ability to fight. Sometimes, through no fault of their own, women cannot hide or escape or fight when they need to. Sometimes they need help. Like her neighbor in Cork did.

Like her family did.

It had been raining when they came. Four men in dark waxed jackets. The air had smelled of apple blossoms and spring rain. The sky beyond the sun-shower had been gentian blue. Emer had been playing in the meadow, flitting through the spray with her cousin Niamh, when the men had appeared at the edge of the forest.

Emer had seen them first. For years, it has haunted her that she did not immediately run inside and warn her mother. Perhaps, if they'd had some seconds to prepare, the women inside might have been able to fight back. They had no use for offensive or defensive invocations because they had chosen a secret, self-sufficient life away from the threats of the regular world. Their magic was gentle, meant to coax plants from the ground and ensure nearby streams ran with clean, fresh water. They were witches of the earth, of soil and root, not of fire and violence.

Only Orlaith, Emer's grandmother, had dabbled in much darker magic—but she was so old by the night of the attack, so feeble, that she, too, was unable to defend herself.

They had been a coven. Not solitary, lonely women who lived in fear like most cursewriters, but a whole *coven*. A rare thing, after the witch burnings of centuries past drove them to the edge of extinction.

Emer had never seen men in real life before, had only heard about them in tales and seen illustrations of them in books. They were taller and broader than she had expected them to be, bigger than any woman she had seen. They each held a hunting rifle, but Emer had never seen those before, either, and did not yet know what they were. So she watched them curiously as they walked across the field toward the house. Niamh ran around them in circles, giggling and asking them questions. Emer hung back, wary. Men were not to be trusted. This much she knew. Men burned women like her mother and her grandmother at the stake. This she knew, too.

Emer stayed outside and climbed the branches of a tree in the apple orchard. There, nestled in the blossoms, she watched and waited. It was not long before the gunshots began, and not much longer still until her mother, Saoirse, burst out of the big house, barefoot and bolting, her skirt hitched up around her knees, one side of her shirt splattered with blood. "Run, Emer! Run!" she shouted, though she could not see her daughter. A man appeared at the door through which Saoirse had escaped and aimed his rifle at her. There was a loud crack that reverberated throughout the clearing. Saoirse dropped midstride, face-first into the grass, and did not move again.

Emer did not run. Not immediately. Frozen with fear, she watched and listened as the rest of her family fought and died inside that house. After the shots stopped around dusk, the four men exited the building and roamed its perimeter in silence, waiting for hidden survivors to flee. There was only one, by that point.

Emer watched as her teenage cousin Róisín, heavily pregnant with her first daughter, shimmied down from a second-story window. Emer watched as she dropped into a flower bed carpeted with pansy and primrose. Emer watched as a man caught her by red hair and wrestled her to the ground. "Andy!" she cried. "Andy, please, Andy, no, no—"

If Róisín had been wearing a spell like the ones Emer writes . . .

Emer touches the scroll pendant at her neck. It is meant for him, if she finds him.

*When* she finds him.

*Andy.*

"Emer?" asks a distant voice. "Emer Byrne?"

Emer lifts her gaze from the page she is reading and looks down over the balustrade to the shop floor below. The asker, a girl with short black hair, is moving around the store, asking the handful of people browsing if they are her.

"Emer?" the dark-haired girl tries again. "Emer?" she asks the next person she passes. Emer watches with raised eyebrows.

"I want it on the record *again* that I do not think this is a good strategy," murmurs the blond girl she is with.

"Oh yeah?" the dark-haired girl asks. "What do you suggest?"

"Go to the occult section. See if she's sitting there."

"That's a terrible idea."

"Actually," Emer says over the balustrade, "it is a very good idea."

They both look up. The dark-haired girl grins. "Hello, Emer Byrne," she calls up. "My name is Jude Wolf. I think you might be able to help me."

Emer motions with her head for them to come up.

When Jude Wolf ascends the stairs and stands before her, there's a sudden fizzing in Emer's teeth, an insect hum in her ears. It is perilous business, trying to get the word around about her services. Each business card that she makes with the coordinates of this bookshop is a clue that could fall into the wrong hands. It is sometimes hard to judge friend from foe—and Jude Wolf, with her sharp jaw and clever eyes, has a definite air of threat about her.

The blond girl surges forward to shake Emer's hand. "My name is Zara Jones," she says. "It is a pleasure to make your acquaintance."

"Sit, both of you," Emer says. They do. "How can I help you?"

"I think you know what I want," Jude answers.

A dart of sulfur stings Emer's nose, and she understands instantly what Jude is and what she has come for. Her gaze falls to Jude's thigh. Beneath the fabric, she can sense wrongness emanating from a bad invocation. It has left the girl's body damaged and her soul necrotic. The curse has eaten her up.

"I cannot help you," Emer says, because the magic is a cesspit too far gone to be redeemed. "I cannot fix other people's bad work."

"Emer. Peach. I will pay you *lots* of money."

"I do not accept payment for this work."

"You don't accept *payment*?" Jude asks, incredulous. Then she stands and unbuttons her suit trousers and shoves them to the ground.

Zara gasps. "You are in *public*," the girl says—but they are buried at the back of the store and no one is around.

Emer leans closer to get a better look.

Jude's entire right thigh is gangrenous. It is black and yellow with rot and split down the middle with gaping fissures in the flesh. Patches of fat and muscle are exposed and in one section near the center, the flesh is so desiccated that it has shriveled away to reveal Jude's femur. There are metal letters inside the most fetid parts of it. Worst of all, it is moving. As Emer watches, the wound shudders and contorts. The letters embedded in it drift across the flesh as though they are boats sailing on a lake.

"Who did this to you?" Emer asks as she hovers her palms over Jude's leg.

"I did it to myself."

"*Why?*"

"Well, I surely didn't mean to. I was a dumb kid messing around with the occult. I didn't think it was *real*. I didn't think it would actually work."

"It is the worst curse I have ever seen."

"Gee, thanks." Jude pulls up her trousers. "I know it's bad. There's no need to rub it in."

"It should have been over a pulse point, to begin with. That is a very basic requirement of spellwork."

"I know that now. There was a mistranslation in the instructions."

Emer lets her gaze travel from Jude's thigh to the ceiling and then to a darkened corner of the room, where she can feel a malevolent presence.

"You're sighted," Jude guesses.

Emer is not a talented seer, unlike her mother and aunts, who could effortlessly hold both worlds in their eyes. Her sight for the supernatural is weak because, unlike her body, she has chosen not to train it. It is much more pleasant to not see the horrors that live alongside humans. Mostly she only sees beyond the veil in the mornings when she wakes. Emer lets her eyes go unfocused. What she sees tethered to Jude Wolf is this: a furious wraith, bound against its will to Jude's soul. It has not made a deal with her. It has not been coaxed from the hellscape in which it dwelled with the promise of feeding on a human spirit. It has not latched correctly to her and is rabid with starvation.

In the few moments that she glimpses it, Emer sees the demon clamber across the ceiling. It stops in one corner and pulls at the tether that binds it to Jude, which makes Jude wince. It moans and froths at the mouth. It gnaws on its own limbs as it tries to break free. It is a confused, trapped animal.

There are two other demons tethered to Jude, bound by the two invocations at her wrists. These ones are more orderly and docile. Jude has given them part of her soul in exchange for some power. As long as Jude lives, they will be happy to provide it. While Emer watches, they suckle away at Jude's spirit, nourished and happy—or at least as happy as two wraiths can be with a third monster furiously and endlessly flailing around them, never giving them any peace. Which is to say, even Jude's two normal invocations, given to her by mediocre cursewriters, are not functioning particularly well.

"It would be very difficult to control," Emer says. "It is angry and starving. Extremely volatile. It would take many more invocations to restrain it. More than your soul could handle."

"I don't want you to restrain it, Emer," Jude replies. "I want you to cut it off. You hear that?" Jude speaks to the ceiling. "Ego te ad tollendum." She draws a finger in a sharp line across her throat. "You're a goner."

*Terrible Latin*, Emer thinks—but the demons still get the idea. All is quiet for a second and then Jude is yanked out of her chair and dragged across the carpet on her back. Zara gasps, because she cannot see what Emer sees.

It is not the starving demon's doing, but rather the doing of the other two. The vow made between them and Jude is supposed to be unbreakable. If Jude rids herself of one of her demons, what is to stop her from ridding herself of all of them?

"Demons!" Emer says, except she does not say it in English, but in Akkadian. Her blade is already in her hand, already cutting the familiar line of pain down her left arm. "Feed!" The demons dragging Jude drop her. Emer holds out her bloody arm and winces as all three of Jude's monsters and Bael, unseen to the others in the room, slam into Emer and begin feeding from her wound.

"What are you doing?" Zara whispers.

"Distracting them," Emer answers.

"With cheap tricks." Jude drags herself up off the floor and smooths down her suit jacket. "There are two ways to pay for magic, Jones, because demons only love two things: souls and blood. Blood is like—well, junk food. A sugar rush. It keeps them going for a few minutes. You can use it to pay for little things. Unlocking a door, that kind of stuff."

"What about souls?" Zara asks. "What are they like?"

"Souls? Souls are like—" Jude thinks for a moment. "Nuclear friction."

"I think you mean nuclear *fission*."

"You are exhausting to be around, Jones."

Emer withdraws her arm and tries to roll down her sleeve. "Prohibete," she says, and then, again, more serious this time: "*Prohibete.*" The demons go back to feeding on Jude's soul. Well, two of them do. Emer blinks away her second sight.

Jude is staring at her. "What do you say, Byrne?"

What Jude wants is impossible.

A tether with a demon is made for life. That is the deal. That is the law. Emer has done patch jobs before—tethering a second, more powerful demon to someone to enhance a weak invocation written by an inferior writer—but severing the link altogether is unimaginable.

"I cannot do what you ask of me," Emer says. She turns to Zara. "Why are you here?"

"I think you knew my sis—" Zara begins.

"Oh, I am *not* done," Jude says as she places her hand on Zara's shoulder. The girl instantly passes out, her head landing heavily on the table in front of her. Jude turns to Emer, her eyes dark. The lights in the store flicker, picking up on Jude's magic. "Why don't you show me a little of what you can really do."

So she does. Without hesitation, Emer stands and knees Jude squarely in her injured leg, right in the soft, infected center of the wound. They never expect it, Jude's kind. Those obsessed with the magic of the occult. They're ready for snakes coiling around their ankles or incantations muttered under the breath, but not crippling physical pain, which is why Emer opts to carry a knife and build muscle instead of searing spells into her skin.

The pattern doesn't fail her here. Jude folds to the floor with an "oof," giving Emer enough time to palm her knife once more. The lights stop flickering. Jude is still gasping for breath when Emer sits heavily on her chest.

"You . . . *bitch* . . ." Jude manages to spit.

"Hey," Emer says, tapping Jude's cheek to get her attention. "I do not like that word." She presses the blade against Jude's throat with just enough pressure to draw a razor-thin line of blood. The demons in the room can smell it, but they cannot partake of it unless given permission first. "You think because you sold a piece of your soul for some meager magic that you are invincible. You are not. There are other ways to protect yourself. Now undo whatever you did to Zara and leave."

Jude stops moaning and goes still. "One million pounds," she says, breathing through her teeth as she extends her hand toward Zara's ankle.

Emer lessens the pressure on the blade. "What?"

"One million. That's how much is in my trust fund. That's how much I can withdraw right now, no questions asked. That's how much I'll pay you for one measly invocation. If you can fix me."

"Wake her up," Emer orders.

Jude's fingertips graze Zara's ankle. Zara wakes up with a gasp to find Emer crouched on Jude's chest, the blade still at her throat. Zara looks from Emer to Jude and back to Emer. "I think you knew my sister, Savannah Jones." The words tumble out of her, as though she has not noticed that she collapsed, as though she must convey this information right this very moment. "I think you knew Rebecca Wright, and Marcella Rossi, and Lara Beaumont, and Yael Mizrahi-Greenwood. Am I right?"

Emer's head is still spinning from Jude's offer. What would she do with that kind of money? It is not something she has contemplated before. She has never planned a life for herself beyond this: living in the shadows at the edge of the world, a rat scrounging to survive so she can write one more spell for one more desperate woman.

"What?" she asks Zara finally, confused. "Yes. I know them." They all came to her, here, in this bookshop and asked to sell a piece of their soul to the devil.

"Emer," Zara says, her face filled with alarm. "They're all dead. Someone is killing your clients."

# NINE

**THE WITCH** is furious.

Zara can feel it in her body, can taste it on her tongue, can see it in the hairline fractures that have appeared suddenly in the overhead light. The bookstore is on edge, the air electric and friable with magic. The witch takes short, sharp breaths through flared nostrils. Her teeth and fists are clenched.

*Magic.* After all these wretched weeks and months scouring books and forums, here it is, the thing Zara has searched so longingly for. She felt it inside her when Jude knocked her out, a long shadow stretching over her mind, dragging her down into the darkness. She feels it again now, a current on her skin: a warning of danger.

"What do you mean they're all dead?" Emer asks in a low voice.

Cautiously, Zara takes a dossier out of her satchel and begins to lay out printed articles and photographs of the dead women when they were alive.

"You brought a multimedia presentation," Jude says. "Of course you did."

"It's been happening for a year," Zara says, ignoring Jude as she hands Emer a photograph of Savannah. "Someone is hunting them. Cutting pieces out of them."

"Invocations," Jude adds. "*Your* invocations, it would seem. You must be good if they're keeping trophies."

"A year?" Emer breathes. "A whole year?"

Zara nods. "I think that's when it started. With Savannah. My sister."

Emer hovers her hands over the women's faces. "How many? How many have been killed?"

"There are five that we know about," Jude says, "but there could be more."

The witch says nothing. Then:

"I warned them."

It is no more than a whisper. Zara kind of thinks that that will be it, that the cascade of energy that has been spilling from the witch will dissipate now into grief, but she is wrong. Emer slams her fist into the table and says, "I WARNED THEM!" The voice that booms from her is no longer human. It is chasm-deep and dark to match, the voice of a god gone mad.

Someone shushes them from the shop floor below.

"Sorry," Jude calls down.

"I warned them all," Emer says as she trails her fingertips over the women's photographs again. "I told them that they might become targets, that I had seen firsthand the violence men wreak on women who choose this path, but I . . ." Emer looks up at them. "I made a decision two years ago to do this work. To give women power when they had none. I have been such a fool."

Zara shakes her head. "You didn't kill these women."

"I marked them, though."

"*You* didn't kill these women, Emer. Somebody else did that. Right, Jude?"

"Oh, yeah, sure. Totally culpable. No, wait, that's not the right word. What's the opposite of *culpable*? *Inculpable*?"

*Shut. Up,* Zara mouths to her.

*What?* Jude mouths back.

Emer looks up and holds each of them in her dark, magnetic gaze. "Tell me everything you know."

Jude dives in and gives her version of events and shows Emer photos on her phone she took at the crime scenes. Jude flicks through and narrates them as casually as if they were shots from a recent holiday. "Oh, this one is particularly nasty, she had three invocations cut out of her. Three! Look at this one, look how carefully the skin from the heartspace was removed. Is he a surgeon, maybe? Or some kind of creepy craft hobbyist who needs steady hands to paint tiny dolls? Who's to know."

"*Heartspace?*" Zara asks. The word is new and piques her interest.

"Oh yeah, sorry, I forgot you're a noob," Jude says. "The area over the heart is reserved for the most powerful invocations. That's where your blood flow is strongest. They're pretty hard-core, heartspace spells. It's big power at a big price. Not easy on the body, not easy on the soul. You'd probably lose—What do you think, Emer?—twenty years of life for a heartspace spell?"

Again, Emer does not answer Jude's question.

While Jude continues speaking, Zara opens the notes she took during the drive from London to Oxford. It had been a short but informative (and rather pungent) trip. There had been no more trading of questions—Jude had gotten everything she wanted from Zara last night, it seemed—so the flow of information had gone one way. Zara had her computer balanced on her knees the whole time, typing quietly but feverishly as Jude answered question after question about the occult.

QUESTION: Why do demons want human souls? Do
    they need them to survive?
ANSWER: Demons are immaterial and immortal. They
    don't need human souls to survive (they don't need
    anything to survive)—but they live a cursed existence.
    Forever starving. Forever gaunt and withered. Shadow
    creatures. In a kind of tortured, miserable stasis—
    unless tethered to a human. They crave human souls,
    human blood.

Zara adds the words *Blood = junk food. Souls = nuclear fission* to the answer.

QUESTION: What are demons?
ANSWER: Unclear. Older than humans, have had
    significant influence on human civilization (see: the
    Bible). Jude thinks: aliens from an astral plane (feels
    unlikely, seems like she is joking).

QUESTION: How do tethers work?
ANSWER: Umbilical cords? (Jude does not seem to know,
    mainly waffling.)

To the end of the document, Zara adds the information about heartspace spells and tunes in in time to catch Jude giving Emer the last details on the most recent death. The cursewriter sits unmoving, her eyebrows drawn, her jaw clenched, her breath still coming through flared nostrils.

"So what do you think, Byrne?" Jude says, arching her fingers in front of her. "I've given you the lowdown, now how about we talk business?"

"You can leave," Emer says. "I have no further need of you."

Jude looks at Zara, confused. "Uh, what? No. Wait. I just gave you the comprehensive history of Jack the Magical Freakin' Ripper, and now, in return, you scratch my back and cut these demons out of me. For a very handsome reward, might I remind you."

"I cannot help you," Emer says. "So you can leave."

"I don't think I will do that, actually, because it's taken me months—years!—to find you, and I'm like, really, really, deeply not enjoying my existence currently. I feel like crap all the time. I'm cold, I'm hungry, I'm thirsty, I'm tired. My throat hurts. My nose runs. I don't think I've had a solid bowel movement in two years." None of this seems to particularly move Emer, so Jude continues, more desperately. "I *miss* my *life*, Emer. I miss . . . the glittery parties. I miss the feel of silk on my skin and the taste of champagne. I miss kissing pretty girls and reading books by the fireplace on rainy afternoons. I miss not reeking of rotten eggs. I miss not being in pain. I even miss my messed-up family. I complain about them a lot, and some of them have done some truly terrible things, but—" Jude exhales. "I am *one* of them. You know? I am a *Wolf*. With them—it's the only place I've ever felt like I belong. I want to go *home*, Emer."

Zara thinks she knows what Jude means, because she understands you can miss people who hurt you. She understands this because she misses her mother sometimes, the woman who dumped her at Pru's and never came back. She misses the smell of her mother's hair when she washed it (shea butter and coconut oil), and she misses her face, so similar to Savannah's and Zara's own. That face—it somehow made Zara's face make sense. She never knew her father and so could see none of him in herself—but Lydia? Zara doesn't think about her mother often, but she would like to know what she looks like now. She would like to see herself—and Savannah—reflected back in the world. A link to something.

So Zara feels like she gets it.

"There's a deal to be done here," Jude continues. "You want to stop the murders, right? Fine. Let's do a girl-power thing and team up. I have resources. That trust fund I told you about—it's real. I can fund your investigation, and you can Poirot your little heart out and catch the bad guy. In exchange, you at least *try* to fix me. Give it a crack, you know. Give it a little noodle, see if anything comes to you."

Emer answers slowly. "You should pledge your resources to help me stop the killings whether I can fix you or not."

"Well, that's not exactly a good deal for me, is it?"

"So if I don't help you, you won't help me find the murderer?"

Jude swallows. "Jesus, Emer, when you put it that way, it sounds pretty bad, but—look. You want something, I want something. We make a trade. It makes me sound like a monster, but . . ." Jude straightens, committing to her line of argument. "If you don't help me, I don't help you, and, uh, well, your clients keep dying, I guess."

Jude looks at Zara with a grimace. Zara grimaces back and lets a breath out through her teeth. It's bad.

"Go," Emer orders. "Leave. For your own sake."

"Oh, come on, please, you can't be serious. I have so much money!"

Emer says nothing, just raises her hand to point at the exit below. Jude looks like she wants to go all dark sorceress again, but that didn't work out so well for her the first time. "Fine," she says begrudgingly, putting her hands up in defeat. "Look, I'm driving Jones home, so I'm just going to sit here quietly." She mimes zipping her lips. "Not another word."

Emer's eyes flick to Zara. "And you? What do you want?"

*I did not come this far to only come this far.*

"I want to resurrect my sister from the dead," Zara says plainly.

Emer blinks at her a half dozen times and says nothing.

"Do you know how to do that?" Zara continues.

"When I was a child, men came to my house and killed my entire family. Nineteen women died. If I knew how to bring them back, I would have done it a long time ago."

"Jesus Christ," Jude whispers.

"Oh my God, Emer. That's . . . It's . . ." Zara cannot find the words. There are no words for a tragedy so great.

Emer nods. "Yes. It is."

"I mean—why?" Zara cannot form more of a question than this.

"Witch hunters," Jude says.

Emer's eyes flash with fire. "*Women* hunters. Calling them witch hunters is far too lenient. My family were much more than witches. They were women. They were human. They were whole and complex and dynamic. They did not deserve to die for a sliver of their identity."

"Spitballing here," Jude says, interrupting. "Any chance it's the same dudes? Your family were witches, your clients are witches. Look at me, I'm helping with the investigation already."

Emer considers this, looks again at the photographs, then shakes her head. "Your killer takes trophies, purposefully leaves the bodies to be found. A hunter would never do that. They live in the shadows, as we do. Secrecy is of the utmost importance to them."

"Do they hunt men who use magic as well?" Zara asks.

"Ah, but there's the catch," Jude says. "Men cannot wield magic."

"What? Really? That's . . . new." After a year of research, of course Zara has come to know that, historically, many more women were accused and punished for witchcraft than men. Burning, drowning, stoning—people came up with all sorts of hideously cruel ways to execute suspected witches. The victims were usually women— but they were sometimes also men. "Why is that?"

"Jesus, Jones, you ask a lot of questions. Why does the sun rise in the east and set in the west?"

"I know you meant for that to be a rhetorical question, but the sun rises in the east and sets in the west because of Earth's rotation."

Emer looks at each of them and sighs. "Even the devil does not trust men to honor a bargain, so it does not deal with them. It offers power only to women."

"What about trans women?" Zara asks, writing the question in her document. "How does that work?"

"Of course I have written invocations for trans women," Emer says. "Demons do not care about bodies. They only care about souls."

Zara nods and makes note of the answer.

Jude's phone starts vibrating in her hand. "Well, look who it is!" she says, showing them both the screen. Reese Chopra's name (flanked by red hearts) crawls across the screen. Zara raises her eyebrows as Jude answers and says, "Reese, darling, I'm so thrilled—"

Jude shuts up immediately. Her smile falls. "Oh God," she says. Then: "How much?" Finally, she looks up at Zara and Emer, and says, "We'll be there."

# TEN

**ANOTHER ONE,** Chopra had said. *No charge. Just get here and tell me what the hell I'm dealing with.*

Jude has suspected, for some time now, that Chopra's motivation for inviting her back to crime scenes again and again was not purely monetary gain. Chopra doesn't believe in magic or the occult—or at least she doesn't want it to be real—but she heard everything Jude told her about witches and demons, and maybe, just maybe, she can't shake the suspicion that Jude was telling the truth.

Jude tightens her fingers around the steering wheel, tries to breathe through a contraction of pain in her thigh. It feels like there's something *moving* down there. Inside of her. Something about the size of a mouse, writhing around. Something that Emer really pissed off when she drove her extremely sharp and knobby knee into Jude's wound.

Emer said there was nothing she could do to fix her, to break the curse—but Jude will not accept that.

Jude *cannot* accept that.

If there is anything she has learned from her father, it is that there is no task too great that it cannot be accomplished by throwing vast sums of money at it. Even obstinate witches can be convinced, eventually—she hopes.

Thinking of Lawrence makes Jude's heart twist. Makes her angry and sad at once. The wedding is this weekend, and she hasn't even been informed, let alone invited. It stings—but then again, it's meant to. You are *meant* to know when Lawrence is displeased with you. It is *supposed* to hurt. Because when something stings, when something hurts, you do what you can to fix it. You do what you can—*whatever* you can—to get back in Lawrence's good graces, because nothing feels better than praise from your harshest critic. Even now, Jude practically salivates at the thought of strolling in, uncursed, to the wedding on Sunday and having her father give her the hint of an approving smile.

*I need to get back into therapy,* Jude thinks. Out loud, she says, "How are we doing on those calls?"

Jones is in the passenger seat beside her, Emer is in the back. Jude has gone from the utter depths of loneliness and despair to having *two people* in her car in the space of a day. Two very annoying people, but two people nonetheless.

Jude glances at Emer in the rearview mirror and cannot help but to scowl. The witch looks so serious, her jaw set, her beady little crab eyes glued to the notebook in her lap—her grimoire, she called it. Jude wanted to roll her eyes. *Witches.* As if a tatty book from a supermarket stationery aisle could really be called a *grimoire*.

"Fifteen out of sixteen," Jones says, sounding pleased with

herself. Of course. Goody Two-shoes Jones loves good marks. "Not bad—but I want to keep trying the one I missed until I get ahold of her." She checks her notes. "Vera Clarke."

They are on the outskirts of London already, bound for Chopra's crime scene. Jones and Emer have spent the drive calling Emer's past clients, warning them that there's a target on their backs. They divided the list of over thirty women and began phoning each of them. Emer told Jones what to say: That the women are in grave danger. That they must try to protect themselves with a sacrifice of blood. Jones—who, a day ago had no real idea that magic existed outside of her hopes—has spent the last two hours explaining wards to the women on her list. How much blood they will need, where to place it, the words to say that will allow demons to consume the blood in exchange for some protection.

"Tell me again about the difference between blood magic and soul magic," Jones said at the start of the drive, laptop balancing on her knees, her reading glasses back on her nose. Such an eager beaver.

Emer went over everything: Demons are immortal, they don't need souls or blood to survive but their endless existence sucks and consuming souls and blood makes them less wretched, blah blah blah.

Jude listened with interest as Emer explained wards, because she didn't know much about them. Emer showed them the unhealed wound on her arm and told them about the blood ward she cast each night to protect herself, how it was weak, more of a warning system than something that would keep intruders out.

More powerful wards require more blood. Around half a liter is enough for a powerful boundary spell that can protect a property for a week. The woman must harvest the blood from herself and then divide it equally into four small jars, each of which must be buried or placed at north, south, east, and west compass points outside the house. There are also several paragraphs of Latin that must be recited while placing the jars, to stop nearby demons from downing them all at once like shot glasses.

Of Emer's thirty-two remaining unmurdered clients, they have managed to reach twenty-seven. Twenty-seven women who answered their phones and listened to what Emer and Zara had to say. Jude expected most of them to think it was a horrible prank phone call, but none of the women hung up. The calls were brief, serious, informative.

"No, we have no reason to believe your children would be a target for any reason."

"Remember to call me back if you see anything strange or feel unsafe. We'll do our best to get to you in time."

That kind of thing.

Jude glances at Emer again. The witch is staring back at her in the mirror, her brown eyes hard. Jude shakes her head and returns her gaze to the road. Jude Wolf is good at getting people to like her. It's a game she's been playing with her father her whole life.

*Okay, Emer Byrne,* she thinks. *You want to catch a serial killer? Let's catch a serial killer.*

# ELEVEN

**ABBY GALLAGHER** had been fifteen years old when she found Emer and asked her for an invocation that would allow her hands to melt through flesh. There had been an abusive uncle, parents who refused to believe her story, and a younger sister she wanted to protect, so Abby had decided to take the matter into her own hands. Literally.

It had taken Emer close to four months to get the spell right, because there were so many ways it could go wrong. What if Abby could not control the power and her hands burned through everything she touched? What if the meaning of the request was lost on the demon and it set Abby's hands on fire or she ended up in constant pain from a skin condition that caused her palms to burn but could not burn others? These were the things that had to be considered when writing a curse. Translation is an art. It is about conveying a deeper meaning, about painting an image in the demon's proto-mind, something deep and visceral that it can understand.

In the end, it had worked as Emer had hoped it would: Abby Gallagher could hurt people with her hands if and when she wanted to. She could control fire. The spell was tight and elegant and brutally effective. It had been some of Emer's best work.

Abby had sent a news article some weeks later about a man named Greg Gallagher whose genitals had melted off in horrific and mysterious circumstances. The journalists theorized about spontaneous human combustion. Little did they know.

That was a year ago. Now Abby Gallagher, whose fingers could melt through metal and bone, is dead. She has been for several days. Her skin is murky, mottled, the color of bones and sap and the green of soft plants that grow on forest floors. Her body has sprung leaks, has begun to sag into the carpet. Her eyes are blank and reptilian, no light behind them. She lies wide-eyed on a five-pointed star painted in her own blood. Around the pentagram, also in blood, is a message: *Thou shalt not suffer a witch to live.*

Emer breathes into her surgical mask, grimaces at the hot, sour stink of her own breath as it washes back into her nose. She rubs hers fingers together. They are cocooned in powdered latex gloves, muting her fingertips' sensation of the world. She feels sick, but she has been warned by Reese Chopra not to vomit.

"This is not the work of a hunter," Emer says slowly, breathing through her mouth. She is more sure of it now than ever. The men who hunt witches are not ostentatious. Not anymore, anyway. Witch burnings have long fallen out of favor, and so the grisly business of killing women is conducted in secret. They do not want the world to know that magic exists. They do not want girls and women to go seeking it. Even the men who killed Emer's family buried them in the apple orchard on her family's land. It was messed-up hunter logic: "cleanse" a woman's soul, then give her a decent burial now that she is "worthy."

"If it were a witch hunter, she would just have disappeared. There would be no crime scene. This is something different." Emer kneels next to her body.

"Don't touch her," the detective warns. Reese Chopra is deeply displeased that Emer is here and has been making her feelings known since the moment the three of them arrived at the crime scene. "Don't touch anything."

They are in Abby's bedroom in the flat she shared with her parents and sister. There had been fighting in the Gallagher family, Reese tells them. Abby had dropped out of school, could not hold down a job, drank in secret and then no longer bothered to hide it. The family was out of town for the week, visiting relatives. They left their eldest daughter at home alone because she had refused to join them. They said her depression prevented her from leaving the house much. Emer is doubly sad for this. That the power she gave Abby was not enough to change what had already happened. That becoming the hero of your own story does not always mean you get a happy ending.

There is a rectangle of skin missing from Abby's chest, about the size of Emer's palm. Her heartspace. Guilt tightens Emer's throat and makes it hard for her to swallow. She does not like heartspace spells and rarely thinks they are worth the price. Why cleave off half your soul for the ability to melt a double-decker bus when you could put the same invocation at your wrist and burn through someone's skin for far less cost?

Abby could not be swayed. Most women, when they decide on heartspace spells, cannot be bargained down. They want power. They are furious. They are willing to burn themselves to the ground to wield what they have never known.

Emer did this to her. Emer made her a target.

"She fought hard," Reese Chopra says. "Look at her nails. She gave him hell."

Abby Gallagher's fingernails are glutted with the flesh of whoever killed her. She was deeply sad, devastated by the abuse her uncle had inflicted upon her—but she did not want to die. She wanted to live.

She had *fought* to live.

Outside, Reese Chopra speaks while they take off their protective clothing. "Well?" she asks Jude. "What does your ever-growing gang of sleuths think?"

"Gee, Reese, I don't know," Jude says. "Looks like a murder to me."

"Very funny."

"You monster." Jude feigns outrage. "A woman is dead. Dead! I don't think it's funny at all."

Reese Chopra lets out a long breath through her nose, her jaw set.

"Still no physical evidence?" Zara asks.

"The skin under her nails—and something else."

"Go on, then, you tease," Jude says. "What is it?"

"Security footage from the building."

"Stop it. You've got footage?"

Reese Chopra nods. "I've seen it. It's glitchy, and you don't see the killer's face, but . . . it might be something."

"Let me see," Jude says greedily.

"I have to be compensated, naturally. How about five hundred pounds for old times' sake and you never hit on me again?"

Jude's smile fades until her expression falls into a glower. She seems to be seriously weighing the deal. "Fine," she says as she gets out her wallet again. "I really thought we had something special, but—"

"Uh-uh-uh," Reese Chopra says as she folds the money and puts it down the front of her coveralls. "No more."

Jude crosses her arms. Reese Chopra takes out her phone, and the three of them crowd around to watch. It is snowy footage captured in black and white, but clear enough to see the terrified girl running into frame. Abby Gallagher slams into the glass door of the lobby, fumbles with her keys, then darts inside and pulls the door closed behind her. She is dressed in a hoodie and baggy sweatpants, a plastic bag dangling from her wrist. For a moment she lingers, watching the street. Then she sees him. Emer sees him, too. The shadow cloaking the figure is so dark it is as though a hole has been punched in reality. Abby holds her phone to her ear.

"Who is she calling?" Emer asks.

"Nine-nine-nine," Reese Chopra replies. "Told them she was being chased by a demon. We're going to run toxicology and see if she was on anything."

Abby Gallagher runs out of frame, deeper into the building. She should be safe. She is inside. The figure is outside. How did he get in?

Reese Chopra answers Emer's unspoken question. "There's this strange moment here, where the video glitches. See that?" Emer watches. The figure disappears from one side of the street and reappears on the other side a split second later. "It happens again when the killer is trying to get inside. Look." The figure is outside the glass door of the lobby and then—glitch—the figure is inside the lobby. A flicker, some might call it. The door does not appear to have moved.

Emer and Jude look up at the same time and lock eyes. They both know.

"I must have watched it a hundred times," Reese Chopra says as she puts her phone back into her pocket. "You never see his face."

Emer wants to watch the footage again. A stone sits in her stomach. What she has seen cannot be true.

"I thought, you know, since you're into some weird occult nonsense—" Reese Chopra closes her eyes and tilts her head to the sky. "I cannot believe I'm about to ask this. What are the chances Abby Gallagher was actually killed by a demon?"

Jude opens her mouth to speak, but it is Emer who answers: "There have been rare occasions when women who are tethered to demons become possessed by them," she says quietly.

"Excuse me?" Reese Chopra asks, looking at Emer for the first time. The initial question was directed at Jude and Zara, not her.

"It happened to Countess Elizabeth Báthory," Emer continues.

"Look, I'm really just looking for a yes or no answer here. The shadowy figure: demon? Yes or no."

"No," Emer says.

Reese Chopra nods. "Because demons aren't real. Great. That's exactly what I needed to hear."

"I never said—"

"That is *exactly* what I needed to hear," Reese Chopra says again.

Jude hands the woman a piece of paper with all of Emer's clients' names on them. "Can't tell you how I know this, but his next victim is probably on this list."

Reese Chopra looks at the list. "What do you want me to do with this?"

Jude shrugs. "I don't know. Your job maybe? Surveil them. Protect them."

"There are, like, thirty names here. You want me to go to my superiors and say, 'Oh, a gang of delinquent youths told me the next victim might be one of these names'? Please."

"Hey, I am *not* a delinquent," Zara says.

The police officer folds up the paper. "Time to clear out, Scooby Gang. Don't call me, I'll call you."

"Give me your phone," Emer orders her. "I want to see the footage again."

Reese Chopra is taken aback. "Uhhh. How about no."

*"Give me your phone."*

Jude nudges her out of the room. "Jesus, Emer, chill. We want to stay on her good side. Not that you have a bad side, Reese, you saucy—"

"Get out, the three of you. *Now.*"


"WELL, HOW ABOUT that," Jude says when they're out on the street. "The killer is a woman. Has to be. Not a witch hunter—a witch. What a plot twist!"

"Wait, *what?* How do you know that?" Zara asks.

The stone in Emer's stomach flips and presses tight against her throat.

"That was not a glitch in the video," Emer says. "It was an invocation. Magic. I know who the killer is."

"What?" Jude says. "Hold up, how? Wow, we solved that so

quickly. Damn, I really wanted to make a murder board with, like, photographs and red string pinned up on a map."

Emer does not answer. She is thinking, trying to put all the pieces together in her head. Why? Why would she do this? There is no good reason she can think of.

"Emer, peach. Care to share with the rest of the class what's going on up here?" Jude says as she taps Emer's temple.

"I wrote that spell. It was an invocation for a woman who wanted to be able to get out of the way of her husband's hands when he was drunk. It allowed her to flicker into the next room."

"God," Jude says, "you'd think a divorce would be easier."

"You might think that." In the beginning, Emer often tried to coach the women who came to her to leave the men who scared them. It was not worth making a deal with the devil when you could walk away. Over time, she stopped trying to convince them that leaving was the easier choice. They would have left, all of them, if they'd felt like that was an option. It was never as simple as packing a bag and driving off into the sunset.

But—for a price—Emer could help them. Emer could grant them power so that they in turn could find their own strength.

"I know my magic," Emer says. "It's like recognizing a piece of music. I wrote that invocation. There's no one else it could be but her."

"Who is she?" Zara asks. "Where is she?"

"Her name is Vera. Vera Clarke. Let me check the exact spell." Emer sits on a nearby bench and opens her backpack. Inside is everything that she owns in this world: a pair of socks, an envelope with £45 in cash, a stolen stick of deodorant, a pen, a box of matches, and her grimoire. The grimoire contains the details of the clients Emer has worked with over the years. She records their names, their phone numbers, the details of the curse they wanted, all of it coded in dead languages so that if a hunter found it, it would take a dozen different scholars years to decrypt and translate it.

Emer scans the invocation she wrote for Vera. It is fourteen looping lines long and complicated, as all of her curses are. The majority is written in Latin. Yet Emer also encircled her spell with some Tamil and some Sanskrit, to tighten it.

Writing for demons is more of an art than a science. There is no rule book about what works and what does not. Each curse-writer in her family approached it differently. One of her aunts exclusively wrote curses in ideograms taken from Egyptian hiero-glyphs and Sumerian cuneiform. This, she said, attracted only very old and very powerful demons, though her spells didn't have the elasticity of a more modern language such as Latin, and the magic they produced was rigid, much as the woman herself had been. Emer's mother, on the other hand, favored Latin and used it to the exclusion of almost all other languages except English, which she occasionally tried to work into her invocations, with varying degrees of success.

Demons do not understand grammar. They do not read left to right or right to left. They have no concept of sentence structure. The order of words in a spell does not matter, nor does tense, nor gender, nor much of anything that gives language structure.

The language that demons speak to each other—voces mysti-cae—has no writing system. No human has ever learned it, because speaking it irreparably damages the soul of the speaker. How, then, can you communicate with them? How can you state the terms of a deal?

Emer understands that it is more about intention than anything else. It helps if you tie that intention to a word that demons know. She likes to build her curses from the outside in. She begins with the most ancient words: Akkadian words for *soul*, for *tether*, and finally, the eight-pointed symbol for *deity*. Emer suspects that this mark is why her invocations work so well. Most cursewriters address demons as some variation of *monster* or *wraith* or *beast*. Emer addresses them as *god*. Next comes the Latin. This does the bulk of the heavy lifting. It is in Latin that Emer states the terms of the deal: a small piece of the bearer's soul in exchange for some particular power. Tamil and Sanskrit and Hebrew and Basque are used as flourishes. Not decorations. That is not the right way to think about them, although they certainly lend beauty to Emer's work.

"Vera Clarke. Yes—a flicker."

Zara taps on her phone screen. She finds a picture of Vera, a corporate headshot on LinkedIn. Vera is as Emer remembers her. In the photograph, she's dressed in a fine gray suit. Black curls fall to her shoulders, shaping a face with warm brown eyes and warm brown skin. She is smiling. She is radiant.

Emer wonders if she was already married when the photograph was taken. If her husband had already hit her for the first time.

Zara is staring at the picture. "Why would she kill my sister?"

Emer does not answer that question, because there is no answer. It does not make sense. A scared woman would not take her new-found power and use it to end the lives of other scared women. "It cannot be her." She is adamant about this. Vera Clarke was petite, around the same height as Emer herself: five foot two on a good day. The shadowy figure in the video was much taller. "The killer cannot be her."

Zara looks confused. "Whoever was on-screen used Vera's magic, right? So it has to be her. Why would she hurt these women?"

Again, Emer does not reply. She is thinking, trying to understand, but she cannot make it make sense. "We need to find her," she says finally.

Jude tries calling Vera on the phone number Emer has recorded in her grimoire. "Line's disconnected," Jude says, hanging up and immediately calling someone else. "Never mind. I have just the incompetent PI for the job."

# TWELVE

JUDE'S HOUSE is a slip of a building, four times as tall as it is wide. Inside, it is decomposing. Persian rugs squelch beneath Zara's shoes, wet with some unidentifiable gelatinous liquid that soaks through the holes in her soles.

"Sorry about, uh . . . Well, sorry about everything," Jude says as she leads them through the darkness.

Jude's PI, Saul, said it would take him a few hours to find Vera Clarke's address, so Jude had invited them back to her house to wait—with the caveat that it "wasn't nice." Zara had thought she was exaggerating, the way very clean people say their rooms are "so messy" when they're not—but the house is repulsive. All the crockery in the kitchen is cracked with spiderweb lines; the water that leaks from the tap is the color of rust. There is mold and damp everywhere, the walls soft to the touch, the furniture moist, and the floorboards sagging beneath her feet. The stink of the place is heavy and rich.

Jude lights a fire—most of the light bulbs don't work, nor is the heating functional—and the three of them huddle around it, warming their hands as the flames catch and grow. The flickering firelight reveals a library, the wooden shelves stretching off into the darkened ceiling and stuffed to bursting with antique books and loose sheets of yellowing paper. On the fourth wall is a giant map of London.

When she can bend her fingers again, Zara sits by one of the windows in a sodden armchair, her feet tucked up beneath her, her hands pulled into her jumper sleeves because even the warmth from the fire cannot touch the cold that gathers in this place. Outside, the moon is lethargic, nodding in and out of clouds. Occasionally it throws a silver beam through the glass, pools for a moment on the wooden floor, retreats again. Jude is stretched out on her stomach in front of the fireplace. Emer sits cross-legged even closer to the fire, seemingly entranced by it.

Zara opens the Voice Notes app on her phone and begins recording. "You said to Chopra—" she begins, speaking to Emer. "You mentioned something about Countess Elizabeth Báthory."

"Yes," the witch says, staring into the flames. "I thought of it because—there have been rare occasions when women who are tethered to demons become possessed by them."

"Tethering and possession are different things, then?" Zara asks.

"Entirely. When a demon is *tethered* to a soul, it exchanges some of its power for a fee. When a demon *possesses* a body, it takes control of it. That is what happened to Báthory."

"Why does that name sound familiar?" Jude wonders aloud.

"She's the vampire woman, right?" Zara asks. "The serial killer?"

"Vampire, no," Emer says. "Serial killer, yes. Báthory was a

Hungarian noblewoman born in the sixteenth century. As a child, she suffered from seizures. The family was heavily involved in the occult, and a curing curse was written for her when she was a teenager. It worked, for a time—but Báthory had the misfortune of being tethered to a particularly powerful and hungry demon who—" Emer bites her lip. "Who consumed her entire soul in a matter of years and then instead of letting her die, climbed inside her corpse and used it as a shell. That's when the killings began."

Jude scratches at her wrists. "Jesus Christ," she says.

Would Jude's demons let her die, when it came to it? Zara wonders. Or would they try to wear her like a human morph suit?

"Báthory—or, at least, whatever bloodthirsty thing lived inside her—murdered many, many young girls. Hundreds of them. Maybe as many as six hundred. They were beaten, mutilated. Báthory . . ." Emer stops to clear her throat. "Báthory *ate* parts of them. Drank their blood. Demons have very little power to affect the physical world, but this one had full control of a human body, and it used it to inflict unimaginable cruelty for years."

"You think this could be happening again?" Zara asks. "You think the demon tethered to Vera Clarke took over her body, killed my sister, and, what . . . ate part of her?"

"It is exceptionally rare. Only a handful of cases over the centuries. There are many risks associated with binding one's soul with a demon, but this has only happened a few times before that we know of. But . . . Báthory preyed on servant girls and later the daughters of other nobles. The women that are being killed now are different. They're witches. They're powerful. Báthory mutilated her victims, yes, but this does not feel the same. Still, it could be something similar. Vera Clarke could be possessed."

"So let me get this straight—Báthory, theoretically, was dead," Zara continues, trying to put the pieces together. "Is that right?"

"Yes. The soul was gouged out, gone."

"Yet her body was animated. Mobile."

"Yes."

"We're not talking about an uncontrollable animal here. We're talking about a restrained, calculating—"

"What about killing six hundred girls feels restrained to you?"

"The fact that it was done methodically, over a period of many years."

Emer narrows her eyes. "What are you fishing for here, exactly?"

"Well, it sounds to me like you're saying that Báthory proves that a body—a *dead* body—can continue to function after death. It can be animated. It can think, reason, even speak."

"Yeah, and it can also *mass murder*," Jude points out.

"I'm just spitballing," Zara says with a faux-casual shrug, her heart racing.

Emer is not appeased. "Perhaps you should ball your spit in the direction of solving these murders," she says acidly.

*Enough probing for one night*, Zara thinks. The thing about puzzle boxes is—you cannot force them open. You must move the pieces gently, feeling each step of the way. Zara stops recording and looks up Elizabeth Báthory online. Demons can fuel dead flesh, that much is clear—but surely *some* of Báthory had to have survived in order for her to pass as human for so many years. The woman dressed in fine clothing, posed for portraits, ran an estate. What if there was a way to *balance* the possession somehow? What if there was a way for a demon to reanimate a human body long after it had died? What if a blood ward—a spell meant to keep intruders out of a designated space—could be used *inside* a person? Inside a skull, for instance, to protect a brain from possession long enough to have a conversation?

Zara writes these questions down, stroking her chin as she does so, then stands and stretches and climbs the ladder and reads the spines of the books that line the walls.

There, nestled right in front of her face, is a little black book with the word *Nekromanteía* pressed into its spine.

"Oh my God," she says as she takes it down. Touching it stings her fingers, as though she's holding something covered in fine cactus hair. "Oh my God, oh my God, oh my God."

This is what she has been waiting for.

"Don't get too excited," Jude says. "That's demon leather, by the way. Don't hold it for too long, it'll give you blisters."

Zara doesn't care about blisters. She's thrilled, her heart racing—until she opens the book to discover that the paper has grown soft and damp with black mold. She tries to turn a page, but it rips, as delicate as wet tissue paper. Much of the ink has run. Very few words are still legible. "No," she whispers. The next book she takes out is in better condition, but still colonized with pinholes of mold that send spores spiraling into the air with the turn of each page. Book after book she tries. They are all the same, each wretched one of them. Each damp, decaying, corrupted by Jude's curse.

"What *happened* to them?" Zara says quietly. A treasure trove of knowledge and secrets. Hundreds of years, rotting away in the dark. Zara doesn't mean for Jude to hear, but she does.

"Oh yeah, shame about that," Jude says, still on her belly by the fire. "Some of them should still be salvageable, but you'll have to sift through. Tends to happen around me. Don't go in the basement. It is absolutely flooded with some kind of viscous liquid that looks a lot like pus."

"Your basement is flooded with . . . pus?" Zara asks.

"Well, of course it sounds weird when you say it like *that*."

"How would you like me to say it so it doesn't sound weird?"

Jude glowers. "I'm going to order some food and take a shower. Emer, do you want to come with?" There is a beat as Jude realizes what she's said. "I mean, not into the same shower as me, obviously. I have more than one shower. Another shower that you can have. That you can be in. That is not the same shower that I'm in."

Jude's cheeks glow like lamps. It's the first time Zara has seen her embarrassed. She was starting to think Jude was entirely incapable of shame.

Zara presses her lips together. Perhaps Jude Wolf has a little bit of a crush.

"No," Emer says.

"Okay," Jude says. "Good. Yes. You stay here while I go shower."

"Maybe *I* want to shower," Zara teases.

Jude glowers at her, then orders them sushi on Deliveroo. While she's upstairs, Zara tries—unsuccessfully—to unstick the pages of *Nekromanteía*. The only readable markings she manages to make out are some numbers on the first page: *4/5*. A date, is her first thought, but perhaps not: four of five, maybe? Which means there could be four more copies of the book out there somewhere. An internet search is entirely unhelpful. *Your search—Nekromanteía book—did not match any shopping results,* Google's shopping tab informs her. Jude mentioned having buyers scouring estate sales, so Zara tries that next, scrolling through lot after lot without luck.

Jude reemerges a half an hour later dressed in silk pajamas and fluffy slippers. The doorbell chimes. Zara goes downstairs and collects the two heaving bags from the delivery driver, then hands them to Jude, who starts laying out all the little dishes on the coffee table in front of the fire.

"What is this?" Emer asks, pointing at one of them.

"This?" Jude points at the same dish. "Tuna sashimi."

"What is that?"

"What is what? Sashimi? Emer, have you never had sushi before?"

"No."

"Well, it's raw fish."

"You cook it yourself?"

"No, you eat it like this. You eat it raw." Jude uses chopsticks to dip a piece of sashimi into some soy sauce, then eats it. "Delicious."

Emer turns to Zara. "Is she making fun of me?"

"Surprisingly, no," Zara says. "Sushi is raw fish. It's a delicacy."

Emer picks up a piece of the tuna sashimi with her fingers. "I spent a whole autumn hiding in the Forest of Dean once. When I could not light a fire, I had to eat raw fish I caught with my bare hands. I do not consider it a delicacy."

Jude groans. "Okay, Mowgli, well, you can poke around the kitchen and see if there's a can of beans or something to heat up, because this is delicious and I will be eating it."

Zara doesn't mention that she, too, has never eaten sushi. Of course she's heard about sushi, but she's never tried it before, at least not the real thing. Prudence was a meat-and-three-veg kind of woman—even pepper was a bit too exotic for her taste. There's a Sainsbury's near Kyle's flat that sells chicken, avocado, and sweet chili sauce wrapped in rice and seaweed, but Zara is pretty sure that doesn't count. The spread that Jude has ordered looks like a rainbow of fish and textures. Jude names all the dishes for her— "Yellowtail sashimi. Toro tartare with caviar. Whitefish tiradito. Ceviche. Squid. Sweet shrimp. Eel. Wagyu nigiri."—and Zara quickly forgets which is which.

Emer reappears from the kitchen a minute later with a loaf of stale bread, a hunk of stinking cheese, and a whole head of very sad-looking uncooked broccoli.

Jude is repulsed. "Oh, so you won't eat raw fish, but you'll chow down on raw broccoli, no problem."

"Vegetables have essential nutrients. I eat them whenever I can find them to stave off scurvy."

"Sheesh. I thought my life was grim. That cheese didn't have mold on it when it arrived, by the way." Jude shoves a big piece of sushi in her mouth and talks around it. "All right. Murder investigation. How do we do this?" Jude pauses. "I know Vera is our primary suspect, but that's just one lead. I really want to do a murder board. You know, like a big corkboard with pictures of the victims and strings connecting all the clues, you know? Does that feel tacky? I'm worried it feels tacky."

All three of them look at one another, and then Zara points at the map of London on Jude's wall. "We could use that." Within seconds, their sushi (and broccoli) is abandoned, and they are pinning up pictures of the women who have died. When they have taped up a picture of every victim on the map, they pick up their dinner and begin to eat again, each staring silently at the web of dead women before them. Zara's gaze lingers on the image of Savannah. Emer holds her grimoire in her hand and moves from picture to picture, writing things beneath the women's faces. Things like *Ability to move through shadows like doorways* and *Ability to burn through metal with bare hands.*

Beneath Savannah's face, Emer writes, *Ability to find anything she wants.*

Why would Savannah want that power? What had she lost that she was desperate enough to sell a piece of her soul to find? Their mother? Their father? Zara has no idea.

The soberness of what they're doing suddenly hits. Until now, Zara has been purely focused on Savannah—but every woman on this wall is somebody's sister. Somebody's daughter. Somebody's mother.

*Somebody.*

Every woman here is mourned and missed as violently as Zara mourns and misses Sav. Even Jude, who seems entirely motivated only by her own self-interest, seems freshly instilled with fury.

"Where do we start?" she says. "If we assume that Vera Clarke is the killer?"

"Well, we know two things the police don't know," Zara offers. "Thing one is Vera, obviously."

"What's the second?" Jude asks.

"That these women are connected. To Chopra and the Met, the killings are confusing. These women live in different parts of London, come from different socioeconomic backgrounds, are different ages, different races—but we know what links them: Emer."

"None of this is new information to me, Jones."

Zara stares at the board a while longer. "How is she finding them?" she wonders out loud. "How is she choosing them? Why these women and not the others?"

Nobody answers. They eat all the sushi and sit by the fire in silence, waiting for Saul to call. When another hour ticks by, Jude makes a show of stretching and yawning. "Well. It's been fun. I think I need to hit the sack. Good night. I'll let you know when Saul gets in touch."

"Good night," Emer says, not taking her eyes away from the board.

Jude clears her throat. "I know you're terrible with social graces because you grew up half wild, but, uh, that was your cue to skedaddle."

"Oh. I am not leaving."

"What?"

"I will stay here and wait."

"Me too," Zara says quickly, because why the hell not?

"Are you kidding me? Does this look like a hostel? You can't all just move in!"

"I have nowhere else to go," Emer says.

"Me neither," Zara adds.

Jude narrows her eyes at her. "Don't you have to be at school, little girl?"

"Don't you? We're the same age. Besides, I think we can all agree that this is more pressing than school." Zara thinks of how disappointed Principal Gardner will be when she doesn't show up to class *again*. She can repeat this year once Savannah is alive once more.

"As soon as we catch who is doing this, you can go back to being miserable on your own," Zara says. "Until then, you have spare rooms with beds in them."

"*Fine.*" To Emer, Jude says, "If you're going to stay, can you at least make yourself useful and ward the house?"

"I can."

"Well, good. Good night."

"You should know that wards are only deterrents. Warnings. If someone is determined to get in here, I can't keep them out forever."

"Gee, thanks, Emer. I'll sleep much better tonight knowing that. Follow me." Jude leads them up another set of stairs to a door leading off a narrow hall. "Jones, you can sleep in here. It's the same as the room across the hall. I've never had guests so the sheets could be moth-infested, I don't know. En suite is through that door. See you in the morning."

"Jude, why is there a bathtub in the bedroom?" Zara asks.

Jude shrugs. "There are bathtubs in every bedroom."

Exhausted, Zara crawls into bed. The mattress is too soft and the sheets feel slick against her skin, squelching slightly when she rolls over. There is a bow in the ceiling above the bed as though it's a fishing net sighing with a heavy load. Zara imagines it collapsing on her during the night. What is up there, groaning through the plaster? What wet, gruesome thing will fall on her?

Zara goes to sleep, as she always does, thinking of Savannah. It is a nightly meditation. A nightly punishment. She forces herself to think of her sister's dead body where it rests beneath the earth. Early on, she read at length about the different stages of decomposition to track what was happening to Savannah as it occurred. There was a medical website that showed graphic pictures of a piglet after death. Its little pink body in the first picture, its white baby fur. Already, the website said, the bacteria that lived in the piglet's gut had begun to digest its intestine. The next stage was putrefaction. Zara stared for a long time at the picture of the piglet at this stage, at how swollen and bruised its body had become, at the pocket of maggots growing beneath a thin membrane of skin stretched over the ribs. Black putrefaction came next. This was the worst stage. The piglet looked like a cooked thing bursting from a sack of flaking skin. Its flesh was bloated, creamy. It looked painful, its whole body a searing sunburned blister. The next two stages—butyric fermentation and dry decay—were easier to look at, because the piglet no longer inhabited the uncanny valley between life and death. When all the gases and blistering red flesh began to calm, finally the creature wore the face of death that she knew, the face of death that made sense to her. All of the soft parts of the piglet had long since turned to liquid and been eaten by maggots and beetles. There was only a dry skeleton left behind, draped with desiccated flesh.

Somewhere along the way, Zara drifts from waking to sleep, but Savannah's decaying body follows her into her dreams. Sometimes Zara is rewarded with dreams of Savannah whole and lovely, but more often than not, she gets nightmares. Tonight she is in Sav's coffin with her, deep underground. She watches her bloated sister as she raises her bruised, swollen arms and begins to rake the wood.

"Let me out," Savannah says.

Zara blinks slowly back into semiconsciousness. The dream ends, but the scratching doesn't.

There is something in the room with her.

Zara's eyes trawl through the gloom. The sound is coming from the copper bathtub at the foot of the bed. Fingernails against metal, maybe. Skittering. Scratching.

She waits for it again to make sure she wasn't dreaming.

There it is. A definite scratching. Not a mouse or a cat. Something bigger. Something with more weight, longer limbs.

Zara squints and watches. A shape moves slowly above the brim of the bathtub.

Zara stops breathing.

A head. A skull with patchy blond hair hanging in lank curtains. A girl with caves for eyes and a dark puckered plum for a mouth. Zara blinks and tries to make it not real, but the shape of the dead girl remains. She stares at her. Tears slip down Zara's cheeks. She cannot move.

The creature unfurls itself. It places a damp, earth-slick hand on the end of the bed and then another. It climbs out of the tub. It moves its way up Zara's body until it is sitting on her chest. Zara feels the weight of her, smells her decomposing flesh.

Savannah says, "You left me to rot." Her voice is a wheeze, a dead thing's growl.

Zara feels her body return to her suddenly. She scrambles to turn on the lamp. Light slams into the room and the decayed remains of her sister dissolve instantly back into the dreamworld from which they came.

Savannah isn't here. Savannah is in a coffin in a graveyard in the ground.

Sleep paralysis, Zara realizes. A waking nightmare.

"I'm coming for you," Zara gasps. Tears stream down her face.

It is then that Jude starts screaming.

# THIRTEEN

**JUDE WAKES** screaming. This is nothing new. Jude is often wrenched from slumber by the vile hell beast yoked to her rotting thigh. All she can do is grunt and cry and yell and wait for it to be over, or knock herself out for half a day and hope it's slightly better when she wakes up.

What is new is that tonight, others are here. Jude is on the floor, moaning and generally feeling very sorry for herself, when her door slams open and Emer and Jones race in.

"Go away," she slurs at them. Jude doesn't want people to see her like this, sweaty and writhing and weak. Jude likes to be seen as suave and sexy, which she still manages to be sometimes, even with a half-rancid soul. These episodes, when the pain gets so bright and sharp that she would like to die, she would prefer to keep to herself.

Emer comes over to Jude and pries her fingers away from her wound. The girl smells of sulfur and woodsmoke from the fire—not a mix Jude would immediately describe as *pleasant*, but on Emer, with those dark eyes and that red hair, it works somehow. She is the embodiment of autumn with a touch of hell thrown in for a bit of excitement. Jude herself smells like rotten eggs and the dankness of old, weeping wounds.

Together they form a *lovely* bouquet.

"Zara, please boil some water," Emer says to Jones, who remains in the doorway. "Find me a towel, too."

"I'm fine," Jude says through gritted teeth. "I've done this before."

"Oh yes, you look perfectly in control." Emer stands. "Wait here."

"I was planning on popping out for a late-night jaunt to a night-club for a boogie, but sure, if you insist, I'll stay here sprawled out on the floor."

Emer returns some time later with her backpack and two bowls, one filled with steaming water, and a towel draped over her shoulder.

"Where's Jones?" Jude asks.

"I sent her back to bed. Give me your arm."

"Why, so you can slice me open? I hate blood magic. It just feels so . . . uncouth. All that cutting of skin and splashing of blood."

"Because soul magic is working out so much better for you. I would give you my own blood, but your demon will not be calmed by that for long. It wants something from *you*. Now, give me your arm and take off your trousers."

"I thought you'd never ask."

Emer draws a resentful breath but her cheeks light up like Christmas baubles, which makes Jude grin even through the pain. Emer isn't her usual type. Jude's usual type is such a cliché she's almost embarrassed by the women she's most attracted to: blond, ample of bosom, overtly feminine—a.k.a. Zara Jones. Emer is short, hard, boyish. Her forehead is constantly furrowed and her resting bitch face is set at a 9.9 out of 10. Yet as Jude shimmies out of her pajama bottoms, she finds herself fixated on Emer's eyes. Perhaps they are not as beady and crab-like as she first thought.

Emer turns on Jude's bedside lamp, and her freckled face comes into full view—as does the wound on Jude's leg. It is a chasm from her hip to her knee, a long crack running through her dead flesh that reveals dead fat and dead muscle and—Jude gags as she looks at it—dead bone beneath. The extent of the infection is catastrophic.

Jude can tell by Emer's expression that it is very bad. "I know it's gross and I smell rank—"

"I do not mind the way you smell," Emer says.

"You . . . don't?"

"I grew up in a house full of witches and demons, for a time. Everything was tinged with sulfur. So, in a way . . . I suppose you smell like home."

Jude finds that she cannot speak. Something has caught in her throat. Emer dips the towel into the steaming water and begins to dab it against Jude's skin, which hurts like hell but also saps some of the sharper pain of its vibrancy.

Emer opens her backpack and takes out her knife. The same knife she pressed to Jude's throat in the bookstore in Oxford. "We must placate the demon," she says.

"No, it's fine, I'll just knock myself out," Jude says, not particularly thrilled at the idea of Emer cutting her open.

"Let me try. Please. It may give you a few days of peace. *Conscious* peace. Give me your wrist."

Peace sounds nice. Jude does what Emer asks.

"It wants to feed on your soul, and it is punishing you because it cannot." Emer runs her thumb over Jude's veins. "It wants to see you suffer. Give it your blood. Give it your pain."

Jude says nothing. If it's her pain the demon wants, it's surely getting a lot of that.

Emer holds the knife against Jude's skin but doesn't apply pressure. "Can I?" she asks. "It will be deep. You may feel woozy."

Again, Jude nods.

"Close your eyes. Hold still. Breathe out as I make the incision."

Jude closes her eyes. She breathes out. It begins as a normal exhale and turns into a gasp as Emer's knife slips into her flesh, opening her. The cutting is over quickly but the pain remains. It is bright and fresh, so different to the black, rotting agony in her thigh.

Emer turns Jude's wrist over and holds it above the empty second bowl.

"Pump your fists," Emer says. "Like this." She demonstrates.

Jude follows her directions and watches as her own blood spits and dribbles.

"It's a lot," Jude says after a few minutes. It's a cup of blood, maybe slightly more. She has never bled so much before. "I feel like a cow being milked."

Emer turns Jude's wrist back over and presses a dry cloth to the wound. Then she holds the bowl in both of her hands and speaks to the ceiling in Latin. The blood is swiftly taken. The bowl clatters to the wooden floor, licked clean. To Jude's surprise, the pain in her leg instantly lessens. It becomes a dull throb, a second beating heart.

"What did you say to it?" Jude asks.

"I ordered it to stay close to you. It is constantly pulling against its yoke. It will settle, for a time."

"Thank you, Emer."

Jude closes her left eye and squints. In the needle of space that appears between her cracked sight, she glimpses the shadow shape of the demon that causes her so much pain. It's not its usual agitated, dickish self, but a purring thing now, huddled up close to Emer in the dark. Jude blinks. There is another shadow shape close to Emer too, this one vast and monstrous. Jude looks up and into the translucent, hollow-eyed face of a waking nightmare.

Jude gasps and scrambles back against her bed, glad that her second sight snaps out when she fully opens her left eye. "What the hell is that?"

"Bael," Emer says. "It is Bael."

"What the hell is a *Bael*?"

"You are partially sighted?" Emer asks her.

"Accidentally and begrudgingly," Jude answers. "Again, what is a Bael?"

"Not what, *who*. Bael is a demon. My demon. My guardian."

"You are going to have to explain that to me in a tad more detail."

So Emer does. She begins at the beginning, with the killing of her family. Bael, she tells Jude, and two other demons followed Emer, only a child then, and spoon-fed her a diet of Latin and sigils and dead languages.

"We have a bond that is unlike any I have read about before between witch and demon," Emer says quietly.

"How so?"

"It has . . . When I was younger I lived for a time in Cork with a woman, Nessa. She was—is—my cousin. She left our family— our coven—as a teenager, before I was born. Some girls do. The life does not suit them. Nessa hated magic. She was afraid of it. Afraid of the old stories of women being burned at the stake. She didn't want to live in a coven, thought it made us a target. So she went to Cork and tried to live a normal life. I don't know what drew her back to Lough Leane. Perhaps she was just checking in on the family. She found me when I was ten, roaming the woods near where my family home had been. I lived three years out there on my own. Mowgli, as you said."

Emer continues her story, telling Jude she might've stayed there forever, drifting and feral, if it weren't for a chance encounter on a spring afternoon. She was ten years old and had not spoken to humans in three years. She was roaming the trees, collecting hawthorn flowers and wild garlic in slips of sunshine. The soles of her feet were thick as animal hide, her limbs bone-thin, her belly filled with sour spring berries after another hard winter. She moved through the forest like a wraith, light as a night predator, each footfall silent.

Then: a flash of red through the trees. Hair, Emer realized. A woman with red hair in a dark coat, traipsing her way through the woodland. Toward the meadow. Toward the house.

The woman, Emer says, looked like her mother had looked.

At the edge of the meadow, the woman stopped and looked back, her eyes finding Emer's instantly.

Young Emer startled and stared back at her, unbreathing, trying to make the image before her make sense. Had her mother not died? Had she gotten up after Emer left and been looking for her all this time? But no, she realized. There were differences. This woman had higher cheekbones, was taller and thinner than her mother had been, her hair a darker tone of red.

"Nessa," Emer says, turning to sit next to Jude, her back against the bedframe. She stretches her legs out and wiggles her toes. Jude notices that she only has eight.

Jude listens intently as Emer goes on. How she lived with Nessa for five years in Cork. How Nessa banned her from practicing or reading about magic, and how Bael continued to bring her books in secret. How she spent her days cooped up inside, a hidden thing, because Nessa feared the men who had killed their family would come looking for them both. How a man and a woman moved into the next-door flat when Emer was fifteen. How her bedroom abutted their living space, so she heard the fights from the very first night. The yelling, the broken crockery, the fists hitting walls and, eventually, hitting flesh. The unmistakable sound of it, the soft horror of it, skin and bone giving in to skin and bone, the accompanying panicked screams from the woman begging him to stop, stop.

How, that very first night, Emer dove from her bed and went to get Nessa so that she, the grown-up, could do something about it. Call the police. Save the woman. How Nessa came and listened for a while, her hands on her hips.

How she said, eventually, "There are earplugs in the bathroom," then turned and went back out into the hall.

"You are not going to do anything?" Emer had asked.

"What do you want me to do?"

"Anything. Call the police."

"If I call the cops, he'll know it was me who called the cops—and then he'll be banging on our door next. I don't know about you, but I don't want him banging on our door."

Jude lets out a long exhale.

"I suppose I cannot blame Nessa," Emer says. "She lived her whole life in fear."

"What happened?" Jude asks.

"It went on for months. Every night, for months, until—until *the* night. It was bad. I thought he was going to kill her. It sounded like he *was* killing her. I could not—how could Nessa ask me to sit there and do nothing? To listen to another woman die? How could she expect me to—" Emer shakes her head. "I was seven when my family died. I was a powerless child. At fifteen I felt—" Emer pauses, looks down at her hands, stretches out her fingers. "I went to their front door. I confronted him, the man. He answered with rage in his eyes, spit flying from his mouth. The woman was cowering in the background. Covered in blood from a head wound. I stood my ground. I told him to stop. He hit me."

Jude swallows, says nothing. Her lips and throat feel dry. She has been in the presence of angry men before. She has been afraid of men before—but no one has ever laid a finger on her.

Emer stares straight ahead. "I ordered Bael—I told Bael in Latin to *kill*. I did it without thinking. It happened very quickly. The man . . ." Emer's voice is barely more than a whisper now. "Bael disemboweled him and consumed him, flesh and gristle and bone, with such speed and violence that he was still alive, blinking at me, the entire time he was being eaten."

"Holy *shit*."

"The woman saw everything. She screamed at me and called the police. I was paralyzed. All those nights she'd endured his violence, and this was the night she chose to contact the authorities."

"Surely the police wouldn't have believed her story."

"That is exactly what I said to Nessa. It was not the police Nessa was concerned about. A story like that—a man disemboweled and devoured where he stood, ripped apart by the power of an angry teenage girl—it was so unbelievable that the police would share it, laugh about it. Eventually, someone would overhear it. Someone who believed it was possible. Someone who would come looking for me."

"Oh."

Emer nods. "I haven't seen Nessa since that night. We packed our bags and went our separate ways. She went into hiding—and I went to Oxford. To learn more about languages and how they could be wielded. To become a cursewriter, like my ancestors had been. Nessa had drilled it into me that the occult was bad, something to be feared—but that night, I came to see it as the only tool I had to fight *against* evil. Bael has been with me the whole time. My family could not control demons the way I can Bael. They could not use them as weapons. Or perhaps they had just never tried. I do not know."

Emer is right. Jude hasn't heard of that kind of connection between a witch and a demon before. Demons don't follow women around for years, untethered, protecting them without payment.

"Why do you think it stays with you?" Jude asks.

Emer undoes her necklace, unfurls the invocation that she wears rolled up on the chain, hands it to Jude. It is a delicate thing, the lead soft and thin from years of handling. Jude holds it like it is a baby bird, afraid even to run her fingers across it lest she snag and tear it.

"This is for Bael, one day. When I find the men who killed my family. I will put this over my heartspace and tether myself to Bael. It is . . . catastrophic power. I imagine it will come at a catastrophic price."

"What does it do?" Jude wonders aloud.

"What *doesn't* it do? It will allow me to crush bodies with just my mind. It will allow me to tear objects apart atom by atom until they are dust. It is a nuclear weapon." Emer takes the invocation, rolls it up, and puts it back inside the locket she wears around her neck. "I should let you rest."

"Emer," Jude says when she stands.

"Yes?"

"Will you . . . stay?"

Emer doesn't answer. Jude thinks she's going to say no—and why wouldn't she? They haven't exactly had the friendliest of introductions.

"Don't worry about it, it's—"

"I will stay," Emer says. "I will—I can watch over you, if you would like."

"Yes. Please. I would like that."

Emer nods. "Try to get some rest."

Jude climbs back into her bed. The sheets are sour and damp with sweat, infested with little dead things that come to her in the night. Emer lies down next to her. The walls groan in the wind. The room stinks of pennies from the blood and rotten eggs from her curse. Jude's blood is hot and acrid as it beats through her leg. She feels terrible, her skin slick, her stomach girdled with nausea. Yet, she also feels . . . What is that?

What is the opposite of loneliness, when you have been lonely for as long as you can remember?

Jude reaches out in the dark, looking for Emer. She finds her.

Her skin against her skin, their fingertips touching. It is the barest of caresses, a thing so small it could easily be passed off as an accident—but Emer does not pull away. For a moment, they are connected, these two lonely girls—and then the moment goes on and on, a second stretching into minutes.

When Jude finally falls asleep, her fingertips are still grazing Emer's in the dark.

JUDE WAKES IN the morning, not with a start, not with a gasp, not clawing at the pain in her thigh, but peacefully. Emer is still in her bed, turned away from her now, her red curls spilling across Jude's pillows. Early November sunlight filters through the windows, casting Emer's hair in a prismatic array of tones: copper, rose, blood. Jude touches the ends of the witch's hair, twists one curl in her fingertips and smiles. So it was not a dream.

There's the sound of quick footsteps on the stairs and then Jones bursts through the door.

"Jude," she says. She looks peaky, rattled. "Your father is here."

Jude stands and lurches across the room, gasping at the crackling pain as the crust of her leg wound splits. Lawrence is here. Why is Lawrence here? He has never visited her here before, and certainly not unannounced—usually a meeting with Lawrence Wolf required several back-and-forths with his PA. How did he even get in? It *is* his house, Jude supposes. He must have a key.

"Stay here," she says to Zara as she shrugs on a robe. "Both of you."

Downstairs, she finds her father standing by a cracked window. Jude looks around at the state of the room, tries to see it as if through his eyes. She has never even invited Elijah here because the house is so obviously . . . *wrong.*

"Judith," Lawrence Wolf says. He is staring out at the city in the distance. Jude cannot see his face, but his voice is thin and acidic.

Lawrence has never been a particularly warm father—but he *is* her father. Despite his distance, Jude cannot deny that the life he has provided for her has been a good one. The best schools, the best tutors, the best nannies. Private chefs, private yachts, private planes. Birthday cakes flown in from master pastry chefs in France, an unlimited spending account at Net-a-Porter. Jude had never been one of those depressed rich kids who felt empty because they had too much. She *loved* her life. She *loved* attending fashion week, flying by helicopter, spending summers aboard her father's super-yacht in the Mediterranean and winters nestled by the fireplace in his Scottish castle.

Then had come the photographs. Jude had been fifteen at the time and at a friend's house for a Halloween party. The friend lived near Highgate Cemetery. Naturally, twenty drunk teenage girls dressed as various sexy interpretations of scary things—sexy zombie, sexy vampire, sexy witch—had the brilliant idea to stumble down to the graveyard with candles and try to perform a séance. They broke into the old West Cemetery and took dumb, bawdy videos of each other—grinding on tombstones, making out with statues—and tried to commune with the undead soul of George Michael whilst playing "Careless Whisper" (alas, George was not roused from his eternal slumber).

Jude's friend posted everything to her private TikTok. Two days later, screenshots from the videos were on the front page of several London tabloids. Jude was a background note in most of the coverage (one of her friends was the daughter of a cabinet minister—apparently her dancing in front of the mausoleum of a long-dead conservative politician proved that her father was both "depraved and incompetent"), but there was a single picture of Jude dressed as a sexy goth with black lipstick and a shirt with the Sigil of Baphomet on it, a.k.a. the official insignia of the Church of Satan.

WOLF HEIR: DEVIL GIRL? a headline asked.

Jude thought this was hilarious. Lawrence, apparently, did not. She was summoned into his office that afternoon, where he slapped the front page down on his desk in front of her.

"You are a Wolf," he said, spittle hitting her in the eye as he spoke. "I expect more decorum from you."

"I'm . . . sorry?" Jude said. It was obviously meant to be a joke, a silly Halloween costume: Jude was not a member of the Church of Satan (though she'd seen a documentary on them and thought they had a lot of smart ideas; they didn't actually believe in or worship the Devil).

Rival papers said all sorts of untrue things about the Wolf family all the time. Jude knew, for instance, that her father was probably *not* the Zodiac killer, despite a rumor that had started on Twitter and spilled into the tabloids a few years earlier.

"I do not want to see this"—he pointed to the photograph of Jude licking a tombstone—"ever again."

"I . . . I don't know what to say." Jude was so rarely lost for words.

"You are not required to *speak*. You are only required to *listen*. *Do not* draw attention to yourself again."

"But—the boys are in the media all the time."

"You are not your brothers. You are to be seen and not heard.

In fact, it would be better for you not to be seen, either. Do you understand? You are to be a wallflower. You are to be a shrinking bloody violet. Do you understand me?" Lawrence was shaking. He slammed his hand on his desk. "Answer me when I ask you a question!"

"Yes," she whispered.

Jude had known for most of her life that Lawrence was a misogynist—it was a strikingly hard fact to miss, after all. Hearing him say it out loud—that "seen and not heard" bullshit—that was something entirely different.

When she told Elijah what had happened, her brother laughed.

"Well, what do you expect? You're not very nice to him."

Jude was stunned. "What does that mean?"

"You don't pay fealty to the lord, Jude. The Horsemen"—their name for their older brothers—"practically get on their knees in front of him, and then you waltz in and eat his food and unwrap his Christmas presents and have the audacity not to fall at his feet wailing with gratitude. It has not gone unnoticed."

"You don't pay fealty," Jude protested.

"Oh, but I do pay. I pay with our brothers' hatred. I bear the brunt of their derangement without complaint. You know about the stupid snake, but so much more has gone on. You know they once held me down and pulled out one of my baby teeth before it was loose? These grown men, torturing a kid. I went crying to Lawrence, and you know what he told me? Be a man, Elijah. Stop crying and be a man. So that's what I did. I kept my mouth shut. Every time those monsters came after me, I took it without complaint. I didn't snitch. Lawrence saw what they did to me, and he liked that I took it like a man."

"Jesus." Jude had had no idea how bad it was for Elijah. Yes, the Horsemen had always been borderline pricks—but this was something else. The thought of them hurting Elijah made her stomach bubble with rage. "Why do we bother?"

"You know why. Because he's the king, and when the king's light lands on you—you're invincible."

Jude did know, because she also took part in the seedy underbelly of favor that made the Wolf household tick.

As she stares at her father standing in her house, she realizes that simply uncursing herself will not be enough. (*Simply!* Jude thinks. *Ha!*) Lawrence is disappointed in her, has lost all respect for her. In order for her to win her old life back completely—Jude's mouth waters at the thought of caviar flown in fresh from the Caspian Sea—she must also win her father's approval.

"To what do I owe the pleasure?" Jude asks eventually.

"I am getting married on Sunday at the house in Holland Park."

"Oh." Jude tries to act like this is new information. "Congratulations!"

"It would arouse suspicions if you were not in attendance."

Jude's heart skips a beat. "Is this you inviting me to your wedding?"

"There will be photographers from the paper"—when he says *the* paper, he actually means *my* paper—"and people have started asking questions about your absences."

"You own the paper. Can't you just stop people from asking questions?"

"The papers are not the ones asking."

"Then who is?"

Lawrence is silent for a beat. "Your appearance clean and well-dressed and smiling will go a long way toward dispelling rumors that you're dead."

"Rumors of my death have been greatly exaggerated," Jude jokes. Her father remains stern, but in her mind Jude is already there, in the Holland Park house. Her heart longs for it. A *party*. With champagne and music and beautiful people, beautiful food. The ballroom dripping with flowers, the smell of delicacies drifting up from the kitchens. Silk on her skin. Perfume at her wrists. Elijah will be there, her constant co-conspirator. They will whisper about the rest of the family, teasing. Everything will be clean and bright. Jude clears her throat. "You know I never pass up the promise of free hors d'oeuvres."

"Clean yourself up. There will be press there. Wear a dress. I will have something organized for you."

"Okay. Thank you."

Lawrence nods and makes to leave. Jude wonders why he has not said anything about the house, about the putrid walls or the dead things that have collected overnight on the floor. When he is next to her, he stops, speaks quietly. "Despite what you may think, I have only ever acted out of a desire to protect you."

"Exile sure is a funny way to show your love."

"Be careful, Jude."

"Of what?"

Lawrence says nothing. Then, with a final glance up at the photograph of his dead wife on the wall, he leaves.

# FOURTEEN

**IT IS** Friday morning, and Zara's nerves are still frayed from her run-in with Lawrence Wolf. When she woke from her restless sleep, she padded downstairs in Jude's cold house in search of strong black tea—a morning habit picked up from Pru—and didn't notice the man, standing stock-still and staring out at the city skyline, until he said, "Get my daughter," in a low voice. Zara, standing at the kitchen sink, yelped and splashed hot water over the back of her left hand. The man—Lawrence—did not even turn around.

Saul calls not long after Lawrence departs. On speakerphone, the PI delivers Vera Clarke's address in a bored drawl and then reminds Jude he will send an invoice via email that is due immediately.

The three of them set off into the dreary morning. The sun rises slowly, a sluggish jelly drifting through a gray sea. Emer carries with her a huge old map book from Jude's house, its pages damp and overgrown with mold. It's part of their plan B. If Vera isn't home, Emer can try to scry for her—but first they'll need something she owned, something she touched, a personal item of hers that only she used.

On the way to Vera's, Jude swings into the drive-through of a McDonald's and buys them all Egg McMuffins and orange juice for breakfast. Zara is afraid to unwrap hers at first. Jude's car doesn't seem like the kind of car you're allowed to eat in. On the rare occasion Zara had no choice but to get into Kyle's car, he always found something to chastise her for. Her shoes were muddy and ruining the carpet. Her BO was seeping into the air-conditioning and the car would smell like her sweat for weeks. Zara hasn't gotten back into the car with him since the time he put his hand on her knee and said, seemingly as some kind of joke, "At least I'm not this kind of uncle."

Then Zara watches Jude as she unwraps her own sandwich and shoves half of it into her mouth at once. Crumbs dust her lap. A piece of egg slips out and onto the seat between Jude's legs, which she flicks into the footwell without a second thought. Because Jude is a wild animal.

Zara eats hers holding the wrapper up to her chin like a bowl as she takes each bite. They sit in the parking lot with the windows cracked, a sliver of crisp air keeping the car from fogging up. Zara does another search on her phone while she eats.

"Vera Clarke," she says, scrolling through the woman's LinkedIn. "She's a corporate lawyer. She left her job about a month ago and hasn't listed a new one yet."

"So she quits her job as a lawyer to start, what, full-time murdering?" Jude says. "Is that when the demon took over, maybe?"

A demon with enough oversight to tender a resignation letter and update her LinkedIn profile is a positive sign, Zara thinks. That

means that some of Vera Clarke—perhaps *a lot* of Vera Clarke—
still has to be intact, to function at such a high level. Two minds
inside one body, the demon with more control than the woman—
but what if there was a way to flip that?

Zara clicks out of LinkedIn, searches for Vera Clarke on
Google Images. There is a picture of her on her wedding day on a
beach somewhere. They look happy, Vera and her new husband.
The photograph makes Zara's skin crawl. That so much misery
can be hidden behind a smile.

FIVE MINUTES LATER, Jude parks the car in front of a three-story
brick building across from a school. Emer stays outside as a lookout,
in case a possessed Vera Clarke tries to make a break for it. When
Zara and Jude get to the front door of the building and find a video
doorbell, Jude nudges Zara in the ribs and says, "Jones, you buzz."

"Why me?" Zara asks.

"Because if the husband answers, well, straight men are threatened by my energy. They rightfully feel inferior to me, and that
makes them angry. Besides, you look like a nice girl with your frilly
little skirt."

"I'm not a nice girl."

"Oh, I know that. I just said you *look* like a nice girl. I know
you are, in fact, insufferable—but the husband doesn't. Not yet
anyway."

Zara sighs and says, "Fine." She buzzes and waits for an answer.
Off-screen, Jude mimes lowering her top and pushing her breasts
together. *Show him your tits,* she mouths.

*Stop,* Zara mouths back. Is everything a joke to Jude?

There's static from the buzzer, then a man's voice: "Yeah?"

"Oh, hello, I'm looking for Vera. Vera Clarke."

No answer. A second passes—long enough for Jude to mouth, *Tits!* again—and then the door buzzes open.

"Not bad, Jones," Jude says as she pushes inside.

"I didn't even have to get my tits out."

"Shame. There's always next time."

Zara shakes her head as she follows Jude. "How do you get away with being like this?"

"It's my natural charm. It's impossible to resist."

"You're a deviant."

"A deviant *with swagger.* Come on."

Upstairs, Zara knocks on the door of Vera's flat. There are footsteps beyond it and then a man answers. He is short, white, disheveled. His gaze slides over the two of them. "You look too young to be cops."

"We're not police officers," Zara says.

"You expecting cops?" Jude asks.

"You know my wife?" the man asks.

"Is Vera here?" Zara asks. "Can we talk to her?"

"Who are you exactly?"

"Oh. I am so sorry." Zara smiles. "How rude of us not to introduce ourselves. We are . . . student lawyers. We are Vera's students."

"I didn't know she had students."

"We're, like, interns, you know," Jude says. "Baby lawyers."

"I haven't seen Vera in a couple weeks. She's not here."

"Excuse me," Jude says. "Your wife is *missing*?"

The man immediately bristles. "No, not *missing*; she's just *gone*."

"Have you reported it to the police?" Zara asks.

"Why would I?"

Jude cocks an eyebrow. "You haven't seen your wife in weeks, and you didn't think that was maybe something you should take to the authorities?"

"You're getting the wrong idea. She left me. She was always threatening to leave. I guess she finally did it. Left her engagement ring on the bedside table. Didn't even leave a note. Bitch."

There's a moment of stillness following the final word of his sentence. *Bitch.* It charges the air with something noxious. Zara feels Jude go rigid next to her.

Zara forces a smile. Plan B it is. *"Women,"* she says, despising herself—but they need something of Vera's if they're to have any hope of finding her now. They need to get inside. "Speaking of the weaker sex—I'm so sorry, but I am absolutely *bursting* for a wee. Can I use your bathroom?"

The husband looks her up and down, apparently deems her nonthreatening. "Fine," he says eventually. "Down the hall. Last door on the right. Don't touch anything."

Zara's heart gallops as she slides past him. When she looks back, Jude winks at her, then leans in the doorway, her arms crossed, and starts talking to the man about sports. Zara heads down the hall and into the bathroom, closing the door behind her. The room smells of bleach and seems to have been stripped of personal belongings recently. Not a good look for when the cops inevitably come searching. There's only one toothbrush on the sink, one bottle of cologne in the cabinet. The dirty clothes in the laundry basket are all men's. Zara opens the drawer under the basin. Again, there's no sign of a woman having lived here recently. No hairbrush, no tampons, no makeup. It's as though it has all been collected and thrown out.

"Damn it," Zara whispers. She goes to the door and opens it a crack. Jude is still prattling away—"How's Arsenal looking this year, do you think?"—buying her more time. Zara steps out of the bathroom and quietly turns the handle of the door across the hall. She slips into the room and tiptoes across the floorboards, looking for something, anything, that Vera Clarke might have owned. The space is neat and orderly, like the rest of the flat. Zara eases open the wardrobe. There are no women's clothes, no jewelry, no high heels. Zara pushes deeper into the room, to one of the bedside tables, but this clearly belongs to the husband: There's men's underwear, lube, tissues.

In the second drawer, finally, there are some of Vera's things: a pot of strawberry lip balm, a purple sleeping mask, a tangled set of headphones. Are any of these personal enough to find her? And there, wedged in a far corner of the drawer, a felt ring box. Bingo. Zara reaches for it—

"Jones, he's—"

"What the hell are you doing?"

Zara whips around, the felt box held behind her back. "I'm sorry. I'm sorry. I got lost."

"No you didn't." The husband snatches the wrist of Zara's free hand. She is utterly shocked by the strength of him. The man isn't tall or particularly muscular. To look at him, Zara would've thought they were fairly evenly matched physically, but his fingers around Zara's arm are concrete. He slams her sharply into the wall, his other arm across her collarbone, his face so close to her face that she can smell the stale coffee on his breath.

Zara pushes against him with all her strength, but he doesn't move, doesn't even seem to register her effort. He's a snake constricting her chest, and she is filled with venom for this small, smug, hairy creature with so much unfair power.

"Get *out* of my flat," he says. He leans his full weight into Zara for a second, digging his elbow so deeply into the soft flesh of her upper breast that she feels the capillaries burst beneath the skin. Then he's off her and she can breathe. She shrinks as she skirts past him, sure he will grab her and pry the stolen box from her fingertips, but he doesn't. When she lurches back into the hall, she begins to run, certain that he's behind her, but he isn't.

"Jones, what happened?" Jude says when Zara stumbles into her.

"Go." Zara grabs Jude's hand and pulls her along. "Just go."

When they are downstairs in the safety of Jude's car, Zara begins to cry. It explodes out of her, uncontrollable sobs that constrict her lungs so tightly that she struggles to breathe. Normally, she would be embarrassed at such an unchecked outpouring of emotion—Zara survives around Kyle by employing an endlessly bright tone, by not allowing him to see her as weak—but right now she can't help it.

Is that what it was like for Savannah? Is that what she felt like on the kitchen floor as the life was wrung out of her?

A part of Zara has always blamed Savannah for not fighting harder. How could you let yourself die? If you really wanted to live, wouldn't you go rabid and let your limbs fill with adrenaline and fight and fight and fight until the last moment?

Zara realizes now that Savannah fought as hard as she could. There were defensive wounds on her hands and arms. Her feet and legs were bruised where she had kicked and bucked against her assailant. There were little moons of bloody skin underneath her fingernails where she'd dug them into her attacker, the DNA samples that came from them so strangely degraded that the police couldn't even confirm if they were human.

For the first time, Zara appreciates the terrible, unyielding strength of the person who decided to kill her sister. Realizes that, once the decision was made, there was nothing Savannah could have done to protect herself.

How dare they.

*How dare they.*

Zara cries. The two other girls in the car comfort her, and she lets them. She lets Emer rub her back, and she lets Jude pat her knee as grief and anger cascade through her. The sobbing subsides as quickly as it began. When it is over, Zara feels cleansed, like a crisp, clear day after a storm. She wipes her eyes, blows her nose.

"Will this work?" she asks Emer as she pulls the ring box out of her skirt pocket and holds it up.

Emer takes the box from her and opens it. Inside is a gold ring, set with a single diamond solitaire. "Yes," the witch says. "This will do nicely."

# FIFTEEN

TO FIND someone, you need three things: a personal item of the missing person, a map, and blood. Emer lays the book of maps open on the back seat of Jude's car and presses the tip of her pinkie finger to the sharp point of her knife. Zara holds out Vera's engagement ring so Emer can squeeze several drops of blood onto the diamond.

"Now you," Emer says, handing the knife to Zara. Zara pouts and takes out her hand sanitizer and uses it to disinfect the tip of the blade before she, too, pricks her finger and squeezes blood onto the jewel. Jude follows suit. By the time they are done, it is slick with red.

Emer speaks to Bael in Latin, her voice low as she tells it who they want to find, then she begins to flick through the pages with one hand while she holds the ring high in the other. Thirty seconds pass. Nothing happens.

"Is Bael broken?" Jude asks.

"What does that mean?" Zara asks.

Emer does not have time to answer. With the turn of the next page, her arm slams down with such force that she yelps. She lets the ring go and shakes the stinging pain from her hand.

"Too rough," she tells Bael grumpily. Demons forget to be gentle with the bodies of mortals.

The ring stands up on its own, diamond down, and rotates slowly on the map, the jewel grinding so deeply that the paper is beginning to tear.

"Hampstead Heath," Zara says. "The Wood Pond, it looks like. Not far."

"Let's go," Jude says, already pulling onto the road.

BY THE TIME Jude parks at the edge of Hampstead Heath, the sky has grown even gloomier, swollen with storm clouds that smother the sun. The streets are cloaked in fog. Car headlights kindle softly in the haze as the three of them plunge into the ancient park full of grasslands and swimming ponds and woods. Emer knows that there is magic here, as there is in all the older parts of London. Old magic, the kind that is tied to the land and the shadows and not to demons. The kind that simply exists and cannot be harnessed by humans.

Jude leads them by watching her phone screen, navigating to the approximate area where Bael indicated Vera Clarke was. Jude and Zara are wary of the shadows, the storm. They do not know darkness as Emer does. They have never worn it as a cloak. They have never welcomed it as a tool. Instead, they carry their phones in their hands and shoot out beams of light at their feet so that they will not trip.

"Turn your lights off," Emer tells them as the heath swallows them.

"Do you want me to end up face-first in the mud?" Jude asks.

"A brutally violent, serial-killing possessed demon may be lurking in the trees. Do you want it to know we are coming? Turn off your lights."

"Fine," Jude grumbles. The light beams snap off.

They have to be still for a minute while their eyes adjust, but soon the gloaming landscape begins to reveal itself to them. A field of long grass swishes downward toward ponds and a wooded area beyond. Thunder cracks and the sky opens, begins again to spit.

"The demon GPS said she was near the water," Jude says as they scan the shore of the pond. "I'm suddenly realizing we're woefully underprepared to meet a demon."

"I am not unprepared," Emer says as she draws her knife and presses forward into the storm.

Jude stays close to her as Emer walks downhill. Presses against her. Emer's ears buzz with tinnitus, and pressure builds behind her eyes. Being around Jude is torture. Yet there is also something else there: a sweetness. A spritz of something chemical above everything else. Jude is wearing perfume, Emer realizes. Perfume to mask the smell of her shriveling body and rancid soul.

It is then that Emer remembers what is often easy to forget: That Jude is a girl. That even though she is grandiose and self-centered and tactless, she is a girl roughly the same age as Emer herself, and she is scared. With her free hand, Emer reaches out to Jude. Jude threads her fingers through hers easily, quickly, without hesitation, like she has been waiting for her. They clip together like magnets in the grayness and begin to move as one creature.

Emer has never defended anyone before. She has only ever had to think about herself. Now, with these two girls here and Jude's hand in hers, she feels at once more powerful and weaker than ever before.

The three of them trail along the fenced shore of the grease-black water, waiting for a sign of movement that does not come.

"Obviously she's long gone," Jude says.

Emer is not so sure.

"What are you doing?" Jude asks as Emer lets go of her hand and climbs the low metal fence around the pond. The trees that grow on its border are shedding their summer foliage. A storm of red and yellow leaves float across the surface. More are shaken free by the gusting wind. Emer walks in the ankle-deep mud along the edge, stepping in the footprints that dogs left behind as they came to play in the water. Jude again: "Earth to Emer, Emer, come in."

"We have to be sure."

"Sure of what?"

Emer crouches by the water and places her palm flat against the tension of its surface. There is no grand revelatory moment, but rather a small, insistent tug: *You must get in. You must look harder. There is something here.* It is the same power that tells her the right days to go to the bookstore in Oxford.

Emer stands and begins to undress. Zara looks away. Jude does not. Instead, when Emer unbuttons her shirt, Jude climbs over the fence. "I'll hold them for you," she says. She takes Emer's coat and shirt.

"Thank you." Emer unzips her skirt and tries to step out of it without caking it in grime. She wobbles. She is unsteady on the slippery ground. Jude reaches out to hold her, her palm warm against Emer's bare ribs.

When she has stripped to her underwear, Emer expects Jude to make a quip to lighten the moment, because that is Jude's defense mechanism, but Jude says nothing.

"Do either of you have something I can keep my hair back with?" Emer asks. Jude shakes her head. Zara steps forward with a hair tie, careful to keep her gaze trained at her feet.

The water is so cold that the moment Emer steps into it, the sensation in her feet is lost to her. It is a vise, squeezing her tight. She steadies herself and takes a breath before diving. Her body screams at her to get out of the freezing water. Cold is no new enemy. She knows it well, inside and out. The way it seeps beneath clothing and soaks in, all the way to the bone. The way it eats through fingers and toes. Cold is a fiercer enemy than hunger or thirst or fear or darkness. Cold has driven her to do some truly stupid and reckless things.

Today, at least, there is a warm house to go back to: Jude's. That is a luxury Emer wished for many, many times. So she bears the cold for now and moves deeper into the lake, even as she continues to gasp with every breath.

"Well?" Jude calls from the shore. "Find anything, Aquawoman?"

"No," Emer manages thinly.

Why did her intuition drive her into the water?

She takes a deep breath and plunges her head beneath the surface. Down here it is dark as night and cold as death.

*Go deeper.*

Emer does—and then her fingers graze something that feels out of place. Not silt or rock or weed, but skin. Flesh. Emer kicks to the surface to breathe, then plunges into the depths again. She does not fear the dead; she only fears the living. This time her fingers close around something that feels very much like a wrist.

"I found something!" Emer yells as she surfaces. "I need help!" On the bank of the pond, it is Jude who kicks off her shoes first and wades into the water, fully clothed. The pond turns instantly to ink. The ugly force of the spell hits Emer like a wave.

"Fuck!" Jude yelps as she flops in. When she emerges again, she continues: "Fuckity, fuckity, fuck! It is cold!"

When she reaches Emer and sees the blackness lapping at her collarbones, Jude says, "Sorry about the water."

"There is a body in the pond."

"Another victim?"

"I don't know. I think it's weighted down. We need to pull it to the edge. Do you have a strong stomach?"

"My own leg is half rotted off, and I manage not to gag at it on a daily basis. My stomach is stronger than most."

"Okay. Take my hand. I'll show you."

Jude gives Emer her hand. Emer cannot see it through the pitch-black water, but she can feel it. They dive together. Emer pulls Jude down and guides her to the corpse. Then she presses Jude's hand to the body and closes her fingers around its wrist.

Emer takes the other wrist. Together, with some effort, they are able to lift the waterlogged body.

Emer can see Zara on the bank, holding a bright white light that guides them through the now driving rain.

"Oh God," Zara says when she sees what they have between them. They drag her, face up, onto the bank, through the leaves and squelching mud, heaving with the effort.

"It's her," Jude says, but Emer already knows this. "It's her."

The cold water has slowed her decomposition, so Vera Clarke's body is still recognizable. Her black hair. Her brown skin. Her white running jacket stained tea-colored by the pond water, an infestation of green algae growing at the collar. One trainer still laced to her foot, the other foot bare, the toenails painted pink, the skin there puckered into valleys. Emer kneels in the mud next to her, hovers her hands over Vera's body, barely able to breathe. The woman who came to her two years ago for a spell that would keep her out of danger.

Dead.

It is too much death. It is too much death to bear.

Zara drapes Emer's coat over her bare shoulders, though the cold is so bitter on Emer's naked body, the rain so persistent, the horror so profound, that it makes little difference.

Jude is shuddering, pacing in the mud, wincing with each step. "The husband said she's been missing for, what, a couple of weeks?"

"Yes," Emer manages.

"How long do you think she's been out here for?" Zara asks.

"That long." Furious tears cut paths down Emer's cheeks. "There is no way Vera could have killed Abby."

"So she's *not* possessed by a demon, then," Zara says, a hint of disappointment in her voice.

"Not unless her corpse was walking around last night," Jude offers.

"Yet she was there." Emer is confused, trying to put the pieces together. "Or at least her magic was there. Whoever killed Abby did so using the invocation I wrote for Vera."

"We know that," Jude says. "We saw that in the security footage."

"It is impossible for someone to use another person's magic. You cannot use what has not been paid for. The moment a person dies, the tether between the soul and the demon is severed and the deal expires. The magic ceases to exist. That is the *only way* to break the deal: to die. It is the same reason why I cannot help you, Jude. So how could Vera Clarke's magic have been used last night when Vera Clarke has been dead for two weeks?"

Jude manages to shrug despite her shivering shoulders. "Maybe you're wrong. Maybe the invocation in the video wasn't the one you wrote."

"It was." Emer's gaze travels to Vera Clarke's chest. Gingerly, she unzips the dead woman's wet jacket and pulls down the fabric of her shirt. Beneath it is a rectangle of flayed skin.

Emer stares at the space where her curse should be.

"Someone is stealing your curses," Zara says quietly, "and taking them for themselves."

"That cannot be possible," Emer whispers.

"It's obvious now," Zara continues. "The killer cuts the invocation out of the victim and then—somehow—they're able to use it themselves. Your clients are being hunted and murdered for their power, Emer. Not a witch hunter or a possessed body but . . . a spell collector."

Emer shakes her head. "That makes no sense. Why not go straight to a cursewriter? If they could find my clients, they could find me. Why kill these women for their magic when they could wield magic of their own?"

"Because the murderer is a man," Zara replies, like it's self-evident.

"Men can't use magic, peach," Jude reminds her. "It's just the way it is."

"I *know*. That's why he's murdering these women. That's why he killed my sister. I know you think it's impossible, but it makes sense to me. Men can't use this power themselves. The only way they can access it is by stealing it from women. By cutting it out of them."

"It just does not work like that," Emer insists. "Power cannot be transferred."

"I don't care how it works. Look beyond your own understanding of this for a minute. Look at what's staring you right in the face."

Jude makes a call to Reese Chopra to report the body while Emer gets dressed.

They wait in a copse of trees on the other side of the lake, all three of them pressed close together in the rain for warmth. Emer's ribs shake and her teeth chatter as she watches. Finally, half a dozen beams of light appear near Kenwood House and begin to bob down the hillside toward the lake. The lights fan out as they reach the shore. It is not long before a woman's voice rings out into the night: "I've got something here!"

"My tits have officially frozen off," Jude says. "Let's go back to my place and get warm."

# SIXTEEN

JUDE COULD get used to this. To Emer Byrne in her house every day, stoking the fire, tending to it until the flames are as bright and wild as her hair. Soon, the fire is roaring, but Emer is still shuddering from the cold. Jude offers to draw her a hot bath. Emer accepts. Jude offers Jones one as well, but Jones cannot be lured away from the library, where, already high up on the ladder, she is nose deep in a half-decayed book about wards.

Once Emer's bath is ready, Jude heads into her kitchen, where the floor-to-ceiling photograph of her mother watches over the space. Jude pours two shot glasses of Becherovka, a spicy herbal liqueur of cloves and cinnamon and ginger that, according to articles about her in the press, Judita used to drink with every meal as a "digestive aid." Jude has kept at least one bottle of it in her house ever since. It tastes, she thinks, like Christmas.

"One for you, one for me," she says to the photograph as she puts one of the shots, like an offering, in front of her mother's portrait. Jude downs her own, neat and warm, then wipes her mouth with the back of her hand. Judita looks down at her, ever inscrutable, holding an infant Jude in her arms as she descends a staircase in a ballgown. It was Jude's first (and only) appearance in a fashion magazine. Jude only knows her mother through fashion shoots and editorials, which are far fewer than she would like, because Judita practically stopped working soon after she met Lawrence, as all of Lawrence's wives and girlfriends are encouraged to do. The mysterious circumstances surrounding her death have ensured that her legacy has been long-lasting despite her short-lived career.

Jude was there when her mother died, sleeping belowdecks with her nanny, but she was a toddler at the time and has no real memories of the event. What she knows she has pieced together from news articles and Wikipedia. Judita, who was not a strong swimmer, had, according to her husband, decided to go for an evening dip as the party floated into the early hours. Nobody saw her get in the water. Nobody saw her alive again. Lawrence passed out and didn't realize until the crew were serving breakfast that Judita was missing. By the time her body was found weeks later, it was so damaged by water and marine life that it was impossible to determine a cause of death.

The unsaid implication in all the news coverage was that Lawrence Wolf had murdered his wife. There was a Netflix documentary insinuating as much, which Jude has never been able to bring herself to watch. It is a tale as old as time: Rich old white dude grows tired of his wife but, to protect his fortune, decides to off her instead of getting a divorce. See: Henry VIII. Jude cannot accept this. She has seen the pictures of their wedding day. She has seen her father's smile, luminous and uncomplicated, so unlike the man himself. Judita's death was an accident. A terrible, tragic accident.

Still, Lawrence was forever telling Jude—when he still spoke to her, that is—that she was "too much like your mother." Knowing what people suspected he did to Judita, this sometimes came across as a thinly veiled threat.

Jude carries the second shot of Becherovka back into the library and sits by the fire. While she is sipping, she notices Emer's leather backpack resting on the couch. Jude opens it, takes out the witch's grimoire, begins flicking through the pages.

"Did you ask if you could touch that?" Jones asks from where she stands on the ladder, her reading glasses on her nose and a thick book open in front of her.

"Did you ask if you could touch *that*?" Jude says, nodding to the book.

Jones glowers but goes back to minding her own business.

Jude keeps flicking through the pages. A paper-thin piece of lead falls out onto her lap. It's an invocation—and some of the most complex spellwork she's ever seen, second only to the beast of a spell Emer's saving for Bael. The whole piece is filled with symbols and icons of women and teeny-tiny writing in half a dozen alphabets.

A work in progress, maybe? Hell, it could be Emer's shopping list.

Jude thinks back to the first time she cursed herself, when she was young and her soul was whole and the biggest problem in her life was that her father seemed not to like her very much.

At fifteen, she had loved horror movies and hosting Ouija

board nights with her friends and, yes, wearing the Sigil of Baphomet because she thought it was funny. She'd been interested in magic the way most fifteen-year-old girls are interested in magic. It was sexy and a little bit dangerous to toy with the occult.

That was when she found the book. A small thing about the size of her palm, its vellum pages handwritten in what turned out to be a variant of Czech that was old enough to be considered Bohemian by the academic Jude paid to translate it. Once translated, it appeared to be a grimoire. It had been hidden in the walls of her bedroom, behind a brick that wiggled like a tooth. It wasn't necessarily a strange thing to find; Jude grew up in the tower of a converted church, one of Lawrence's many luxury properties around London. It felt right that a priest had hidden something they considered dangerous in a holy place.

Jude had been ecstatic. It was no folklore nonsense about rubbing manure and molasses on your temples to cure a headache. It spoke about magic and demons in a plain, authoritative way that made it seem, well . . . real.

So Jude had decided to give it a go (despite the extensive warnings that curses should only be written by cursewriters, whatever they were, and should never be phrased in the "common tongue," whatever that was). The necessary tools weren't hard to gather: a piece of lead beaten paper-thin on which to engrave the invocation, something to scratch the words into the metal, a few drops of blood to guide a demon to the tether point.

The grimoire was careful to outline that invocations should only be used for great needs or great wants. For anything short term, the book encouraged blood magic instead.

Soul spells should only ever be used for the heavy stuff.

Due to a quirk in the translation from Bohemian to English, the translator had not understood that the curse needed to go directly over a pulse point, so Jude decided to whack it on her upper thigh so no one would be able to see it if something went wrong. (Jude was more concerned, at the time, that her lovely legs might be marred by a scar, not that her soul would be desiccated by a demon.)

Though the spell felt real, she also knew that it wasn't, obviously. That it couldn't be. It was no different from the manifesting spells she did with her friends, where they'd put shells and rose petals and drops of bright red blood in glass vials and bury them in the soft soil of their parents' expansive gardens. Everyone in medieval Europe had believed in magic to some degree. Even King James I had written a dissertation on necromancy and black magic that was published in 1597. The grimoire felt the same: like something written by someone who had really *believed* in magic because it had been real to them, had been a genuine part of their world and life. But, for Jude, there was no reason to believe it was any more legitimate than the "very authentic!" Ouija board she had bought off Amazon for £25.95, Prime shipping included.

So Jude shut herself in her en suite with it and scratched the stupid spell she wanted to try into the lead she'd ordered off the internet:

*Make my father love me.*

And, as something of an afterthought:

*Make me his favorite child.*

She lit red candles and had a YouTube video of druids chanting playing in the background. Like an idiot.

Jude had laughed at herself, at the childishness of her request—but what was the harm, she thought, of putting that desire out into the universe? Wasn't that what manifesting was all about?

In the hands of a gifted cursewriter like Emer, someone who was fluent in Latin and a number of other ancient and protolanguages that demons understood, perhaps the invocation could have worked. There was a way to curry favor with a relative, to soften the hardness of their heart, though Jude would later learn that love spells were notoriously bad under almost all circumstances.

A demon could not make her father love her. A demon could not reach inside a man's heart and warm it. So even if Jude had gotten all the other stuff right—even if the spell had been written in Latin or Proto-Balto-Slavic or bloody *Wingdings*, even if it had been correctly placed over a pulse point at her wrist or neck or groin or heart—it still would not have been worth the sacrifice she ended up paying in pain and sickness and life and soul.

Jude strokes her chin in an imitation of Jones and finds that it does, indeed, help her think.

What Jude knows is this: Vera Clarke is dead. Vera Clarke's power is being used by the person who killed her. Ergo, power *can* be shifted from one soul to another. The bond between human and demon broken and then transferred. Somehow. The thing Emer thinks is impossible appears to be possible after all—and the killer knows how to do it.

"I could," Jude says as she stares at the piece of lead in her hand. They have no other leads, after all. They're at a dead end. So why not give it a crack? "It would be deranged—but I could."

"Are you talking to yourself?" Jones asks.

"What are you doing?" Emer asks, emerging with her hair wrapped in a towel, her cheeks petal pink from the hot water.

Jude grins, twisting the lead in her fingertips. "Ladies, I have a *very* bad idea."

THEY BOTH HATE it, of course. Emer vetoes it immediately. Jones calls Jude all sorts of things that are synonymous with the word *fool*. When they have calmed down enough to listen, Jude tries again.

"The killer is exclusively hunting women with curses written by Emer," she says, explaining it to them like they're five. "We want to find the killer. Thus, it makes perfect sense to set a trap to lure them in—with me as the bait."

"What, pray tell, do you intend to do with a supernatural serial killer once they show up to murder you?" Jones asks.

Jude holds up her hands. "Knock them out with these bad boys."

"Great plan," Jones says. "All the other victims had power, too, remember—and it made no difference."

"Well, then, we have Bael as a backup plan."

To Jude's surprise, Emer does not protest. She simply says, "Oh."

Jones looks confused. "I'm sorry, that is the second time you've said that word. What is a *Bael*?"

"Turns out Emer has a big, bad guardian demon doing her bidding," Jude explains. "We know Bael can disembowel a dude in, what, five seconds flat? So this is how it goes: I curse myself, the killer shows up, I have a conversation with them, because they think I'm about to die, they give an evil monologue explaining *exactly* how they transferred untransferable power from one soul to another. I knock the killer out when they attack me and/or Bael eats the killer starting with their spine, I uncurse myself with our newfound knowledge, we all live happily ever after. Except for the killer, who will be dead. We could wrap this up *tonight*."

"You are *unhinged*," Jones whispers.

"How would the killer even find you?" Emer asks.

"The same way they've found all the other girls—" Jude clicks her fingers and points at Jones. "With Savannah's power."

Jones takes off her glasses and climbs down the ladder. "I have been wondering if that's how he's been tracking them down."

"The killer cut an invocation out of Savannah Jones and has used it ever since to hunt his victims."

"I still don't understand why she wanted *that* power," Jones says quietly, more to herself than anyone else.

"All of your other clients are warded," Jude continues. "All of the ones we were able to reach, anyway. I will be a tempting, easy treat—a girl, alone, at night. What's the spell?"

"Unfinished, is what it is," Emer replies.

"You know what I mean."

"The woman who commissioned it wanted power. Literally. It's electricity. From the hands."

Jude considers the piece of lead with newfound awe. *"Wicked,"* she says.

"It is *unfinished*," Emer insists. "It is a *draft*, Jude. The power will be unstable, potentially even unusable."

"How long, theoretically, would it take you to make it perfect?"

"Weeks. Months."

"We don't have weeks. Will it kill me? If I whack it on today?"

"You speak so casually of cleaving off more of your soul. Losing more years of your life."

"Emer. *Will it kill me?*"

Emer sighs. "No. I do not think it will kill you."

Jude grins again. "Let's do it, then."


JUDE STEADIES HERSELF with a few deep breaths because she knows what's coming. There's a sacrifice every time you give one of these bastards a bit of your soul to gnaw on. It ain't pretty. The cursewriters she found before Emer both told her there would be a physical price to pay for the power she wanted. Jude had known that, but she had thought it would somehow be much . . . sexier. A fainting spell or fevers, perhaps.

The cursewriter she had commissioned her second curse from, the retired doctor, specialized in chronic pain relief. It was unclear if magic could even be used to combat magical pain, which the cursewriter was quick to point out. No one had come to her with a problem like this before. She usually helped women with endometriosis and postpartum recovery, not necrotic souls. Jude had paid her £10,000 for an invocation to ease her agony. A second demon attached itself to Jude's soul and seemed to do absolutely nothing outside of cracking her eyesight. A fun side effect of the occult.

The third time she seared herself with magic, she really should have known better, but the songwriter she found on the internet—on a Reddit forum, no less—claimed to know what she was doing. Never commission spells from a songwriter. Bob Dylan may have won the Nobel Prize for literature, but a cursewriter he was not. After that demon started suckling on her soul, granting her the ability to knock herself out, Jude was sick for weeks with what her nannies might have called "an upset tummy" but actually consisted of Jude passing nothing but liquid and mucus. Food would go in and turn into fire inside her, so she stopped eating, which made her stomach cramp and her muscles begin to eat themselves.

Eventually she was hospitalized again. The tabloids reported that she was suffering from an eating disorder and printed pictures of her looking gaunt. Another starving socialite. Like that was even interesting. After a colonoscopy (all her dignity was gone by that point anyway) revealed no reason for the volcano, doctors diagnosed her with irritable bowel syndrome and put her on a special diet to help control her symptoms. Jude ate nothing but porridge for a month, and slowly the dysentery stopped (the mucus, however, remained for much longer).

All this is to say it is not without appreciation for potential dire consequences that Jude takes the roll of lead into the bathroom and watches in the mirror as Emer uses her fingertips to find the place on her neck where her pulse is the strongest. Then, before she can reconsider, she lets Emer nick her flesh in that spot and observes as her blood beads to the surface. It's not much. Just a scratch. That is all you need.

The blood will bring them. Every wraith within a quarter mile will crowd into this bathroom in moments, such is their thirst for the red juice.

Jude waits. She cannot see or hear or feel them, but she knows they must be there.

"I cannot believe I'm doing this," she says with the lead pressed against her bloody skin.

"You must say the words," Emer instructs.

"Hanc potentiam volo," Jude whispers. *I want this power.* The devil never got around to learning English, but he can, apparently, understand Latin. Jude rolls her eyes. Magic is so tragically cliché. "Animam meam offero." *I offer my soul.*

Jude removes her hand, but the lead stays against her neck. It has taken. She can feel the magic biting her, a thousand tiny leech teeth burrowing into her skin. Somewhere, beyond the veil through which she can occasionally see, a flurry of hungry demons are vying for the opportunity to tether themselves to her soul for the rest of her natural life. Jude imagines the scene as a kind of auction, with a podium and a gavel and demons in business suits shouting bids for her immortal soul. She imagines it this way because what is really happening beyond the veil is dark and frightening. The biggest, baddest demon is fighting its way through the others to get to her. She feels it first at the back of her neck, a hot prickle that spreads up and over her scalp, and then something invisible slams into her and she knows it has begun.

What does it feel like to bind your soul to a demon for the fourth time? The soul is not a separate entity to the flesh. It inhabits every cell, every fiber of the body. And so when the soul is cracked open and something foreign crawls inside, it is felt everywhere, all at once.

Jude takes off her clothes and staggers to the shower. She does not mind Emer and Jones seeing her naked. She is already in the realm of pain.

At first the body thinks the invader might be in the gut, and so it violently purges the contents of the stomach and the bowels. Jude is used to shitting herself at this point, so no big deal. Next, the immune system reacts, fast and hard. Jude sits on the tiled floor under the stream of cool water as she feels her temperature climb from normal to feverish in minutes.

Jude's body continues to purge that which isn't necessary: Several of her fingernails wash away in the spray, a couple of toenails following not long after. A tooth loosens in her mouth, though she has learned to keep her jaw shut, to ride the wave of shedding.

When the pain grows too great and her brain too hot, she passes out.

When she comes to, shuddering and shaking and naked, Emer and Jones are watching her with concerned expressions.

It is evident immediately that Emer is a far superior cursewriter to those she has used before. The bind is clean and strong. There is new weight in her body: The demon the invocation summoned must be a big bastard. Beneath the horror of what she's just done, there is something else. Something that Jude is unfamiliar with. It fizzes through her like sherbet powder, lighting her from the inside out. It is power. Power dancing in her fingertips, sparking through her muscles. The power that she exchanged a good chunk of her soul for.

Strangely, unlike her previous three curses, Emer's curse leaves her feeling somehow . . . stronger.

"Emer," Jude whispers as she runs her fingertips over the neat lines of leaden letters that have melted into her neck. "You are Walter Goddamn White."

The witch is good. Damn good. With Emer and Jones's help, Jude staggers to her feet. She can feel her new power coursing through her muscles, electrifying them. She likes the feel of it. When she spreads her fingers, little snakes of static dance between them.

She is electric.

She is lightning.

"Let's take you out for a spin."

# INTERVAL

**A GIRL** walks alone at night.

Though her soul is cracked, a new power seethes beneath her fingertips. It gives her a false sense of security, of invincibility.

Electricity. There is no part of her that is not alight with it. She is an electric eel, sleek as she parts the night spaces that have been closed to her all her life because she is a girl.

For the first time, the girl doesn't hover at the edge of the dark; she plunges into it, is swallowed whole by it. The gift of fear was given to her by the women she grew up around: nannies, teachers, friends, lovers. From them all, she learned to carry her keys between her fingers like knuckle-dusters. She learned to pour her own drinks at parties and keep them close to her, always in sight, never unguarded. She learned to walk in busy, well-lit areas at night and to wear bright, memorable clothing so that if—when—she disappeared, she would stick in the minds of those who'd witnessed her final hours.

The girl enters Regent's Canal down a ramp near her house in Hoxton. It is long after sunset, and the towpath is deserted. Old fear, ingrained in her from childhood, tells her to go back to the light, but she fights the fear and pushes on, on past one closed restaurant and another in the final stages of being packed up by a lone staff member stacking chairs inside. Tonight she's an explorer plunging into uncharted territory, exhilarated to be welcomed into the sloe-black. There's a whole new world to be discovered, here in the dark.

It takes some minutes for her eyes to adjust. When she can see better, she kneels by the canal's edge and spies bloat-bellied city fish drifting in the current, their homes made in discarded tires and waterlogged bicycles overgrown with green sludge. She places her palm flat against the dreggy water and—

Lightning guts through her. It begins as a ball of bright pain beneath the right side of her skull and hijacks her nervous system to scream down her arm and out her fingertips. For a second, the entire canal is luminol bright, the electric blue of eels and bioluminescence. The water boils and seethes. The tips of the girl's fingers blister, the skin singed by the force of the electricity. She shoots backward as though hit by a wrecking ball and slams into the wall behind her. Steam rises from the surface of the lightning-struck water. The fish, who were just minding their own business, float to the top, cooked and scalding.

When the girl comes to, shaking and haggard, she swallows and holds her burning hand against her chest. That's not what she meant to do.

"I'm so sorry," she whispers to the fish. "Oh God. That is so unfortunate."

"*What* are you *doing?*" asks a figure looming over her. Jones, she realizes. Yes, Jones and Emer are trailing her. Watching. Waiting for the emergence of the killer.

"Get out of sight," the girl mumbles.

"Stop killing fish and just walk up the damn towpath like we talked about," Jones says, before disappearing back into the darkness under a nearby bridge.

It takes her some time to gather herself, to stand, to keep being bait. Several hours pass. The night is cold as she walks back and forth in the darkness, waiting.

A girl walks alone, but not alone.

She feels him before she sees him, the way women do.

Her eyes find the figure immediately, standing stationary on the towpath. He's a slip of shadow, nothing more. No face, no weapon, nothing to indicate that he might do her harm. Just a man.

The girl rolls her eyes and continues on. She's deeply disinterested in men, not only on a sexual level, but also on an intellectual one. It's not that she despises them exactly, but rather that she doesn't quite see the point of them. They're violent and brutish and arrogant. They walk though spaces as though they own them. Why? As far as she's concerned, they're inferior to women in almost every way—women are better lovers, better leaders, better investors, better communicators. Yet she's seen firsthand the power that men gather and wield. She knows it's not their fault—the patriarchy has damaged them—but still.

The girl looks up and stifles a yelp with her hand.

The figure has followed her and is standing on the sidewalk directly in her path. Closer now than he was the first time.

The girl stops again. Stares. How could he have followed her? How could he have overtaken her without her noticing? How could he have moved so quickly?

A flicker, she realizes.

It is him.

It is *him*.

"All right," she says, her voice shaking more than she would like it to. "You've got me right where you want me."

The man doesn't react, doesn't move. That is, somehow, more threatening.

"How are you doing it?" she tries again. "How are you taking their power?"

Again, the figure says and does nothing.

The girl's immediate response is a heady shot of anger infused with fear. Anger that a man can make her afraid. For a half dozen heartbeats, she's scared—and then she looks down at her ragged hand, at the electricity dancing between her fingertips, and the fear crumples to smug knowingness. Oh, he wants to scare her? *Just try me, buddy.*

The girl lifts her right arm and lets her new power sizzle through her again. It yanks out of the bottom of her brain, howls down her arm and explodes out, cracking each of her remaining fingernails in half. She screams as electricity arcs through the air, thick and twisted as a hedgerow, and slams into the figure with all the force of the girl's hatred. Then, a split second after it has started, it stops. The power sputters out. She calls for it again and again, but it is like a motor that keeps turning over but will not start.

The figure is in a steaming pile on the ground. He twitches. He rises to one knee and then pulls himself to standing. He takes a step toward her and then another.

"Holy sweet mother of Jesus," the girl says. She thinks about all the dead women she has seen, their throats crushed and mottled with bruising.

Even this close she cannot see his face. It's masked by smoke and shadow, as though he's conjured pure darkness to hide his features. She understands, then, that he is not human. She understands that he has come to kill her and that despite the new power raging through her synapses, she has no real way to defend herself. Not alone, anyway.

Now she is truly afraid.

Now she turns to run.

# SEVENTEEN

**JUDE RUNS.** The shadow wraith follows her, flickering out of Emer's sight in an instant.

Emer swears in Latin and gives chase. This was not part of the plan. Jude was supposed to wait until Emer set Bael on the killer—but it is hard to do nothing when you are terrified. Jude bolts up a set of stone stairs to the road above. By the time Emer reaches street level a few seconds later, both Jude and the killer have disappeared.

"Where are they?" Zara is on Emer's heels, drawing heavy breaths.

Emer turns frantically on the spot.

A bolt of lightning suddenly splits the sky. It shoots *up* from the ground, as thick as a tornado, spiraling high into the atmosphere. A second later, it zaps out, spent.

"Holy *hell*," Zara breathes.

"There," Emer says at the same time.

They both run toward the lightning. Emer's muscles respond with glee at being unleashed. She is small and hard and very fast. When they round the corner, they know instantly where it has come from: Jude's house. The power she used has split the building open, left it charred and burning. Emer does not see how the girl herself could survive such a catastrophic burst of voltage. Surely her body could not handle it. Surely her heart will have been cooked.

"Wait here," Emer says, pressing her knife into Zara's hands. "If he comes this way, stab him."

"You want *me* to stab *him*?" Zara asks.

Emer does not answer. She is already inside the house, stumbling through the choking smoke and heat.

"Jude!" she cries. "Jude!"

There is no answer. Emer ascends to the next floor—and that is where she finds her. A smoking heap on the ground.

"Jude," Emer says frantically, turning her over. There is a ring of red, angry skin around Jude's neck, a spider's web of broken blood vessels branching out from her eyes. The killer tried to strangle her. "Jude, can you hear me?"

Jude moans. "Am I dead?" she rasps.

Relief thrills through Emer. "No," she says. She could cry. She could laugh. "No, you are not dead."

"That is unfortunate." Her voice is hoarse, forced through her swollen windpipe.

"Get up." Emer tries to help her stand. "Get up and get out of here."

"Emer," Jude says. "*Look.*"

Jude points through the smoke. Near them, a wall is gutted by a funnel of black char where Jude's power has cut through it. There is a second body crumpled on the floor in the next room.

"Is he dead?" Jude whispers.

"Be quiet," Emer orders.

"Ask him. Ask him how—"

"*Quiet.*" Emer steps through the melted wall and approaches him with caution. Up close, he does not look as tall or broad as he did on the canal when he was cloaked in shadow. His shoulders and hips are narrow, his height diminished from the towering form he becomes when covered in Emer's stolen magic. The fabric of his dark jacket is crisp, burned by Jude's immense power. The color of his hair is impossible to discern beneath the layer of dust and ash that coats it.

Emer reaches out to touch his shoulder. To roll him over and witness his face, this killer of women. He is heavy. He does not move easily. She has to push his shoulder back with all her weight, even though he is not much bigger than her.

Emer turns him. The man groans. Alive, then.

Yet—is he a man? The face beneath the blood and falling ash looks young.

A boy, Emer sees. He is a boy. A boy around her age. Perhaps a little older, but not by much.

His eyes start to open. They are blue, set into bloodshot whites.

Emer frowns. She cannot comprehend him. She cannot understand.

For a second, there is peace between them as they consider each other. The witch and the witch killer, each within arm's reach of the other.

Then a shadow falls instantly over his features, hiding his face in total blackness. With shocking speed, he shoves Emer hard across the room. It is all she can do to keep on her feet. It is lucky she does not fall, because he is already scrambling to his knees.

"Run," she tells Jude. There is no need for the instruction. Jude is already moving, plunging unsteadily down the stairs into the smoky house below. Emer follows her and loses her almost immediately to the haze. The smoke here is thick, small fires burning everywhere. The force of Jude's magic punctured walls, ceilings. It has left scars of fire burning in its wake.

Emer could outrun him, she is sure of it—but it is not herself she fears for. It is Jude he wants. It is Jude's magic that drew him here.

"Bael," Emer says as she moves. There is no need to whisper. The man will be dead before he can catch her. She brings her wrist to her mouth and bites the skin there, tears a small hole in it with her incisors to feed her demon its payment. "Occide."

Emer scurries around a corner and presses her back against the wall, her heart a darting thing. She chances a peek, to see if Bael has done its work yet. The hall is gloomy but not entirely devoid of light. The man is still there. The man is still following her. She can make out the contour of him, standing there in the haze land. He seems to take up the whole corridor with his height and breadth, so much bigger now than when he was an injured boy on the floor moments ago.

Emer takes shallow sips of air and lets her eyes go unfocused. The world beneath the world hits her like a flood, the stench and power of it raking over her, stripping her skin, burning her hair. The bile yellow of brimstone, the sting of it in her eyes and nostrils, so potent she has to raise her hand before her face and look through her fingers at the scalding power before her.

Bael stands in front of her in a protective stance, wild and fuming. There are needle-fine hackles raised all over its chest and shoulders. Its tar-dark organs beat wildly inside its translucent body. It screams at the boy in voces mysticae, its tone so vile and loud Emer's brain lurches instantly into the vise of a migraine.

"Bael," Emer says again, more forceful this time. "Occide!"

Bael does not move. Bael does nothing.

It is afraid, Emer realizes.

Bael is *afraid*.

The shadow boy turns around and looks at Emer. Or at least Emer thinks he is looking at her.

"Oh," she whispers because she cannot understand what she is seeing.

There is the boy, and above him is what he has taken from the women he has killed.

A swollen nest of demons is tethered to him. There are dozens. Too many to count. A vast bloated balloon of pale-bodied creatures bobbing above his head, each bound to his soul by a filament-like string. They are stuck together like mice on a glue trap.

Emer once found glue traps in a farmhouse on the outskirts of Killarney that she was raiding for eggs. Squares of sticky yellow paper set by the door, seven small bodies stuck to them and stuck to each other. Two were already dead. The others were still fighting to free themselves. They gnawed their own flesh down to the bone.

The demons are not dissimilar. They move where he moves, bound to him. They are not docile, as they should be. They are starving, furious. They snap and gouge at each other. There are so many tethers that they have all twisted and snagged into a gruesome rat king. They break one another's bones. They eat one another's limbs. They gouge one another's insides. It is a feeding frenzy, and because they are immortal, it goes on and on and on, forever.

The reality of the underworld bends around the boy. The weight of so many curses.

It is an abomination. No human soul could support so many curses. Not when each curse costs so much life. The only person Emer has seen with anywhere near as many demons is her grandmother, Orlaith, who had six—though she was alive into her eighties, she was a withered straw of a woman.

It is impossible.

It *should* be impossible.

Yet here he is. Walking toward her.

Emer blinks away her second sight and breathes into cupped hands to stop herself from vomiting.

A face appears in a doorway. Jude. Jude, who should be gone, who should have run. Jude, her bleeding arm cradled against her chest, her eyes big as an owlet's. Jude is here, beckoning Emer toward the stairs. Emer follows her as quietly as she can. They go down, down, spiraling into the depths of the ruined building together. There are footsteps above them. Not hurried but loud, assured.

He is coming. He wants them to *hear* him coming.

Emer and Jude slip through a door. The room beyond is cluttered, a basement of some sort. As Jude says, it is flooded with half a foot of viscous yellow liquid. Emer takes Jude's hand, leads her into a cupboard filled with mops and buckets, pulls the door closed behind them.

They wait.

"Where is Zara?" Emer breathes.

"Outside," Jude rasp whispers. "I made it out before—before I came back for you."

"You should *not* have come back."

"Believe me, I regret it already."

They are looped together in the dark, their arms around each other, their hearts beating madly as one.

"He is coming," Emer whispers.

There are footsteps. They grow closer and closer as if he can see them like a beacon. Emer thinks of all the other women he has killed. How afraid they must have been, hiding and running just as she is now. Emer had touched each one of them when they were alive. She had pressed her fingertips to their wrists and necks to look for the point where their pulse tripped beneath their skin. All that life. All that power.

All snuffed out by this man.

This *boy*.

There is a slit in the door through which Emer can see the room beyond. He moves like a slow beast through the dark. Emer can hear him breathing. He is looking for them. She cups her hands to Jude's mouth to muffle her vital sounds.

Emer burns with anger and fear. There are flames and thunder inside her. She is too bright. She is too loud. He will find them where they hide, and he will crush them.

They cannot hide from him. They cannot hide from him because he can find anything he wants, like Savannah Jones could.

Jude buries her head into Emer's neck. Emer can feel the girl's racing heart in her own body. Her cheek to her throat, the two of them one trembling creature. It is easy, in these moments, to remember that Jude is a girl. A girl who is scared, who wants to go back to her family.

The shadow man wades toward them. He knows where they are.

Jude's power cannot fight him. Bael cannot destroy him. Emer does not even have her knife.

What will they do?

The figure reaches out in the dark, his fingers brushing the handle of the cupboard. There is the scream of sirens in the distance, bound for the smoking house. They will be too late. By the time the police arrive, they will all be dead. And then, suddenly—a second wraith in the dark.

No sound or breath escapes Zara's lips as she raises Emer's knife and sinks the blade into the figure's back. The weapon digs in all the way to the hilt. The attacker gasps and twists away from her. Emer swears she can hear the knife grind against the man's ribs as the blade sucks out of his body. He stumbles backward, gasping, and then he flickers and is gone.

Emer and Jude let go of each other but do not move apart. Jude had been holding Emer so tightly there will likely be bruises across her ribs. They are still very close. Jude is looking at her intensely. Her breath is warm against Emer's lips. Emer wants to reach out and touch Jude's face. Emer wants to put her lips against Jude's lips. She has never wanted anyone in this way before, but in that moment, she wants Jude.

Zara opens the cupboard door, panting, the bloody knife still in her hand.

"Well, that," she says, then she pauses to suck in a breath, "did *not* go as planned."


"So what do we do now?" Jude asks an hour later, her voice still hoarse. It is Friday night, and the three of them are tucked at the back of a bar near Jude's house, none of them drinking the beers they ordered. They all smell of burning, of brimstone, of Hell. Jude looks like she has been electrocuted, her hair standing on end, her skin charred, the tips of her fingers raw. The ring of red around her throat is growing darker by the minute, splotches of blue bruises blooming beneath her skin. In the distance, Emer can still see the flashing lights of fire engines.

"I do not know," she answers. The thought of the killer with his hands around Jude's lovely neck. Emer grits her teeth, flares her nostrils. It should not have happened. Not on her watch.

Zara has her laptop open in front of her, searching the internet incessantly for information she will not find. Emer watches as she types dozens of search terms that return nothing but Bible websites trying to save the souls of the wayward.

Eventually Zara snaps her laptop shut and rubs her temples. "What *exactly* are we dealing with here, Emer?"

"*I do not know,*" Emer says again, perhaps for the tenth time. Because she truly does not know. The killer—he was an abomination. An impossibility.

"Explain to me again what you saw," Zara says, like it is somehow going to make a difference.

"Dozens of stolen demons tethered to a young man. So many invocations that I have written for women, now feeding power to . . . someone else. Bael, cowering. Afraid of him."

An immortal demon. Afraid of a *boy*.

Jude opens a photo on her phone. It is of the murder board they constructed in her house. She zooms in on each different stolen power. "It's quite an impressive arsenal," she says. "One man collecting all of these curses, using all of these curses. Jesus."

"How would you ever be able to stop him?" Zara asks.

It is a good question. "The knife you drove into his back seemed to slow him down," she offers. There was pain and mortal fear in the way he gasped and retreated after the injury. Catching him off guard again might not be so easy—but it was good to know he could be hurt. That he was not entirely impervious to harm.

"Is there anyone we can go to for information on the occult?" Jude asks.

Emer thinks of Nessa. Wonders, for the millionth time, where her cousin is now, if she is safe and settled or still on the move because of what Emer did. How much would she know about the world she shunned?

"Anyone who's . . . I don't know, into really dark stuff," Jude continues. "Who might be able to shed some light on what the hell we're dealing with? Or some kind of, like, witch encyclopedia or something? There have to be *some* resources *somewhere*."

"Lough Leane," Emer whispers. She has been thinking about it since they found Vera Clarke. Since it became apparent that a transfer of power had occurred. A spell taken from one soul and tethered to another.

"What?" Jude says.

"We could go to Lough Leane," Emer says. "My family home. In Ireland. The house still stands."

"Not to be insensitive but, um, is anyone even . . . there?"

"Something is happening here that I do not understand," Emer says quietly. "That I have never come across before." Emer nods at Jude. "That *you* have never come across before. You have read all the books in your library, yes? Looking for a way to uncurse yourself?"

"I have," Jude says grimly.

"You have never seen anything like this before?"

"No—but to be fair, ninety-nine percent of those books aren't real witch books. They're junk speculation written by people who have no idea what they're talking about. We need *real* resources."

"There is—was—a library at the house at Lough Leane." Emer's voice is a thin thread. That place is a tomb. It is not somewhere she ever thought she would go back to after Nessa took her away, and now here she is, suggesting it. "My grandmother, Orlaith—she was from a different time. I didn't know her well— she was a shell by the time I was born—but my cousins whispered stories. A dark witch who practiced dark magic, they said. The library—it had grimoires and diaries and books stretching back hundreds of years. All of my family's knowledge, including Orlaith's." Emer looks up. "If we are going to find information anywhere, that is where it will be."

# EIGHTEEN

ZARA HAS never been on an airplane before, let alone a private plane.

The family "holidays" of her early childhood had been to "visit" ailing relatives in small, damp villages on the outskirts of London. Zara and Savannah were left at these homes for increasingly long stretches of time as their mother's various addictions crashed over her like waves, until, inevitably, she dumped them at Pru's and then just never came back. Had it been any of the other five or so distant relatives with whom Zara spent much her childhood, her life might have turned out quite differently.

"I can't believe my first plane ride is on a private jet," Zara says as she runs her hands over the shiny marled-wood table in front of her.

"Sorry it's so utterly tacky," Jude says, tapping her fingernails on the wood. "Why my family insists on making our planes look so douchey I will never know."

"Your family owns this plane?" Zara asks.

"My family owns a lot of planes."

It is Prudence whom Zara thinks about as the plane's engines begin to swell with heat and sound. Pru, who'd wanted to spend her twilight years somewhere warm, like Spain, but had instead spent them raising two angry, damaged girls to be slightly less angry and damaged. There is lift, a buoyant feeling in Zara's insides, pressure against her chest and head as the machine climbs.

The wing follows a wide arc, and for a minute she is suspended over London, her face pressed against the glass. The light changes. The way the rising sun hits the Thames gives it a hard quality, sets it somehow, turns it into a vast snake of slate. There's nothing soft about it anymore, and for the first time Zara understands how people jumping from bridges can die when they hit water at speed. The city's rivers look like trails of almost set black lava, smooth and flat. Everything is solid from this height.

Emer isn't doing well on the flight. It's her first time on an airplane too, though for her it seems to hold no wonder or excitement. She is breathing laboriously, her fingers curled white-knuckle around the armrests of her seat.

Zara goes to say something, to help the frightened witch—maybe something about the statistics of plane crashes and how unlikely they are—but Jude beats her to it. Jude, who can come across as so cool and aloof, slides her hand beneath Emer's and pries it from the armrest. It's a gesture of such unexpected warmth. They sit like this for the rest of the short flight, Jude running the pad of her thumb in small circles on the back of Emer's hand.

After takeoff, Zara opens her laptop and returns to her notes about Elizabeth Báthory, to the question she wrote down two nights ago: What if there was a way for a demon to reanimate a human body but for the mind to still have full control? What if a blood ward could be used *inside* a person, to protect the brain from possession?

Zara taps her nails on her laptop and chews on her bottom lip as she thinks. *There is a library at the house at Lough Leane.* Emer's words turn over and over in her mind. *Grimoires and diaries and books stretching back hundreds of years. All of my family's knowledge.*

A dark witch who practiced dark magic, she's called her grandmother. It's a long shot—but what if another copy of *Nekromanteía* is there somewhere? They are going to Lough Leane with a goal— to find out what the heck is going on with the killer, how they have learned to do the impossible—but it won't hurt to do a little research of her own on the side.

Jude answers a call from her father, gives a very bad performance pretending she has *no idea* what happened to the house she split in half with her magic. By the time they begin their descent, Jude is gloomy, muttering as she scrolls through her phone looking at pictures of a woman on Instagram.

"Who's that?" Zara asks.

Jude looks up. "Oh. The leggy bombshell? Just my new stepmother, as of tomorrow." She shows Zara her screen.

"Oh my," Zara says, scrolling through the woman's pictures. She is very beautiful. At the top of her profile, her bio reveals that she's twenty-three and from Spain. "You really want to go to the wedding and watch this happen? No offense. I mean, I'm sure, under his utterly terrifying exterior, your father is a nice—"

"Oh, he's not. He's not a nice man."

"Why bother, then? Don't you have better things to do? When someone shows you who they are, believe them the first time. That's a Maya Angelou quote. When I heard it, I knew I was done with my mother. She showed me who she was when she left Savannah and me. If your dad isn't nice—"

"Why do you think your mother is the way she is?"

"I guess . . . I don't really know. Alcoholism?"

"Before that, though. Like, why did she *start* drinking? My grandfather was a bad guy. Like, a really bad dude. I never met him, he died before I was born, but—Lawrence has cigar burns on his arms from his father. So—I don't know. Lawrence is cold and can be a bit of an arsehole, but—"

"It could be worse?"

Jude shrugs. "I've always been willing to give him the benefit of the doubt. I try to think of him as a scared little kid. I don't know, I feel . . . looked after. I didn't understand that for a long time—if I had, I wouldn't have bloody cursed myself, I wouldn't have wanted so much more from him—but I think he loves me in the best way he knows how."

Zara hands Jude her phone back. "You're more enlightened than me."

"A lot of people tell me that," Jude says, reclining in her chair and swinging her feet up onto the marled wood of the table in front of her. "A regular walking, talking bodhisattva, that's me."

# NINETEEN

**THE DRIVE** from Cork to Lough Leane takes around two hours. The road is narrow and bordered by hedgerows, beyond which lie the fields and forests in which Emer grew up wild. When they reach the southern end of Lough Leane, their driver parks the black SUV that collected them from the plane and says he will wait for as long as they need.

The three of them plunge into the forest on foot. The sun sits low above the trees. Emer enjoys the pleasure-pain of bright golden sunshine and cold air on her face. The dew reveals a vast kingdom of spiderwebs cast like nets across every shrub, every tree. Garlands of carmine-red vines swing between branches like decorations. Every stone and root is covered in a carpet of moss. Ravens, thick-beaked and glossy, follow them curiously. There is a sense that the world is closing down, exhaling, readying itself for sleep. Winter is coming.

Emer cannot remember the exact location of the house, but she knows they are heading in the right direction. The closer they get, the taller and thicker the trees become until they stretch above the trio like cathedral arches. The trees have been made unnaturally tall by the magic of the women who lived in these woods.

"Not far now," Emer says to the others. They follow her in silence.

Minutes later, the forest gives way to a meadow. It is a barren space. Empty and desolate.

"Um . . . There's nothing here," Jude says.

"That is what you are supposed to think," Emer says. The ward was Nessa's doing. A spell to hide the house and orchard from anyone who might stumble across them accidentally. "Give me your hands," she says to the others. "We can push through the ward together." They clasp hands and take a step forward. The ward begins to repel them. A curious sensation creeps into Emer's mind: sudden fear. *Leave this place*, it seems say. The wind picks up. The way it moves through the trees makes it sound like whispering voices.

"I don't like it here, Emer," Jude says.

"I agree." Zara tries to work her way out of Emer's grip. "We should go."

Emer holds them tighter. "Push through your fear. It is not real." They take two more steps. Shadow pulls across the meadow until it is as sunless as twilight. Grisly black shapes move between the trees, twisted things with yellow eyes. "They are not real," Emer whispers to the others, though she does not sound convinced. "Do not look at them. They cannot hurt you." Jude and Zara are both fighting her now, whimpering. They want to flee. Emer does not let them. She takes another step. Another step. Her blood is thundering, her brain screaming at her to run, run, *run*.

One more step—and they burst through to the other side of the ward. The wind quiets. The shadow recedes. The meadow's secrets are revealed to them: a slumping house, a withered orchard, the skeleton of a greenhouse. The forest has spent a decade working to consume everything Emer's family spent generations building.

Jude clears her throat. "That wasn't so bad. I don't know about you, but I definitely didn't wee in my pants *at all*."

Emer gravitates first toward the orchard. The stand of apple trees where she hid ten years ago as she watched her family die. The trees still grow in the straight lines in which they were planted, though the boughs are all but wicks, bone white and gnarled. The branches that droop from them are the legs of dead spiders. Leafless, wretched, curled. There are no graves marked, but Emer knows her family is buried here among the roots. Buried by the men who killed them. Her mother. Her cousins. Her grandmother. Emer watched them work into the night, laying to rest the women they had murdered.

When the coven lived here, the apples were harvested by hand in September or October. It is November now and apples still grow heavy on the naked trees, but they have changed. Emer picks one. It is matte black, as though cloaked in mourning. She takes a bite. The flesh beneath is sour and soft as mucus. Emer spits it out. She kneels and places her palm against the earth. There is so much anger here. It boils out of the ground. It congeals in the roots of the trees.

Emer pushes her hand softly into the dirt. Thick red liquid swells out of the ground around her fingertips. It runs across her knuckles and creates a complicated crosshatch of rivulets across the surface of her skin. Blood. There is blood here in the dirt.

The witches have infected the grove with their fate. The ground has been poisoned by the murders that took place here and now the trees that draw their nutrients from the soil are sick with it.

"Emer," Jude says quietly. "Look."

Emer follows her line of sight. There is something sticking up out of the ground.

The arm is bilious and withered to leather—but it is still covered in flesh. The bodies have been preserved by the fen in which they are buried.

Emer draws closer. The hand wears a gold claddagh ring. Emer knows immediately who the body belongs to. "Róisín," she whispers as she slides her hand into her dead cousin's palm. The skin is cold but still remarkably soft. "She knew him," Emer says quietly. "The man who killed her. I heard her say his name before he . . ." She shakes her head. *"Andy."*

They were an isolated coven who had very little contact with the outside world. How on earth did Róisín know him?

That is when Emer sees it. A rectangle of skin missing at the wrist.

The invocation that once lived there has been cut out.

Emer lets the hand go and presses her fingertips to her mouth. *No.*

Jude and Zara have seen it too.

"Jesus," Jude whispers.

"What does that mean?" Zara asks. "What does that *mean*?"

Emer stumbles back and sinks to the ground and tries to take deep breaths.

"It means . . ." Jude does not say it out loud.

It has always been Emer's understanding that hunters do not cut bits of witches out. They do not keep trophies. They seek only to destroy, not to memorialize. There is not a part of a witch they would keep.

"They are . . ." Emer whispers. "They could be . . . linked?"

Could the murders of her family at Lough Leane ten years ago and the murders of her clients in London be *linked*?

"Did you recognize him?" Jude asks. "The man who attacked me? Did he look like the men who came to your house—the men who came *here*?"

"No." Emer cannot quite remember what Andy and his accomplices looked like, cannot quite remember the shape of their faces or the color of their eyes—but she is certain, if she were to see them again, she would know them instantly. The boy in Hoxton who came for Jude—the new killer of women—was not one of the men who murdered her family.

The wind picks up, bringing with it the sigh of leaves as they are plucked from their branches. Emer pushes her palms into eyes, uses the heel of her hands to drive them inward. Shattered neon shapes leap out at her in the darkness. Her head aches.

Some time passes in silence. Jude sits next to Emer on one side. Zara sits on the other. They huddle together in the November chill, three strangers bound and bonded by horror. They do not speak. For this, Emer is grateful. There are no words in her, no breath to send them from her lungs to her throat to her mouth.

Eventually, Emer stands and moves toward the house. Rotten apples pop and spread beneath her boots. She stops at the front door. It is sealed shut with a thicket of vines. She takes out her knife and slides it through the greenery. The door opens with a sigh, releasing air that smells earthen and damp. Emer is relieved by this, relieved that it does not smell of blood or gunpowder, but of things that grow.

She steps inside. Into the house she spent the first seven years of her life in. Into the house where her family lived and died. She moves deeper into the darkness, Jude and Zara trailing close behind. The air is cold from ten years without heating, yet it does not feel like a tomb. Everything is almost as it was, almost as she remembers it being. Everything is frozen in time, as though it is still that same spring afternoon ten years ago.

Here is the living room. Always cramped and crowded with women chatting and working around the hearth. The furniture, like all the furniture in the house, is old, inherited from another generation. The couches, still in situ, are big and lumpen, stuffed with grass and feathers. Emer felt like she was being swallowed whole when she sat in them. A book sits open on the leather of one, a sock mid-darning on the arm of another. There are only small hints of struggle: A little table is turned over on its side, the kerosene lamp that once lived atop it now sideways on the rug.

Emer heads forward, down the hall, to the kitchen. It overlooks the vast greenhouse, where many of her aunts and cousins spent their days, often from dawn to dusk. Here they cultivated exotic plants for tinctures and hallucinogenic mushrooms for brewing teas, along with many of the fruits and vegetables that would keep them alive through the bitter Irish winters. Again, it is like the day she left it: A chopping board and knife on the bench, whatever was being cut long since rotted away. A pie tin left to cool on the windowsill. A cupboard door left ajar, a drawer not quite closed.

The dining room is across the hall. Everyone prepared their own breakfasts and lunches, but dinner was a family affair. They gathered here, all twenty of them, each night around the long ebonized wood table to eat bread and drink wine. Candlesticks still run down the middle, the beeswax candles in them ready to be lit. Several chairs are turned on their sides, one curtain rod ripped down. Two bullet holes puncture the limewashed walls—

but that is all. If you did not know, you would not know.

There had been a whole small world in this house. It had been cut off from the rest of reality, but they had been happy here. They had been driven into hiding by the men who had persecuted their ancestors. They had found a way to live completely self-sustained. They relied on no one but themselves. Instead of withering in their exile, they had thrived.

And this had brought furious retribution upon them.

"Where is the library?" Zara asks.

"This way, I think." Emer leads them to the very end of the hall, where she finds what she is looking for: a room with floor-to-ceiling shelving on each wall. The books are thick with dust and cobwebs, and part of the ceiling has fallen in, strewing debris across the floor—but the library is there.

"Jackpot," Jude says. "Let's find out how our boy's doing this."

They read for hours. They are methodical about it, sorting tomes into stacks of those written in English and those written in other languages. Zara and Jude scour the English ones, Emer everything else. Anything that seems vaguely promising, they put into a much smaller third pile for all of them to review together.

In the afternoon, the light becomes threadbare. Emer starts a fire and ignites several kerosene lamps, brings them flickering into the library, where they cast a ghostly dancing glow on the ceiling. The wind winnows through cracks in the window glass, making disturbing singsong whispers. Emer's eyes ache. She stretches, decides to carry a lamp through the rest of the house to see what else she can find.

Upstairs are the bedrooms. No one had their own, not even Orlaith. They shared every space. The little ones even shared beds, three or four of them curled around each other in the winter months for warmth. Emer enters the room that was once hers, sits on the edge of the bed she shared with Niamh.

Emer allows herself to imagine an impossible life: coming back to this place and building it all again. Constructing a greenhouse to grow delicate angel's trumpets and planting a new orchard to grow apples. Tilling fields to plant potatoes and milking a cow each morning to make butter, cheese. For some reason, Jude is suddenly in this fantasy, flitting through the spring blossoms in a linen dress.

For ten years, Emer has not allowed herself to want much of anything beyond helping desperate women and writing her spell for revenge. Now that she is here, a part of her begins to want this.

To come home. To settle in one place. To rebuild what was stolen from her.

Emer thinks about what she said to Jude. She touches her necklace, the spell that lives there, over her heart. The spell that may very well destroy her and allow her to ruin her enemies in the process.

What if her place in the world is right here?

"Emer?" Zara is calling her. "Can you come here, please?"

Downstairs, she finds Zara pacing the library. Jude is sitting down watching her, arms crossed, frowning.

"Did you find something?" Emer asks. "What is going on?"

"Beats me," Jude says. "Jones has been in a right huff for a few minutes now."

"Zara?" Emer says.

"It's just that—well, I suppose I have an idea. A bad idea that you're going to hate, but an idea."

Jude scratches at the invocation on her neck. "Why does this trio only seem to have bad ideas?"

"Yes?" Emer says.

"If Róisín knew the man who killed her and we think the man who killed her is somehow linked to the murders in London—we could . . ." Zara pauses, bites her bottom lip, clears her throat, gathers herself. "Well, we could ask her who he was."

Jude points out the obvious: "Uh, newsflash: Róisín is dead."

"I think . . ." Zara continues. "Well . . . I might have figured out a way for that to not be the case." From behind her, she pulls out a book. Emer spots the word *Nekromanteía* on the spine.

Emer recoils, all the air sucked from her lungs.

"We're back on the necromancy bandwagon, I see," Jude says. "Jones, is there anyone you *don't* want to resurrect?"

"If we could speak to her," Zara says quickly, giving her explanation directly to Emer, "we could ask her who Andy was, how she knew him. This book—it's the same one that Jude has in her library, except this one is pristine. The rituals are all in Latin, but from what I've been able to translate so far—it looks like we weren't too far off with our Elizabeth Báthory theory. A demon can reanimate dead flesh, if there is still flesh. It's a good lead, Emer. It's worth trying."

"It is *not* worth trying," Emer says. "You speak so casually of things you do not understand in the slightest. Offering up an empty human vessel to a demon to wear as a skin is not the same as resurrection. It would *not* be Róisín."

"It might be *partly* Róisín," Zara insists. "Elizabeth Báthory was possessed, and she was still at least *partly* human. Look, I just did the translation on my phone, so I can't be one hundred percent sure it's right, but the book gives a pretty detailed account of the author bringing back a murder victim for long enough to ask them who killed them."

"Wait, really?" Jude asks.

"*Yes.*"

"Your sister is *dead*, Zara, just as my family is *dead*." Emer is harsher than she means to be, her voice low and barbed—but how can Zara not understand that if there was a way to resurrect loved ones, Emer would have done it long ago? "There is no way to bring them back."

"I think you are wrong."

Emer shakes her head.

Zara clears her throat again. "Did you hear what I said? I think you are wrong."

"No," Emer says sharply. She hooks a kerosene lamp into the crook of her elbow and walks out of the room. She needs air. She cannot be here any longer, cannot deal with this silly girl and her obsession. This is madness. *Madness.* She wants to run, hit something, hurt someone, hurt herself. Instead, she goes to the greenhouse, sits alone in the ruined beauty. All of the glass panes have been broken, the plants that once grew here long since withered to husks. Emer stares at the apple orchard as moonlight skims over the ground, at the exposed hand that punctures through the soil.

"Hey." Jude finds her, drawn by the lambent light of the lamp. She sits next to her. Stretches her legs out, mirroring Emer's pose. Knocks her shoe against the edge of Emer's boot.

Emer stares straight ahead. She does not look at her. "Nothing you say will convince me that bringing Róisín back from the dead is a good idea."

Jude takes a breath, sighs it out. "I don't disagree with you—it's a bloody terrible idea—but I still think we should do it."

Emer turns to face her. Jude's voice sounded serious, but surely this must be a joke. "You cannot suggest such things to me."

"Just think about it," Jude pushes. "The women in London don't know who's killing them. Abby Gallagher told the police she was being chased by a demon. She didn't give a name. She must not have known her killer. We saw ourselves that he hides his identity somehow in darkness. So if the murders really are linked—which we think they are now, right?—well, the men who came to your house that day weren't cloaked in shadow, were they? Róisín knew them, or at least one of them. Maybe, if we asked her, she could give us a name."

"You really want me to bring a dead member of my murdered family back to life?"

"Yes," Jude says simply. "I do. If we could get information. If we could get a name. I do." Jude presses the necromancy book into Emer's hands. "Jones was in there trying to translate it, but I thought you would probably do a more accurate job. At least have a skim. See if what she says is possible."

Jude holds the kerosene lamp up while Emer reads. Corpses, the book says, are best when fresh, useless once decomposition has stripped them of skin and gristle. A skeleton cannot speak. Normally, Emer guesses, a body ten years in the ground could not be reanimated—but the women of Lough Leane have not left normal corpses. She reads on. At first she thinks the ritual requires five cups of blood—but no, it is five liters. *Five liters.* As much blood as there is in a human body. It makes a gruesome kind of sense. To reanimate a dead body, the body must first be flush with blood. A life to bring back a life.

"We cannot do this." Emer snaps the book closed. "We do not have enough blood. Even between the three of us, we could not give so much without—"

"There was a lot of blood in the soil," Jude points out. "We could bail it out, see if that works. Look, I know this won't be easy for you. It's a really messed up thing for us to ask of you, and if you want to sit this one out and let Jones and me take a crack at it, that's fine— but we both know I'm rubbish at magic and Jones is probably even worse than me. You're a genius. We need you to make this work."

Emer looks through the gloom at the hand emerging from its shallow grave and thinks of the dozens of women who wear spells of her creation on their skin. They will be huddled in fear tonight, the ones who know. Trapped in their warded houses, waiting for a force they cannot stop to come and strangle the life from them, cut the power from them.

It seems a reprehensible evil, to give a demon a dead human body, to allow it full access to the corporeal realm.

It is a greater evil, though, to stand by and allow women to be killed.

"Bring out all the kerosene lamps," Emer says eventually.

"Is that a yes?" Jude asks.

"Kerosene lamps, spirits, rubbing alcohol, oil—anything that burns hot and fast."

"Emer, what are we doing?"

"If we are going to raise an undead, we need a contingency plan. Demons hate fire. We need to soak it with flammable liquid before we . . ." Emer swallows. "Before."

"That sounds very much like a yes."

Emer nods. If it saves even one more woman. "It is a yes."

# TWENTY

THE NIGHT is heavy when they begin to dig. Kerosene lamps burn softly around them, lighting the orchard where Emer's dead family sleeps. The sounds of the forest come to them, leave them on edge: the screaming of foxes, the rustle of wild things drawn near, curious about these strangers in their midst. The earth is soft as a bruised peach and parts easily beneath their hands. The mire is wet with blood. Each handful of removed mud leaves a pool of red in its wake, like digging in wet sand at the beach.

There are huge clots within the soil, gelatinous pillows of black-red tissue. Emer watches Jude as she pulls one out, births it with a sucking sound. It is the size of her head. It wobbles for a moment in Jude's hands, fetid and placental, then splits and slumps out of her grasp, falling back to the ground with a splatter.

Jude goes pale. "Yeah, that'll be a no from me," she says.

For the rest of the hour it takes to bring up part of the body, Jude sits and watches from the roots of a nearby apple tree.

Eventually, Róisín's face and shoulder begin to emerge from the fen. Emer has seen many springtime births on this very land, slimy, feeble creatures slipping from their mothers in the dawn light. This is like that, but more foul. The earth does not want to give her up. This is a good thing. Emer wants most of the corpse's body to remain buried, its other hand and both of its legs trapped in its grave just in case.

Emer pours water over the body and wipes the blood and mud from its face. The muck comes away slowly. For a time, it feels as though she is doing nothing but pushing sludge around. Soon, though, bare, clear skin shows through. It is waterlogged from soaking for so long, pale and puckered but freakishly whole after a decade in the ground.

*Róisín.*

Emer places her palm against her cousin's cold cheek. She was not much older than Emer when she died. "Hand me the lamps."

Jude and Zara do as she asks. Emer opens each of them and pours the kerosene over the exposed parts of Róisín's body.

"Is this part of the ritual?" Zara asks.

"No," Emer says. "A contingency plan. In case she gets out. In case *it* gets out. You two need to stand far away."

"Why?" Zara asks.

"What comes back will not be human. If it gets free of its grave—the book says, it will not eat me. They do not seem to consume their creators." Emer hopes that this is true. "I cannot promise you the same amnesty."

"Eat you?" Jude says. "*Eat you?* Can't you just sic Bael on it if things get out of hand?"

Emer shakes her head. "Demons will not eat the undead. The book makes that clear also. Bael cannot stop it. Nothing can stop it."

The ritual is brutal and requires more blood than any spell Emer has ever seen. She hopes the demons in the vicinity will not be too picky about the freshness of it. That they will still accept it as payment, that it will flow, clotted and gelatinous as it is, through her cousin's veins for long enough for Emer to ask the woman's corpse who killed her.

Once the pail they found in the house is full of blood from their digging, Emer opens her backpack and presses a box of matches into Zara's palm. "Just in case," she says. Zara nods grimly.

Emer crouches by Róisín's corpse and forces its mouth open.

"You pour the blood into her mouth while I recite the spell," Emer says.

Zara looks faint and peaky, her brow beaded with sweat.

"Begin," Emer says.

Zara swallows and starts to pour.

Emer reads the words from the book. Wind begins to whip around the clearing. Emer lets her vision go unfocused and tries to see beyond the veil. The faint stink of sulfur drifts to her. Bael is near her, as always. It noses at the bucket of dead blood. It snorts in disgust and tries to knock it from Zara's hands. Zara yelps. Emer steadies the bucket.

"Hey!" she says to her demon. "That's enough from you. I know you're too high-and-mighty, but some of your friends might be interested."

Bael does not understand her words, but it must understand her tone. It huffs at her and drags its long arms along the ground as it skulks away.

There are not many hell creatures out here in the woods. They prefer to be in cities. They like to hide in the dark crevices of human homes. In attics, under beds. They like to lie in wait, like bats, for witches to throw scraps of human souls their way.

Still, some are out here, out in the woods. One comes cautiously to the edge of the clearing and watches them for a time. Emer beckons it to her. "Come," she says in Akkadian. "Come and see what I have for you."

It does not want to come. It smells the old blood, is not enticed by it.

Emer watches as Bael goes and speaks to it. They are too far away for her to overhear any voces mysticae and so she does not double over and vomit from their demon language. The wary beast looks over Bael's shoulder. It stares at Emer, or at least it seems to, but it does not have eyes. It speaks to Bael some more.

Emer raises her eyebrows and sucks her cheeks in between her teeth to stop herself from smiling.

Bael is telling it who and what she is, she thinks. Bael is convincing it to trust her.

The creature comes out from the wood. It is a feeble thing, no taller than Emer herself and skinny as a reed.

It sniffs at decade-old blood pooling in Róisín's mouth and recoils. Bael huffs. Emer swears it rolls its nonexistent eyes, as if to say I told you so.

"Drink it, you ingrate," Emer mutters. "You'll never get so much blood again in one sitting."

"Drink," Emer says again, this time in Latin. "Drink of the blood and take up the body."

Emer motions to the corpse of her cousin.

The demon looks suspicious. Rightfully so. It is not a fresh corpse. It is not fresh blood.

Still, the offer is too good. It is not every day a witch wanders through the woods and offers blood and the chance to inhabit a corporeal form. The chance to have hands and teeth and a gullet that work in the human realm. The chance to feed whenever and wherever they choose.

The demon nods. It is such a human gesture that Emer is taken aback. It must have spent some time around people, watching them.

Zara continues pouring the blood into Róisín's open mouth. The blood gurgles down what remains of her throat with the sluggish speed of water through a blocked drain.

Emer resumes chanting the words from her the book. The spell is written in Latin by an excellent speaker of the language, someone almost as good as Emer herself.

Zara finishes pouring the blood. Emer finishes speaking the words.

They watch.

They wait.

The demon climbs into what is left of Róisín. The corpse sucks in a great gasp of air. The eyes open. The lips peel back to reveal the teeth, yellow as corn.

Róisín Byrne lives again.

The creature turns its head an inch. Its dead eyes slide over Emer and lock on to Zara. Its nostrils flare as it takes in the scent of the girl. The teeth begin to gnash. Already it hungers for blood, but it is trapped in the sucking fen of its grave, entangled with the bodies of the rest of Emer's family.

"Listen, demon," Emer says in English. Róisín spoke English; the demon should be able to understand her. "Who killed the body you inhabit? Do you know?"

The corpse gnashes at her. Emer takes out her dagger and slices a familiar line of pain down her left arm. She drips blood into the creature's mouth. It splutters and chokes on it, disgusted by the offering. It will not feed from her because she has created it. It wants someone else. Anyone else.

Emer wipes her blade on her sleeve and hands it to Zara.

"It wants your blood," she says.

Zara riffles around in her satchel and pulls out a little tube of hand sanitizer and starts vigorously disinfecting the knife.

The demon creature snaps and wrestles as Zara works. Emer watches it with increasing concern. She hoped, because her cousin was small and spent so long desiccating in the ground, that her body would be a weak vessel for the monster that now inhabits it. That is not the case. It is unsticking itself from the mire. It is squirming and writhing and gnashing with such vigor that soon its arms will be free of the muck and it will be able to use them to dig itself out.

"Enough," Emer says to Zara. "We must hurry."

"Okay, okay, fine!" Zara touches the tip of the knife to the inside of her arm and looks away.

"Wait," Jude says, suddenly with them again, before Zara has made the cut. "Take mine."

"Are you sure?" Emer asks.

"I'm used to pain—and what's another scar at this point?"

Jude kneels in the blood and mud next to Emer and offers up the translucent skin of her forearm. She gasps when Emer's knife cuts through. Emer turns Jude's arm over and holds it above the corpse's mouth. Its lips part greedily as drops of Jude's blood fall onto its teeth and tongue.

Emer leans close to the demon's ear. "Tell me who killed you," she says quietly, "and I will feed you the blood of ten men."

"Volkov," the corpse rasps.

"Who?"

"Volkov," it says again, louder this time. "Volkov, Volkov, Volkov."

"Volkov?" Emer asks. The name sounds familiar but she cannot place why. "Andy Volkov."

"Yes," the creatures growls. "Andy Volkov. That is the name."

"Who is he? How did he find us?"

The creature's free arm shoots up from the mud. It grasps Emer's face, pulls her down close to its lips. "I will eat the world," it says in guttural Akkadian.

It shoves her away so hard that she falls. By the time she rights herself, the creature has both of its hands free and is shimmying its legs out of its grave, its pregnant belly bulbous in front of it. Its eyes are locked firmly on Zara.

"Zara!" Emer yells. "Burn it!"

"I'm trying!" There is a match in her hand already. She stabs it again and again against the striking surface, but it doesn't light. Her shaking hands drop the box. Matches spill everywhere, ruined by the wetness of the earth. Zara swears. The creature births itself, a rush of clots and muck slipping into the hole it leaves behind. Zara is kneeling, fumbling in the fen—and Róisín is free.

Then—the sound Emer has been waiting for. The strike and flare of a match lighting.

Zara says, "Yes!" as she throws the flame.

It finds its mark. The creature is so soaked in kerosene that it goes up in an instant.

Emer closes her eyes and saves herself the horror of watching her cousin's body die for a second time, but that does not block out the screams. The demon is furious. It has been betrayed. It runs across the clearing, into the trees, looking for a way to douse the flames that consume it. It does not make it very far before the screaming stops.

Emer opens her eyes. A small flame burns just beyond the tree line.

The meadow is quiet once again, inhabited only by the dead.

Róisín Byrne is gone.

# TWENTY-ONE

*HELL OF a day,* Jude thinks as they open the door to their hotel room in Killarney. Private jet in the morning, zombie in the evening, lousy hotel for the night. It's not the kind of place she used to stay at when she was traveling with her family. It has no suites, no personal butler, no champagne or chocolates waiting in the room when they arrive—but after the day they've had, it's practically heaven.

Nobody has spoken since the meadow, since they reburied Róisín's burned body and Emer set new wards to keep the whole place hidden.

The room is a triple with a double and a single bed. Jones heads straight for the single, immediately shoves on her glasses, and begins furiously typing on her laptop. The three of them saw necromancy today, up close. They saw its rotten teeth and yellowed bones. They smelled its putrid insides, leaking from its orifices, its eyes roaming hungrily over flesh.

If necromancy is what Jones has been planning since Savannah died, today had to have sucked for her. No one should see someone they love like that, their skin a puppet for a hungry demon.

Jones on the single bed leaves only the double for Emer and Jude.

They both stare at it. It is much smaller than the one they shared at Jude's house.

Emer says nothing, just drops her bag on the bed and goes into the bathroom to clean up.

Jude sits down on her side of the bed and twiddles her fingers. Occasionally, she glances at the bathroom door.

"If you like her," Jones says, "maybe you should just tell her."

"Who says I like her?"

"Jude, for goodness' sake. You stare at her all the time."

"I *do not* like her. I loathe her."

"Sure."

When Emer is done, Jude showers away the day's grime. The shallow cut Emer made on her arm stings beneath the stream of water, but in a good way. It's the kind of pain that Jude's brain understands. Normal pain. Mortal pain. Not pain caused by a demonic force.

Jude puts the plug in the drain and sits under the searing stream of the shower while the tub fills. The water that rises around her is black as ink, as always. Jude watches as it rises up her thigh, a tide flooding a barren island.

Tomorrow, she will see her family. Tomorrow, she will see her father and older brothers, her nieces and nephews and cousins. Tomorrow, she will walk into Wolf Hall and drink champagne and eat caviar and wander like a ghost through her old life. All this she wants, but what she longs for most is this: Elijah. To spend time with Eli, to be the way they used to be, them against the world. Jude can hardly believe it. There's a cavern inside of her, a huge, aching emptiness that can only be filled by home—and for her, home is a person. Home is him. Finally, finally, she will fill the abyss in her chest, even if only for a night. It won't be the perfect reunion she has longed for. There's still the matter of her decomposing soul—but it is something.

Jude turns the shower off and soaks in the dark water. She messages Eli, asks him what he's wearing to the wedding. Elijah messages back a picture of Harry Styles in a dress. **Do you think Lawrence will approve?** he asks. Jude laughs, but her smile soon turns to sadness. She wonders who Elijah would be if he'd had the luck of growing up in another family. A kinder, warmer family. A family who supported him to become an artist, instead of packing him off to Oxford and expecting him to become a banker or whatever it is Lawrence deems appropriate for his progeny.

**I think you should secretly transfer to fine arts**, Jude messages back. **I'm being serious by the way.**

Elijah responds with a bunch of eye roll emojis and then says: **Artists don't get banker bonuses, Jude. Nor do they get included in Lawrence's will. I'll do some watercolor painting in my retirement. Only five decades to go!**

When the water turns cold, Jude pulls the plug.

When she's re-dressed, Jones tells her she couldn't find anything on the internet about anyone called Andy Volkov. A fake name, maybe? Or maybe witch hunters just don't have social media profiles or podcasts or TikTok accounts dedicated to their killing of women. Jude's stomach growls. There's no room service—of course—so after Jones has also showered and changed, the three of them walk in search of food. Killarney is a small place, the kind of town that only seems to have one main road.

They stop at an Indian restaurant and order food to go. When they're back in the room, they turn on the TV and lay out their feast on the floor and eat in silence. The news comes on. There are vigils in London for the murdered women. There are also protests. Protests at the lack of police transparency in taking so long to publicly link the crimes and protests at the suggestion that women should not go out alone at night.

Jude snaps a picture of the banner crawl—*Women given curfew in London as new Ripper rampages*—and sends it to Reese with a message: **I told you so.**

Jones mutes the TV but lets the news footage keep rolling. "So how does this guy—the London Ripper—who is somehow linked to Andy Volkov, but not Andy Volkov—figure out how to do what has never been done before?" she asks.

"He would need to have in-depth knowledge of and access to the occult," Emer says. "A greater understanding of it than even most witches do. Andy knew Róisín—but she was a teenager, she would not have known how to do what the Ripper is doing."

"The next generation of hunter, maybe?" Jude ponders. "Emer said he was young. Could he be Andy Volkov's son? Taking the family hunting business to the next level?"

An image of Vera Clarke flashes on the TV screen. "Oh," Jones says quietly.

"What?" Jude asks. "What does *oh* mean?"

"I just . . . we might've missed something."

"Yes?" Jude pushes.

"At all of the other crime scenes, the killer made no attempt to hide the body. And the crime scenes are becoming ostentatious, dramatic. The killer *wants* people to find his victims. So why did he hide Vera Clarke at the bottom of a lake? What makes her different?"

"No clue," Jude says.

Jones exhales. "You don't watch enough crime shows. The killer *knew* her. *Personally.* That's why he hid her. Because he didn't want her to be found. Because she is the first victim that can properly be linked back to him somehow."

"So who the heck is he, and how is he connected to the hunters—and Vera?" Jones muses.

"Let's see if we can't find out," Jude says. She calls Saul, who grumbles for a while about how she takes him for granted, doesn't treat him right. Jude offers to pay him a nice little bonus, which perks him right up, and then she tells him what they need: a deeper dive into Vera Clarke. Why she left her job. What she did in her spare time. Who her friends were.

Once Saul is on the case, the three of them dive into the pile of books they carted back with them from Lough Leane, in search of how, exactly, this bastard is pulling this off.

"I think . . . maybe I've found something," Jones says after a while. "At least, maybe I have a theory?"

"You sound so confident," Jude says. "Lay it on us."

"There are a few passages in this book about the link between the soul and the body. It's all in Middle English, so it's hard to parse, but I *think* it's talking about people who've died briefly and come back to life."

"Pray tell, what does it say?"

"That they 'wander in search of their lost souls.' "

"The soul and the body separate at the moment of death," Emer confirms.

Jude doesn't follow. "Explain."

Jones takes off her glasses and rubs her eyes. "How about this," she says after a while. "We know from Chopra that he kills them slowly. Why? Because right when the women are about to die, he makes the demons tethered to them an offer. They can stay attached to the dying woman and have their meal ticket ripped away. Or they can tether to him."

"Demons do not make deals with men."

"Maybe, in this case, the demons don't have much choice in the matter." Jude gets down on her knees and puts her hands out in front of her as though she is choking someone trapped beneath her weight. She tightens and loosens her grip on her imaginary prey over and over again. It is what he did to her, when he was on top of her in her house. Coaxed her toward unconsciousness and then eased off. She would suck in a great lungful of air and see the black spots dimming from her vision. Then it would begin again.

Jones looks sick. "Is the demonstration really necessary?"

An idea falls into Jude's head: "He's loosening the soul from the body."

"What?"

"If you stab someone or shoot someone and they die instantly, their soul is immediately released from their flesh, right? Ripped away, gone to some netherworld."

Emer nods.

"If you coax them toward death slowly, if you take them to the brink and then pull them back from the edge over and over again—you might reach a point where the body and the soul are only very tenuously linked. That's when he cuts the invocations out of them—and gives them to himself." A stunning realization hits her, a possible way to save herself: "I have to die," she says suddenly.

"What?" Emer says.

Jude smacks herself in the forehead. Of course, *of course*. "I have to die. Or at least get really, really close to death. Just for a little bit, a few seconds." Jude clicks her fingers and points at Emer and Jones. "I need one of you to kill me."

They both stare at her. "Yeah, I think that's our cue to go to bed," Jones says.

"No, I mean it, listen to me. We can do exactly what he's doing to them to me. Take me to the edge of death, cut my invocation out of me, bring me back to life, and—"

"May I remind you that your last brilliant plan almost got us *all* killed," Emer says, "and this plan is even more spectacularly bad than that one. Besides—how does this help us catch the killer? How does this help anyone but Jude Wolf?"

"Jesus, Emer, you act like I'm not here resurrecting dead broads with you to try and catch this guy. What's so wrong with trying to fix myself along the way?"

"If he is doing it the way you are suggesting—which we do not know for sure—you would need to attach your bad invocation to someone else. Do you see any volunteers in this room?"

"I . . ." Jude sinks down onto the bed. "Shit." She had forgotten about that part. It's not enough to die. You have to somehow tether your unwanted demon to someone else as well.

Another day, another crushing disappointment.

In bed, Jude scrolls through Instagram, looking for Volkovs in London. "'Richard Wortley-Volkov III, a.k.a. Dickie,'" she reads from her phone when she finds a suitable candidate—the only youngish Volkov in London whose socials aren't private. "Jesus, what a name. He's twenty-four, Oxford grad, works for his daddy's finance company, naturally. God, he even seems like a serial killer." Jude shows his pictures to Emer, who squints at it and says, "Maybe," which is good enough for Jude. "Jones, give me your phone."

"Why?" Zara asks.

"I'm going to make a fake Instagram profile for you and slide into Dickie's DMs."

"Me? Why me? Why don't one of you do it?"

"Well, Emer can't do it in case Dickie recognizes her, and I can't do it because he'll definitely recognize me. Our families travel in the same circles. He'll be like, 'Aren't you that billionaire's junkie-lesbian daughter?' It won't work. It has to be you."

"Why does it always have to be me?"

"What's a sexy name?" Jude asks as she's making Zara's fake profile. "I always wanted a girlfriend called . . . Scarlett. Yes, you can be Scarlett. Scarlett . . . Twisleton-Flynn. Dickie will love that. You are an up-and-coming young lawyer with an Oxford education."

"I can't be a lawyer."

"Why not?"

"Because I don't know anything about the law!"

"Please, Jones, you know everything about everything. Read some Wikipedia pages before the date. It's fine, he's not going to ask you anything about the law, he's going to be staring at your boobs and telling you everything he knows about hunting witches and breaking tethers with their demons."

Emer sits in silence at the foot of the bed, turning the pages of her grimoire, again calling the numbers of the women they weren't able to warn that first day. There are no more answers. Emer must be thinking what Jude is thinking: that these women are already dead. Splayed out on bloody pentagrams or hidden away in dark ponds, their corpses weighted down among the weeds and eels.

Emer wards the hotel room before they go to sleep, walking around the perimeter of the room and splashing her blood at the walls. When the warding is done, Emer comes to check on Jude's wounds. Between appeasing Jude's angry demon and the hungry dead, Emer has opened Jude's flesh twice now. It has bonded them, this sacrifice of blood and pain. Jude feels it. That something has shifted between them. Emer sits closer to her than is necessary and her fingers linger on Jude's skin as she re-dresses her cuts.

They turn out the lights and fall asleep as they did in Jude's bed, turned to face each other on opposite sides of the mattress, a single arm outstretched toward the other. In the low light, Jude studies Emer's face. Emer watches her watching her and does not look away, does not seem to mind Jude's unbroken gaze. There is depth to Emer's brown eyes that Jude never appreciated before. Perhaps you need to know someone's history before you can see the fathoms in their eyes. Jude sees it all now, Emer's story laid bare. The horror, the sadness, the loneliness—yet something new is there, too.

A twinkle, perhaps, when she looks at Jude.

A spark.

# TWENTY-TWO

**IT IS** early, pre-dawn, on Sunday morning. In the airport bathroom before they board Jude's family's plane, Zara sits on the toilet and opens the book she stole from Emer's family home. The pages are tissue thin and nicotine yellow with age. Zara's heart is a thing lodged high in her chest, jumping hard inside her throat.

She could bring Savannah back *tonight*.

Can she do this?

*Should* she do this?

Seeing Róisín brought back from ten years in the ground was gruesome. Zara's insides feel wet and sagging at the thought, infested with some unnamable darkness. She puts her hands on the book, lets it sear her palms. The hurt feels good. Grounding. There is a sound coming from inside of it, or maybe it's just in Zara's head. A hiss, a gurgle. A whisper that says, in a voice that is not her own, *You did not come this far to only come this far.*

Should she really go further?

For a year, she has been determined to bend the rules of reality itself to bring Savannah back. She tracked down a witch. She confirmed that magic is real. It seems impossibly cruel that she should not get what she wants now.

Small memories flicker through her. The time she skinned her knee and the wound crusted to her pajama pants overnight, how Savannah put her in the shower with her clothes on and then peeled the wet fabric away so the scab wouldn't rip. A terrible burn on Savannah's hand, small but deep and bubbling, Zara only learning later that it was from hot glue dripping onto her sister's skin while she made decorations for Zara's surprise birthday party. The time they sliced open their palms and pressed their hands together and mixed their blood like they'd seen in a movie, their souls and bodies forever linked.

Love was pain. Pain was love.

That was the way it had always been with them.

Róisín had been long buried in her grave. It hasn't even been a year for Savannah. There must be more of her left. There has to be. More memories. More essence. More strength. Zara feels certain that if she brought Savannah back, Sav would be able to fight the demon for control of her body. She could win. It seems improbable—but so many improbable things have happened to them.

*We are magic,* Sav said the night after they both got their period on the same day. *We can do anything.*

Why should this be any different? Why shouldn't Savannah be special? She *was* special. Lightning-haired, a girl crackling with energy.

Zara peels her stinging fingers from the book.

*I did not come this far to only come this far.*

Outside the bathroom, she finds Jude grinning. This is never a good sign.

"What?" Zara asks.

"Guess who's going on a lunch date with Dickie Boy when we land?" Jude makes finger guns at her.

"I can't today." Zara plans to go straight to the cemetery. The thought of Savannah being alive by tonight is too great a temptation to ignore. "I have plans."

"Oh, you have plans? You have *plans*? I'm sorry, I didn't realize stopping the serial killer who murdered your sister was second on your list of things to do today. I, for one, have a wedding to get ready for, but I'm still making time. What are you so busy doing?"

Zara can't come up with a good excuse in time, so she relents. "Never mind. What do I need to do?"


IT'S MIDDAY WHEN Jude pulls up in Soho and points across the road to a restaurant with big Art Deco glass doors.

Jude chose a dress for Zara from a store down the street. It's a mustard minidress with a black lace collar. It cost £2,400. Zara feels exposed in it. It's slightly too small for her and sits tight at the waist and shoulders.

"Remind me again why I couldn't wear my own clothes?" Zara asks as Jude puts the car in park and Zara tries to pull the dress down over her black stockings.

"Because you are trying to convince him you're a slick young lawyer," Jude says, "not a Virginia Woolf impersonator."

"Gee, thanks. I don't know. I don't look anything like myself."

"That, my dear, is precisely the point."

"I've never been on a date before. What am I supposed to say? 'How do you feel about witches?'"

"You ask him what his favorite TV show growing up was, and he'll answer with something banal and boring that he thinks makes him sound interesting, like *The Wire*, and then you say, 'Mine was *Sabrina the Teenage Witch*. Love the reboot, by the way.' Then you wait and see how he reacts."

Zara exhales. "This is a really bad idea."

"We've all got to do our part, Jones."

"Wait, I think I see him. Emer, what do you think? Could that be *him*?"

Emer stares at him and shakes her head. "It . . . is hard to know. I only saw him for a moment, and his face was covered in ash. It *could* be him."

"Okay. Great. Date with a possible supernatural serial killer. Easy. I'll see you soon."

They meet on the street in front of the restaurant that Dickie has booked for lunch. Dickie is handsome in a way that none of the boys around Zara's age are handsome. The girls at her school fawn over boys who drive cars or sell weed or have lots of followers on TikTok. Dickie is dressed as though he's never rolled a joint, in sockless brown leather brogues, a finely woven sweater, and a bone-colored trench coat that looks very expensive. His blond hair is slicked back and parted harshly, in a style that was probably popular a century ago. He is tall and broad-shouldered and very clearly a *man*. A man, not a boy. A totally different species from what Zara is used to interacting with.

Zara feels suddenly very seventeen and very vulnerable. How the hell was this ever supposed to work? How the hell is she supposed to convince this actual man that she's a twenty-three-year-old lawyer?

"Scarlett?" Dickie asks when he sees her. He does not smile.

"Yes, hello, I'm Scarlett." For some reason, Zara's accent comes out affected, like the Received Pronunciation of the royal family. Yikes. Now she has to keep that up the whole date. "Nice to meet you, Dickie." She sticks her hand out to shake his, which he ignores.

"You look lovely. I like your dress. Is it Alexander McQueen?"

"Yes," Zara says, though she has no idea. She was in such a tizzy in the store she never actually managed to take in the brand. "McQueen is my favorite designer."

"*Was*, you mean. Before his death."

"Yes, that's exactly what I mean, obviously. Is yours . . ." Zara racks her brain for a designer. Any designer. "Valentino?"

Dickie laughs, but in a smug way that makes Zara feel stupid. "Have you ever seen a Valentino coat before, Scarlett? No, this is Brunello Cucinelli. I like to support British designers as much as I can, but you can't go past the Italians when it comes to cashmere."

"Silly me. How could I not have known?"

"Right, well, it's rather cold out. Shall we?"

Zara watches him as they walk inside and hand their coats in. Dickie's hands are soft, his fingernails manicured. Did this man—this marble statue with slick golden hair—close his pretty fingers around Savannah's throat and wring the life from her?

The restaurant is gold and opulent. Zara and Dickie are seated in a blue velvet booth by the window. Zara can see Jude's car parked across the road.

"Can I get you anything to drink?" a waiter asks.

"Bollinger," Zara says quickly. "Please."

"Sparkling water for me."

When the waiter goes, Dickie leans forward. "You look younger than I was expecting."

"Well, I'll take that as a compliment. You, however, look far older than I thought you would be."

Dickie does not take this as the joke it was meant to be. "Do I?"

"No. I'm just teasing you."

"Oh. Right."

Zara clears her throat. This is not going well. "So, this is a nice restaurant."

"Well, it wasn't my first choice, but you know how difficult it is to get reservations in London on short notice. I would have preferred the Dorchester, but beggars can't be choosers, can they?"

Dickie flicks out his napkin and folds it over his lap. "So, Scarlett Twisleton-Flynn—wonderful name, by the way, I think I know a few of your cousins—what's your story? Give me the lowdown. Who are you? Where are you going?"

Zara forces a laugh. "My name is Scarlett Twisleton-Flynn, and I'm an alcoholic."

"Oh God, are you? You probably shouldn't have ordered Bollinger, then."

"No . . . That was a joke."

"So, wait, sorry, you're not an alcoholic?"

"No. It's just what they say at—"

"You have an odd sense of humor."

"Okay, well. Let me try again. I went to Oxford—"

"Which college were you at?"

"Um . . ." Zara tries to remember the name of a college. Is Jesus one? There are several that sound religious, she thinks. One about saints? "Magdalen," Zara says eventually. That's one, she is sure of it. But the way she says it—like Mary Magdalene—feels wrong.

Dickie frowns at her. "It's pronounced *maudlin*."

"Right, yes. Of course. I—sorry. I always get confused, even now. It trips up my tongue. How about you?"

"Corpus Christi."

"Oh yes. I love the . . . grounds of Corpus Christi."

"Yes. They are nice, and the architecture is spectacular. Anyway—back to you."

"So I went to Magdalen"—Zara is careful to pronounce it *maudlin*—"and I decided to become a lawyer. So that's what I do now."

"What area of the law?"

Zara tries to remember what Amal Clooney does. "Human rights and lots of . . . international . . . stuff."

Dickie scoffs. "No money in that, is there?"

"I'm really only in it to marry George Clooney one day."

"I do believe he's already married."

"That was another joke."

"Oh." Dickie forces a pained smile.

*God*, thinks Zara. *Put me out of my misery.*

The waiter arrives then. Dickie orders for them both, without asking Zara if that's okay, without asking her if she has any allergies or preferences. Sturgeon caviar, a dozen of the Jersey rock oysters and steak tartare to begin, none of which Zara has ever eaten before. Then lobster, crab, and shrimp pelmeni (Zara does not know what this is until she checks the description on the menu—Russian dumplings, apparently) and stinking cheese soufflé. Last,

the mains: the lobster macaroni and cheese to share and a chateaubriand each, complete with truffle jus and truffle French fries
on the side. Zara has also never eaten lobster or soufflé or truffle
before, nor can she recall ever ordering steak at a restaurant (that
is what chateaubriand is, according to the menu). Whenever she
and Savannah could afford to eat something they hadn't cooked
themselves, it was at a chicken shop or a PizzaExpress if they were
feeling fancy.

As unpleasant as Dickie is, this may be the first and last time
Zara gets to eat like this, so she figures she will enjoy it.

There is some more small talk, and Dickie says some more
obnoxious things. Zara presses the button on the table that says *Press
for Champagne*, and more Bollinger arrives. The caviar is served,
along with the oysters and steak tartare. Zara doesn't tell Dickie she
has no idea what she's doing. Instead, she watches him—the way
he squeezes lemon juice onto his oyster and then a dash of Tabasco
before downing it in one go—and copies what he does. The oyster is
good and salty, not as gross in texture as she expected it to be. Zara
eats a second and a third, and would have liked more, but Dickie has
already eaten the rest. Next she tries the steak tartare, with some
trepidation, because she has always been told you're not supposed
to eat uncooked meat or raw eggs, and here both are served as a delicacy. The tartare, too, is surprisingly delicious, with tiny pops of salti-
ness from the capers. Dickie keeps talking about himself, and Zara
keeps pretending to listen, all the while savoring the expensive food.
Eventually, when their plates are cleared away and Dickie seems to
be in a better mood, Zara decides to press on.

"Let's do some rapid-fire questions," she says. The champagne
is making her feel bubbly and light.

"Okay."

"Favorite color."

Dickie fake laughs. "I'm a grown man. I do not have a favorite color."

Douche. "Okay, then. Favorite TV show when you were growing up."

"Oh, I didn't really watch TV. My favorite book, though, was Proust. *In Search of Lost Time*. You could not pry it from my ten-year-old hands."

*Douche douche douche.* "Mine was *Sabrina the Teenage Witch*." Zara says it so quickly it comes out like one long word, like *supercalifragilisticexpialidocious*. "I loved the reboot, too, by the way. The one on Netflix. It's a crime it was canceled, I couldn't get enough of it."

Dickie goes silent and leans back in his chair.

"Did I say something wrong?" Zara asks.

"Tell me, what is there to love about the depiction of a teenage girl offering her soul up to the devil?"

Zara almost laughs. Jude was right. "It's not real, it's—"

"What if it was real? Bear with me for a moment, Scarlett. What if the devil and witchcraft were real, and Sabrina the Teenage Witch encouraged innocent young women to seek them out, to the detriment of their immortal souls?"

"I've always thought of witchcraft as more feminist and empowering."

"It's not," Dickie snaps, before taking a breath to regain his composure. "It is not empowering. It is damning. I don't expect you to understand, but my family has done a lot of work to . . . combat the occult."

Holy hell. "Oh? Tell me more."

"Well, I can't speak about it too freely."

Zara shifts toward him and presses her breasts together with her elbows. "Now you're just teasing me, Dickie." Dickie looks at once suspicious and like he wants very badly to brag about how many women his family has murdered. "Come on, you can't just dangle a treat like that in front of me. Spill."

Zara's previous attempts at flirting have failed, but this one seems to work.

Dickie smirks and leans in. Their faces are close together, conspiratorial. "I come from a very old family. We can trace our lineage all the way back to King James. King James, of course, was the author of *Daemonologie*."

Zara knows this. *Daemonologie* was one of the first books she read after Savannah died.

"We hunted witches for him, and in return, he gave my ancestors their land. Most of which we still hold today."

"I mean, who wasn't a witch hunter in medieval Europe?"

Dickie seems offended by this. "Most people, actually."

Damn it, Zara. Get it together. "Sorry. Go on."

"Anyway, it's become a sort of . . . family tradition. Something passed down from father to son. It seems very archaic in modern times, I know, but there is still a surprising need for it."

Zara's heart is beating fast. "For . . . hunting witches?"

"Well, the *reeducation* of witches. You would be appalled at the number of young women who are interested in the allure of the occult. I will never understand it."

Zara can't help herself. "Well, it's about power, isn't it? About how disenfranchised you are and how much you're willing to sacrifice to change that."

"The sacrifice of one's soul is never worth it."

"That's easy for you to say. You have power already."

"Are you telling me you would side with the women who offer up bits of their immortal soul to the devil?"

"All I'm saying is, why does it have to have anything to do with you?"

"Scarlett, you don't need to be personally offended on the behalf of these women. We are not talking about women like *you* here. We are talking about uneducated, impoverished women in unfortunate circumstances who—instead of working hard to pull themselves up—make the easy choice and turn to the devil for salvation."

"That sounds like bullshit, Dickie."

"Excuse me?"

Zara clears her throat. "One more question, if you'll indulge me."

Dickie draws a sharp breath through flared nostrils. His lips are tightly pursed. "Fine."

"Let's say I believe you, which I don't, by the way." Zara smiles, tries to soften the sharp edge of her voice. "Are you trying to tell me that *you* hunt—sorry, *reeducate*—witches, Dickie? You, personally? You're out there like some Batman-type vigilante, ridding the city of evil women?"

"I wish. My grandfather was the last real hunter in our family. My father was morally opposed—a bleeding-heart liberal. Everything I know is through my grandfather, may he rest in peace. The glory days of witch hunting are long past—bring back public burnings, I say—but my grandfather certainly had some tales that would put hair on your chest. God, if I knew how to track one down, I'd happily—"

The mains arrive then. The lobster mac and cheese, and the truffle fries, and the dish Zara has been waiting for: the steak. They do not talk about witches or witchcraft or demons or the devil while they eat. Dickie has not killed a witch, does not seem to be the Ripper—Zara is certain he'd brag about it if he was—so she decides to enjoy the food. Dickie drones on and on about his job in finance. He talks a lot about cryptocurrency and NFTs, how he bought and sold a Bored Ape at exactly the right time and made several hundred thousand pounds in a couple of weeks. Zara tries to ignore him, tries to savor the taste of the chateaubriand with truffle jus. Everything is rich and decadent and delicious. When the bill comes, Dickie pays. Zara makes no offer or attempt to contribute, not that she could even if he had expected her to.

"You've intrigued me, Dickie." Zara makes one last attempt at being flirtatious. "Let's say I want to find out more about, uh, combatting the occult. Where would I start?"

"Really? You didn't seem all that interested."

Zara shrugs. "If witchcraft really is as bad as you say it is, I feel like I should be doing something to . . . save these women's souls. You know?"

"Exactly, Scarlett." Dickie hits the table with his palm. "That's exactly what I'm talking about. They need our help. They need their souls to be cleansed. Well, I'm thrilled. We don't have many women involved in our society, unfortunately, but we're pushing hard for diversity."

Dickie pulls out a pen. Zara tries not to scowl.

"Go here." Dickie scribbles down an address on a napkin. "Speak to them. It's all very hush-hush. We have to be very underground these days. You can imagine what the feminazis would have to say about what we do. Go along, meet some people, see how you can get involved in the cause."

"So there are people here—hunters—who've actually . . . you know . . . 'reeducated' a witch?"

"Oh, yes, definitely. A lot of the younger generation haven't popped their cherry yet, but all of the old guard are active. Some of them are against the idea of female hunters, but they're dinosaurs. They need to get with the times. Well, Scarlett, it was interesting meeting you. I have an afternoon engagement, so I had better get going."

"Oh sure, yeah. Well, goodbye, Dickie. Thanks for lunch."

"Right, well. I have your number." Dickie looks down at the napkin in Zara's hand. "Perhaps—Don't tell anyone there about your soft spot for Sabrina."

Zara nods as he stands and leaves her at the table alone.

# TWENTY-THREE

**JUDE CHECKS** the time on her phone again.

Sitting in the car outside the restaurant waiting for Zara feels so . . . stagnant. She wants to be doing something other than drumming her fingers against her steering wheel and grinding her teeth. Her heart feels full of little hollows. The blood is pumping wrong, leaking into her lungs, something in her chest flapping with each beat.

The wedding is tonight.

Jude tightens her fingers around the wheel until all the little bones in her hand begin to ache. *Hurry up, Jones.*

"Relax," Emer says, touching Jude's shoulder. "Eat your food."

"Do you think she's still alive in there?" Jude asks a minute later around a mouthful of egg salad sandwich. Eating Pret prepackaged lunches while Zara gets to chow down on caviar and oysters. Such is the injustice of Jude's life. "Oh, wait—there he is."

Dickie emerges from the restaurant looking miffed. Then again, he looked miffed going in, so perhaps he just has resting dick face. A sleek black car pulls up. Dickie climbs into it, glides away into the early afternoon. Zara comes out a minute after him, looking peaky, and crosses the road to get into the back seat of Jude's car.

"Anything?" Emer asks.

"An address." Zara hands Emer a napkin. "He said to go there and speak to them. I don't know what it is—but he's the real deal. Definitely mixed up with witch hunting."

Emer nods. "Let's go, then." Emer stares out of the front windshield, her shoulders drawn back like she's in a chariot, ready to ride into battle.

Jude clears her throat. "Look, I can drop you off if you really want but . . . well, I've got the wedding."

"I will come with you, then," Emer says resolutely. "To the wedding. You can bring a guest, I am sure. I will come with you, and when it is over, we can go here together."

Jude laughs, because the thought of it is so laughable. Emer the wild witch in the ballroom of Wolf Hall! "No offense, Emer, but I'm trying to get back in my father's good books, and I don't think showing up with *you* in tow is going to do anything to help my case."

"Why?" Emer asks.

Jude doesn't quite know how to answer. "Well, because . . . you're so . . . you're so *Emer*. You're not . . . You obviously wouldn't fit in there, okay? They're like . . . fancy people. Why would you even want to come?"

Emer's gaze is dark. "I see."

"Not fitting in there is a *good* thing. We can pick up the trail first thing—"

"Sure." Emer cuts her off. "Zara?"

Jones hesitates. "I can't today. I have to—I have plans."

"Neither of you? We have this"—Emer shakes the napkin with the address—"and neither of you will come with me?"

"Emer, it's not—" Jude tries, but Emer is already out of the car, already stomping down the street.

"Can you go after her?" Jude asks Jones with a sigh.

"Oh, but it's not me she wants to follow her," Jones says, batting her eyelashes.

"You're so immature." Jude gets out of the car and goes after Emer. "Emer, wait!" she calls. The witch does not wait. "Come on, please! Just stop."

Emer rounds on her. "Women could die tonight, Jude. *You* could die tonight. Have you forgotten that? What if he comes for you again?"

Jude runs her hand through her hair. "I mean, you weren't exactly a great help last time."

Emer says nothing for a beat. Then: "Fuck you, Jude."

Jude raises her eyebrows. "Fuck *me*? Fuck *you*, Emer. Just because your family is dead doesn't mean I shouldn't get the chance to be a part of mine for a night."

"Wow." The witch turns again, begins stalking off.

"Emer. *Emer.* Look, I'm sorry, okay? That was too harsh. Emer, Christ, would you wait?"

Emer rounds on her. "What for? There is clearly nothing here worth waiting for."

"Can I just—this has gotten way out of hand. Let me give you the address where the wedding is happening, okay? Take the afternoon off, then we can meet outside at midnight and get back on the trail. What do you think?"

Emer's lips are puckered. She says nothing. Jude sighs and scribbles the address for Wolf Hall on the same napkin Jones brought out of the restaurant.

"I've been waiting for this for two years," Jude says as she hands it back. "It might be my chance to get my family back. Wouldn't you take that chance?"

Emer is stone-faced. "I wouldn't know, Jude. I never will."

Jude winces as the witch walks away. The comment leaves her stinging.

"I know, I know," Jude says when she gets back in the car. "That was pitiful, there's no need to—"

Jones gasps and makes to shove something into the footwell of the car. Jude snatches it, knows immediately what it is from the way it stings her palms. It's the book with the ritual they used to raise Róisín Byrne from the dead.

"Well, well, well," Jude says. "How on earth did you nick this? I'm impressed. You're a better thief than I gave you credit for." There are several Post-it notes marking the pages that Jones has been reading, each with extensive notes written on it. "You cannot be serious."

Jones snatches the book back. "What does it matter to you?"

"Are you unhinged? Did you not see the creepy demon cousin lady climbing out of her muddy grave literally yesterday? It wanted to eat us, Jones. It was going to eat you first. Literally *eat* you. Tear out your throat with its teeth."

Jones holds her chin high. "I will admit it didn't go exactly how I had hoped it would, but I have an idea for how to improve it this time. Besides, Savannah could know who the Ripper is."

"Oh, bullshit. How would she know that? Most likely he was a stranger. You'll wake her up, ask her the question, she'll shrug—

and then the demon inside of her will start moving through London like it's a big ol' buffet!"

"What if Savannah *did* know who killed her?" Jones is angry now, pink-cheeked. She pushes back. "She had a new boyfriend in the weeks before she died. It could have been him. Besides, there is something fishy about the spell that she chose. *What was she looking for?* If I could talk to her—"

"No," Jude says resolutely. Enough zombies. "Emer's following your clue from Dickie, let her—"

"I'll kill you," Jones says quietly.

"What?"

"I'll do it. I'll kill you. If that's still what you want. I'll, I don't know, drown you in a bathtub or something, and then I'll bring you back."

"We established that that brilliant plan won't work unless someone is willing to take my curse just before I die, so no thanks."

"I will. I will take your curse from you if you help me bring Savannah back."

"Don't screw with me, Jones." Jude's voice is low, sharp, her nostrils flared. "Don't dangle that in front of me unless you mean it."

"I mean it. If you help me bring Savannah back. Just for one minute. Just so I can say what I need to say. I will kill you, I will take your curse, I will bring you back. You can throw in the money you promised to Emer to sweeten the deal."

Jude glares. She can see the girl's desperation, knows it is her irrational desire to reunite with her sister that is driving her. Knows also that she shouldn't accept the deal. The curse is not something she'd wish on an enemy, let alone a—God, does she really think of Jones as a *friend*? Annoying, goody-two-shoes, know-it-all Jones? Still. Jones is not the only one being driven by irrational desire. This moment is the closest Jude has ever felt to breaking her curse—and she's not going to let it slip through her fingers. "Where exactly are you planning on getting five liters of blood?"

Jones exhales. "That's the biggest part of the problem right now. I don't know yet. A blood bank? A hospital? I could disguise myself as a doctor, I suppose. Hospitals aren't that hard to get into."

"That is a very bad plan."

"Well, have you got a better one?"

Jude thinks for a moment—and then it comes to her instantly.

Jesus. It's a terrible plan. A truly terrible plan—the worst plan she's come up with yet—but it might work.

"Not that I've decided to help you, because I think you've actually gone off the rails but—there's a panic room in my family's house. The house I'm going to tonight for my father's wedding."

"Okay. So?"

"So because Lawrence Wolf is a paranoid billionaire, he keeps a fresh stock of blood in that panic room at all times in case he's shot or stabbed by intruders or something."

"How much?"

"A lot. Many liters. He doesn't take any chances with his life."

"That's brilliant! Jude, you're brilliant!"

"Always the tone of surprise."

"So you go to the wedding, steal the blood, and meet me at the cemetery afterward, and then—"

"How do you plan on containing her?"

"What?"

"Your sister. When a big, hulking, hungry demon crawls inside of her skin and starts using her as a puppet, what's your grand plan to stop her from eating me?"

"I have a theory. I think I can ward her brain so that the demon only has access to her body but not her mind."

Jude shakes her head. "Come again?"

"Róisín had been in the ground for a long time. Maybe, because Savannah has only been dead for a year, there'll be more brain matter left. More processing power, more reasoning power. She'll be more docile, she'll be—"

Jesus. The girl is deluded. "It's not going to work the way you want it to just because you have a theory. You saw how strong and hungry that skinny little broad was. If Savannah is even half as wild as her . . ."

"I assume you have a better plan? You seem to be the queen of better plans today."

"I can't believe I'm going to say this, but—" Jude lets out a long breath. "The panic room comes to the rescue again. We dig Savannah up. We put her body in a suitcase or something. We bring her to the house. We lock her in the panic room with you. You bring her back, you find out who the killer is, if she knows. If your little warding trick works, great. If it doesn't, you off her again and she doesn't eat you or me or anyone else."

Jones actually laughs. Jude doesn't blame her.

"Oh, you're just going to sneak a dead body into your family's mansion on your dad's wedding day? That's a really great idea, Jude. Nobody will notice at all!"

Jude shrugs. "We don't sneak it in. We walk it in through the front door. Well, the side door, actually. We pretend it's a gift. It's actually the best day of the year to get a dead body into Wolf Hall. Everyone will be busy, looking elsewhere."

Zara's mouth hangs open. "You're actually serious. You're not joking for once."

"I am."

"Jude—your family would be at risk."

"Not if you follow the plan. There's no way out of that room unless you let her out—and you won't do that. Will you?"

"No. Of course not."

"Good."

"Do we, uh . . . do we tell Emer about this or . . . ?"

There's no way that Emer would go for this—and there's no way Emer would go for Jones drowning Jude and taking her curse, either. "I wouldn't bother her with it. You know? Give her the night off." Jude takes out her phone, dials a number she knows well but has been expressly instructed not to save.

"Who are you calling?" Jones asks.

"If we're going to do this, we're going to need some help."

The call is answered after two rings. "I told you never to call me, you wretched little—" says the voice on the other end of the line.

"Hi, Reese," Jude says. "I've missed you, too."

It's a silver afternoon, the world cast in grayscale. Mist hangs heavy over the city, everything fading away into the distance, bare-branched trees swallowed by gloom. Jude drives to the cemetery where Savannah is buried, parks on the street out front. Shadow people move about in the haze. Jude starts at each new dark-cloaked figure emerging from the vapors, expecting them to be the killer, wondering if he has found her again. Emer wasn't exactly much help when the Ripper attacked, but now that she's gone, Jude finds that she's more nervous to be without her than she expected. She's grown used to her stabby presence.

It's a good day to rob a grave, if there can be such a thing. The fog will keep them hidden.

Jude pays the attendant at the front gate to finish early, to give them "privacy" while they "mourn." Of course, a thousand pounds for private mourning has to be odd, but the attendant doesn't ask any questions.

Chopra meets them at the entrance, her arms crossed and face grumpy. She's in bootcut jeans and a brown leather jacket, an oversize suitcase at her side. Jude has never seen her out of PPE before, and it strikes her now, how much older Chopra is, how very teenaged she feels next to this woman.

Jude gave her the pitch over the phone. Of all the responses she expected from Chopra—*You want me to do what? Are you batshit?*—her immediate agreement wasn't one of them. But two things Jude said had made Chopra eager to help. Thing one: Digging up Savannah could help them identify the serial killer today. Chopra asked, "How?" and Jude said, "I can't tell you because you won't believe me, but I literally promise it could totally potentially work."

Thing two: Jude offered to pay her £30,000 to help them. Chopra was silent after Jude said this, silent for so long that Jude asked if she was still there. All Chopra said was "You better not be fucking with me, you little grave-robbing weirdo." Then she hung up and texted one minute later: **I'm in.**

So there they are. The strangest little trio of grave-robbing body snatchers that has ever existed, each with a shovel slung over her shoulder as they make their way through the cemetery to the grave of one Savannah Jones, a big ol' suitcase trundling along behind them.

The sun is low in the sky, the trees around them naked and mean-looking. Ravens jump from headstone to headstone, following them as they move through the oldest parts of the cemetery toward the newer graves. Jude pulls her billowing greatcoat tighter around herself, breathes into her cupped hands.

They walk in silence. Even for Jude, it is too weird to crack a joke. What they are about to attempt is bonkers. The foul wound at her leg can feel her anxiety, feel her skepticism. It feeds on her apprehension, sharpens it, turns it into physical pain that shoots up her femur and into her hip socket. A toothache, barbed and driving, but in her thigh. Jude imagines herself taking her shovel and using it to hack her leg off, which brings her a strange, maniacal kind of comfort.

At Savannah's grave, Chopra looks at the headstone and says, "Are we really fucking going to do this?"

Zara says nothing, just starts to dig. Chopra lets out a long breath. There are no words in it, but Jude understands it perfectly well—*How the hell did my life come to this?*

Jude wonders, for the first time, if Chopra has children, if perhaps that is the reason the divorce from her wife is so ugly, and why she has sunk to accepting cash from teenage girls to dig up bodies.

Zara and Chopra do most of the digging. Jude tries for a few minutes and then complains that she's not cut out for manual labor, but really, she grows breathless quickly now. That last curse really sucked a good chunk of her life away, has left her feeling more feeble than ever before. A few scoops of dirt, and her lungs feel like they're under the weight of several cinder blocks. Zara and Chopra don't scold her for giving up. They can see how weak she's grown, how withered.

They work quickly, both of them sweating and breathing heavily as they shift shovel after shovel of dirt. The soil is soft, not yet frozen from winter frosts and not yet fully settled from being dug the first time, when Savannah was buried a year ago.

Jude sits on a nearby headstone, watching and waiting anxiously. It takes two hours for Jones and Chopra to hit the solid lid of the coffin. The time Jude is supposed to be at Wolf Hall to get ready is rapidly approaching.

"My arse hurts," Jude complains, the headstone she sits on making her whole body ache. Sharing this makes the other two scowl at her, which is fair enough she supposes.

Then, finally, they are ready for the exhumation to begin.

"Open the suitcase," Chopra says as she begins prying at the coffin lid.

"Hey, Jones, why don't you take a break?" Jude says. Jones is standing at the edge of the grave, staring at the place where Savannah's dead face will appear in a moment's time. "We can do this bit without you."

Jones considers for a moment, then nods. "Thank you. Just . . . be careful with her, please. Don't cut her up to fit her in the suitcase or anything."

"You think so little of me," Jude says—though hacking off Savannah's hands and feet has certainly crossed her mind. Not a bad contingency plan in case things go a bit . . . funky.

Jude helps Jones out of the grave, watches as she wanders off into the mist and is quickly swallowed.

"You got the stomach for this?" Chopra asks.

"We're about to find out," Jude says.

Chopra puts on gloves and a mask. Jude does the same. Then Chopra opens the lid. Loose earth tumbles in on top of the body, getting into Savannah's hair, her clothing. A plume of stench rolls off her, hits Jude like a wall. Jude takes two steps back, breathes through her mouth but can still taste it, the solid stink of it in the air.

"Oh God, oh Jesus," Chopra says as she hooks her arms under Savannah's armpits and lifts her. A bell tinkles in Savannah's dead hand. Something bursts beneath the pressure of Chopra's grasp. Runnels of dark fluid run over her leather jacket, her gloved hands. Jude gags and looks away.

"Help me get her out," Chopra says.

"Give me a second," Jude says, trying to breathe.

It isn't easy to maneuver Savannah out of the grave. Chopra pushes the body up the side, the face pressed into soft soil, as Jude lifts from above while trying not to rip off the corpse's arms. By the time they get her onto the grass, she is filthy and covered in her own putrefaction.

"Careful with her," Jude says as Chopra lifts Savannah into the suitcase, begins to fold her limbs so that she is tucked in the fetal position. When Jude expresses her surprise at how flexible the corpse is, Chopra explains that rigor mortis usually doesn't last long—hours, a day at most—before bodies become malleable again.

Chopra zips up the suitcase and wheels it behind her as they walk back to the entrance. Jones meets them there, solemn faced, and helps lift the bag into the back of Chopra's SUV. One corner has already stained and begun to leak. They wash their hands with a water bottle, change into the spare clothes Chopra brought for each of them, apply a liberal amount of her perfume—the heady scent of clove and burned balsam wood—then drive to Holland Park in silence, the windows down even though the air that rushes in is frigid. Being cold is better than the smell of Savannah's body.

"The daughter is here," a woman dressed in black says into a headset when Jude, Jones, and Chopra arrive at the service entrance to the Holland Park house. It's busy today with vendors wheeling in crates of champagne and Lawrence's favorite cheese that he has flown in from France. "What's in the suitcase?"

Jude slaps the bag. "A big, big gift, to show Daddy how much I love him. It's too heavy to haul it up the front steps. We need to use the service elevator."

"What is it?" the woman asks.

"The gift? The gift inside this suitcase?"

"Yes."

"Oh. It is a . . . marble statue . . . of my father . . . posing with . . . a . . . falcon."

"A falcon?" the woman and Chopra ask at the same time.

"Yes, actually. A falcon. To symbolize . . . taking flight . . . into . . . a new marriage."

"There's also a dove," Jones adds quickly. "To symbolize peace and reunion. I'm the artist. The marble sculptor. My name is Scarlett Twisleton-Flynn."

"A falcon and a dove?" the woman asks.

"Multiple falcons and doves," Jude says. "He's just covered in them. You know how much my father adores birds."

The woman's gaze turns to Chopra. "And you are?"

"My assistant," Jude says. Chopra sucks on her teeth. She's going to love that.

"Right," the woman says. "I don't have time for this. I'll have someone come and pick it—"

"No. No, no. It needs to be delivered to him specifically by me—and the artist needs to stay with her creation to make sure it doesn't get broken."

"Fine," the woman says, waving them through, more interested in the arriving boxes of fresh oysters than she is in the suitcase.

The three of them take the service elevator up to the level of Lawrence's bedroom. Jude checks that the coast is clear—all of the bedroom doors are closed—and then they wheel the bag to the entrance of the panic room.

From the outside, the door looks like a big gilt-framed mirror. Jude fumbles behind it, looking for the latch that opens it. The room beyond is small but luxurious. There's space enough for a brown leather Chesterfield sofa on one side, a desk on the other (in case Lawrence wants to get some work done during a home invasion?), a TV mounted on the wall, a door that leads to a tiny en suite, a bar cart with spirits and crystalline glasses (probably dragged in by younger members of the Wolf family, to impress the dates they bring here), and—crucially—two small, glass-fronted refrigerators on the back wall. One with food and water, the other with medications and—Jude breathes a sigh of relief when she sees it—a dozen bags of bright red blood.

"You weren't kidding," Jones says.

Chopra lifts the suitcase into the room while Jude talks to Jones: "The keypad is here, by the door. Once we leave, you hit the lock button. Then only way in or out of here is with the passcode."

"What's the passcode?" Jones asks.

"I'm not going to tell you that until you know for sure that Savannah isn't going to eat everyone in this house."

"Yeah, I'm going to wait in the hall for this conversation," Chopra says. "Sounds like something I do not need to be hearing."

"You don't trust me?" Jones asks.

"Frankly, no, Jones. I don't trust you. Not with this—and besides. Demons are wily. It might try to convince you to let it out, and I'm not sure you wouldn't listen." A beat. "Are you sure you want to go through with this? Are you sure you want to see Savannah that way?"

"I can handle it."

"Okay, then. Well. Bring her back. Say what you need to say. Find out what she knows. Then I'll tell you how to get out. Got it?" Jude really hopes that Emer was right and that the zombie won't eat its creator. Otherwise—she grimaces, can't think about it for too long.

Jones nods but looks distracted. "Fine."

Jude steps out into the hall, swings the heavy mirrored door closed, waits until she hears Jones press the button that slides the pins into place like a vault door. For better or for worse, they're locked in there now, the baby necromancer and the dead sister she's been trying to bring back for a year.

Jude and Chopra leave the same way they came in, through the web of service elevators and corridors that lead to the side entrance. They slip past harried staff, barely getting a second glance. On the street, Jude walks Chopra to where her car is parked. Chopra watches closely while Jude transfers her the promised money.

"If anyone asks me about this," Chopra says as she gets into the driver's seat, "I'll have you arrested for desecration of a corpse. It'll be my word against yours. You got that?"

"I always love our little chats," Jude says. "By the way, do you have kids?"

"Is that some kind of threat?"

"Jesus, chill *out*. I'm just curious. I'm trying to humanize you under that harsh exterior."

Chopra shows Jude the lock screen of her phone. Two dark-haired children in pumpkin Halloween costumes look out at her.

"Twins," Chopra says. "My eggs but Brooke carried them. Now she's trying to take them away from me."

"I'm sorry. That sucks."

"Don't be sorry. You've been helping pay for lawyers for a year."

"Good. Screw Brooke. I hate her."

"You must really like her."

"I literally just said I hate her."

"Not Brooke—whoever it is you have a crush on. Is it Jones? Or the redhead, maybe?"

"What?" Jude says. "Who says I like anyone?"

Chopra smiles. "You haven't hit on me once all day."

"Yeah, well, maybe I'm just not a raging pervert."

"Anymore, you mean."

"Rude."

Chopra closes the door and winds her window down. "Call me with the name of the killer or don't call me at all."

"There's the Chopra I know and love," Jude says, but Chopra is already driving away.

Jude heads back to Wolf Hall, this time to the front door, which is bedecked in white flowers so abundant that the doorway itself is barely visible. Anxious florists are still making adjustments, shoving in more roses, more lilies, more baby's breath. Full tree branches twist up on either side of the door, draped in moss and white wisteria.

Jude takes a step over the threshold into the house she has wanted to come back to every day for two years. The house that her brothers and nieces and nephews are allowed to come and go from as they please. It is as though a piece of herself has been missing all this time, a piece roughly the size and shape of her lungs. She takes a deep breath—and catches the scent of herself.

*I need a shower,* she thinks as she moves down the hall.

There are glossy black double doors that lead off into various reception rooms and libraries and drawing rooms with huge fireplaces and chandeliers. At the end, giant pocket doors open into the ballroom (yes, there is a ballroom), which overlooks the sprawling gardens beyond. The decor is still painfully rich-white-old-person chic, shades of beige and taupe with occasional pops of brown and blue, but today it has been made beautiful. Plus the walls are not leaking sulfuric pus and there are no bodies of small, dead creatures decomposing underfoot: heaven.

The place is busy with frazzled staff shouting about the coming rain, murmurs of "Plan B" chanted through headsets. Jude walks to the glass elevator (yes, there are *multiple* elevators) that runs up through the spine of the building, bound for the room that was hers, once. Not her bedroom—no one lives at Wolf Hall full time—but hers in spirit, the place she slept after family gatherings.

While she is waiting, wondering if Savannah is already groaning back to life, she hears them: two men talking somewhere on the stone stairwell that wraps around the glass elevator shaft like a corkscrew. A quirk of architecture and acoustics: You can eavesdrop on conversations here, catch snippets of gossip from two or three levels up.

"Of course not," says the first voice, distorted by the echo.

Something, something . . . "the family at risk," says the second.

The first laughs, but not mirthfully. They are angry with each other, these two. How juicy.

"Reckless," someone hisses. Which one, Jude cannot tell. "Stupid and reckless." It sounds like one of her older brothers. Or is it two of them, perhaps, each having a go at the other? Is something rotten in the state of Denmark? Jude chuckles to herself. Of course there's some fucking drama. They are Wolfs. Maybe they're sleeping with each other's wives.

They keep arguing: Something, something . . . "made your bloody point. Stop. Before I stop you."

More muffled words. Another spiteful laugh. "You could try."

Then it is over. There are stomped footsteps, a parting of ways. The elevator comes, and Jude gets in and tries to see, through the glass, who was speaking as she's propelled to the upper floors, but whoever was on the stairs is gone.

Upstairs, in the hall, Jude finds Elijah. She almost collapses at the sight of him, calls his name too loudly, starts walking toward him with her arms flung wide. He turns and grins, thinks she's joking and being overly dramatic, begins running toward her in slow motion like they're in a movie.

"You idiot," he says when she crashes into him. "You should have turned down his invitation. Hey. Hey, Jude, what's wrong?"

"Oh nothing, nothing." She mashes her palms into her misty

eyes. "It's just the decor is so hideous, it moves one to tears, you know?"

Eli grins again. "Oh, I know what you mean. Have you seen the live peacock yet? They have it on display in a gigantic Victorian birdcage in the ballroom."

Jude cry-laughs. "Subtle, our family. You would never know they have money. That's what I love most about them."

"Did you meet our new stepmother?"

"Not yet. What's she like?"

"Like a lamb to the slaughter. I tried to convince her to escape, but the Stockholm syndrome is strong with this one. She even said she loves Lawrence. Can you imagine?"

Jude fake gags. "Where does he find these women?"

And then she smiles. This. Him. Them. The two outsiders, the two outcasts. Them against the world. This is what Jude has longed for. This is what Jude has missed more than anything.

Elijah draws her close, presses a quick kiss to her forehead, rests his cheek against her temple. "Okay, Judebug. Front-row tickets to the freak show. Let's go get our money's worth."

# TWENTY-FOUR

**IT DOES** not take Emer long to find the address.

It leads her to a redbrick townhouse overlooking Soho Square Garden, a neat and unassuming building with large windows and a green door. Fog clings to the trees, rolls across the leaf-littered road. It hides Emer from attracting too much attention as she sits on a bench in the square, a figure in the mist. The smell of rotting leaves and animal shit clings to the air. Emer watches people as they come and go from the house. The men are mostly young and finely dressed, arriving in pairs or threes, smiling, cordial, clapping each other on the back. Some go in for half an hour, an hour. Some she does not see leave.

It feels familiar to be on her own again. Not good or bad, but familiar. It is the way she knows best how to navigate the world.

She watches the windows as the sun sinks and the streetlights come on. The townhouse is lit from within. Honeyed light spills through those big windows. Beyond the glass, men sip amber liquid and smoke cigars and laugh with each other in a wood-paneled room. It is a member's club, she thinks. A member's club for witch hunters. They are here, in this nice building on this nice square, meeting on a Sunday afternoon to drink.

What to do now? It would be wise to wait until tomorrow, when Jude or Zara could sit where she sits now and watch her go inside. To what end, though? To call the police if Emer does not come out?

She stands. Her body groans. Her fingers are stiff from the cold. They feel like they don't belong to her. She loops once around Soho Square Garden, past a small, octagonal gardener's hut that has been built to look like it is from the Tudor period. The ground in the park is uneven, the roots of trees churning the earth, restless. She sweeps through the mist, and finds herself back where she started.

Near the green door in the nice house. She crosses the road. She breathes out and steps in.

The room she enters is small and warm, heated by an open fireplace off to one side. There is a dark wood reception desk, a man standing behind it. Behind the desk is a wide staircase. A mural stretches up the wall. It is beautiful and horrific, impossible not to stare at. A field of wildflowers on a bright summer's day. At the center, softly painted flames reach toward a blue sky and lick at three bodies bound to stakes. Three witches burning. Three women.

There is a sensation in Emer's chest of hands riffling around inside her rib cage, squeezing down hard on her heart. It is so blatant. Emer has spent her whole life in hiding and here is this abomination painted large. The brazenness of it unsettles her.

The man looks up and smiles at her. "Welcome," he says. He is not much older than her. "Who are you here to see?"

"I was invited by Dickie Volkov," Emer says. "Richard Wortley-Volkov III." She makes no attempt to hide her accent. The result of trying to fake an English one would no doubt be terrible. "My name is Scarlett." Emer can't remember the rest of the name Jude made up for Zara and hopes the man does not ask her for it.

The man checks a ledger in front of him. "Dickie isn't here today unfortunately. I'm afraid guests are only allowed in when the inviting member is present."

"I'm not a guest. I'm a prospective member."

The man raises his eyebrows. "You want to join?"

"Yes. I want to join."

The man is momentarily confounded. "Well, in that case, I'm sorry, but we only hold prospective member tours once per—"

"Dickie told me to come by today. I just saw him, a few hours ago. He gave me the address." Emer holds up the napkin he gave to Zara.

The man smiles tightly. "Of course. One moment." He makes a phone call. "Hello, Richard, it's Rupert. I have a young woman named Scarlett here at reception, and she says—oh, okay. I see. Yes, well, when you put it that way, I agree. Yes, absolutely." The man hangs up the phone and smiles tightly again. "Richard is delighted that you've taken him up on his suggestion. I'm Rupert."

"Em—" Emer begins, before remembering that she is not Emer. "Scarlett," she says again.

"Richard would like for me to show you around. If you could just fill in the guest register here, and then . . ." Rupert looks her up and down. "I hope you don't mind, but I—well, I can't let you in unless I check. It's policy, the first time an *unvetted* woman comes inside the House."

"Check what?"

"That you have not been desecrated by the devil."

Invocations. He wants to check her body for invocations. To see her pale, bare flesh. "Why would a witch ever come here?"

"To do us harm, of course. The policy exists for a reason. Several years ago there was a—let's just say, she was a woman whom the men believed they could trust. She was allowed in. There were some . . . unfortunate consequences."

"Oh dear," Emer says.

"Indeed. Anyway. Now we always check. Your wrists, please."

Emer pulls back the fabric at her wrists to show Rupert that she has no invocations there. He frowns at the scabbed cut and healing puncture marks he finds there. "My cat gets carried away," Emer says.

"Your neck," he says next. Again, she shows him. "Your heartspace."

This is more difficult. Emer wears a turtleneck and does not want to untuck her shirt and pull it up and bare her breasts to this man. She stretches her top down as best she can, hides her leaden pendant in her palm as she does so. Rupert leans over, too close, pulls the neckline down further to expose Emer's skin to the light.

"Okay. Lastly, the back of your knees—and, well, I'm sure you know, your groin."

Emer stares at him, hard, until his cheeks burn and he clears his throat, shifting from one foot to the other, but he does not concede. She had been expecting him to ask, had known it was coming, but she had not expected him to follow through.

"Please, Scarlett," he says. "We are almost done. I don't like this any more than you do."

*I somehow doubt that,* Emer thinks.

Emer pushes down her black stockings to bare her legs. She

turns to show Rupert the backs of her knees—the popliteal arteries beat here—and then faces him and lifts her skirt to show him her upper, inner thigh, where the femoral artery thunders deep beneath the skin. It is fertile ground for invocations. Not as powerful as the heartspace, but a close second. A secret, sacred place favored by witches in medieval times, when invocations on wrists and knees and necks and hearts were certain death sentences.

"Excellent." Rupert claps his hands together. "Great. Again, I am so sorry about that. Let's get started, shall we?"

Emer is still pulling her stockings up when he starts climbing the stairs, starts prattling about the "house" and their "values." Emer trudges after him, her jaw set tight.

"I assume Richard has already explained what this place is and what we do here?" Rupert asks.

"Only briefly."

"We call this the House. It is a gathering place. A safe haven for like-minded individuals to come together to express an opinion that has become—controversial."

The tour of the House is rambling and grandiose, Rupert explaining how its members come from old families, good stock, but that their numbers are growing less every year. They have new member targets, are hoping for more diversity in their ranks, more women. The space is sumptuous and faux old, everything made to look vaguely medieval though the House must be postwar.

Rupert leads Emer from room to room. There are men in each of them, laughing, drinking, smoking cigars. Men who go silent when Emer enters. Men who grin and raise their eyebrows and elbow each other at the sight of her. Emer looks each of them in the eye. Makes a mental note of their faces. Perhaps, one day, she will come back here and follow these men into the night. Follow them home. Set Bael onto them.

"Here we are," Rupert says as he opens a huge pair of wood doors. "The main room. I would suggest starting here. You can introduce yourself to some of our old regulars, get to know—"

"Who is that?" Emer asks. A huge portrait hangs above the fireplace. The man is handsome and young. His eyes are pale blue and clever, his hair dark and casually mussed. He wears a long black coat. His right hand is in his pocket, his left reaching down toward the head of the large gray dog that circles him, its yellow eyes menacing and face cast in shadow. It is a strange portrait, at once arresting and disturbing. Emer cannot put her finger on why it unnerves her so much. The man looks familiar, though she cannot place him.

"Him?" Rupert asks. He pauses and returns to where Emer is standing. "That is one of our founding fathers. Victor Volkov. One of the best."

Emer's skin prickles, goose bumps instantly rolling down her body. The ancestor of the men who killed her family.

"Volkov," she says quietly. She takes a steadying breath. The air smells stale, of old men and old leather. "They were not so good at painting dogs in those days, were they?"

"It's not a dog," Rupert says with a snide little laugh. "Volkov means—"

"I know," Emer says sharply, suddenly, ice-cold dread plunging through her veins. She steps closer to the painting, examines the creature more closely. Its gray coat. Its yellow eyes. Its sharp teeth, bared in a snarl. "I know what *Volkov* means."

"Would you like to see the gym facilities and the rooftop?" Rupert asks as he continues on. "We have squash courts and a heated pool and—Scarlett?" Rupert realizes that Emer is not next to him. That she is halfway down the hall, heading in the opposite direction, barreling back toward the entrance. "Scarlett, is everything okay?" he calls after her.

No. Everything is not okay. Emer is incandescent, white-hot on the inside—because she knows.

She knows who the London Ripper is.

And she knows who killed her family.

# TWENTY-FIVE

**ZARA IS** alone in the room with the suitcase that Savannah's body has been folded into.

Savannah is here, with her. She can hardly believe it. So close and yet so far. Only the fabric of the bag and all the fathoms of the afterlife separate them now.

Zara runs her hands over the suitcase. A sharp edge on the zipper pricks the soft pad of one of her fingertips. Zara squeezes the wound, watches as a beet-red bead of blood comes to the surface.

She takes a step backward. The carpet beneath her feet is so thick and sumptuous she sinks into it with each footfall, like when she walks through the layers of moss that coat the cemetery in the colder months. She stares at the bag, trying to savor the moment, though perhaps *savor* is not the right word. Resurrecting your murdered sister is not a thing to savor.

It is happening. The impossible thing she has worked toward for a year is happening.

Zara places her shaking palms on the suitcase once again. She does not want to see what has become of Savannah. She wishes she could skip the next part, wake up in half an hour when Sav is alive—but that is not how the world operates, and Zara has never shied away from hard work.

"I did not come this far to only come this far," she says.

She unzips the bag.

The stink hits her like something physical. A wall of noxious gas that bowls her over, pushes her toward the other side of the room, coughing. It feels wrong to inhale it, like simply inhaling death might kill her. The air is soupy. The room is rancid. Zara takes several deep breaths through her mouth. She can feel the thickness of the air in her throat. She wants to run, to run away from this reality.

When Savannah's body was released by the police to the funeral home, Zara immediately requested that her sister be embalmed. The relentless process of decay had already begun, bloating her body from the inside. The embalming would slow the rate of rot and keep Savannah from sloughing away to nothing, for a while at least.

Zara doesn't want to see. She doesn't want to look. She can't look. She can't not look.

She feels she owes it to Savannah to witness the horror of what happened to her, again and again and again. You do not get to look away because it is unbearable. You do not get to shield your eyes or nose from the grim reality of the violence that is wreaked upon women every day.

Look. Look at what was done to your sister.

Zara forces her eyes open. The body in front of her is very obviously a corpse. It is sunken and sucked dry, all sinew and withered leather, tucked up inside the suitcase in a fetal position.

Saponification has begun. The process by which human fat seeps out of the skin and coats the body in a layer of wax. Zara is relieved to see this taking place. It is a natural kind of preservation. It happens often in cold European graveyards. There are stories of corpses being dug up thirty years after burial in Germany, looking fresh as the day they were buried. There are parts of Savannah that are encased in a waxen cocoon, the skin beneath it remarkably well preserved. Her face, though hollow and drained, is surprisingly intact. Other parts have not fared so well. The bones in her left arm are visible, most of the flesh over the radius and ulna gone, some sinew and cartilage still keeping the limb together like a puppet threaded through with string. The rest of her body is deflated like a punctured balloon, her limbs somehow flat.

The mouth is open, the lips dry and pulled back over the teeth. There is a folk legend that says corpses' hair and fingernails continue to grow after death, but this is not true: The skin simply dries and shrinks away, making the hair and nails look longer. This has happened to Savannah. She was always thin, but now she has been made gaunt by death, her cheeks sucked in, her collarbones pushing through her tight skin.

Zara saw Emer's cousin, and there was only a sliver of her left. Only enough of Róisín to give them a name: Volkov. Savannah hasn't been dead for nearly as long.

*I did not come this far to only come this far.*

There are dozens of bags of blood in the little fridge, each labeled and dated so they can be swapped out when they expire. All this blood, kept here for Jude's family, just in case.

Zara finds a small bin in the bathroom. Then she begins cutting open the cold bags of blood and dumping them into the bin.

It is woozy, gag-worthy work. The smell of cold blood is worse than when it is warm. It reminds Zara of her biology classes, of slicing into a sheep's heart and smelling the intense hospital scent of its deadness. A sharp, iron tang. There is something clinical about it. She has to take a break. She goes back into the small bathroom and splashes water on her face, hangs her head in the sink while the water runs.

When her head clears and she no longer feels on the edge of fainting, she returns to her work. Zara wasn't the only one who fainted in dissection class—but she was the only one who went back into the classroom again and again. She would not let blood stop her then, and she will not let blood stop her now.

When she has roughly five liters of blood sloshing in the bin, she takes out the book. She has studied the spell, recited its words over and over again, checked the pronunciation of each syllable.

Again, reason finds her, very briefly. Savannah's decaying body will soon be inhabited by a demon. That is how this works.

Zara shakes the thought from her mind.

*I did not come this far to only come this far,* she thinks.

Before she begins, she wards Savannah's head. Four plastic cups—two by each of her ears, one close to the top of her skull, one balancing on her breastbone—each filled with a few teaspoons of blood. Zara recites the same words that Emer recited in their hotel room, the same words Zara taught to Emer's clients to keep them hidden from the killer.

"It'll work," Zara says. Savannah, Savannah, Savannah. So close. Here and not here, on the other side of death. "It's a good idea. It'll work."

Zara opens Savannah's mouth and wedges the funnel she

brought with her between her dead sister's teeth. She does not want to take her out of the suitcase, to handle her any more than is necessary at this stage. Zara takes careful breaths through her mouth and focuses entirely on her work. To acknowledge the situation too directly would be to fall apart, and so Zara shuts off several parts of herself. She is simply a scientist in a lab, testing a hypothesis that she has been working on for a year.

The bin is heavy with blood, too sloshing and unwieldy to hold with one hand, so Zara stands over the suitcase, the bucket held in both of her hands, the spell book flipped open on the carpet next to Sav's head.

Zara pours the cold blood into Savannah's throat. The words she speaks in Latin don't sound half as impressive coming out of her mouth as they did when Emer said them. She stumbles over the pronunciation, squints, and exhales in frustration when she gets something wrong. She hopes the demons in the room, if there are any, will be able to decipher what she means, what she wants them to do.

Then the spell is finished. The blood is poured. So little has gone into Savannah's mouth. Instead, the suitcase is flooded with an inch of cool red. Zara's shoes are flecked. Blood has leaked through a hole in the corner of the bag, a shocking pool of crimson against white.

The blood bubbles and flows out of Savannah's mouth, her blond hair staining as it sinks in.

"Come on," Zara urges. "Come on."

She waits.

And waits.

And waits.

# TWENTY-SIX

**IN JUDE'S** room, there is a stack of boxes on the bed, the largest of which is a black one from Net-a-Porter that has been tied with a ribbon. She opens it to find a high-collared Valentino gown in screaming neon pink. It is comically un-Jude, with dainty pink bows down the sides. Mercifully, it is long-sleeved and will cover the lightning-shaped wounds jolting down her arm—and conveniently also hides her invocations.

The price tag is still attached, because Lawrence loves you to know how much money he spent on you: £6,100. The dress is very deeply not to Jude's taste, which Lawrence would have known—and he bought it anyway. It's his wedding, his chance to dress her up like the doll daughter he has always wanted her to be. In four other smaller boxes, Jude finds a pair of gold-and-pink-sapphire drop earrings (£1,500), a pink Judith Leiber Couture clutch in the shape of a giant bow (£5,275), a pointy pair of mercifully flat René Caovilla satin sandals (£915), and a delicate gold headband encrusted with tiny diamonds (a staggering £6,144). Jude tries not to do the mental math to calculate how much it cost all together, which she succeeds at, because she hasn't really been at school for the past two years and her brain is turning to mush. Still, it's a lot, and also so pink and delicate and feminine. She has made it clear to her father, since she was eleven or twelve, that this is not her. Jude likes tuxedos. Jude likes tailored suits. Jude likes greatcoats and patent-leather brogues and to wear her hair slicked flat against her skull.

Jude showers. A woman arrives soon after to do Jude's hair and makeup. She does not ask how Jude would like to look. No doubt she has already been given instructions by Lawrence, because when she is done, Jude's black hair falls in soft finger waves over her forehead and her blue eyes shine beneath lids shellacked in shimmery pink powder.

Jude looks like a sweet, pretty girl. Which is to say, Jude looks nothing like herself. She feels a pang of guilt for making Zara wear that stupid yellow dress on her date with Dickie.

A bell is rung, like it's the bloody theater or something, and Jude knows that it is time.

It is beginning.

Downstairs in the ballroom, the wedding of Lawrence and Luciana is small but extravagant. The bride wears custom Elie Saab, an exquisite gown of white lace and crystal beading and delicate organza flower appliqués that seem to cascade from the woman's very skin, as though she is a garden in summer—and she is in bloom. The dress doesn't hide her growing bump, nor does she want it to: She touches it during the ceremony, presses Lawrence's palm to the small but obvious roundness of her. Twins, Elijah said. Jude grimaces. Poor creatures.

The woman herself is also exquisite. Luciana is tall and bird-boned and deeply tanned, with light brown hair that frames a face so lovely it is difficult to comprehend. When she speaks to say her vows, it is with a Spanish accent. She cries as she tells Lawrence that she will love him forever. Jude thinks crying is the appropriate response to marrying Lawrence Wolf, but Luciana smiles through her tears, dewy-eyed and radiant.

The wedding was supposed to take place outside, but it's raining because it's London, so the festivities have been moved indoors to the ballroom. The bride and groom stand before a roaring fireplace, facing each other, clasping hands. There is, as Eli said, a huge fucking birdcage in the room, a peacock wandering around inside of it, its plumage on display.

There are few attendees. Jude recognizes all of them. None of Luciana's family have come to see her wed an old, rich man. There are no children, either, none of the squalling younger siblings from Lawrence's most recent flings. Jude's older brothers are here, their wives orbiting around them dressed in silken gowns and diamonds. Eli is here, obviously. Some of Jude's aunts and uncles are in attendance, the ones that Lawrence still speaks to, anyway, the ones who grovel at his feet in the hopes of scavenging his scraps. There are some of Lawrence's creepy business associates, some even creepier people from his papers, men who have leered at Jude since she was what, eleven? Twelve? Their gaze flitting to her budding breasts, lingering there too long. It is the inner sanctum only, the two dozen or so people that Lawrence Wolf can tolerate—and, for some reason, Jude.

Soon the vows are over, the contract is signed, the bride is kissed, Luciana's fate is sealed. Everybody claps. Confetti is thrown. A string quartet begins to play. Elijah hits on one of the wedding planners, is leading her out of the ballroom within minutes of starting up a conversation. He winks at Jude as he passes. Jude mouths, *Traitor*, at him. It's him she most wanted to spend time with, and now he is gone already.

Waiters glide through the small crowd with trays of impossibly gold champagne. Jude snags one, gulps it back, snags another immediately. The room smells intensely of the lilies that overwhelm the space. It is sickly sweet, the air too thick and close, but at least it hides Jude's own scent. Her violently pink dress itches at her neck, her wrists. For two years she has ached to be back in this room with these people, but now that she is here, it is difficult to put on a smile and pretend that her years of horror didn't happen.

People flit past her, tell her she is looking well (*The makeup is working hard*, Jude thinks), it's so lovely to see her here. Jude's gaze travels to the ceiling, to the three grand chandeliers that hang there, all more expensive than the average London flat. She wonders if Zara has revived Savannah yet, if there is a zombie demon monster banging around in the panic room.

Jude takes her phone out of her bow-shaped clutch and messages her: **Any luck?** There is no response. Maybe Savannah has eaten her after all.

The bride and groom make their way around the room, greeting their guests. When they get to Jude, Lawrence's lips pucker.

"Congratulations," Jude says. She steps forward to hug him, lightened by the two glasses of champagne. It is perhaps only the third or fourth time she has been this close to her father. Lawrence does not hug her back. Instead, his gaze flicks across the ballroom, then to her. "You've shown your face. You should leave now."

"*Laurie*," Luciana scolds.

Jude's heart becomes a swollen thing. She takes another glass of champagne from a passing waiter, something to stop the prickles in her eyes from turning to tears. "No. I don't think I will."

"Don't make a scene." Lawrence's face is turning red, his hands curled into fists at his sides. *"Go."*

Adam saves her. He claps their father on the shoulder, shakes him jovially, smiles at Jude. "You're not sending my beloved sister away, are you? I've barely seen her for years, and you want to pack her away already?"

Lawrence chews on his cheeks, his mouth a sour plum. "Judith," he says eventually. He stares hard at Jude. His voice has changed, cracked, become a stream running over sharp rocks. *"Get. Out."*

"Father, that's enough," Adam snaps. "Why don't you go and greet the rest of your guests?"

Luciana pulls Lawrence away, chastising him.

"What is his problem?" Jude says as she watches them go. "Why does he hate me so much?"

*"That* is a good question," Adam says as he too stares after their father. "One I have been asking myself for some time. Now, let me look at you." He holds Jude's face in his hands, smiles grimly as he searches it. "You look well."

"You're a bad liar."

Adam laughs. "Okay. Fine. You look like hell."

"I *feel* like hell."

"How's school?"

"I've been taking a break from school to focus on my health. You know, after the accident."

"Oh yes, of course. I was very sorry to hear about your car accident. Did we—"

"You sent flowers, don't worry," Jude assures him. "At least, your assistant did."

"I'm pleased to hear that." Adam pauses, seems to be struggling to find a thread of conversation. "Which university are you planning on attending?"

What Jude would normally say: *Whichever one Lawrence can bribe my way into.*

What she says instead: "Oxford, obviously. I want to go where you all went. Carry on the family tradition."

Adam nods approvingly. Jude scratches at her neckline, where her dress irritates her fresh invocation, making it weep into the fabric.

"You . . . have a tattoo," Adam says, nodding at her neck.

"Oh." Jude pushes her collar over it. "Yeah. Rebel without a cause and all that."

Adam leans in close and pulls down the fabric to get a better look. "How unusual. What does it say?"

Lawrence is back suddenly. Jude does not see where he comes from, just feels the crushing strength of his fingers as he grabs her arm and yanks her away from her brother, pulling her so abruptly and with such force that she stumbles and falls face-first into the ground. There are gasps in the crowd. The string quartet stops playing, bows drawn sharply across instruments in a moment of shock. The room is quiet, time suspended by the violence.

Nobody comes to her to aid. Nobody dares to challenge the king. Nobody says anything or does anything or moves at all. They are all waiting. Waiting for Lawrence to speak first.

Jude touches her face, can feel the wetness spreading from a split lip. She holds her fingers up in the light. They are slick, red with blood. "What the fuck?" she whispers.

Lawrence is a grade-A prick, but he's never hurt her physically before. Before this moment, she'd have thought him incapable of actual violence, just of sneers and barbed words—but here she is, on the ground, bleeding, her father towering over her. "You shouldn't have come." His voice catches. His hands are shaking at his side. He looks desperate, deranged. "I didn't *want* you to come."

Jude is confused. Why did he come to her house and invite her, then?

"*Lawrence*," Adam says sharply. "That is *enough*." Adam helps Jude to her feet, then stands close to their father and says in a low voice: "Go outside. *Now*. Cool down. You are embarrassing yourself and embarrassing this family."

Lawrence doesn't take his eyes off Jude. His jaw is set, his nostrils flared, his shoulders heaving. He doesn't move. Jude doesn't understand what is happening. Is he going to lunge for her again, drag her out by her hair? It looks like he wants to. He is coiled tight, a snake about to strike.

"*Go*," Adam orders.

Lawrence relents finally, lets a crying Luciana pull him toward the towering glass doors that lead into the garden. The whole way he does not tear his gaze away from his daughter. His expression is at once menacing and desolate, full of meaning that Jude cannot comprehend.

"Sorry about that, everyone," Adam says to the crowd with a forced laugh. He motions for the string quartet to start up again. "The old man can't hold his champagne."

There is a titter of stilted laughter. The music begins once more, hesitantly, one of the violists starting before the other three musicians eventually join. Adam leads Jude to the side of the room, sits her on a bench there and turns her head left and right, assesses the extent of her injuries.

"Let me get you some ice," he says.

"No, it's—" Jude starts, but her brother is already striding toward the hall. Seth, Drew, and Matthew trail after him like sharks slicing through the crowd, no doubt going to confer about whatever the hell just happened. Wolfs are very concerned with public image. If it gets out that Lawrence split his daughter's lip at his wedding, it will not look good.

Other relatives lean in close to each other to whisper. Jude glowers at them all, these people who thought she was sick and ravaged and did not come to her, did not message her or call her even once in two years to see if she was okay. They do not come to her now, either. They do not say, *Fuck that old prick, you didn't deserve that*; they do not ask her if she is all right. They drink their champagne. They eat the oysters waiters offer them. They murmur, tickled by the drama.

Jude wishes Elijah was still in the room so they could make fun of them together.

When Adam returns, it's with a champagne bucket filled with ice and one of Lawrence's chambray linen napkins (£25 each) that he handpicked for the house and that he despises guests actually using as napkins. Adam puts a handful of ice inside the square of fabric and then gives it to Jude to press to the split in her lip. It hurts like a bitch.

"Are you okay?" Adam asks.

"Oh yeah, just peachy," Jude says around the napkin. "I love it when I'm physically assaulted by my own father in public. Has he lost the plot? Is that why you're taking over?"

"No, it's—you know how he gets sometimes when he's stressed."

"Are you kidding me?"

"Sorry. I shouldn't minimize. If it's any consolation, apparently Luciana is now yelling at him in the garden. Somehow I don't think they will be consummating their union tonight."

"Good. He doesn't deserve to get laid. Why the hell did he invite me if he so desperately didn't want me here?"

"Probably because I asked him to."

"You? Why?"

"I wanted to know why he keeps you away from us. Why you suddenly disappeared off the face of the earth. Why he reacts with such vitriol whenever I inquire after you. That's why I made him invite you."

"How do you *make* Lawrence Wolf do anything?"

Adam grins. "Oh, I have my ways." He pulls down the collar of Jude's dress again to get a better look at her invocation. "It's a strange tattoo."

"Just a bit infected." Jude shrugs away from him. "It'll heal."

"A tribute to your mother, no doubt."

Jude freezes. "What?"

"Judita had one just like it, in the exact same place. I imagine Father got quite a shock to see a similar tattoo on you. I assume that's what set him off."

Jude sits very still, trying not to show any discernible reaction to this revelation. "I didn't know that."

"Oh. An odd coincidence, then. Another champagne?"

"No. I—" Jude's phone vibrates. The incoming call is from Saul. Why the hell is *Saul* calling her? "Sorry." She stands, smooths out the front of her blood-flecked dress. "I need to get this."

# TWENTY-SEVEN

**EMER'S HEART** feels like it might burst, all the air from her lungs sucked away.

From the outside, the house does not seem ostentatious. It is three levels of red brick with white window frames, a black door, and neat hedges in the small front garden. Emer knows from her time in Oxford that the richest people are often the most unassuming. They do not need gaudy estates or helicopter pads or limousines to communicate their wealth, because they are so secure in it.

There is a passage, down the side, to the right of the house, that leads beneath it. The servants' entrance, no doubt. Emer slips down and tries to get inside.

"You. Stop." Emer turns to find a woman who is blond and beautiful, smoking a cigarette. "You're very late."

"I'm sorry," Emer says.

"What are you wearing? The dress code is all black for female servers."

Emer looks down at her clothing. "Sorry," she says again.

"It's fine, for tonight. We're two waitstaff short. On a normal night, though, I would have sent you home. Follow me."

So it is that Emer does not have to break into the house at all, but she is ushered in through the front door, which is wreathed in flowers. The hall beyond is wide and bright, full to bursting with more blooms. The smell of the place is intensely sweet. There are sounds of a party. People laughing. Violins playing. Emer follows the woman. There is a wine cellar next to the kitchen, though Emer supposes *cellar* is the wrong word for it. Two of the walls are glass, the bottles showcased like jewelry in a store.

"Do you or your cousins have a black dress at the house?" the woman asks a blond teenage girl.

"I think Eugenie's Alexander McQueen is in one of the guest wardrobes. The leather-and-lace one."

"No, something simple. Not a gown."

"Oh, I have the dress that Daddy got me for my internship interview. The silk wrap with the leather belt."

"Perfect. Please give—what's your name?"

"Scarlett," Emer tells them.

"Please give Scarlett the dress for the evening and show her the staff quarters so she can get changed."

The girl looks suddenly angry. "Mummy . . . *really?*"

"Yes, really, now hurry up."

The girl pulls her mother close and whispers furiously in her ear, though not so quietly that Emer cannot hear what she says: "That dress cost four and a half thousand pounds." Her eyes land on Emer, on her poorly fitted coat. "What if she steals it?" Emer supposes that she should not be offended, given her history. Still. Something inside her twists.

The mother rolls her eyes. "Honestly, sweetie, you didn't pay for it yourself, and you've worn it once. I do not have time for this tonight."

The girl leads Emer back past the wine cellar, back past the winding staircase, to a door that reads STAFF. Beyond this is, apparently, a whole other house: another lobby, another hall, more bathrooms.

"The staff bedroom is that way," the girl says, pointing down the hall. "There's an en suite where you can get changed. The staff kitchen is that way." The girl points to the other end of the hall, through which Emer sees a second kitchen bustling with uniformed people and women in black dresses pouring champagne. "Wait here. I'll bring you the dress."

The girl leaves. Emer stays put. It would be easy to slip away. No doubt there is a staff staircase hidden back here somewhere, so that the domestic helpers do not have to be seen by the family or their guests as they move about the house. Yet Emer does not leave. She wants to put on the disguise the girl will bring her. She wants to move among the predators, seeing but unseen.

The girl returns a few minutes later with a plastic garment bag draped over her arm. "Here," she says. "Don't spill anything on it, okay? It's very expensive."

"Four and a half thousand pounds," Emer says.

The girl glares at her. "Make sure you wear deodorant. You smell like rotten eggs."

Emer changes quickly. The dress is a black wrap made of silk with a thin leather belt at the waist. It looks nice on her, but she cannot fathom how it cost so much money. Emer rolls her stolen clothes up in a ball and leaves them in a corner on the floor.

"Oh good, you're here," a woman dressed in black says when Emer enters the kitchen. "The devil is absolutely losing his shit tonight. Take these out." She hands Emer a tray of champagne glasses and tells her to follow the other servers.

Usually when she trails her prey, she feels the weighty meat of her muscles as she moves. Now her heart beats hot and hard with fear. The woman that has been growing inside her for the past ten years is replaced by the frightened seven-year-old who watched her family die. There is a boiling, sour tide in her stomach. There is the painful scream of blood through the needle-thin capillaries of her ears. The thin skin that stretches over all the soft, wet parts of her.

Is she right? Will they really be here?

"Start with the guests by the string quartet," says the server in front of her as they walk into a large ballroom bedecked with flowers. Emer stands next to a table, breathing quickly.

A woman says, "Oh yes, I will have a champagne." Emer goes to her and lowers the tray. The woman takes a glass. Emer looks up, out across the extravagant room—and there he is. Staring right at her.

*Andy.*

She knows him the moment she sees him. The past decade has been kind to his features. He barely looks older than he did the day he came to her home in Ireland and murdered everyone she knew. Emer's mouth parts in a gasp. Andy narrows his eyes, as though he is trying to place her, and then begins making his way through the crowd toward her.

The others are also here. These four men killed her family. The four of them walked into her house with guns and hatred and undid her world. They have been here the whole time. Eating oysters and drinking cold champagne served to them by other people. While Emer starved in forests in Ireland. While Emer's toes rotted off in the cold. They were here.

And among them, surrounded by them, in this nest of witch hunters—Jude.

"Volkov," Emer whispers to herself. From the Russian *volk*. How could she not have seen? *"Wolf."*

# TWENTY-EIGHT

"SORRY, I need to get this," Jude tells Adam. Adam nods as Jude stands and wends her way through the crowd and steps out into the flower-infested hall to answer her phone. The music from the string quartet still resonates here. Waiters bustle past with trays of champagne and hors d'oeuvres. Jude closes the huge pocket doors behind her so she can hear.

"Saul," Jude says when she picks up. "Listen, if you've racked up another debt with phone psychics, I swear I'm—"

"She worked for your father," Saul says breathlessly.

"What? Who worked for my father?"

"The woman you wanted dirt on. Vera Clarke. She worked for your old man, or at least she was about to. She'd just been brought on as a lawyer at one of his papers."

Jude had entirely forgotten she'd asked him to go digging on Vera Clarke. "Are you sure? You've so rarely brought me useful information before."

Jude looks up from the marble floor just in time to lock eyes with Emer, standing next to the entrance to the service stairs, a tray of empty champagne glasses in her hand.

Emer—is here?

Why the hell is Emer *here*? Jude is bewildered.

"Emer?" she says. The witch's expression is hard, fearful. *Get out*, she mouths—and then she pushes through the door and disappears without a word.

"Are you there?" Saul says on the phone. "Just listen, you little shit. Another one of the victims—what's her name?" Jude hears the sound of rustling paper. "Oh yeah. Savannah Jones."

"What about her?" Jude's thoughts are blurred, looping. The hall is cold, and she cannot make anything make sense. Emer is here? Yes, Jude gave her the address.

"She was hired as a PA at another one of your father's companies just before she died."

Something unpleasant settles in Jude's stomach, slimy as an eel. *A tribute to your mother, no doubt.* "Wait, slow down, who are we talking about?"

"Savannah Jones worked for your father. Vera Clarke worked for your father."

"Oh."

A man strides past where Jude sits. She does not look up in time to see his face, but he pauses at the entrance to the service stairs and glances back at her before he pushes through the door.

Drew.

"That doesn't sound good," Jude says.

Why is Drew going into the service corridors?

"No, it doesn't, does it."

"Surely—if this was really a lead, the police would have followed it by now."

"I looked into that, too."

"Oh?"

"Lawrence Wolf has been making significant fundraising contributions to Met charities for years. It's not unusual for rich folk."

"This isn't a gangster movie, Saul. This is real life."

"Do you know who your father is?"

Jude touches her split lip. "I know who he is."

"I'm not saying he's a killer. I'm not saying this is any more than a coincidence. But I'd tread carefully if I were you."

The lights go out suddenly. There are screams and laughter from the ballroom, titters of excitement, the thrill of the darkness interjecting into the normal world. Jude tries to keep her breathing steady and waits for the lights. There are generators in this house and backup generators should those fail.

The lights stay out.

Instead, there is a screeching sound as heavy metal screens begin to lower over the windows and doors. Jude stands and whispers, "No."

Red emergency lighting pumps on. An alarm begins to blare. It's all very *Star Trek* red alert, which is probably where her father got the idea. Jude makes a dash toward the front door, trying to get there before the grate comes all the way down. There is time for her to escape, to save herself—but Zara is in this house. Emer—for some bloody reason—is in this house.

Jude stops running and watches as the grate groans to the floor and locks into place. Locks her inside. The house is a fortress now. It is designed to survive nuclear fallout, to protect the Wolf family in case of civil unrest or, like, the fucking Purge. They rode out the first few months of the pandemic here, ready to bring up the drawbridge in case things went pear-shaped and the peasants decided it was time to eat the rich.

There is no way in. There is no way out.

Jude turns. The hall is red, red, red, the color of arterial blood.

Eerily, the violinists are still playing in the ballroom. There is still chattering and laughter.

The rest of the Wolf family is not afraid. Only Jude is afraid.

The double doors at the end of the hall slide open. A figure emerges into the redness. A tall, shadowy figure.

Suddenly Jude knows why the grates have come down.

The pieces click together in her mind in a way that makes sickening sense. Emer, here. Her father's fury. A strange tattoo like her mother's. Drew. *Andrew.*

Of course, of course, of course.

"Please," she says as he approaches her in the gloom. "Please."

She wants to run—but there is nowhere to go.

The figure knocks her hard against the head.

Jude gasps and tumbles down, down, down into darkness.

# TWENTY-NINE

**THERE IS** nothing.

There is nothing.

There is nothing.

It hasn't worked.

Why hasn't it *worked*?

Zara screams and tears out a chunk of her hair. Froth and spittle fly from her mouth as she pounds Savannah's chest, commanding her heart to beat.

Zara is gasping, choking. The sobbing will kill her. Good. *Good.* She wants to die. Right here, close to the remains of her sister.

And then, from the darkness, a thin sound.

A whisper.

A tinkle.

Zara gasps and stops breathing. She waits. She waits.

There, again. The softest of chimes. Zara swallows and wipes away a bead of snot with her hand.

"Sav?" she whispers. Savannah is unmoving. Zara watches and

waits. Watches her sister's desiccated remains and waits for the bell to sound again.

The fingers curl. The bell rings. Zara wails with joy.

She collapses on top of her sister's chest.

Savannah is alive.

Zara watches the recomposition of her sister with awe.

Black, milky eyes stare into the light. She blinks. She blinks! The eyes drift like sea jellies in their sockets. They are wet, gelatinous things. The fingers twitch and curl like dying spiders as the great electric nervous system sparks back to life. Zara helps her to sit up. Savannah is like a newborn, fresh into the world, slippery with earth. She slides along the floor and stays there for a while, jerking like a fish out of water, her face buried in the carpet.

The clothing she was buried in has decayed on her body so it hangs off her in strips. She is mostly naked, her dead flesh aglow in the soft light of the panic room. Her thighs shake, her knees buckle.

She does not look well or whole or human. Though she moves as if she's living, her body remains shriveled from months beneath the ground. Zara holds her sister's face in her hands and tries to get her to look at her.

"Sav?" Zara asks. There is no flicker of recognition there. The eyes are bulbous and unfocused. The mouth opens and closes without passing sound. Black sap leaks out of her, the liquefied remains of her gut seeping from her mouth and nose and eyes. It carries with it a tide of all the things that were eating her insides only minutes ago: the pale eggs of things that live under the soil and never see sunlight. Savannah gags and vomits all over herself. The smell of it makes the air feel hot and thick.

Zara steps back.

Savannah's tongue, her gums, her lips—all are the color and texture of autumn leaves, dry and crackling. The teeth sit exposed, each a little yellow tombstone.

The creature is monstrous.

Savannah is monstrous.

Zara wipes the liquid from Savannah's face with the corner of her jacket. "There you are," she says to her sister. "There you are."

But is Savannah there? She moans. Her head begins to dip from side to side, a predator taking the scent of prey it cannot see. Her eyes lock on to the empty bin of blood. She shoves Zara off her with surprising strength and buries her whole head in the bin, rabidly licking at the leftover blood.

"Oh, right," Zara says, remembering that Róisín wanted payment in someone else's blood before she would answer any of Emer's questions. Zara goes to the mini fridge and takes out the last remaining bag of chilled blood.

"Savannah?" Zara tears open the bag. Savannah is on her in a heartbeat, her teeth snapping at Zara's fingers to get at it. Zara throws it on the floor, watches as the blood spills across the rich white carpet. Savannah is already on her knees, her lips and tongue against the floor as she sucks blood from the fibers.

Zara watches in horror. When as much of the blood is sucked up as possible, the creature looks up at her, its face slicked red, its eyes hungry for more. When Zara speaks, her voice is wavering. "I need to tell you something. Can you understand me?"

"Yes." The sound that comes from Savannah's mouth is not Savannah's voice. It is low and raspy, air forced through vocal cords that have been decomposing for a year. It is slow, a growl from a thing that is not quite human.

"I'm so sorry," Zara whispers. She doesn't know if Savannah is really there, can really hear her, but she has to say what she came here to say. "I'm so sorry for everything I said to you that night." The fight had started when Zara spotted the dressing covering Savannah's tattoo. *A neck tattoo.* Zara can't remember exactly what she said to her sister, though she knows it contained the phrases *trashy* and *no class.* For a long time, Zara had wanted more for Sav. She wanted her to go back and finish high school. She wanted her to go to university. She wanted her to quit working dead-end jobs and dating deadbeat boyfriends.

Zara wanted her sister to be more like *her.* Studious. Ladylike. Respectable. A promising young woman.

"Don't you get it?" Savannah said before she left, before she slammed the door behind her, before Zara never saw her alive again. "I sacrificed everything for you. I quit school and got that dead-end job to keep a roof over your head so that *you* can stay in school. So that *you* can go to Oxford one day. So that *you* can follow your dreams. I don't have dreams, Zara, and that doesn't bother me at all—because I gave them all to *you.*"

"I didn't mean any of it," Zara says, tears welling in her eyes. "I was so awful, and I didn't mean any of it, and I've been sorry for everything I said every day since you died."

The creature stares at her with those big, yolky eyes, then finally breaks eye contact and stands and goes to the door. She drops to her hands and knees and presses her nose to the base of the door, tries to draw in the scent of the hall beyond.

Zara becomes suddenly aware of her own body, the adrenaline that's been driving her beginning to fade. The dryness of her throat, the salty smell of sweat from her armpits. Her heavy limbs. The too-cold air in the panic room. An enormous fear swelling inside of her chest.

"Are you there, Savvy? I need you to be there. I need you to hear this."

The lights snap out, plunging the room into solid blackness. Zara yelps and holds her hands up to her face, expecting the demon inside Savannah to come for her in the dark.

"What's happening?" Savannah asks, her voice husky.

Red lights flicker on. Zara can see again. Savannah hasn't moved, hasn't lunged for her, is still crouched by the door.

"I don't know," Zara says. An alarm begins to sound, a long and bone-chilling wail that lifts and lowers and lifts again, over and over.

Have they been found out?

"Why did you want a spell to find things?" Zara asks, stepping closer to Savannah. "What were you looking for?"

"Let me out," Savannah says.

"What did you need to find so badly that you sold part of your soul for it?"

"Let me out, and I will tell you."

"Do you know who killed you? What was his name?"

"I won't hurt anyone," the creature says. Its eyes are black glass. Something like a smile tugs at one corner of its mouth and Zara can see, in that moment, that it is not Savannah. "I promise."

*Oh God.* A tear slides down Zara's cheek. "I don't know the passcode," Zara whispers. "I really don't."

This makes the creature angry. Savannah had a quick temper, but not like this. The creature launches across the room and begins smashing things. It puts its hand through the TV. It knocks over the bar cart, sends all the glasses and bottles of alcohol clinking across the floor. When it is done, it slumps to the carpet amidst the wreckage and begins to howl. The sounds are violent and terrible, and it squalls on and on, competing with the alarm for shrillness.

Zara puts her hands over her ears and cries silently as she watches.

The alarm stops. Savannah stops. They sit and say nothing for a long time, at an impasse. Zara waits and waits for the door to spring open, for Lawrence Wolf or the police to come, but nobody does. Savannah stares at her with devilish eyes.

"Savannah," the thing says eventually. It places a hand to its chest, as if remembering who it is. It looks at Zara. It crawls over to her and holds Zara's face in its corpse hands. "Zara. Yes?"

"Yes," Zara says, her heart racing. More tears slide down her cheeks, coming hot and fast now. She has wanted to hold her sister for a year. To touch her skin, to pull her close. To fold into Savannah's body like she did for the first sixteen years of her life. "That's right." Something of Savannah is in there. "Now try to remember for me. What were you looking for? Who killed you?"

"Here." The creature's eyes slide from one side of the room to the other as if slowly accessing a memory. It is like watching Prudence's old desktop computer whir. Savannah pulls away from Zara and stands and trails her fingertips along the Chesterfield. She picks up a glass from the toppled bar cart and holds it up to the red light. She mimes taking a sip, mimes laughing, then lets the glass fall to the carpet. She sits down on the sofa and leans back and closes her eyes. She touches her left breast, squeezes it. She runs her palm up her neck, over her jaw, turns her hand around and kisses it, bites the dry skin there.

"Savannah?" Zara whispers. "What are you doing?"

What is she remembering?

Savannah's eyes snap open, her gaze narrowed on the panic room door. She goes to it again, presses her palms and cheek against it, closes her eyes.

"The door is steel." Zara can barely speak, does not understand what is happening. "The walls and ceiling, too. You can't get out. Not without the passcode. Please, just talk to me."

Savannah's eyes open. Her fingers walk across the wall to the keypad. She presses a button, and then another, and then another, and then another. She looks back at Zara.

"Here," she says again. "Do you understand?"

The keypad beeps. A light goes from red to green. There is a heaving sound as the door unlocks and swings open on heavy hinges.

"Oh my God," Zara whispers as the wraith slips into the corridor.

Savannah is out—and there's only one way she could have known the passcode.

She's been here, in this room, when she was alive.

She's been here before.

# THIRTY

**EMER GOES** down the service stairs again, to the basement buried beneath the house.

There is a lavish indoor pool here, past the staff kitchen. It is very long and narrow, flanked by deck chairs. Emer presses on, deeper into the underground. She passes a sauna. A steam room. A gym. A home theater. Two more staff bedrooms. The boiler room. A surveillance room, all of them coming off the pool room. And then, finally, what she is looking for: a locked room, right at the very end. No attempt has been made to hide it. It is not concealed behind bookshelves or a painting. A vault door—metal with a pronged spinner to open and close it.

Emer sinks her teeth into the old wound on her arm, opening the scab. She drips her blood onto the locking mechanism and allows Bael to feast upon it. In exchange, the demon unlocks the door. The metal door swings open, and Emer steps inside.

It is a trophy room. There are no heads mounted like game. Instead, it is a museum of stolen artifacts. There are many books, all displayed on shelves with their covers face up. Beneath each is a plaque with a location and a year. *Ipswich, 1988. Inverness, 1995. Marseille, 1996. Sarajevo, 1998.*

The dates and locations of massacres, Emer realizes.

Emer stops by a plaque that reads *Killarney, 2013.* The book above it is old and bound in soft red leather. Emer reaches out to touch it. She opens the cover. The title page reads *Leabhar Byrne.*

*The Book of Byrne.*

Emer keeps moving around the space. There are other trophies, too. A tray with locks of hair tied together with ribbon. A tray with jewelry, talismans stolen from witches. Then, at the back, the proof Emer has been searching for: trays and trays of invocations cut from the flesh of dead women. The rectangles of skin are stretched and pinned like butterfly specimens. Not just one tray, but many. Emer scans them. She finds the spells they cut out of her mother, her grandmother, her cousins. Strangely, she does not see any of her own work.

"Good evening, little Byrne."

Emer whips around.

It is him. He is here, in the doorway. The man who has haunted her days and nights for a decade. The man who killed Róisín.

"Andy," she says.

"No one has called me Andy since university. My real name is Drew. Andrew Wolf. And you—you are the girl from the orchard in Lough Leane." He steps inside the room. "I'm pleased to see you. I've thought about you often." There is a red button on the wall by the entrance. Andy Volkov presses it. The lights around them go red. An alarm begins to sound. "I won't let you sneak away so easily this time."

Emer touches the leaden spell on her necklace. He thinks she is trapped in here with him, but really he is trapped in here with her. "How did you find us?" she asks.

Andrew Wolf smiles. "I was in Cork on business eight months before you and I met for the first time. Do you understand?"

"No."

"I met your sister. Or cousin, I don't know how you're all related. Róisín. I was happy to provide her with what she wanted. I saw her in a nightclub, drunk as anything, slipping around the dance floor in her little clothes. I took her back to my hotel. I may never have known what she was, except I overheard her in the bathroom, holding commune with the devil. One of the necessities of my line of work: fluency in Latin. I realized, then, what she was—and what she'd come to Cork for. She wanted a baby. Not many modern covens are as isolated as yours was. Most have integrated now. They live in cities, they have jobs, they get married and have children the normal way. Your family was old-school, sending dopey virgins out on missions to get knocked up. I could've killed her that night— one less witch in the world is always a good thing—but I smelled a larger prize: her coven."

Andrew Wolf's eyes go unfocused, as though he is remembering. "Róisín wanted so desperately to be loved. In the morning, when she woke up, she told me she had to go, but I convinced her to stay a while longer. We spent the day together. We spent another night together. I whispered sweet nothings in her ear. I tried to remember the sappiest quotes from movies, because I knew she probably hadn't seen them. *To me, you are perfect. You complete me.* And the real kicker: *You have bewitched me, body and soul, and I love . . . I love . . . I love you.* That was the one that got her."

The wolf draws closer to Emer. She steps each time he steps. They circle the table in the center of the room.

"I had my father post me to Cork for business so I could be nearby when she came looking for me. Slowly, I gained her trust, and slowly, she revealed herself to me. She told me she was pregnant. I told her how much I loved her and how much I would love our child. She told me about her isolated childhood and how I was not like the monstrous stories she'd heard of men. Eventually, when it became too conspicuous for her to keep traveling to Cork, she told me that Killarney would be an easier meeting place, that her strict family lived on a farm on Lough Leane and she could slip away more frequently if I went there, so I did. Right before she was due to give birth, I followed her home, to the secret house where your family lived. My brothers and I came back the next day. The rest of the story you already know."

The way he tells his tale is monstrous. There is no feeling in it at all. It is bare facts. He is not gloating or proud, he is simply recounting things as they are.

"You are a monster," Emer says. Her fingers go to the spell at her throat. Her back is to the door now. The basement room with the pool is behind her. How quickly can she move? How quickly can she dart out of the door and close it? How quickly can she attach the invocation to her heartspace and invite Bael into her soul?

"No," Drew says. "I loved Róisín. Don't you see that? I loved her and our unborn daughter—and in the end, that is why I had to end them both. They were tainted by magic. Their souls were bound to the devil. I freed that which I loved most from evil. It was the hardest thing I've ever done. Now I am going to do the same for you."

Drew looks over Emer's shoulder, to the opening door at her back. She begins to turn, but she is not fast enough. A strong hand closes over her mouth.

Wolves. They hunt in packs.

# THIRTY-ONE

**JUDE COMES** to in low light.

The space inside her skull feels like a puffer fish: spiky, oily, pressurized. She tries to move but finds that her wrists are bound behind her back, which makes her panic and yank hard at her fastenings, but they don't budge.

There is someone close to her. A man, staring at her. The same person who smacked the side of her skull and knocked her out cold.

"Lawrence?" she asks, but as her sight clarifies, she sees that it is almost her father's face but not quite.

"No," Adam says. "Not Lawrence."

"Adam." The memory of how she got here slides through her head, a slick, slippery thing she cannot quite grasp. There was a figure in the hall. Not her father's face; her eldest brother's.

They look so much alike.

There are other faces in the ghostlight. Jude blinks and tries to bring them into focus. Where is she? She cannot quite remember. The room is lit by flickering candles. Shadows shift and jitter, making it hard to see. Still, Jude knows the elaborate cornicing, the enormous marble fireplace, the gilt bronze and Baccarat chandeliers sourced from a nineteenth-century French palace.

The ballroom. The house that no one lives in, that family members pass through only for glittering parties and long summer lunches catered by famous chefs. There is a party tonight. The room is bedecked in flowers. There are brothers and nieces and nephews. Adam, Matthew, Seth, Drew. The Horsemen, Jude and Elijah call them, a.k.a. the Four Horsemen of the Apocalypse, because they're all so serious and ridiculous. She looks for Eli, but he is not there, nor is her father. Everyone is dressed in suits and dark evening dresses made of silk and velvet. Everyone holds a crystal glass filled with champagne. Everyone stares at Jude with hungry eyes.

A wedding. Yes, that is why she's here. Her father's wedding. An alarm was going off, but the room is quiet now. The red sirens have been replaced by the eerie candle glow. Some time must have passed.

With a start, Jude realizes that she's inside the enormous gilt peacock cage.

"What the actual hell is going on?" she asks as she again pulls hard at her bonds. "Why am I in the bloody birdcage?"

"'Thou shalt not suffer a witch to live,'" Adam says softly.

Jude stops still. Something deep inside her shudders.

*They know.*

They know what she is.

Of course they do.

They are witch hunters.

"Oh," Jude says, her eyes landing on Drew. To his family he is Drew. To the world he is Andrew Wolf.

*When I was a child, four men came to my house and killed my family. They burned the house to the ground. Nineteen women died.*

*Andy.*

"It was you," Jude whispers. "The four of you." She looks at each of her brothers in turn. Adam. Drew. Seth. Matthew. "You killed the Byrne family. You went to Ireland ten years ago. You massacred nineteen women."

"Massacred?" Adam says. "No, Jude, you misunderstand what we do. We liberated those women. We saved them from themselves."

There's movement from behind her. A tug on her bonds. There's another body in the cage with her, Jude realizes, tied behind her, their wrists bound together. Jude looks over her shoulder and tries to get a look.

"Emer?" she whispers.

Emer doesn't answer. The witch is gagged and slumped forward, unconscious.

That's when Jude knows. That's when Jude fully understands.

They are witches. They are in a cage. They are surrounded by witch hunters.

"You're going to kill us."

"Lawrence tried so hard to keep you away from us," Adam says. "I see that now, the sly old bastard. He knew what you'd become and knew what we'd need to do to you if we found out. So he spun the tale of a damaged heiress with a drug problem, and—like fools—we believed it."

"Why?" Jude asks. "Why do this?"

"That is the deal we made with God and Crown when we were first granted our lands hundreds of years ago. We had a different name then, when we first came to this country and offered our services to the king."

"A different name?" Jude asks.

"Volkov," Adam says. "Wolf. Then there were witches aplenty. A man could make a good living as a hunter—and we did. We slaughtered them by the dozen, and with each fresh kill, our favor grew. We were granted more land, more wealth, more power. We ushered this country out of the Dark Ages of devil worship and into the light. Modern Britain was built by our work. Now your kind are much harder to find. They scurry and scatter when we try to hunt them. Sometimes, though, they hide in plain sight, right beneath our noses. Like you. Like your mother."

Jude shudders.

*A tribute to your mother, no doubt.*

"You . . . murdered Judita." Jude almost laughs even as a twist of pain spikes through her—how could she not have seen? "You killed my mother."

Not an accident, after all. Not Lawrence, either. *Adam.*

Fifteen years ago, Jude's eldest brother would have been in his late twenties. There are photographs and videos of him from that week on the yacht. In them, he is tall and taut, his sandy hair bleached by the sun, his young muscles certainly strong enough to push a drunk woman off a boat into the sea—but perhaps it isn't that simple. Perhaps Judita didn't slip silently into the ocean and drown in the dark. Perhaps she had also woken in a shadow-slicked room like this one, her head thumping, the hungry eyes of wolves picking over her body, desperate to feast on her power.

Adam nods. There is no need to rush, no need to hide things now. They have her in a cage.

"Lawrence brought his devil bride into our family and hoped we wouldn't notice what she was. It took some time to figure out, I will admit. Who would have expected him to squirrel her away in plain sight? But eventually, it came to light. She was fighting with our father on the yacht, so drunk she couldn't stand. I put her to bed. I saw the marking on her neck. Lawrence spent the night collapsed in his bed. Judita spent the night being cleansed of her sins, just as you will be this evening." Adam looks at her sadly. "I love you, Jude. I know we have never been close, but you are my blood. I want you to know that we are only doing this because we care *so deeply* about you and about your soul. You have damaged it beyond repair; this is the only path to salvation."

"How exactly are you going to 'save' me, huh? How did you 'save' her?"

"I cut her throat." Adam's eyes do not leave Jude's. He looks so sad, the hangdog face of a grieving man. The bastard. "The art is to kill them quickly, before they can use their blood magic against you. I drank her blood. Through my holy body, her soul was purified. Everyone who was on the boat that night took part—even you. We placed a drop of her blood on your tongue while you slept so that you, too, could help save your mother."

Jude's stomach is sour. She cannot help the tide of sickness that rises in her throat, washes past her lips. She coughs and spits. Champagne and hors d'oeuvres dribble down her chin, down her dress. She half expects the vomit to be tinted red with her mother's blood. God. *God.*

"Our greatest find came a decade ago," Adam continues. "The Byrne coven in Ireland, one of the last remaining bolt-holes of the old ways. A family of rats, living and breeding and poisoning their young with the occult. That year, we purified nineteen. Nineteen souls saved. Do you remember what it was like in the months afterward? Maybe not, since you were still a child, but our wealth increased nineteenfold." Adam laughs in wonderment. "Do you see? Our family is blessed. We have a divine mandate to release the souls of witches from their bodies, and we are rewarded for it, as we have always been."

Jude spits, tries to get the acid taste out of her mouth. "You can't all be okay with this." Jude locks eyes with her niece Dove. They are the same age, they went to the same school, they moved in the same circles. Dove, the pretty TikTok star who makes videos about ending factory farming and saving the whales. "Dove. You can't honestly be cool with this. You're going to stand there and watch them cut my throat? This is fucking unhinged, and you know it."

The girl swallows and looks at her mother.

"Don't listen to her, Dove," the woman says. "Don't listen to the devil using her tongue to speak."

"Oh, screw you, Karen," Jude says. "You've never liked me."

"You see?" Karen says. "Foul language betrays a foul soul."

"I once walked in on you doing cocaine in my childhood bedroom, and somehow *I've* got the foul soul?"

"This isn't my first cleansing, Jude," Dove says quietly. "I was inaugurated five years ago, when I was twelve. I found the woman myself. She was the grandmother of one of my nannies. When she came to visit from Poland, I saw the marks on her wrists, and I knew what she was. I knew what had to be done to save her."

"You're a goddamn vegan influencer!"

Dove pouts. "I don't consider human blood an animal product."

Adam places his hand on his daughter's shoulder and squeezes. He is proud, Jude thinks. Proud of the murder that his daughter instigated and took part in.

"You were supposed to be there, but Lawrence sent you away the weekend of the ritual," Adam says. "I should have fought harder to make sure you didn't stray down the same path as your mother. I failed you—we all failed you—and for that I'm sorry. Tonight, we pay our penance with your blood."

"Stay the hell away from me," Jude says as Adam goes to the fireplace mantel and takes down a box made of dark wood. Inside is a silver dagger with a wolf's head carved into the hilt. "Stay the fuck away from me, Adam, I swear to God." It doesn't sound like a threat. It sounds shaky and desperate, because it is. Jude tugs at her bindings again, but they are too tight to break free from. "Emer, now would be a fan-bloody-tastic time to wake up and do something," she says. The witch stirs behind her, her movements slow, but she says nothing.

"Viktor Volkov's knife, presented to him by the king, upon the burning of his first witch. Tonight, it will spill your blood and cleanse you of your evil, as it has done for hundreds of women before you."

Jude is crying as Adam approaches her. She draws on the power that Emer's spell seared into her soul. The spark, the ball of nested pain, the burn of electricity gutting through the nerves of her arm. There is a static spark from her fingertips—and then nothing more. Again she tries, and again little webs of light hiss at her fingertips, gentle as the tongues of snakes. The invocation was unfinished, unstable. Sometimes it is a match, sometimes it is a bonfire. In this moment, it fails to light altogether.

Everyone is holding empty glasses. Glasses into which Jude's blood will be poured, warm and fresh as syrup tapped from a maple tree.

Everyone begins to chant. It is a soft sound at first, sweet as a lullaby, but it becomes more and more discordant as Adam draws nearer to Jude.

He reaches the cage and takes her by the hair. If only he was touching her skin, she might be able to knock him out using her invocation. The chanting becomes wailing, weeping, animal.

"I absolve you of your sins," Adam says.

*I can't believe I'm going to die in this ugly dress,* Jude thinks.

Her brother tips her head back and places the point of his blade against her jugular.

Jude screams as it breaks the skin.

# THIRTY-TWO

**"SAVANNAH!" ZARA** says to the shadowy hall. "Get back here!"

The creature doesn't listen. It barrels down a spiral staircase, pushing farther into the dark house. Zara gives chase. The wraith moves impossibly quickly, a ghost always just out of reach. Finally, several floors down, the staircase spits Zara out into another hall, this one grand and marble-clad.

There is flickering light at the end of the space and . . . the sound of people chanting? Savannah is drawn to the thrumming noise. Zara darts after her. She can still stop this. Coax Savannah back upstairs, lock her in the panic room somehow, fix this—but how, if she knows the bloody code?

*"Savannah!"*

The creature doesn't stop. Its pace is picking up.

Zara is on the verge of tears now, panting, desperate. "Savvy. Please!"

The corpse of her sister pauses. She turns back toward Zara. For a split second, Zara thinks she sees something in her eyes.

Something familiar. But then the creature snarls, bares its rotting gums. It turns and opens the doors and steps into the room beyond.

It is too late.

Zara approaches the rectangle of light that Savannah has left in her wake, the gap between the doors. The scene beyond is a dream, a blur. Zara cannot make sense of it. It's a ritual of some kind, attended by glamorous people in gowns and suits. Each holds a candle in their hands. They sway as they chant the same haunting, hissing prayer.

Zara's gaze lands on Jude and Emer.

Jude and Emer.

Jude . . . and Emer?

Here.

At the center of the vast ballroom.

In a . . . cage.

A human-size gilded cage.

Both are bound. Emer is gagged. Jude bucks furiously as a man approaches her with a knife.

"I absolve you of your sins," the man says as he places the tip of the blade against Jude's neck and breaks the skin. Jude screams. The blood beads, swells, drips to the floor. The wound is deep but not lethal, not yet.

It is at that moment that all hell breaks loose. The wraith inside Savannah hurtles through the crowd with gnashing teeth, tearing out chucks of flesh from all the beautifully dressed people. Blood flies in arcs, slashing across the walls. Candles fall from the hands of shrieking victims, each snuffed-out light leaving the room a little darker than before.

Savannah is . . .

Savannah is *eating* people.

"Jones!" Jude shouts, snapping Zara from her daze. "Open the bloody cage!"

Zara doesn't want to go into the room with that thing, doesn't want to get closer to the blood and the violence and the gurgling sounds of death, but she does. She stumbles over the bleeding body of a girl who looks no older than her and staggers toward the cage. It is closed but mercifully not locked. Zara climbs inside it and yanks Emer's gag down.

"Bael," Emer gasps. "Occide." Though Zara cannot see the demon, she can see the violence it begins to wreak. Savannah is slamming into people and tearing at their flesh, but Bael lifts them clean from the floor and eviscerates them. It opens their backs and pulls out their spines and leaves the skin to last. People scatter into the house, fleeing the ballroom while Savannah feeds and Bael destroys.

Half a minute passes while Zara works at undoing Emer's and Jude's bonds. Suddenly there is silence. No more screams, no more desperate attempts to escape. The floor of the ballroom is slick with blood, ruby-bright in the candlelight. There is no one left living in the room now but the three girls in the cage at the center of it.

Finally, the knots in the rope give and Jude and Emer are free.

Jude rubs her wrists. "Jesus, Jones. Talk about a well-timed entrance."

"Quiet," Emer warns. Zara and Jude turn to face what she is staring at. "Stay very still."

Savannah turns her dead eyes toward them. Blood and black bile weep from Savannah's mouth. The whole front of her is soaked red, the ends of her long blond hair dip-dyed in arterial blood.

"What did you do?" Emer breathes.

A tear slides down Zara's cheek as her sister's corpse sniffs the air, grunting like a creature in search of prey.

"The demon has her," Emer says. "The blood has sent it wild."

Savannah's head cocks sharply in their direction.

"It will come for Jude," Emer continues.

"What?" Jude whispers through clenched teeth. "Why *me*?"

"Because you are bleeding. Press your hand to your wound, very slowly."

Jude does as Emer says, moving her hand to the gash at her neck.

"Can't you stab it?" Jude breathes. "You're always threatening to stab things."

"They took my knife."

"Can we make a run for it?"

"We cannot let it leave the house. It will not stop killing until it is destroyed. Besides—" Emer lifts a hand. Savannah's gaze locks on to it immediately. She snarls and launches toward them, instantly rabid, though the floor is slick now and she slips with the sudden motion and lands face-first in a pool of blood. When she draws herself back up, she seems to have lost their location again.

"Good thing we're in a cage," Jude whispers.

Zara swallows, thinking. "I'm going to open the cage door. I'm going to let her in."

"The hell you are."

"She wants Jude, right?" Zara whispers. "We open the cage door, Emer and I get out, Jude stands in the doorway and dives out of the way at the last second. Then we trap Savannah in the cage and—" She cannot finish the sentence. Burn what is left of her into oblivion?

"You want to use me as bait?" Jude whispers furiously.

"Yes," Zara says.

"I do not like that plan, Jones."

"Do you have a better one?"

A discarded candle, rolled beneath one of the heavy curtains, chooses that moment to set the fabric on fire. It grows quickly, then begins to smoke and climb in seconds.

"Okay." Jude breathes a sigh of relief. "We just stay in here until she burns."

Zara looks around the room: There is a lot of wood. The room is a tinderbox. It will go up in minutes.

Another curtain, even closer to them, also catches alight.

Emer shakes her head. "We will die of smoke inhalation long before she does."

The curtains are already blazing. The flames lick at the paneled walls, curling tongues into the wood. The ceiling begins to fill with storm clouds of smoke. Already Zara's throat is burning, her eyes full of stinging nettles.

The three of them share a look. Very soon it will be too late.

A second later, the decision is made for them. A bead of Jude's blood wells up through her fingertips and falls to the cage's floor. Savannah's head snaps in their direction.

"Move," Emer orders, but Zara is already in motion.

The two of them launch out of the cage at once, throwing the gate wide as Savannah careens toward them. Jude staggers to the mouth of the cage, wincing as she lands on her cursed leg.

"Come at me, you zombie bitch," she says.

Savannah hurls herself at her. Jude twists out of the way at the last moment. Savannah slams into the opposite side of the cage, the force and weight of her sending the whole thing toppling with Jude still inside. Then they are on top of each other. Jude kicks her off and scrabbles for the gate, now more of a hatch, while Savannah tries to get her teeth into Jude. Jude almost makes it, but Savannah gnashes at her fingertips, clamping down hard on two of them as Jude tumbles backward out of the cage: She rips off Jude's fingers and lunges for her throat, but this time Jude is faster. She gets out of the cage. Zara and Emer slam the bolt shut, shutting Savannah— still crunching on Jude's finger bones—inside.

Jude wails, clutching her bleeding right hand to her chest. Emer drags her toward the pocket doors and out of the blazing room.

Zara is only vaguely aware of what's going on around her. She watches the flames approach her sister's cage, watches as the fire twists and leaps higher. The undead creature finishes its meal and then realizes, when it touches the bolt, that the metal is searing hot. It hisses and rears back. It is trapped. It bucks in its cage. It froths at the mouth. It screams in foul, unknown languages.

The fire licks at its feet. The scraps of clothing it is dressed in begin to melt on its body.

Finally, it comes to stillness. It locks eyes with Zara. It is haunted and ghostly, its eyes wide. It is frightened. Zara knows then that some of Savannah has survived inside of it. That her sister is about to die again, and this time she will have to watch. That this time it will be her fault.

Jude and Emer are at the door now, Jude still bleeding, still swearing. Emer is calling to Zara. "Hurry," she says to her. Her voice is muffled as though underwater. "Zara, hurry, come." Zara barely registers her. She cannot look away. It is only when Emer puts her hand on her shoulder and physically steers her back that Zara stirs. The curtains are serpentine things, whipping about in the flames like adders ready to strike.

If she does not move, she will stay here and burn with her sister. It is what she deserves—but she lets Emer pull her back anyway.

They teeter across the room. They step over exsanguinated bodies, their necks opened by human teeth.

They hear the hiss of the water quenching flame, feel the welcome coolness on their skin, before they understand what is happening.

"It's raining," Zara says, holding her hands out in front of her. *How curious*, is her first thought. *Rain indoors.* She looks up. The ceiling is a storm of smoke and gusting darkness. It is pouring from a dozen little clouds. Absolutely bucketing down, as Prudence would say, the droplets big and sharp as sleet.

Sprinklers, Zara realizes. The fire is being doused by sprinklers.

Emer looks frightened. Zara turns and stares through the rain to see what she sees. Savannah has stilled. Steam rises from the suddenly cooled metal of the cage. The creature is looking up at the ceiling, watching the water, slowly coming to understand its own salvation. It drops its gaze. It looks at them. It is no longer frenzied by blood and fire. It has longer to think, longer to plot.

It looks at the bolt, no longer red hot. It considers it for a moment.

And then it slides it open.

# THIRTY-THREE

**EMER SLAMS** the pocket doors behind her and ties the handles together with the cord of a nearby lamp.

Jude is swearing, cradling her injured hand to her chest. "Your dead sister bit off my bloody fingers!"

"Oh God, oh God, oh God," Zara chants.

"These doors will not hold her for long," Emer says as they turn and run. They have an obligation to kill it, that undead thing—but they cannot do that if they are dead. They need a plan.

Dozens of Wolf family members and wedding guests lie wounded and groaning in the hall. The three girls surge over them.

"Witch," one man spits, his mouth full of blood. "Witch, witch, witch."

Emer slows and kneels before him. He is not one of the four men who came to her house that day, but he looks similar enough to be a relative. "I know what I am. Now, you keep quiet or I will unleash hell on you again."

The three of them scramble for the front door only to find that it is hidden now behind metal shutters.

"Are there any other ways out of the house?" Emer asks Jude as they swing back to face the hall.

Savannah crashes into the doors, making all three of them jump. The people in the hallway scream and stand and begin to scatter into the darkness, up the stairs.

"It's a nuclear bunker when it's shut up like this," Jude says. "No way in and no way out."

"How do we lift the grates?" Zara asks.

"I don't know."

The undead girl throws herself against the ballroom doors again.

"Perhaps you want to make an educated guess," Zara says tersely.

"There's a surveillance room in the basement," Jude says. "A kind of security room with CCTV screens and buttons and important-looking junk. We might be able to open everything up from there."

"That'll do," Zara says. "Lead the way."

Jude goes. Emer and Zara follow. They race into the service corridor, barrel toward the basement stairs. They run as if something is nipping at their heels. Jude winces as she moves, but she does not let up.

There is a crash from above them, wood splintering, a bovine groan. Screams follow.

"This way," Jude says. They bang through a door, then another, then they are heading downstairs. Suddenly, a body is in their way. A man, huffing, his shoulders tight with fear as he turns to make sure they are not Savannah.

*Andy.*

Andy is running.

Andy is afraid.

"You did this, you little bitch," he says when he sees Emer. He lunges for her, but Emer has the upper ground. She shoves him, hard. The combination of his own instability and her push sends him tumbling, limbs flailing, down the stairs. Andy lands with a nauseating crack on the basement floor. He is face up, eyes as wide as coins. A pool of dark red blood spreads out from the back of his head, the edges of it flowing into the little canals made by the grout between the tiles.

"Drew?" Jude whispers.

"No," Emer breathes. She walks down the stairs to stand over the man she has dreamed of killing for a decade. Andy Volkov does not move. Emer nudges his shoulder with her boot, expecting him to leap up. Andy Volkov is still. She crouches next to him and digs her fingers into his neck, looking for a pulse, but there is none.

"Get up," she orders him.

Still he does not move.

"GET UP," Emer says again, lifting him, shaking his shoulders. The mash of hair and skull and blood at the back of his head makes a soft, wet sound when he slumps back to the floor.

"He's dead, Emer," Jude says.

It is obvious. It is clear.

She cannot believe it.

"No," Emer says. *No.* He does not get to die like *this*. He does not get to die instantly, without pain.

Emer lifts him again. Again he slides back to the tiles with a splatter, his body heavy with death.

Emer lets out a strangled cry and slams her palms against his chest.

Andy Volkov is dead.

More screams come from overhead.

"Shit," Jude says. "We need to hurry."

It is over. How can it be over? The man who came to her home when she was a child, who slaughtered her family. How could his skull have broken so easily? How could he have been so utterly mortal?

"It was not supposed to be this way," Emer says to herself.

"Come on, Emer, we need to get out of here," Jude urges.

"Close your eyes, Jude."

"We don't have time for—"

"*Close* your eyes."

"Damn it." Jude shuts her eyes. "Okay."

"Bael," Emer says. "Occide."

Jude's eyes remain closed, but Emer stares, taking in the impossible speed of Andy's consumption. There are terrible sounds: bones breaking, flesh tearing, the bursting of organ sacks. There are terrible smells: a rush of bile, undigested food and alcohol, feces. Within a handful of seconds, there is nothing left of the man except his watch, his shoes, and his clothing. Even that has been sucked dry of his blood. A coin turns on its edge and then clatters to the ground.

"I think I'm going to be sick," Jude says.

A fresh crop of screams overhead, farther away this time. Savannah is heading upstairs—for now.

The three of them run past the long indoor pool, toward the end of the basement. The entrance to the surveillance room is unlocked. They go inside and survey the black-and-white chaos that unfolds on a dozen screens from a dozen video feeds.

"Okay, let me figure out how to get us the hell out of here," Jude says, the fingers of her uninjured hand hovering over the keyboards in front of her.

Emer reaches out to touch her shoulder, stays her. "We cannot open the grates," she says quietly. "Not yet."

"What? Why? The whole point of finding the surveillance room was opening the grates!"

"If we let that out now"—Emer nods at the array of screens—"it won't ever stop."

Jude and Zara step back to take in what Emer is seeing. They all watch as the creature moves from screen to screen before them, a slick-bodied specter. It is a horror movie unfolding in real time. Bathed in blood, Savannah finds people where they hide. In closets, under beds. She beats down doors and gives chase. No one escapes her.

"Oh," Jude says. "Oh fuck!"

"What?" Emer asks.

"Eli! Eli must be in the house somewhere, in one of the bedrooms! Oh Jesus, he left after the wedding, went upstairs with a girl! I have to go and find him, I have to warn—"

"Jude, wait," Emer says. "Look."

Emer points to a screen toward the bottom of the array. It is flickering and staticky, cut through with lines. A shadowy figure lurks at its center. It is in one of the service corridors. It is making its way toward them.

The killer.

"Oh, you've *got* to be kidding me," Jude says. "How is Adam still alive? Oh God, oh God. My brother is going to murder me, isn't he?"

As she sees the fear rack Jude's face, as the shadowy figure stalks closer, as the three of them, hunted, nestle together in this room with the acrid smell of burning, Emer has a moment of clarity. Emer feels serene. Because she sees now what she must do.

"Jude, don't be afraid," Emer says.

"Don't be afraid? That prick is here to kill me!"

"We will not be hunted any longer," Emer says with a finality that seems to calm Jude. Emer will not get revenge for herself—Andy's death was an accident, too quick and painless to truly count—but that does not mean she cannot be an avenging angel for each of the vulnerable women who came to her and died because of it. It does not mean she cannot be an avenging angel for Jude. "I have a plan."

"Well, it's about time!"

"Look at me. Look at me. You have to let him kill you."

Jude is staggered. "That's your plan? That was my plan—and you told me it was a bad plan!"

"Yes."

"I'd actually rather not die today!"

"I'm serious. This is how we uncurse you. Let him do to you what he has done to all the others. Let him take you to the edge of death. Then we will cut out your invocations—and bring you back."

"I thought we all agreed that was a stupid idea. Like, how do you even plan on bringing me back?"

"CPR."

"Do you know CPR, Emer? Do you even know what CPR stands for?"

"I know CPR," Zara offers.

"Oh yeah, how many people have you performed it on?" Jude asks.

"One."

"Did they live?"

Zara says nothing.

"Did they live, Jones?" Jude asks again, shrill this time.

"Well . . . no, but that was only because she'd been dead for a long time when I started."

"Jesus Christ, I'm really going to die."

"He's coming for you, Jude," Emer says. They all watch the screen again. He is almost at the basement stairs now. "One way or another."

"What are you going to do with the invocation once you cut it out of me?"

"Stitch it to him, like all the others." Emer pauses, her eyes slightly wild. "Use his own method against him."

"How, pray tell, do you plan to hold him still for long enough to do that?"

Emer takes Jude's hand and places it against her chest, wraps her fingers around the invocation she wears on her necklace. "With this."

Jude draws her hand back. "You said it was catastrophic power at a catastrophic price."

"It is. It will be."

Jude shakes her head. "I won't let you pay that. Not for me."

"It's not just for you. It's for all of us. For all of them, too. The women he killed."

"Emer . . . I don't want you to die."

Emer says nothing. She does not want to die, either—but death is here. Death has found her at last.

"Emer," Jude whisper. *"Please."*

"Be brave, Jude. Go out and meet your death—I will see you on the other side."

# THIRTY-FOUR

"FUCK," JUDE whispers as Emer shoves her out of the surveillance room, back into the bleach-and-chlorine glow of the vast pool room. "Fuckity fuck fuck fuck."

Her gut feels bubbly, slippery. It always does when she's nervous, like she's eaten a spicy meal that's begging for its exit.

"I hate this plan, Emer," she mutters to herself. "I hate this plan so, so much. Just go and die, Jude, no big deal. I'll totally give you CPR on the other side if you're lucky."

The door slams open. Smoke rushes down the stairwell, a drifting haze. For a moment, Jude hears the screams and chaos from upstairs as Savannah makes short work of what remains of Jude's family, her father's wedding guests. The door closes. The basement is quiet again, apart from the Ripper's footsteps as he strolls, rather fucking casually, down the stairs.

He is here.

He is inside.

Jude is going to die. She is going to *die*.

Her jaw shakes. She has lost so much in the last few hours. Her family. Her future. Her fundamental understanding of her reality.

Step.

Step.

What will it feel like to hover at the edge of death? To tip over into it? When the Ripper attacked her in Hoxton, she never lost consciousness. This time she will have to, if Emer's plan is to work. She remembers the feeling of the man's hands around her throat, how desperately her lungs wanted oxygen, how her eyeballs bulged and nearly burst from her skull.

Jude acts a fool, but she is not one. She knows that this plan is not as simple as Emer makes it out to be. How long without oxygen before the brain is permanently damaged? Four minutes? Five minutes? Not many minutes, that's for sure.

Step.

Step.

Jude thinks of her mother on the night she died, young and beautiful and surrounded by danger.

"Come on, you bastard," Jude mutters under her breath. "Come and get me."

A shadow appears at the foot of the stairs, tall and broad.

The man lets the obscurity fall from his features. Jude sees him and struggles to make his face make sense. Even now he is sweet-faced, handsome in a gentle way that makes women love him, trust him.

"Eli?" Jude murmurs.

Jude does not understand. This is a trick, surely. Elijah loves to prank her. It is part of the fabric of their relationship. They have always been this way with each other.

"Hey, Jude," Elijah says. He does not sing it the way he usually does when he greets her. He is sad. The words are heavy, full of regret.

Jude still doesn't understand. "What . . . are you doing here? It's not you. You're not . . ." Jude takes a step backward. "What the fuck, Eli?"

A memory comes, swift as poison. Christmas a decade ago at the castle in Scotland, all the decorations tartan, though they have no Scottish roots to speak of. Jude, sent to bed hungry and sulking because she poked her tongue at her father before dinner, called him a bully, which he didn't like because it was true.

A knock on her door that night. A grin in the dark. Elijah sitting at the end of her bed like a mischievous elf, his pajama top stuffed and lumpy, a strange pregnant belly bulging out of the silk.

"Here," he said. "Look what I got for you, Judebug."

Treasure spilling out from his clothing. Pfeffernüsse dusted with white icing. Crystalline sugarplums shimmering like jewels in the low light. Aniseed humbugs, each a mini striped Beetlejuice suit.

They ate until their heads ached with sugar fuzz, until their bellies cramped and groaned, and then, bloated and thrilled, they slept. Jude was unable to imagine loving anyone more than she loved Elijah in that moment.

Her brother. Her ally. Her best friend.

A killer of women.

"You tried to kill me?" Jude says. It sounds so absurd. Of course that wasn't Elijah. Even as he approaches her now, even as he reaches a hand toward her, Jude cannot bring herself to be afraid of him.

Elijah pushes a strand of hair behind her ear, then touches his fingertips to the invocation that hides on her neck. "I wish you hadn't done this," he says quietly. He does not take his eyes off hers.

Jude wriggles away from his touch, her skin suddenly flushed with goose bumps. "Done what?"

"These I have never had any interest in." He turns her wrists over and touches the spells there. "Nor the abomination on your leg. But this one?" He places his hand on his own neck, in the same position as Jude's invocation. "The power of it is astonishing. Unbridled. I have seen and felt what it can do."

"You're one of them," Jude says quietly.

"No," Eli disagrees. "I'm *nothing* like them."

"But you . . ." Jude sobs. "Eli, I don't understand!"

"Oh, I know what they are and what they do to keep their power."

"And you? Do you . . . ?" Jude can't even finish the sentence. Not Elijah. Elijah hates the Four Horsemen, hates Lawrence, hates everything they stand for.

"There was a time when I wanted to be what they were—but you know what our brothers are like. You know how they treat me. They've always hated me. Lawrence had an affair with my mother while their mother was dying. Then I had the audacity to be born. An accident, born to a drug addict. I brought shame to the Wolf family name, they said. They never accepted me. They never allowed me my birthright."

"Your *birthright*?"

"You know, by now, that you come from a very old family with a very old craft. Do you know what you're promised when you kill a witch? Why do you think our family is so wealthy? So powerful?

Why do you think every one of them is so handsome? It is the spilling and taking of witch blood that makes it so. I wanted a part of that. I *deserved* a part of that. The Horsemen refused me. I had no choice but to prove to them that I am worthy. To show them what I could do. Now I know: What they do is so crass, so simple. What I do—I *appreciate* the power of these women. I harness it. I don't let it go to waste. I am an artist, and this is my art."

"Eli." Jude's eyes are welling, her voice low. "*What* did you do?"

"I met Savannah Jones on a dating app. She was . . . exactly what I was looking for. There was no real life ahead of her, no real prospects—and she so badly wanted to be loved. I told her all about my little sister. I told her about your drug addiction. How you had disappeared off the face of the earth two years ago and how I was so desperate to find you."

"You convinced her to get an invocation to help her find whatever she was looking for."

"I did not *convince* her. I *suggested* it to her. I gave her some advice on how to start looking—but you know as well as I do that I would never get very far if I tried to find a cursewriter myself. Savannah was . . . brilliant. Dogged in her search. She went looking and found the witch up in Oxford."

Jude closes her eyes. "Then you killed her and stole her power."

"It was all a theory, up to that point. Was it possible to transfer an invocation that had been granted to another?" Elijah pulls back the cuff of his shirt to show Jude his wrist.

"My God," Jude breathes.

There is a piece of flesh there that is not his own. Elijah is as pale as his mother; Savannah's skin clearly had a more olive undertone. There is a patch of her . . . stitched onto Elijah. *Into* him. A part of him. "It was . . . traumatic. Awful for me. I'll never forget . . ." The pain on his face and in his voice makes Jude sick with rage. "You know me, Jude. I'm not . . . violent. I'm not that kind of man."

Jude barks a laugh. "Listen to yourself!"

"I don't—it's not *easy*. I don't *enjoy* it. I need you to know that."

"You take your *time*, Eli. I have *been* to your crime scenes. I've seen what you do."

"The pentagrams and the Bible quotes were for our brothers, not for me. I wanted—I needed the killings to make the news. For the Horsemen to see and know what I was capable of, so that they . . ." Eli curls his hands into fists at his sides. "I wanted them to fear me. To fear what I was capable of. I wanted them to cower before me the way I have cowered before them my whole life."

"It was you," Jude realizes. "On the stairs, earlier tonight. You were fighting with Adam." What were they saying to each other? "Adam was warning you to stop."

"Adam can't make me do anything I don't want to do anymore. I've made sure of that."

"Adam is *dead*," Jude tells him. "They're all *dead*. You don't have to do this. There is no one left to prove anything to."

"I love you, Jude. I was willing to overlook your foolishness. To help Father protect you from our deranged, idiot brothers."

"Until I had something you wanted."

"Until you had something I wanted."

"Jesus, Eli. Don't you have enough power now?"

"When you have been powerless your whole life—how do you know when it is enough?"

They stare at each other for a handful of breaths, waiting.

"It's a bit of a garbage invocation, just warning you," Jude says.

"Half the time it conks out entirely, the other half it screams out of me like lava and rips off my fingernails. I wouldn't recommend it." Still Elijah does not respond. "Are you really going to do this, Eli? For a shred more?"

Elijah looks heartbroken, the prick. He nods.

Jude's bottom lip quavers.

"All right." Jude knows she should go without a fight. It's part of the plan—but she'll be damned if she doesn't inflict at least a little pain on this entitled little brat on her way out. "Get it over with, then."

# THIRTY-FIVE

**JUDE DOES** not go easily. Emer watches from the shadows, her heart pressed high in her throat. Elijah has not seen her. He is too focused on his sister.

Emer does not take her eyes off Jude.

Jude is shocked at the revelation that her most beloved brother is a killer, but Emer is not. There have been many sweet-faced boys who have catcalled her. Boys who have followed close behind her at night. Boys who have laid their hands on her without her permission.

Emer listens as he tells Jude the horror of what he has done. The atrocities he has committed in the name of power he feels was owed to him. His birthright.

She lets her eyes go unfocused so that she can see beyond the gloaming light of the pool room into the world beyond the veil.

They are there en masse, the demons he has stolen. The power. He has cut pieces out of women and stitched them into himself. The monstrous creatures gather above him like thunderclouds. They are furious. When he moves, they are forced to move.

A man with everything: wealth, good health, access to education. Still it was not enough for him. Still he felt hard done by. Still he had to take more.

Now he has power beyond comprehension. Power that Emer herself wrote. Each word was chosen carefully, agonized over, to constrain and enhance the spell.

The spells are still glistening in their clarity. They are sharp and perfect. Emer is too good at what she does—but she has a spell that she hopes will be enough to bring him down. A spell made so powerful that she will not be able to wield it for long before it kills her. Before Bael sucks dry the marrow of her soul and leaves her body a husk.

Emer undoes her necklace and slides off the leaden pendant she has worn around her neck every day for two years. She unfurls the scroll and reads over her work one last time.

She has never written anything so beautiful before.

She has never written anything so gruesome before.

Like with much of her other work, there are figures in this spell. Images of women, nineteen of them dancing in a circle around the edges of the vile words.

It was meant so she could crush a mortal man with her mind. So she could hold him still and dismantle him atom by atom without even touching him. It is nuclear power, unbridled, unrestrained.

The only problem is that Elijah is not a mortal man. Zara stabbed him and he did not die. Emer set Bael on him and Bael cowered in fear. Jude electrocuted him and he rose again.

Will it work?

Elijah is on top of Jude now, his hands around her throat. Emer does not look away.

Jude fights. It is hard to die, even if that is the plan. Her legs buck. Her fingernails rake lines of raw red into her brother's smooth-skinned hands. Her electricity gutters and spurts. Her body writhes like a snake beneath Elijah's weight as he throttles her to the edge of death.

"Bael," Emer whispers. "Hora vindictae est."

*It is the hour of vengeance.*

To Emer's surprise, Bael is solemn. She expected it to lope around the room with glee. It has worked toward this moment for a decade. It fed her and educated her and protected her so that it could one day feast upon her. It has worked hard. Emer almost feels like it deserves its payment.

Bael watches as Emer uses her knife to slice open the front of her black dress so that her breastbone is exposed. Then she grits her teeth and drags the tip of the knife through her skin. The wound is deep, to the bone. There is no need to make it shallow. There is no need to think of beauty or infection or how the wound will look when it has healed, because it will not heal.

Emer knows that there will be no after.

Jude has stopped fighting. Elijah checks her pulse. There must be a beat there, a thin thread of life. Satisfied, he takes a scalpel from his coat and kneels by his sister's side and begins to flay the invocation from her neck with practiced skill. Soon, Jude will die and the power granted to her by the spell Emer wrote will be taken from her.

To save Jude is also to risk losing her. To save Jude is to die herself.

Life instead of death.

It is an easy choice for Emer.

Emer places the lead against her bloody skin and holds it there with one hand. The other hand she stretches out to the demon that has cared for her all these years. The demon that she has loved. Bael is contorting, the dark blood of its insides thrumming. Emer hovers her palm near its hot cheek. It reaches up its own hands and closes hers in them, though it does not touch her. She stares into the empty sockets in Bael's head where its eyes should be.

"Hanc potentiam volo," she says directly to it. *I want this power.* "Animam meam offero." *I offer my soul.*

*Be kind, Bael,* she thinks, though the thought is quickly lost as the magic rips through her.

Emer's body cracks clean down the middle. Her rib cage butterflied apart, her heart and lungs suddenly exposed as Bael climbs into her. Of course, this does not happen—but that is what it feels like as Bael slams into her body, tears her apart, disintegrates into her. It is a curious sensation, to be ripped apart for a moment and then be reassembled the next, slightly different.

Emer screams and doubles over and falls forward. She vomits. She hears Elijah say, "What the hell," as he looks for the source of the noise in the shadows. He leaves Jude's side, comes looking for her. The lights in the room shudder out. Emer isn't sure if Elijah turned them out or if it was the power surging through her, out of her, all around. She cannot breathe. Her soul cannot bear the weight of the terrible magic she has conjured and pulled into herself. Her flesh is suddenly heavy on her bones.

Then she feels something strange, a sensation like an eel moving around the borders of her heart. A warmth spreads from it. A sensation of . . . lightness.

*You have never been alone,* Bael says to her in voces mysticae.

Emer gasps. She has never been able to understand this language before, but now that her soul is cracked and Bael is inside it, she can.

It is ancient. It feels fragile in her mind, a piece of papyrus from long-forgotten lands. Now that it is a part of her, she no longer finds it vile. Language carries history, and the language of demons is as old as the world. Emer sees flashes of Bael's past as the demon continues to fold into her.

The weight lifts from her bones, and Emer is raised from the ground against the will of gravity. She no longer feels bound by the rules that have governed her all her life. She feels no need to walk upon the floor.

Bael is strong. So much stronger than Emer could have imagined.

By the time Elijah turns the lights on, Emer is upright and hovering six inches from the floor.

"You," Elijah says.

"Me," Emer snarls back.

She flings him across the room with her mind before he can get the first hit in. Bael feeds her power, its exceptional strength crashing through her veins like a river that has broken its banks. While Elijah is pinned against the wall, Emer slides him up and cracks his head into the ceiling.

Elijah is dazed and confused. He is used to being the hunter. He is not used to being attacked first. Emer has caught him by surprise.

Power ripples through her. For a handful of moments, Emer thinks it will be easy. She thinks because Bael is so strong and because she is filled with so much hatred, that fate will give her what she wants. What she deserves at this point in time: an easy win.

With her new power, she begins to peel Elijah, atom by atom. To dust away the particles that encase him. They come away quickly, because the invocation she wears over her heartspace is extraordinary. Because she is extraordinary.

Elijah feels what is happening to him. He feels his own disintegration. He screams as the outer layer of his skin begins to flake off and flutter away from him—and then he comes to his senses. He remembers that he is a man and Emer is a girl and that this is not the way the world is supposed to work for him. He remembers that he has powers stolen from the women he has killed.

Emer sees his left hand just in time. It begins to glow the same molten, fluorescent red as flowing lava. She tries to restrain it, but it is too late. She drops Elijah from the wall and dives into the pool just as he conjures Abby Gallagher's power from his archive of stolen spells. Heat. Fire. Burning.

Emer plunges deep into the water and looks up as a firestorm rolls across the surface. The world turns bright gold and black as fury. It goes on and on and on, a ceaseless explosion. The water begins to warm, and her lungs begin to beg for air.

This is how witches die. How her ancestors died in centuries long past, cast into rivers by threatened men to see if they sank or swam. Witches can fight, but their bodies are still vulnerable to the world. Emer can still drown in this water. Her flesh can still burn in the fire above.

The fireball recedes. The room is plunged into blackness. Elijah has turned off the lights. He can move through shadows like a wraith.

Emer moves cautiously to the surface. She needs to breathe.

She breaks the surface as slowly and quietly as she can and looks around. The basement is pitch-dark. She cannot see Elijah. She cannot see Jude. She hopes Zara has reached her.

Occasional screams still ring out from upstairs. Savannah has not finished hunting the Wolf family and their guests. Soon, though, there will be no one left to sate her. The undead creature she has become will be drawn by the scent of blood.

Bael lifts Emer's body from the water. Her toes trail across the surface as she comes to the pool's edge.

Where is he?

Then Elijah is right there, right in front of her, so close that she smells the remnants of champagne on his breath. There is a bright, horrific slash of pain across her chest and then he is gone. Emer gasps. He slips through the shadow as though it is a doorway. Another one of her spells, used against her. Another slash of pain across her back. Emer whips around, makes to hold him against the wall once again, but he is gone.

Emer bolts across the room. She needs the light switch. In the dark, he is a phantom that cannot be contained. Elijah catches her Achilles tendon with a blade as she runs and she comes down face-first, hard, and slides across the tiles.

He does not mean to kill her quickly. If he did, he would have driven his blade into her heart. He means to play with her, because he can.

Emer shudders. He does not fear her. Despite her strength, he dares to mock her.

"You cannot beat me, you little witch," comes his voice. "I am too powerful."

Emer knows that it is true. For ten years she has studied ancient languages, hunched over books late into the night—and for what? Even with Bael tethered to her heartspace, it is not enough to defeat this abomination with so many demons fueling him.

*You have never been alone*, says a voice in her head.

The wound cut into her heel is bad. An artery has been nicked and it belches blood onto the floor. Savannah will come, drawn by the smell.

Elijah steps out of the shadows. He kneels over Emer and buries a knee in her gut. She gasps. The blow steals all the air from her lungs. He holds her face in both hands.

*You have never been alone*, Bael says again, with more urgency.

Still, Emer does not understand.

*Look*, Bael says. *Look. They have come for you. They always come for you.*

Emer's vision blurs. She does not do it on purpose. It is easier to see when she's woozy, and right now she is light-headed with pain and the blood loss from the cut at her ankle.

The room is packed with demons. They have come to watch her die.

Or have they come to watch her live?

*We have come*, they say as legion. *We have come for you, Emer Byrne.*

They have come because they need her. They rely on her. They cannot let her die.

*Ask them*, Bael says. *Ask them what you asked me.*

"Me salvate," Emer croaks. *Save me.*

There is not enough blood to feed them all, but they do not seem to care. Emer has never seen a demon act without payment before—but these ones do.

They pull Emer out from under Elijah so quickly that he stumbles backward. They are not gentle with her body. It takes her a few moments to understand that she must not fight them. That she must go limp, become a puppet, let them move her.

Elijah is on his feet again. He comes for her.

That is when Emer begins to dance. Her feet do not touch the ground. Her body is plastic, malleable. The demons yank her out of Elijah's reach. They are faster than her, faster than him, their reaction times supernatural. They twist her out of the way of Elijah's blade. They move her before Elijah's magic can hurt her. Elijah flits between shadows. He unleashes fire in her direction.

Emer is like a possessed thing. There are demon hands are all over her, burning her skin, but she does not cry out. The pain is a dull and distant thing. They tear her limbs so brutally she thinks they will dislocate her joints. They do not understand the limitations of a human body.

Elijah is breathless with the effort of trying to land a blow, any blow, on her. He is frustrated. All the cockiness has gone out of him. He lunges for her, his fury evident in the pinkness of his handsome face. He spits as he moves. Sweat drips from his forehead. His teeth are clenched, his eyes wild with anger, his flanks heaving as he sucks in air.

He cannot touch her.

Now it is Emer's turn to fight.

# THIRTY-SIX

**EMER IS** dancing in space. That's what it looks like. She spins and lifts and dips, unbound by gravity. Her eyes are closed, but the man—Jude's brother—cannot seem to touch her. Elijah flickers in and out of existence, jumping from one well of shadow to another. It is a terrible ballet from which Zara can't look away.

Zara hooks her hands beneath Jude's armpits and drags her into the surveillance room. Though Jude is thin, she is also very tall, and Zara grunts and huffs with the effort of moving her weight.

She checks Jude's pulse. It takes a few seconds to find, but it is still there, a trembling thing slipping beneath Zara's fingers.

"You are one stubborn witch," Zara says with relief.

Jude seems impossible to kill. She is so big and brash. She fills every room she enters, much like Prudence did.

Though Zara's heart is racing, her hands are steady.

"Sorry," she says to Jude as she pushes up the girl's pink dress to reveal the curse on her thigh. The wound is grotesque, a chasm that falls away to the bone. The sheep organs Zara dissected in science class—its heart, its brain, its kidney—were nowhere near as repulsive.

Zara presses the tip of Emer's knife into Jude's thigh. The skin—if the crispy bark that covers Jude's leg can still be called skin—gives immediately with a rush of pus. Zara dry heaves and tries to hold her breath. The wound stinks of rot and sulfur. It hurts Zara's fingers to touch it, the same burning acid tingle that comes when in contact with undiluted bleach. The tips of her fingers go red. Her fingernails begin to split and flake at the ends.

Still Zara works through the pain, flaying the flesh from Jude's leg.

# THIRTY-SEVEN

WHEN ELIJAH lunges for Emer again, she catches him in midair using her mind, with the raw power that Bael feeds into her. Elijah gasps and shudders to a halt once more, the force of his sudden stop squeezing all the air from his lungs. He struggles a foot off the ground, but he is tired now. He squirms and thrashes, a rat in a trap. He tries to jump into shadow, but Emer floods the room with light so there is nowhere for him to run.

She squeezes him, feels his body in her mind. He is a sack of soft organs and sharp bones. His insides begin to burst as she constricts him tighter. She pins his arms to his sides, locks his legs together. She feels his bones as they snap beneath her power, feels his heart as it is crushed inside of him. A velvety piece of fruit at the center of him. So fragile, so easy to destroy.

*Not yet*, Bael says.

Emer lets Elijah go. He falls to the floor with a soft thud, his body ruined. His insides leak out of him. Blood seeps from his eyes, his nose, his ears, his mouth. His face is beet red, his limbs all bent at unnatural angles. He is more a pile of flesh and broken bones than a man—but he is still alive, and that makes him dangerous.

Emer caves in on herself. She is weak with blood loss from the wound at her heel. She feels hollowed out. It will not be long now before Bael drains her soul. She stands, limps to the surveillance room, bangs on the door. Zara lets her in. Jude is sprawled on the floor, her leg wound oozing pus and blood.

"Is she alive?" Emer asks.

"Yes. Barely. We need to do this quickly. Is *he* alive?"

"Yes. Barely." Emer looks up at the surveillance screens. "Zara," she says darkly.

"What?"

Emer doesn't respond, just points. Zara's gaze flicks to the screens, immediately locks on to the convulsing, blood-drenched figure lurching toward the basement door.

"Oh," Zara says.

"Help me get Elijah in here. Before it gets to all of us."

They drag his limp form into the room and lay him next to Jude, top to tail. They look so much alike now that she sees them together, the sharp, gaunt, raven-haired siblings.

Together, Emer and Zara barricade the door, push a low, heavy cupboard in front of it. While they work, they watch as the wraith in Savannah's body careens down the basement stairs on the screens, drawn by the blood that has been spilled. It finds slashes of it, slams its face into the tiles to lick it up, is done with it too quickly.

"Are you ready?" Emer asks. She is already kneeling by Elijah's side.

"Almost," Zara says, the end of the word turning to a gasp as the door behind her shudders. Savannah has found them.

They hear the wraith beat its head against the door.

"Zara," Emer says urgently. "I need your help."

Zara kneels next to Jude. They both try to ignore the buckling door, the demonic screams that ring out from beyond it. "Let's do this."

Jude lets out a rattled breath. Emer and Zara both hold theirs, waiting for Jude to inhale again. She does not.

"Start CPR," Emer says. Zara does. Emer can tell immediately that Zara is good at it, has done it before. She counts silently as she compresses Jude's heart. One, two, three. Thirty compressions, then she gives Jude two breaths and starts compressions again.

"I won't be able to keep this up forever," she says, already breathless.

That is the least of their problems. The door is shuddering on its hinges. The wraith will get through to them long before Zara is exhausted from administering CPR.

Emer lets her vision slip beyond the veil. The threads that bind Jude to her demons are tenuous now, delicate and wispy as cirrus clouds. Jude's life is drifting farther and farther away. Soon there will be nothing left of her to save.

Emer finishes Zara's work of cutting away the bad curse from Jude's leg. With a final slit, the skin comes loose from her body. It is thin as waterlogged tissue, so degraded that it has become translucent and worn through entirely in some areas. Normally invocations are an inch or two wide by an inch or two long, but this one has ballooned across Jude's entire swollen thigh, its cursed leaden letters drifting from her groin to her kneecap. The piece of skin that Emer holds up is roughly the size of printer paper.

Emer tears opens Elijah's shirt and gasps. Beneath his fine clothing, he is a patchwork of a man. There are dozens of stolen invocations stitched into his flesh. Rectangles of magic and power harvested from women Emer knew. Some are fresh, the stitches red and raw. Many are old, the raised scars that border them faded to white now. Each one a dead woman.

Each one a power he could not stand seeing a woman carry.

Zara pauses her CPR for a moment to hand Emer a stapler. "I looked everywhere—this was the best option I could find."

"Please let this work," Emer says. Then she flays off a huge piece of skin from over Elijah's heart, the same size as the piece of skin she removed from Jude. Next she lays Jude's skin over Elijah's open wound, straightens it out, and begins to staple it to him. Elijah flinches and moans, his mouth twisting in unconscious pain. Emer works quickly but carefully, her eyes on Elijah's face even as she forces staples into his chest.

When it is done, she sits back, her legs tucked beneath her. The job is messy and grotesque, not the neat stitchwork Elijah would have performed on himself.

The tether between Jude and her disgruntled demon wavers and stutters, shimmering in and out of existence.

"Come on," Emer chants. "Come on."

It does not work. It's not taking.

"Stop CPR," Emer orders Zara.

"If I stop, she *will* die."

"I know. Stop."

Zara lifts her palms away from Jude's chest and wipes her forehead with the back of her hand. She is sweaty with the effort of keeping Jude alive, her breath coming in ragged gasps as she tries to catch it.

Emer presses her fingertips into Jude's neck and feels the dull pulse there as it fades farther and farther away. She watches the thin tether. As Jude's life fades, it flickers between her soul and Elijah's, jumping back and forth like static electricity. It is hedging its bets, waiting to see who is stronger, who will die first.

"Come on, Jude," Emer says. "Stop being so stubborn. Let go. Let go."

Jude's pulse goes out. The tether shuts off, released from her soul. Emer holds her breath. It flickers to Elijah. It goes on and off like a match in the breeze. Finally, finally, it takes root in him, digging its power into his soul.

"CPR!" Emer shouts at Zara as she lurches to her feet and hooks her hands beneath Elijah's armpits. "Bring her back!"

Zara immediately begins compressions again, grunting with the effort, but she looks doubtful. "You can't just bring someone back with CPR, Emer." Zara pauses, tilts Jude's head back, breathes into her mouth, begins compressions again. "It keeps blood flowing to the brain, but it won't restart her heart on its own."

"How do we bring her back?"

"We need a defibrillator. There's one upstairs in the panic room."

"And your undead sister is outside the door if you hadn't noticed!"

"I *have* noticed," Zara says quietly.

They take turns compressing Jude's chest and breathing into her mouth until their arms ache. Zara is right. Jude does not come back. No matter how furiously Emer pumps blood around the girl's body, her heart does not restart.

The door shudders and groans beneath the wraith's furious pounding. The wood begins to splinter and split.

"What does a defibrillator do?" Emer asks.

"It shocks the heart back into rhythm."

"Electricity?"

"Yes. Electricity."

Emer sweeps Jude's collar away to reveal the curse there. The skin is badly bruised from Elijah's second choking attempt, but that should not matter. Emer looks up and shares a look with Zara. Zara understands without her having to say anything.

"It's worth a try," the girl says.

Emer nods. "Give me the knife." Emer pauses. "Do you think she can come back from this?"

"I don't know," Zara says. "She's the most stubborn and annoying person I've met. If anyone can do it, it's her."

Emer suddenly understands Zara's wild desire to bring Savannah back to life. Jude cannot be *gone*. It does not compute. How can someone with so much life force simply cease to be?

Blade in hand, Emer kneels by Jude's side and carefully cuts the stolen invocation out of her skin.

Emer breathes quickly as she removes a piece of skin from her own wrist and lays Jude's rectangle of flesh over her open wound. Then, as she did with Elijah, she staples the skin to herself. Each staple screams as it punches into her skin, biting through layers of flesh and nerve to seal a piece of Jude to Emer.

She is sweating and shaking by the time the final staple goes in, her body riven by adrenaline. Does she have enough soul left—enough life left—for another curse?

"Come on," Emer wills it. "Come on."

It catches like a fire on a winter's night. Slow at first, then bright in the darkness, as the tether transfers from Jude's soul to Emer's.

Again, Emer tastes her own magic as it bounds through her body, the new demon binding itself to her bones, her nerves, her teeth, her skin.

She holds her hands in front of her and watches ribbons of bright filament coil around her fingertips. "Yes," Emer says as she watches it grow stronger and then feels the power flooding into her body. "Yes."

Zara is still giving Jude CPR, still keeping oxygenated blood pumping around her lifeless body. "Did it work?" Zara asks breathlessly.

Emer puts her hand over Jude's chest. She has seen Jude cleave a house in two with this power. It is an unpredictable, unstable spell. Even now, Emer feels it move through her like an electric eel. It wants to be free, all at once.

Emer releases a quiet breath and tries to slow her heartbeat. At the same time, she lets some of the power leak out of her and into Jude. A zap. A spark. Enough to slip into the girl's heart and jolt it back to life.

It is too much. Jude's back arches off the floor, her nervous system overload by electricity. Emer smells burned hair, the unmistakable stink of blistering flesh.

The electricity leaves a lightning web of burn marks across Jude's chest in the shape of Emer's hand.

Zara shakes her head. "Again."

Again Emer lets a thin thread of power jolt into Jude. Again it burns her skin, arches her back.

"It's not working," Zara says.

"I do not want to cook her!" Emer despairs.

"One more time," Zara urges.

Emer closes her eyes and lets the power leave her fingertips again, except this time she does not lose track of it. She imagines it as an extension of herself, a thread from her fingers finding its way into Jude's heart.

Zara checks Jude's pulse again.

"Anything?" Emer asks. The thread holding Jude to this life feels so tenuous. Emer wills breath into her lungs, life into her bones.

"Anything?" she asks again, her voice faltering now.

Zara's eyes are squeezed shut in concentration. "Hold on," she says. Then: "Yes! I feel it!"

The wraith is slamming Savannah's body into the door over and over again, trying to widen the hole it has made. The hinges rattle and groan, desperate to give way. Emer turns and unleashes the full force of Jude's power on the closed door. The wood disintegrates, splintering into matchsticks and fire. The undead wraith beyond it crashes into the opposite wall, then falls into the pool— but even this is not enough to end it. The creature thrashes in the water, furiously making its way to the edge.

Emer discharges the power again, aiming for the water this time. The whole pool is electrified, the dead girl within it jolting and convulsing—but still moving, still trying to fight her way out. Emer holds the power on, turns it up even higher. Shards of lightning thread through the water. Bolts of electricity strike the ceiling and bounce around the room. The power begins to cook Emer's insides. The wraith sparks and starts. Its hair catches fire. It screams and battles but the electrified water holds it. Its eyes broil, its skin chars. All of the soft parts inside of it begin to leak from its nose and mouth.

Emer's power gutters out. She collapses to her knees, her body shaking. The arm the electricity shot out of is badly burned, the fingernails cracked from the catastrophic damage. The pain is surreal.

Emer waits, breathing as softly as her agony will allow.

All is quiet. All is still.

Then—movement.

The top of Savannah's head emerges slowly from the water, followed by the hollows where her eyes used to be. Emer wants to cry. She is exhausted, and the wraith, though blind now, is still alive. It moves silently through the water until it finds the edge of the pool and then lifts itself out. It inhales, taking in the scent of the room it cannot see. Its head snaps to where Emer lies on the floor. It screams and lopes toward her.

With one final push of effort, Emer holds it with her mind and rips it apart. Elijah could fight Bael's power, could fight Emer, but the wraith cannot. It reaches her and goes for her throat and then, suddenly, it disintegrates, all its atoms coming apart in an instant.

Emer is left gasping on the tiles as Savannah's body rains down on her, no more than dust.

# THIRTY-EIGHT

"JUDE? JUDE, talk to me. Are you there?"

A voice, far away, coming from everywhere. A figure standing on the opposite shore of a black river. Jude lets in a sharp breath. It's dark where she is, wherever she is. Why is she here? Why is Emer here? Emer is the figure, Jude thinks, beckoning her across the glassy water.

"Jude, come back," Emer says.

Someone is shaking Jude's shoulders. She can feel hands on her, though she can't see them. She wants to sleep—everything hurts—but someone is being very annoying and shaking her from her slumber.

Jude blinks her eyes open. The river recedes, washes away. Light burns her eyes. Too strong, like vinegar. She has grown accustomed to the darkness of the land across the water, doesn't like the cold fluorescence that shines from above her now. A storm of red hair, then, close to her. Brown, worried eyes peering out of a pale face.

Emer.

"A zombie ate two of my fingers," Jude rasps. "Can you believe that? A *zombie*."

Emer laughs. It is a wonderful sound.

Jude stares at the stinging stumps. She can see that the fingers are gone, but she swears she can still feel them bend and flex as she moves her hand. "Huh. We're kind of the same now. You lost two toes."

"How do you feel?" the witch asks.

"I feel like I just died and came back from hell." It hurts to talk. Everything in Jude's throat feels crushed, like she's breathing through a straw. A straw covered in thorns. There is more agony in her chest: broken ribs from the CPR, perhaps also a broken sternum. Every breath she takes presses against the fractures, sending sharp nettles of hurt through her. The finger stumps throb.

Pain, though, means she is alive. Pain means she lived.

"Oh God, ow, what is that?" Jude says as she tries to move. Another injury, this one different. Gingerly, she bends her knee and cranes her neck to stare at the bloody mess of her leg from which a bright stinging radiates. She blinks, trying to understand what she is looking at. There's a huge piece of skin cut out from her thigh—but the deep fissure that once resided there is gone. The bone and muscle and fat that were visible in the chasm have been concealed by red flesh. New flesh. Raw, skinless, *uncursed* flesh.

"It worked, Jude," Emer says quietly.

Jude's chest shakes, her jaw—with laughter or sobs, she cannot quite tell. It is both. It is both at once—and it bloody hurts, all of it.

"It . . . worked?" Jude puts her hand to her chest. It stings. A burn, it feels like, blistered and hot to the touch.

Jude turns her head—and that is when she sees him, sprawled

out on the floor next to her, his chest exposed. Her own rotten invocation is stapled into him, over his heart. Around that are dozens of stolen pieces of flesh, stitched into his own.

Elijah. Eli. Her ally. Her former favorite person in the world.

"Is he . . . ? Jude asks.

"He's gone," Emer says.

The grief of it feels like . . . nothing. It is too huge to fit inside of her all at once, and so she cannot comprehend it. Jude is not well-practiced at losing people. She lost Judita before she knew her; a mother had always been little more than concept, a thing that other children had but that Jude did not. A dream of a woman she has known only through photographs and snippets of information found online. It does not make sense to her that Elijah is *dead*. He is right here, next to her. His body. Jude reaches out and touches him. He is still warm.

"Are you sure?" Jude whispers.

"I am sure," Emer says.

Jude's bottom jaw shakes. "How do I do this, Emer?" Jude looks up at her. "How do I keep going after this?" After everything she's found out. After everything that's been taken from her. On the screens, the house is a horror movie. Her entire family, decimated. Jude thinks about the little girl in the apple tree. Here, a decade later, in a basement surveillance room, they are linked by the immensity of their losses. Jude does not know what to do with the vastness of it. Who is she, now? Who is she now that everyone is dead? Grief and relief crash together inside her.

"You just do," Emer says. "You get through today, and then you get through tomorrow, and you keep doing that over and over again."

"Emer . . ." Jude's gaze falls to the witch's heartspace, where the invocation she wrote to tether her to Bael is now seared into her skin. "How do *you* feel?"

Emer looks down. Places her hand over the burned words she spent so long learning to write. "At first I did not understand. Bael . . . has taken no payment. Not yet. It has granted me power—not in exchange for my soul, but something else."

"What?"

"To build an army," Emer says simply.

Jude blinks a few times. "Um. Wow. That's, uh—"

"We have hidden in the shadows for too long. Bael has showed me its plan. For the hunted to become the hunters. For me to . . . for me to be the head of the spear."

The enormousness of that is too much for Jude to process. "Where's Jones?"

Emer nods toward the door. Beyond it, Jones sits by the pool, her legs tucked up to her chest, her chin resting on her knees.

Both of them wait where they are while Emer wanders from room to room, quietly inviting demons to devour the bodies of the dead. Jude watches the gruesome, silent cleanup on the CCTV screens. Soon, there is no evidence of the massacre that has taken place here. The demons are thorough. They suck blood from the carpets, lick it up from the walls.

It's dawn when the cleaning is finally done and Jude instructs Emer on how to lift the security doors. Jones walks outside and calls an ambulance. They wait together, Jude's hand in Emer's, as Emer pats her head and tells her it won't be long, it won't be long now. They watch the paramedics arrive on screen, watch as Jones leads them down into the basement. They give a bad cover story—Jude was electrocuted, needed CPR—that fails entirely to explain the huge piece of skin missing from her leg. The paramedics inject her with her painkillers. Jude cries happy tears with the relief of it. Pain that can be met and bested by drugs. What a phenomenal thing.

Outside, the morning is crisp and clear. The sun rises into the blanched autumn sky as Jude is wheeled out to the waiting ambulance and rushed to the hospital.

Then there is only darkness.


WHEN JUDE WAKES, there is a black-haired woman in her room, sitting near her bed.

"Mama?" Jude whispers. Her eyes are parched, her throat dry. She cannot see well, and for a moment, in the liminal state between sleep and waking, she forgets that her mother is long dead. Jude wants the woman to stand and put down her book and come and kiss her on the forehead. "Is that you?"

"You have serious issues," the woman says.

Not her mother, then. Not the woman she only knows through photographs. Judita *is* dead. Jude remembers this now. Judita is dead, killed by Adam—and Jude is alive.

Improbably, miraculously alive.

"Reese?" Jude's voice is raspy and thin. "You came to see me? You *do* love me."

Reese Chopra stands and comes to Jude's bedside and helps her take a sip of water. "I already took statements from your friends. They didn't give me much. All they'd tell me is that your brother is—or was, rather—the London Ripper. I don't suppose you want to divulge more?"

"Are they here?"

"No. They wanted to stay, but I sent them off. They were both a bit banged up and looked like they could use a rest. As could I."

"What do you want to know?" Jude asks.

"What happened at your family's house last night?"

"What do you mean?"

"I mean, many members of your family have been reported missing. All of the security footage from the house has been wiped. There's a giant cage in the middle of a ballroom that has been gutted by fire. Dozens of people went into that house, Jude—and only you and your friends came out. The inside of the house looks like it's been ransacked, but there are no bodies. No blood."

"How mysterious. I'm sure the investigative geniuses at the Met will figure it out."

"Well, you weren't the only ones who got out, actually—your father is alive as well."

"Lawrence lived?" Jude's head spins. How is that possible? But of course—he was outside in the garden when the grates came down. "I'll be damned. It is hard to kill a cockroach."

"He's here. He's outside, in the hall. He's been here since they brought you in."

"Jesus, *why*?"

"Probably because he's your father and he's worried about you."

"No, that can't possibly be it."

"Shall I send him in?"

"I don't know. Maybe? Several members of my family have

attempted to kill me recently. I wouldn't put it past him to have a go as well."

"I'll be by the door. If you need help, yell out and I'll shoot him for you."

"Thank you, Reese. That's so nice."

Chopra stands, heads toward the door. When she gets there, she pauses and turns back. "We're done. Right?"

"It doesn't have to be the end if you don't want it to," Jude says.

Chopra gives her the finger, but she does so with the hint of a smile on her face. *I knew I'd crack her eventually,* Jude thinks. Chopra ducks out.

Then he is there. The oxygen is sucked from the room as Lawrence steps inside of it. He remains by the door, as far away from Jude as possible. He doesn't rush to her. He doesn't say or do anything.

"You knew my mother was a witch," Jude says eventually.

"Only after we married. Only after you were born. Then I could do nothing but try to keep her safe."

"You didn't try hard enough. You could have sent her away."

"I did try. She wouldn't go. She was not afraid when she should have been. I tried to protect you both." Lawrence checks his watch. "I don't have much time. Luciana and I are going to Tahiti for our honeymoon."

"You have a private jet. You can leave whenever you want."

Lawrence takes a single step closer. "I found you. Do you remember that? After you cursed yourself like an idiot. I was the one who found you and took you to hospital."

"No." Jude had woken up in hospital in terrible agony. Everything before that was a blur, deleted from her mind. "I don't remember that."

"I knew what you'd done. I knew I had to keep you away from them. Away from Adam. Didn't you ever wonder why I made up a cover story?"

"I just thought you . . ." What *did* Jude think? "I just thought you kind of assumed the worst about me."

Lawrence's eyes turn even colder. "I know you think me callous—but when I was your age, I had horrors visited upon me such as you could not comprehend. I spared my own children the same fate. Perhaps I have not been a good father—but I have never been intentionally cruel to you. If you knew my past, you might consider that a miracle."

"What is your past?" Jude asks. It seems an opportunity to know her father. To understand him on a deeper level. On any level, for that matter.

"Next question," Lawrence says, enunciating every syllable.

"How did the Horsemen get involved in witch hunting if not through you?"

"Who?"

"Your sons. Adam, Seth, Drew, Matthew. When did they start killing women? *Why?*"

"I kept my children far away from my father their whole lives. It was his dying wish, to meet his grandsons. I allowed it. I should not have. I thought he was too weak by then to do any more damage. I was wrong. He passed a message, in secret, to Adam, who was a teenager at the time. It ruined him."

"What about Elijah? Why didn't you protect him from them?"

"Because I wanted them to hate him and for him to hate them. I thought it would keep him safe. I thought, if they did not accept him, he would not become like them."

"I loved him." Jude cannot help herself. She begins to cry. In front of her father, who despises such weakness. Her whole body aches with the pain of it. "He deserved better than this family."

"I'm glad it was you, Jude," Lawrence says eventually. "I'm glad you won." It is the closest Lawrence has ever come to saying *I love you*. "Luciana is waiting for me. I should—"

"Okay."

"I think I can do better. For the two on the way. Be a better father for them."

"Thirteenth time's the charm, right?"

Lawrence nods, and then he is gone.

# THIRTY-NINE

ZARA AND Emer sit at a café near the hospital, both of them bruised and blood-soaked.

Outside, the morning is nicer than it has any right to be after the night before. The fog has cleared, revealing a blue sky, a scattering of opaline clouds. Hedges are hung with red winter berries, the sidewalks dusted with bright yellow leaves.

Zara's hair smells like smoke, and her fingers are blistered from touching Jude's cursed wound for too long. She feels like she's been hit by a car or dropped from a great height. Her eyeballs ache. Her rib cage feels too small. Emer looks even worse than Zara does. There are puckered red burns in the shape of demon hands all over her arms and an angry red rectangular wound at her wrist, a flayed piece of skin held in place by staples. The witch did a butcher job on her hair, too, patches of her scalp visible where she cut it too short.

"Late Halloween party this year," Zara says when the waiter stares at the dried blood on their clothes.

"Sure," the man says, then takes their order.

They eat in silence. Jazzy Muzak plays in the background. Everything is comically normal.

"What a night," Zara says when they both find that they can eat no more.

Emer laughs, then stops. She puts her fingers in her mouth, deep at the back, and pulls out a loose tooth.

"*God,*" Zara says. "You can't just pull out your teeth in public. Are you falling apart, like Jude was?"

"No," Emer says. "I think Eli knocked this one loose."

"You don't look like you're going to die imminently. I mean, you do look terrible—but you don't look like death."

Emer looks at her hands, marvels at them. "Bael will not let me die. I have become too valuable. Demons have poured too many resources into me to let me die so soon."

"You're like the demon chosen one."

"There is, of course, an expectation of repayment for the power I have been granted."

"Which is?"

"Write more invocations. Make more witches. Build covens. Hunt hunters. Restore what has been lost." Emer looks up at Zara. "I don't suppose you're interested in selling part of your soul? Joining the cause?"

"Never say never, I guess—but I think I might take a break from the occult for a while. What happens now? Will you go back to Oxford?"

Emer shakes her head. "Oxford was not my home. I will go to Lough Leane, I think. There is more left there than I thought. There could be—something that looks like a life there."

"When will you go?"

"Today. Now."

"Don't you want to wait and say goodbye to Jude?"

Emer takes a deep breath. "Jude—" she begins, struggling to find the words. "Jude got what she wanted. Her curse is broken. She is free, now, to—" Again, Emer can't find the words. "The life she has ahead of her will be extraordinary. Do you understand? Jude is wealthy and beautiful and brilliant. There is a place for her in the world."

"But not for you?"

"No. Not for me. Not in her world, anyway."

"Why don't you let her decide that?"

"Because I have my own work to do right now."

Zara nods. "Fair enough."

Emer stands and stretches. "Goodbye, Zara Jones. I hope I will see you again."

Zara stands, too, pulls Emer in for a hug that the witch returns stiffly. "Maybe we could visit you," she says. "Me and Jude. We could come to Lough Leane, when you're ready."

Emer nods. "I would like that. Next year, perhaps. In the summer." Then she picks up her bag and walks out. She does not look back.

Zara sits at the table for a while longer, wondering where she will go now, what she will do. She knows she can't go back to Kyle's. There's nothing there for her—but it doesn't feel like there's anything for her anywhere else, either. There's no one in the world who cares about her, except perhaps for Jude and Emer, and the tethers that bound the three of them together so closely are beginning to fray now.

Where do you go when you've got nowhere else to go?

Zara puts her hands in her jacket pockets—and it is in one of them that she finds a crumpled piece of paper, slipped to her across her school principal's desk a few days—and a lifetime—ago.

"OH MY GOD," Principal Gardner says, her hands clasped over her heart, when she arrives at the coffee shop half an hour later. The coat she wears is bright pink with tigers and ferns and blossoms all over it. She looks, as she often does, like the embodiment of sugar and sunshine. "I was so worried about you!"

Zara bursts out crying the moment she sees her. Everything she's been holding in for a year rushes out of her at once. Gardner pulls her into a hug, crushes her against her chest, allows her to cry and cry and cry for everything she has lost. "It's okay," Gardner says, over and over again as she holds her and—by the time Zara's tears have dried and her body is wrung of its grief—she actually believes her. For the first time in a long time, it *is* okay. As okay as it will ever be without Savannah.

Gardner sits her down, orders them both a cup of tea. Zara sits, threadbare and wan from crying, barely able to hold up her own weight. It is a school day. That is where Gardner came from. She calls work, tells them she won't be back in until later, or perhaps not at all. The tea arrives. Zara takes a sip and then tells Gardner, as best she can, about everything that's happened, everything she's been through. She leaves nothing out. Whether Gardner will believe her does not matter to Zara in that moment. What matters is the telling. What matters is the release of the truth, in its entirety, to someone outside of the story. The feel of

Savannah's desiccated skin. The smell of her fetid breath. The horror of what happened last night at Jude's family home, all that blood on Zara's hands.

"I wish you'd come to me sooner," Gardner says when she is done.

"You would've told me I was crazy."

"Probably."

"Do you believe me?"

"I believe that you believe that all of this is real. Which means I believe you've been through hell. I'm not so ignorant to think that my way of understanding the world is the only way."

"I don't know what to do now. I don't know what to want anymore. I've always had a goal. First it was to have the best grades, get into the best university. Then it became—"

"Be the best necromancer?"

Zara nods.

"Type A all the way." Gardner smiles. "You don't need to know all the answers right now. You're allowed to take time to find your way through, just like everybody else your age. Hell, I'm still figuring my life out."

"Everything I do—everything I've worked toward—I've never actually *achieved* anything. I've just wanted and wanted—and what for?"

"Zara." The way Gardner says it—it's not hung with weight, like before. It's threaded with pride. Zara sits up a little straighter. "You *literally* raised the dead."

"Well, yes, I suppose, but—I'm not sure it worked, though. I'm not sure Savannah really understood—"

"It didn't work out the way you planned, no—but you set your mind to something. You set your mind to something impossible, something beyond the realm of possibility or understanding—and then you did it. I have no doubt that your sister knew you loved her— and I have no doubt that whatever you decide to do next, you will achieve it."

# EPILOGUE

**WHEN EMER** returned to Ireland in November, the meadow at Lough Leane was barren, the house still an overgrown shell. The winter that followed was lean and hard, but filled, for once, with purpose. With Bael's help, Bael's strength—and the extravagant amount of money that appeared, suddenly and without her asking for it, in a bank account that had been set up in her name—Emer spent the coldest months repairing the tumbledown walls, replacing shattered windows, shipping in new furniture. The days were long, the nights spent by herself curled up in front of the fire, but Emer relished the physicality of it.

Now the land around the renewed farmhouse is bursting with life. Wildflowers have colonized the meadow that looked so dreary in the winter. Emer builds and plants, remaking what was lost. Bael speaks to her about its plans for this place. For her. One day a coven will flourish here, and she will be the matriarch of a large family of witches who will go out into the world and hunt those who wish to destroy them.

Emer practices using her sight every day. At first looking beyond the veil for more than a few minutes at a time makes her eyes ache and gives her migraines, but soon she finds she enjoys seeing what Bael gets up to during the day or watching ghosts drift across the plains at night, bound for the doors that will take them to the realms beyond death.

More demons come from the forest. At first they watch Emer and Bael from afar, hissing and snapping at one another. Emer leaves blood offerings for them until they, too, begin to gather stones and stack wood. Emer must do all the intricate work of hammering nails and thatching the roof. The days are long and backbreaking. She falls into her bed each night an aching ball of muscles.

Bael hunts for her, as it did when she was a dying child. It brings her fish from the river, which she likes best, but also hares and birds and squirrels. Emer cooks them over the fire. Sometimes, when she asks for it, Bael brings her fresh fruit or vegetables, but mostly Emer is able to find these things growing wild. Sour crab apples and rose hips and wild strawberries.

Emer's body becomes more powerful with the work. Her legs and arms become stronger than ever. Calluses form on the palms of her hands. Her skin picks up the sun, freckling like a storm of fallen autumn leaves. Emer likes all of this. She feels she is a tool built to do this exact job. Each day the labor becomes easier. Each day the house becomes more whole. Each day she wakes with a smile, ready for the good, simple tasks ahead of her.

By the time Jude and Zara arrive in the early summer, the house is finished, surrounded by gardens of lavender.

"Wow," Jude says when she sees the place. "It's actually a lot less terrible than I was anticipating."

Emer grins broadly when they arrive, hugs each of them tightly. "Thank you."

"It looks like something out of a fairy tale," Zara says.

Emer knows that they have been living together at Jude's house. That Jude invited Zara to move in. The three of them had only a handful of days together in autumn, and now Jude and Zara have had months. A whole winter, a whole spring. Emer wonders if they are still just friends or if they have become something more.

They bring with them the first haul of real groceries. The three of them unload it all together. Sacks of flour and bags of salt and sugar. Boxes full of canned goods and fresh produce. Several crates of champagne. A cheeping cage of fluffy yellow chicks.

"No idea what these are," Jude says as she holds the cage up. Her right hand, two fingers less, has healed well. *We're kind of the same now,* she said when it happened. Does she still feel that way now, all these months later? "Ducks, turkeys, quails, chickens. Could be anything."

They are, Emer thinks, very obviously chickens.

By the time everything is put away, Jude is breathless and sweaty.

It has been so long since they've seen each other.

Jude looks well. The curse had gutted her. After its removal, she has grown fuller. She is no longer so peaky and pale. Emer finds that her heart swells with longing at the sight of her.

Jude leans in the doorway and looks around. Emer tries to see it through Jude's eyes, as if for the first time. The walls are bare stone. The floor underfoot is wood, rough oak planks hammered by Emer's own hands. The hearth is large, good for cooking and heating in the winter months. All the furniture is simple, built to last.

It has nothing of the grandeur Jude is used to, yet Emer feels a great fondness for this place she has created.

"You really built this all by yourself?" Jude asks Emer.

"Yes. Well, me and my demons."

"A woman who can build. That's, just, so attractive." Jude grins her wicked grin. Emer holds her breath. She thinks, maybe, that Jude will come to her and kiss her—but she does not.

They spend the long summer afternoon outside. The heat persists into the evening, keeping them out in the breeze. Both of Jude's thighs are scarred now, her other leg harvested for fresh skin to graft over the gaping wound Emer left when she cut out the bad invocation. There is a scar over Jude's heart, too, this one in the shape of Emer's hand. It is a puckered and pearlescent thing, a handprint with gossamer threads of lightning branching from it.

Zara cuts up an outrageous number of strawberries. They sit together, the three of them, on a blanket on the grass, eating strawberries and drinking champagne. Emer cannot fathom that this moment exists in her life. No part of her story has led her to believe that her path was heading here.

To this.

To them.

To *her*.

"Oh, I almost forgot," Jude says as she stands. "We brought you a present." Emer watches as she runs back to her car. Jude returns with a parcel wrapped in brown paper and twine. Emer opens it. It is a plaque that reads PHOENIX HOUSE. "We weren't sure if you wanted to call it something different, but we thought, you know . . . from the ashes."

Emer cannot remember the last time she cried, but she cries then.

They have both been accepted to go to university. Zara to Oxford, Jude to Cambridge. Emer is happy for them. Emer is also jealous of them, knows that their paths must split here, after this summer. They are bound for education, for normal lives. Emer is bound to rebuild what was lost here and then, sometime soon, bound to hunt those who kill witches.

After a few days of relaxation, Emer puts them to work. That is what they are here for. They spend the summer tilling fields and sowing crops of beetroot and carrot and fennel. They construct a greenhouse that Jude orders online. It is not as large as the one that stood here before, but it is more beautiful, with lacy Victorian fili-gree across the spine of the roof.

It is not a luxurious lifestyle. There is no running water, so they wash together in the cold stream nearby. There is no electricity, so Jude's champagne is drunk warm, by candlelight. Yet the days are pleasant and long, and everyone is happy.

Emer watches them grow harder, their muscles responding to the daily work. Jude's skin tans in the sun. There is a patch of skin at the nape of her neck that is darker than the rest of her. It's here that Emer most wants to kiss her. Zara goes tan, and her blond hair lightens to almost white. Their hands blister and then go callused. The soles of their feet become thick from walking barefoot in the forest. Emer teaches them how to live out here. She teaches them how to catch fish from the stream and set traps for hares.

Too soon, the days begin to shorten. Soon it is September, and it is time for Jude and Zara to leave. They will be back, they say, at break time, but Emer knows that the lives that are waiting for them will begin to consume them.

Zara leaves first, hiking out of the woods to meet her waiting taxi, and then, later that day, it is Jude's turn to go.

Jude lingers for a long time. She packs slowly. She dawdles. Emer wonders and hopes, but in the end, Jude leaves. She says goodbye and gets in her car and drives away, and then it is just Emer again. Emer and Bael and a host of demons.

Not long after Jude goes, there is a knock at the door.

Emer opens it.

Jude is standing there.

"How would you feel," she says breathlessly, "if I wanted to stay longer?"

"Longer?" Emer asks. She is confused. "Another night? Another week?" There is a bright big world waiting for Jude Wolf. Surely she can't mean—

"Forever," Jude says. "How would you feel if I wanted to stay forever?"

Emer grins.

She is still grinning when Jude leans in—finally—to kiss her.

# ACKNOWLEDGMENTS

THIS IS, WITHOUT a doubt, the hardest book I've written. It was my pandemic book, started in a dark winter lockdown in London. I had Covid three times while writing and editing it, always, always when I was on deadline. Many people kept me propped up so that I could, eventually, get it over the finish line.

Immense gratitude to:

Catherine Drayton, my agent at InkWell Management. My ally, my advocate, the brace who kept me standing through the tougher months.

My editor, Stacey Barney, the earliest champion of this book and its guardian through many of its forms. Thank you for giving these girls, and me, a home.

Caitlin Tutterow, who held so much of this story in her head when I struggled to hold it in my own. You have magical powers that I don't fully understand.

My copy editors and proofreaders: Cindy Howle, Ana Deboo, Chandra Wohleber, Bethany Bryan.

The rest of the incredible team at Penguin Teen/Nancy Paulsen Books: Olivia Russo, Felicity Vallence, Shannon Spann, James Akinaka, Mary McGrath, Becky Green, Christina Colangelo, Suki Boynton, and everyone else who works tirelessly behind the scenes to make and sell books. I'm grateful grateful grateful that I get to work with each of you.

The cover dream team: Aykut Aydoğdu for the art and Theresa Evangelista for the design. I'm awed once again by the beauty you have created.

Everyone at Penguin Australia, but especially Amy Thomas, Laura Harris, Tina Gumnior, Laura Hutchinson, Tijana Aronson, and Lisa Riley, for your continued support from across the seas.

The stellar team at Hot Key in the UK, particularly Emma Matthewson, for your warmth and encouragement at every turn. Also: Emma Quick, Amber Ivatt, Tia Albert, Pippa Poole.

Everyone at InkWell, but especially Sidney Boker, for your feedback, Lyndsey Blessing, for selling my books in so many countries, and Hannah Lehmkuhl, long-suffering chaser of overdue foreign tax forms (they're coming, I promise!).

My film agent extraordinaire, Mary Pender.

My London crew, who listened to me complain about the aches and pains of writing this book for literally years. Harriet Constable, Owen Ensor, Anna Russell, Alex Hourdakis, Lee Kupferman, Lizzie Pinkney, Alex Palmer, Brett Hatfield, Angharad Thomas, Arran Schlosberg, Arianna Reiche, Lyle Brennan, Noel Fettingsmith, Julie Fettingsmith, David Leipziger, Trevor Alton, Rahul Chatterjee. Being on deadline was 95 percent of my personality for so long; thank you for not holding it against me.

Chethan Sarabu, for the celebratory bottle of Clase Azul tequila.

Melissa Albert and Katherine Webber, who read the early chapters of this book before just about anyone else and gave me the first sparks of fire I needed to keep going.

Also Samantha Shannon, Holly Bourne, Alwyn Hamilton, Nina Douglas, who are always there to celebrate the highs and commiserate the lows.

Louise O'Neill, for the pep talk on the future.

The other authors in my community who have been such pillars of support: Kiran Millwood Hargrave, Saara El-Arifi, Karen M. McManus, Ayana Gray, Faridah Àbíké-Íyímídé, V. E. Schwab, Katherine Rundell, Anna James, Juno Dawson.

Also Renee Martin, Cara Martin, Alysha Morgan, Kirra Moke, Sarah Maddox, Sally Roebuck, Danielle Green, for being my foundation, still.

Unwavering gratitude, always, to my family: Sophie, Phillip, Emily, Chelsea, Diane, Lisbeth, Aruna, Lauren, Tom, Srimathie.

Finally, this book would simply not exist without Martin Seneviratne, because I would be flat on a floor somewhere, crying and/or dead. Thank you for listening, consoling, editing, therapizing, enduring, encouraging, celebrating. Everything, basically. Thank you for everything. I love you extravagantly.